D1600896

IVAN GONCHAROV

AN ORDINARY STORY

INCLUDING THE STAGE ADAPTATION
OF THE NOVEL
BY
VIKTOR ROZOV

Translated & Edited by
Marjorie L. Hoover

ARDIS

Ivan Goncharov, *An Ordinary Story* and Viktor Rozov's stage adaptation of the novel
Translated by Marjorie L. Hoover
Copyright © 1994 by Ardis Publishers
All rights reserved under International and
Pan-American Copyright Conventions
Printed in the United States of America

Ardis Publishers
2901 Heatherway
Ann Arbor, Michigan 48104

Library of Congress Cataloging-in-Publication Data

Goncharov, Ivan Aleksandrovich, 1812-1891.
[Obyknovennaia istoriia. English]
An Ordinary Story / Ivan Goncharov ; translated by Marjorie L. Hoover
p. cm.
"Includes a translation of Viktor Rozov's stage adaptation of the novel which premiered
in Moscow in 1966"—CIP data sheet.
ISBN 0-87501-088-1 (alk. paper)
I. Rozov, Viktor, 1913- Obyknovennaia istoriia. English.
1994. II. Hoover, Marjorie L. III. Title.
PG3337.G60213 1994
891.73'3—dc20   93-11284
CIP

PG
3337
G6
0213
1994

3 3001 00779 0115

CONTENTS

Introduction

By date of birth, 1812, Ivan Alexandrovich Goncharov was thirteen years younger than Alexander Pushkin and two years older than Mikhail Lermontov. He met both writers while studying at Moscow University, read their work as it appeared and felt their literary concerns as a contemporary. Goncharov's first important novel, *An Ordinary Story* (*Obyknovennaia istoriia*), was also conceived in the first half of the nineteenth century and in 1847 began to appear in installments in *The Contemporary* (*Sovremennik*), the magazine founded by Pushkin. Yet despite these ties to an earlier era, the author and his novel anticipate the second half of the century, the period following the bourgeois revolution of 1848 which so incisively changed government and society in Western Europe and reverberated in Eastern Europe as well. Goncharov rightly belongs, then, alongside Ivan Turgenev, Lev Tolstoy and Alexander Ostrovsky in the group photograph of contributors to *The Contemporary*. At mid-century they were considered a promising new generation of writers.

These new writers have been called realists because they described the contemporary scene as they saw it in a critical light, in so far as the censorship allowed. The most quoted literary critic of the 1840s, Vissarion Belinsky, strongly concurred in the criticism implicit in *An Ordinary Story*, hailing Goncharov's first novel as "a terrific blow struck at Romanticism, day-dreaming, sentimentality, provincialism" (in a letter to Vasily Botkin, 15-17 March 1847). Nikolai Dobrolyubov, the arbiter of the next decade, the 1850s, made the title hero of Goncharov's next and best-known novel famous by entitling his article about it "What is Oblomovism?" Though the novel's hero, Oblomov, like Hamlet, sees what he must do to set the time right, he relapses ever more into inaction and ultimately fails to do anything. The same conflict between romantically idealistic plans and the practical action needed to realize them obtains in *An Ordinary Story*. Here this conflict, so relevant to the early industrialization of Russia, is embodied in the confrontation between a younger idealist, Alexander Aduyev, and an older pragmatist, his uncle Pyotr. Alexander's experiences and discussions with his uncle form a significant part of his education and he develops to maturity under Pyotr's tutelage. In essence, then, this is an ordinary story familiar since the Greek myths of Jason, the medieval epics of Parsifal and the Renaissance picaresque novels about heroes from *Simplicissimus* to *Tom Jones* and on.

Here, though, we have a specifically Russian hero set against a Russian background. The realist Goncharov confessed himself incapable of fantasizing either character or event, so both derive from his image of the reality he knew: "...there opened before my eyes, as if seen from an elevation, a whole region, with cities, villages and a crowd of people...."[1] How much of this author's experience of reality is used in *An Ordinary Story?* Certainly Alexander Aduyev's history is partly autobiographical. Like him Goncharov came from the provinces, though he was not born on a farm, but was the son of a tradesman, a grain dealer in a river town, the provincial capital of Simbirsk on the Volga (now Ulyanovsk). Goncharov's father died when he was seven, and his education and that of his sisters and his older brother Nikolai was left to his energetic mother and a godfather, an estate owner and much-traveled retired naval officer with wide experience and an interest in the humanities. At the private boarding school to which he was sent at age eight with his brother Goncharov gained a fluency in French, German and English and a background in literature. Both boys, however, were then made to spend eight years at the Moscow Commerce Institute, supposedly in preparation for earning a living. Their mother withdrew Ivan from the course two years early at the time that Nikolai finished, whereupon Ivan studied literature and philosophy at Moscow University. He read widely there and went often to the theater (1831-34). Alexander Aduyev's university experience reflects that of his creator.

After finishing his studies at the university, while awaiting his diploma, Goncharov spent the summer at home and at his godfather's prompting he took the post of secretary-for-all-work to the provincial governor in Simbirsk. The governor strikingly showed off the virtues and vices of his aristocratic heritage. Trained for nothing but the military, he cut a dashing figure with his pretty wife and sixteen-year-old daughter, for whom Goncharov had to serve as dancing partner, in addition to taking practically sole responsibility for the government. The figure-head governor might have survived longer the crush between mortgage payments on his impoverished estates, gambling debts and his extravagant Parisian tastes, had he not carried on in full view his final profligacy, womanizing. Upon the governor's inevitable reassignment Goncharov followed the family to St. Petersburg in a second coach. Throughout that long journey in May 1835, with its numerous stops, he had to tend to an impossible coachmate, the governor's gifted alcoholic ghost writer, who alternated between flat-out unconsciousness and violent attacks of delirium tremens. Like his fictional hero, then, Goncharov first arrived in the capital by coach, but one loaded with difficulties, not with the gifts of a solicitous mother.

Again like Alexander Aduyev, Goncharov at once entered government service. Until his retirement in 1867 he worked there full-time, first as translator for the Ministry of Finance; after 1856 he served as government censor and rose finally to the fourth highest rank of Actual Councillor of State with the appellation "Your Excellency." Known for his writing, Goncharov obtained the assignment of secretary to an admiral who in 1852 went round the world to inspect Russian possessions, including those in North America. This resulted in Goncharov's travel journal, *The Frigate Pallada*, which has at last been translated into English, whereupon it was praised as a near masterpiece.[2]

At first Goncharov supplemented his government clerk's pay by tutoring two sons of the painter Nikolai Maykov. He was soon also spending his free time in the merry Maykov circle with weekend picnics and parties where he met writers and contributed to an in-house literary magazine. He never founded a family of his own, for in 1855 he was rejected by the one love of his life, Elizaveta Tolstaya. However, his housekeeper, Alexandra Treygut, who was with him at his death from pneumonia in 1891, and to whom he left his estate, is sometimes assumed to have been his commonlaw wife. Society at the Maykovs freed him from a bachelor's solitude. He discussed his literary plans there, as he did also with Turgenev, whom he first met at Belinsky's. Goncharov talked to Turgenev and others several times about his ideas for his third and last major novel, *The Precipice* (*Obryv*, 1869). But in 1858, before his novel had been completed, he accused Turgenev of plagiarizing it in the latter's *A Nest of Gentlefolk*. Twenty years later he wrote an account, not intended for publication, of the accusation against Turgenev, which included similar suspicions of widespread literary plagiarism. His account, entitled *An Unusual Story* (*Neobyknovennaia istoriia*), was obtained for publication in 1924. However paranoid Goncharov's charges seem at first glance, they point to the kind of parallels that do exist in literature.

Though Goncharov conceived all three of his major novels while still in his forties, the second and third were completed and published much later, partly because of his several occupations. The changes which took place in Russia between the novels' conception and completion were incorporated most notably in the final novel. The character Mark Volokhov, for example, a nihilist whom Goncharov undoubtedly owes to Turgenev's *Fathers and Sons* (1862), was added to the original cast of characters in *The Precipice*. In addition to his writing Goncharov held many jobs. He worked in the civil service, edited the magazine *The Northern Mail* (*Severnaia pochta*), twice served as judge for the Uvarov Prize, awarding it both times to the writer Alexander Ostrovsky. Goncharov wrote a perceptive citation for the award given in 1860 to Ostrovsky's play *The Storm*. Well aware of the social and political injustice of the time, Goncharov wrote essays about servants, as did his contemporaries Turgenev and Tolstoy. Goncharov's collection *Old-Time Servants* (*Slugi starogo veka*, 1889), written towards the end of his life, combines fiction and nonfiction.

An Ordinary Story ought to be classified as more than a straightforward picaresque tale wherein a young man sets forth to seek his fortune. Goncharov shows how his initially naive hero learns from his successive encounters until he masters the ways of the world; hence *An Ordinary Story* is also an education novel (*Bildungsroman*).

Moreover, the author has an implied message and has therefore written a novel of ideas as well. Early in *An Ordinary Story* the magazine editor to whom Pyotr Aduyev has sent Alexander's manuscript returns it with a comment which summarizes a message to be endlessly repeated in the confrontations between Alexander and his uncle. Goncharov elaborated on this message over thirty years later (1879) in an article "Better Late than Never": "Here [in *An Ordinary Story*] that idea is expressed—the weak flickering consciousness that *work* is essential, real work rather than routine work, an *active undertaking* in the fight against the eternal Russian stagnation (*zastoi*)."[3] This message is preached by Alexander's uncle, who realizes the work principle in his way of life, and it is most pertinent to Goncharov's Russia which was facing the death of feudalism, the impending liberation of the serfs and the rise of capitalism and industrialization

In the end, however, Pyotr must change his life. In the novel's almost schematic action the uncle and nephew exchange positions. Pyotr loses the firm ground of his reality when his wife, Lizaveta Alexandrovna, loses interest in life and falls ill from her submission to the calculatedly luxurious routine he has made of their marriage. Out of the devotion he has felt but never been able to show her outwardly, in the end Pyotr will resign his government office at the height of his career, at the point of becoming Minister of State, and will sell his profitable factory—all so as to go abroad and devote himself completely to her. Alexander, on the other hand, comes down to earth at last and decides to follow his uncle's footsteps by entering government service. He now rushes in to announce his engagement to a fabulously rich girl, not out of love, but for money. He has arranged the marriage with her father without asking her. Whether she will love him and whether Lizaveta Alexandrovna will live—in sum, whether the romantic or the realistic way of life is right—remain unanswered questions. As in reality, the answers lie in the course of life itself, and life goes on after the novel's end. The reader may find the last aboutface of the central characters not wholly credible, more a fresh start than an end. How different the omniscience with which a Dickens or a Thackeray finalizes his characters' fate.

The unresolved ending of *An Ordinary Story* is not the only testament to the author's realistic style. Though but few, his vignettes of nature tangibly evoke moments of vivid experience: the stillness before the wild wind and cloudburst of a thunderstorm in the village, or the twist of a big fish as it gets away with hook and line. In his descriptions of people Goncharov often singles out a physical trait or a gesture to reveal personality or state of mind. So Alexander's loss of his silken blond hair marks the loss of his initial high hopes. When he drops out of society after being rejected by his young love, his carelessly Bohemian dress reflects his apathy, as his reluctance to don tailcoat, stock and white gloves shows his reluctance to re-enter the world of high society. Similarly, Nadenka, Alexander's first serious love, dramatically demonstrates her wilful nature by impulsively spilling the cup of milk Alexander reaches out to take from her. Decades before Chekhov, who is often noted for this technique, here is a single detail which can reveal a whole mood. Goncharov does not always use details only once however; sometimes he repeats them like a Dickensian leitmotif, as when Alexander's mother keeps asking about her son's lost silken curls.

Though women are central to the action of *An Ordinary Story*, the most important woman enters the novel almost in flashback; that is, Pyotr tells Alexander of his marriage to Lizaveta Alexandrovna only after it is an accomplished fact. The couple's mutual love, the psychological basis of their relationship, is never described. Lizaveta Alexandrovna longs for Pyotr to make the telling gesture of love and midway in the novel draws him to her, but he frees his hand from hers. In the end he desperately needs to show his devotion, but late in life he cannot fall on his knees before her, as he would like, because so melodramatic and passionate a gesture would be incredible at his age. Lizaveta Alexandrovna's need for a gesture is explicitly stated in her interior monologue, as well as in the author's narration: "... could he [Pyotr] have married only to have a hostess, to give his bachelor apartment the fullness and weight of a family home...? With all his intellect could he possibly not comprehend that love is inevitably one of a woman's positive goals?... Oh, let me pay for feeling with tortures, endure all the sufferings inseparable from passion, if only I live a full life...." The luxury with which Pyotr surrounds her "seemed to her a cold mockery of true happiness. She bore witness to two terrible extremes in her nephew and her husband, the one exalted to the point of folly, the other icy to the point of cruelty." In the mind of this crucially important woman the two men are reduced to abstract antitheses. But then every woman's sensibility, including hers, is likewise reduced to an abstract principle early in the novel, when the narrator states: "It was proven long ago that a woman's heart cannot live without love."

Society and education turned many women of Goncharov's time into romantics. While he does not explicitly criticize the role of upper-class women in society, who have nothing to do but live for their feelings, he does mock their genteel education, or lack thereof. Nadenka suffers a total lack of discipline, while

Alexander's second love, Yuliya Tafayeva, receives a "good education." Goncharov describes in detail not only her three language tutors, but also specifies, with ironic comment, the telling differences in their reading lists and assignments. Yuliya's later typically loveless marriage of convenience to a man old enough to be her father makes a mockery of her "good" education, which was all for the sake of love. The husband's complacent self-satisfaction is ridiculed in the interior monologue in which he proves himself suited to be her husband. Has he not been subjected to a similar education (though he hardly remembers a thing)? Although they have no cultural interests in common, she is pretty, and most importantly, their marriage will create a considerable sum of money. Alexander decries such a loveless marriage between an older man and an adolescent girl he doesn't even know, but at the end of the novel he joyfully announces that he too will make a similar late marriage—also for money.

To discuss the action, ideas and characters of *An Ordinary Story* so abstractly can make Goncharov's novel seem schematic, "ideological," and psychologically superficial. *An Ordinary Story* does revolve mainly around a triangle of principal characters and two locales, city and country, with only brief mention of the larger panorama of reality which Goncharov had visualized. The two central characters, Alexander and his uncle, stand out against a less distinct background of secondary figures, such as the Count and Kostyakov, for example, who are largely accessory to the action. The county emissary, the extraordinary Anton Ivanych, who can never refuse to give advice or sit down to a meal, seems a mere target of Goncharov's criticism of provincial inefficiency and indolence. The action of *An Ordinary Story* comes neatly full-circle, unlike the picaresque meanderings of plot in earlier novels. Alexander renounces love for his uncle's role of success, while Pyotr abandons success for love; the uncle also accepts his nephew's embrace for the first time, while the younger man yields at last to the older man's offer of a small loan, largely, it seems, to please his uncle. Without the vast panoramas of a Tolstoy, the action moves unilinearly to a neat conclusion, avoiding, as well, the violent aboutfaces and crises of passion frequent in Goncharov's other contemporary, Dostoevsky. Rather than examine the psychology of his characters, Goncharov invites the reader to observe them ironically at times. One character, Lizaveta Alexandrovna, escapes irony; she remains uncriticized and unexplored in her function as the unfulfilled wife. Yet it is she who lends the novel its essential claim to realism by questioning whether the older Aduyev will restore his wife to life by renouncing his own lifelong pursuit of success. Certainly the practical Pyotr's insistence that his romantic nephew not just dream his ideals but actually "do something" to make them real was intended for Goncharov's contemporaries at a crucial point in their history. This advice still holds for our own time.

Marjorie L. Hoover
New York City

Notes

1. I. A. Goncharov, *Sobranie sochineniia v 8 tt.* (M. 1977-80), vol. 7, p. 353.

2. See John Bayley, "Oblomov's Travels," *New York Review of Books*, 3 March 1988, XXXV, 3:34-35.

3. The italics are Goncharov's. *Op. cit.*, vol. 8, p. 108.

AN
ORDINARY
STORY

Part One

I

One summer day in the village of Grachi everyone on the modest estate of the landowner Anna Pavlovna Aduyeva got up at dawn, from the lady of the house to the watchdog Barbos.

Everyone except Alexander Fyodorych, Anna Pavlovna's only son, who went on sleeping the heroic sleep of a twenty-year-old while the others in the house hustled and bustled about. People were moving about on tiptoe, though, and speaking in a whisper so as not to wake the young master. As soon as someone banged something or started to speak loudly, Anna Pavlovna appeared at once like an aroused lioness and punished the careless offender with a strict rebuke or an insulting name, or she sometimes gave him as hard a push as her anger and strength allowed.

Three servants were cooking in the kitchen, doing the work of ten, even though the whole family of masters consisted only of Anna Pavlovna and Alexander Fyodorych. In the barn the carriage was pulled out and greased. Everyone was busy and sweating from work. Only Barbos did nothing, though in his own way he took part in the general bustle. When a lackey or coachman or a maid passed by, he wagged his tail and carefully sniffed the passerby, all the while seeming to ask with his eyes, "Will you tell me at last what the excitement today is about?"

The excitement was because Anna Pavlovna was sending off her son to enter the civil service in St. Petersburg, or, as she said, to see people and let himself be seen. A murderous day for her! That was the reason she was so sad and distraught. In the midst of her turmoil she often opened her mouth to give some order and suddenly stopped in the middle of a word; her voice betrayed her, she turned and—if she was in time—wiped a tear, or—if not—let it fall into the trunk she was packing with Sasha's linen. The tears had been swelling in her heart for a long time, they rose into her throat, pressed upon her chest and threatened to burst forth in three streams, but somehow she saved them for leave-taking and let out only a few drops from time to time.

She was not alone in weeping over the departure. Evsei, Sasha's valet, was also in deep mourning. He was leaving for St. Petersburg with the master, losing the warmest corner in the house behind a comfortable stove bench in the room belonging to Agrafena, the prime minister of Anna Pavlovna's household and—most important for Evsei—her head keeper of the keys.

In the household the story about Agrafena and Evsei was already an old one. People talked about it, as they do about everything in the world, slandered both, and then, as they also will do about everything, kept quiet. The mistress herself got used to seeing them together, and they enjoyed all of ten happy years. Are there many who count ten happy years in the sum of their life? For all that, now the moment of loss had come! Farewell, warm corner; farewell, Agrafena

Ivanovna; farewell, card games, and coffee and vodka and homemade liqueur—
farewell to everything!

Evsei sat in silence and sighed deeply. Agrafena, frowning, was busily going
about her household work. Her grief was revealed in different ways. She was bitter as she poured the tea that day, and instead of serving the first cup of strong
tea to the mistress as usual, she threw it out with a splash: "No one shall have
you," she said and staunchly suffered a scolding. The coffee she made boiled
over, the cream was scorched, she broke teacups. She did not place the tray on
the table, but put it down with a clatter. She did not open the closet and door, but
banged them. Still, she didn't cry, but got mad at everything and everybody. This
was, by the way, the most striking feature of her personality in general. She was
never content, everything was not as she would have it, she was always protesting,
complaining. But at that—for her—fateful moment her character was revealed in
all its pathos. Most of all, it seems, she was angry at Evsei.

"Agrafena Ivanovna!" he said pitifully and tenderly in a way which did not at
all suit his tall, solid stature.

"Why have you sprawled out there, you idiot?" she answered, as if he were sitting there for the first time. "Get gone, I have to find a towel."

"Oh, Agrafena Ivanovna!" he repeated lazily with a sigh, and got up from the
chair and immediately sat down again once she had fetched the towel.

"He only whines! Look at the idler we're saddled with. God, who wished this
on us! And we can't get rid of him!"

And with a clatter she dropped a spoon in the slops cup of the tea service.
"Agrafena!" came the cry at once from another room. "Have you gone mad!
Don't you know dear Sasha is sleeping? Have you quarreled with your beloved as
a farewell?"

"Don't you move a muscle, sit there like you're dead!" Agrafena hissed like a
serpent, and wiped the cup with both hands, as if she wanted to break it in pieces.

"Farewell, farewell!" said Evsei with a huge sigh. "Our last day, Agrafena
Ivanovna!"

"And thank God! The devil take you away from here. We'll have more room.
Just get gone, there's no place to step the way you've stretched out your legs!"

He was about to touch her on the shoulder—how she answered him! He
sighed again, but did not move from his place; indeed, he would have moved in
vain—Agrafena didn't want him to. Evsei knew this and was not disturbed,

"Will someone sit in my place?" he ventured, still with a sigh.

"You demon!" she answered abruptly.

"God forbid it be Proshka. And will someone else play cards with you?"

"What if it is Proshka, what's the harm in that?" she remarked ill-temperedly.

Evsei got up. "Don't you play cards with Proshka, Heaven help me, don't!" he
said anxiously and almost threateningly.

"And who'll stop me? Do you think you will, you eyesore?"

"My dear, Agrafena Ivanovna!" he began in a pleading voice, embracing her—
I would have said around the waist if she'd had even the slightest sign of a waist.

She answered the embrace with an elbow to his chest.

"My dear, Agrafena Ivanovna!" he repeated, "will Proshka love you as I do?
Look what a playboy he is, doesn't let a single woman get past him. But me, oh!
You're the apple of my eye! But for the will of the masters I'd... Alas!"

At this he groaned and hopelessly waved his arms. Agrafena broke down, and
at last her grief revealed itself in tears.

"Will you get away from me, you devil?" she said weeping. "What's this nonsense, you fool! Me team up with Proshka! Don't you see yourself that you can't get a sensible word out of him? He only knows how to paw you with his big hands."

"And he's tried it with you? Oh, the scoundrel! And you don't even tell me! I would have..."

"Let him try it, he'll find out! Aren't there women among the servants beside me? I should team up with Proshka! Look what you've dreamt up! Even sitting beside him nauseates me—pig of pigs! He's likely to try and hit you or he'll gobble up some of the master's food right under your nose—and you won't notice."

"If something like that happens, Agrafena Ivanovna—Satan is strong, after all— then better let Grishka have my place; at least, he's a quiet, hardworking fellow, not a grimacing fool..."

"What have you thought up now!" Agrafena stormed at him, "saddling me with any and everyone. Am I some kind of... Get out of here! There are plenty of the likes of you around, and I'm supposed to run after every one of them: I'm not that kind. Only you, you demon, did Satan clearly tempt me to get entangled with for my sins, and I repent it... and you've dreamt this up!"

"God reward you for your virtue! It's a stone off my shoulders!" exclaimed Evsei.

"You're happy ! she cried again furiously. "There's something to be happy about—be happy!"

And her lips whitened with anger. Both were silent.

"Agrafena Ivanovna," Evsei said hesitantly after a short wait.

"Well, what is it?"

"I forgot to say, not a grain of food has crossed my lips since morning."

"Is that all that's the matter!"

"From grief, my dear."

From the lower shelf of the pantry, behind the sugar, she fetched a glass of vodka and two enormous slices of bread with ham. Her loving hand had prepared it all for him long before. She thrust it at him as she wouldn't even to a dog. One slice fell on the floor.

"Here, serve yourself! Oh, that you'd... and quiet, don't chomp to wake the whole house."

She turned away from him with an expression that looked like hate, and he slowly began to eat, sullenly watching Agrafena and half-covering his mouth with one hand.

Meanwhile, a driver appeared in the gateway with a troika of horses. An arched yoke had been thrown over the neck of the center horse. The bell tied to the harness swung its tongue dully and with restraint like a drunk who has been bound and thrown into the guardroom. The driver tied up the horses under the overhang of the shed, took off his hat, took a dirty towel from it and wiped the sweat from his face. Anna Pavlovna, seeing him from the window, went pale. Although she was expecting this, her legs gave way and her hands fell down. Getting hold of herself, she called Agrafena.

"Now go on tiptoe, very quietly, and see if Sasha's asleep," she said. "My darling will likely sleep late even on his last day. I'll never tire of seeing him that way. But wait, why you! I'm afraid you will clamber in there like a cow! I'd better go myself..."

And she left.

"Go by yourself, then, you non-cow!" objected Agrafena, returning to her quarters. "Imagine that! She's discovered a cow! Are there many cows like that?"

Coming toward Anna Pavlovna was Alexander Fyodorych, a blond young man in the flower of youth, health and strength. He merrily greeted his mother, but upon seeing the trunk and bundles, he looked troubled, went silently to the window and started tracing on the glass with his finger. A minute later and he was talking with his mother again and he was carefree, even joyous, looking at the preparations for the road.

"What's this, my dear, how you've overslept," said Anna Pavlovna, "is your face a bit swollen? Here, I'll wipe your eyes and cheeks with rosewater."

"No, Mama, please don't."   .

"What do you want for breakfast: tea first or coffee? I also asked for sautéed meat balls with sour cream. What do you want?"

"I don't care, Mama."

Anna Pavlovna went on packing linen, then stopped and looked with sadness at her son.

"Sasha!" she said after a moment.

"What is it Mama?"

She delayed speaking as if she was afraid of something.

"Where are you going, my dear, why?" she finally asked in a low voice.

"What do you mean where, Mama? To St. Petersburg, so as to... so as to... in order to..."

"Listen, Sasha," she said excitedly, putting her hand on his shoulder, apparently with the intention of making a last try, "there's still time. Think it over, stay!"

"Stay! How can I! And look, my things are packed," he said, not knowing what to say.

"Your things packed! Why, look... look... see—and they're not." In three moves she took everything out of the trunk.

"What have you done, Mama? I was all ready—and suddenly again! What will people say..."

He grew sad.

"I'm arguing against it not so much for myself as for you. Why are you going? To seek happiness? Are you really so badly off here? Doesn't your mother think day after day about satisfying your every wish? Of course, you've reached the age when a mother's indulgences alone are not enough for happiness; and I don't ask that. But look around you—they're all looking at you. What about Marya Karpovna's Sonya? What... you blush? What about her, how she—may God keep her—loves you, my darling. They say she hasn't slept for three nights!"

"What do you mean, Mama! She..."

"Yes, yes, as if I don't see... Oh! don't forget she's the one who hemmed your handkerchiefs. 'I', she said, 'I'll do it myself, I'll do it, I won't let anyone else, and I'll embroider the initial.' You see, what more do you want? Stay!"

Looking down, he listened in silence and played with the tassel on his bathrobe.

"What will you find in Petersburg?" she went on. "You think your life there will be the same? Oh, my dear! God knows what you'll see and suffer. Cold and hunger and need—you'll endure them all. There are lots of wicked people everywhere, and you won't find the good ones soon. And respect is respect—whether in the village or in the capital. As soon as you see life in Petersburg, you'll think that you're best off living here, and in all ways, my dear! You're well-educated and clever and handsome. The only joy left me as an old woman will be to look at you. If you marry and God should give you children, I'll be nursemaid to them—and I'll live without sorrow and without worries; I'll live out my life in peace, quietly, not envying anyone. But there, maybe it won't be good, maybe you'll remember my words... Stay, dear Sasha—won't you?"

He coughed and sighed, but said not a word.

"And look here," she went on, opening the door to the balcony, "aren't you sorry to leave such a spot?"

The smell of fresh air wafted into the room from the balcony. A garden extended from the house far into the distance, with ancient lime trees, thick wild roses, bird cherry trees, and lilac bushes. Flowers of all different colors bloomed among the trees and little paths led in various directions; further on, a lake quietly lapped against its shores, bathed on one side by the golden rays of the morning sun and smooth as a mirror, and on the other side, dark blue like the sky, which was reflected in it, and barely marked by a ripple. And there in the distance meadows of variegated waving grain spread out, to form an amphitheater, adjoining a thick forest.

Anna Pavlovna shielded her eyes from the sun with one hand and with the other pointed out each thing in turn to her son.

"Look," she said, "with what beauty God has clothed our fields! From those fields over there we'll harvest up to three hundred bushels of rye alone, and there is wheat and buckwheat. Though the buckwheat is not as good as last year—it will be poor, it seems. And the forest, how the forest has prospered! Consider how great is the wisdom of God! We shall sell close to a thousand pieces of wood from our plot. And the wild game, the game! And indeed, it's all yours, my dear boy! I'm only your estate manager. Just look at the lake—what splendor! It's really heavenly! It's so full of fish there—we only buy sturgeon, but perch, bass and carp abound both for ourselves and others. Over there graze your very own cows and horses. You alone are lord of everything here, but there anybody might start to order you about. And you want to run away from such bliss, without even knowing where—perhaps to some abyss, God forbid... Stay!"

He was silent.

"But you're not listening," she said. "What are you staring at so intently?"

Silently, pensively, he pointed into the distance. Anna Pavlovna looked and her face changed. There the road wound like a snake between the fields and disappeared behind the forest, the road to the Promised Land, to St. Petersburg. Anna Pavlovna remained silent for several minutes in order to regain her composure.

"So that's the way it is," she managed to say at last, disheartened. "Well, my dear, God be with you! Go then, if you feel so strongly the urge to get away! I am not keeping you! At least you won't say that your mother consumed your youth and life."

Poor mother! So this is the reward for your love! You didn't expect this! That's the point: Mothers don't expect rewards. A mother loves without reason and without knowing why. If you're great, glorious, handsome, proud, if your name is on everyone's lips, if your deeds are renowned round the world—your old mother's head will shake with joy, she'll cry, laugh and pray long and fervently. And her boy for the most part won't even think about sharing his fame with his parent. But if you are poor in mind and spirit, if nature has branded you with ugliness, if the sting of illness bites at your heart or body, in the end people will reject you and there'll be no place for you among them—then all the more place you'll find in your mother's heart. She will press the deformed, failed offspring the closer to her heart and will pray still longer and more fervently.

How can we call Alexander heartless because he resolved to leave? He was twenty years old. Life had smiled upon him since infancy. His mother sang him lullabies and spoiled him as an only child will be spoiled. His nurse always sang to him in his cradle that he would walk in gold and know no pain. His teachers affirmed that he would go far, and after his return home his neighbor's daughter smiled at him. Even the old cat Vaska was friendlier to him than to anyone in the house.

He knew about grief, tears, and misfortunes only by hearsay, as one knows about some disease which has not yet broken out, but which lurks imperceptibly somewhere among the masses. And so he saw the future in a cheerful light. Something beckoned him from afar, but precisely what—he didn't know. He couldn't quite make out the alluring spirits that fluttered there. He could hear mixed sounds—first the voice of fame, than the voice of love, and all this put him in a state of sweet agitation.

His domestic world soon began to constrain him. Nature, his mother's kindnesses, the awe of his nanny and all the servants, his soft bed, the tasty delicacies, even Vaska's purring—all these blessings so highly esteemed in our declining years—he was happy to exchange for the unknown which was full of alluring and mysterious charms. Even Sophie's love, a first, tender, and rosy love, could not keep him here. What was this love to him? He dreamed of a colossal passion which knows no limits and moves men to perform celebrated feats. Meanwhile, while awaiting a great love, he loved Sophie with a small one. He dreamed, too, of the good he would do his country. A diligent student, he had learned a lot. His diploma documented his knowledge of some dozen subjects and some half-dozen ancient and modern languages. Most of all, he dreamed of a writer's fame. His poetry astonished his comrades. Numerous paths spread out before him, and each one seemed better than the other. He didn't know which one to rush on to. Only the direct path was hidden from his gaze; had he noted it, then perhaps he wouldn't have left.

How could he have stayed? His mother wished it—that was another matter again and a very natural one. All the feelings in her heart had died but one—love for her son—and her heart clung fervently to this last object. What would she do without him? Simply die. It was proven long ago that a woman's heart cannot live without love.

Alexander was spoiled, but he had not been ruined by his life at home. Nature had done so well in creating him that his mother's love and the adoration of those around him had affected only his good sides, prematurely developing, for example, an affectionate tenderness in him and implanting an excessive trust in everything. These same causes, perhaps, also aroused self-esteem in him, but self-esteem in itself, after all, is only a form; everything depends on the material you pour into it.

A much greater misfortune for him was the fact that for all her tenderness his mother was not able to give him a real view of life and did not prepare him for the struggle which awaited him and awaits everyone. But that would have required a skillful hand, a subtle mind, and a store of much experience not limited by the narrow horizon of the village. She would even have had to love him less, not think for him every minute, not avert every worry and unpleasantness from him, not weep and suffer in his stead, so that even in childhood he might have felt the approach of a storm himself, managed with his own forces and thought about his destiny—in a word, come to know that he was a man. How was Anna Pavlovna to understand all that, let alone carry it out? The reader has seen what sort she was. Still, shouldn't we take another look?

She has already forgotten her son's egoism. Alexander Fyodorych found her packing linen and clothes for a second time. In her frantic efforts to prepare things for the road she seemed to have quite failed to remember her grief.

"Now, Sasha dear, note carefully where I'm putting things," she said. "The sheets are at the very bottom of the trunk—a dozen. Look, are they listed?"

"Yes, Mama dear."

"All with your initials, see, A. A. All done by darling Sonya! Without her our foolish servants wouldn't have moved so fast. What next? Yes, the pillowcases. One, two, three, four—yes, a dozen here. Here are the shirts, three dozen. What fabric—it's a pleasure to see! This is Dutch material. I went to Vasily Vasilich's factory myself; he picked out three pieces of the best. Check them, dear, by your list each time you fetch them from the laundress; they're all new. You won't see many such shirts there—they might substitute others. There are, after all, people so low they have no fear of God. Twenty-two pairs of socks... Do you know what I thought of? Putting your wallet with the money in one sock. You won't need it before St. Petersburg, so if—God forbid!—somebody rummages around, he won't find it. And the letters to your uncle I'm putting in the same place. I expect he'll be delighted! After all, not to exchange a word for seventeen years is no laughing matter! Here are your neckerchiefs, here are the handkerchiefs; Sonya still has a half a dozen. Don't lose the handkerchiefs, dear; they're made of splendid material—half-cambric. I got it for two and a quarter at Mikheyev's. Well, we're done with the linen. Now the clothes... Now, where's Evsei? Why isn't he watching? Evsei!"

Evsei lazily entered the room.

"Madam wishes?" he asked even more lazily.

"Madam wishes?" said Mrs. Aduyeva angrily. "Why aren't you watching the way I'm packing? And on the way there, when you have to get out something you'll go turning everything topsy-turvy. Can't tear yourself away from your beloved—that treasure! The day is long, you'll have time! Is this the way you'll be taking care of the master when you get there? Watch me! Here, look, this is the good dress coat—see where I'm putting it? And you, Sasha dear, take care of it, don't pull it out every day; they were asking sixteen rubles for this cloth. Put it on when you go to see proper people, and don't sit any old way, the way your aunt, almost deliberately, never sits down on an empty chair or sofa, but manages to plop down where there's a hat or something like that; the other day she sat down on a plate with jam, made such a mess! When you go to see more simple people, wear this cotton coat. Now for the vests—one, two, three, four. Two pairs of trousers. Well, then! That's enough clothes for about three years. Oh, I'm worn out! It's not easy to rush about the whole morning! Run along, Evsei. Let's talk, Sasha dear, about something else. If guests come, there won't be time for this."

She sat down on the sofa and made him sit down beside her.

"So, Sasha," she said after a moment's silence, "you're going to a foreign land..."

"What kind of 'foreign' land is Petersburg! Come now, Mama dear!"

"Wait a minute, wait—listen to everything I want to say! God alone knows what you'll encounter there, what you'll look upon with pleasure—both good and bad. I hope my Heavenly Father will give you strength; and above all, dear, don't you forget Him; remember that there's no salvation anywhere and in anything without faith. If you rise to a high rank there, or join the nobility—after all, we're not worse than others: your father was a nobleman, a major—all the same, be obedient to the Lord God. Pray, whether in good or bad fortune, and not according to the saying, 'The peasant won't make the sign of the cross if it doesn't thunder.' Some men won't look into a church as long as their luck lasts, but as soon as they suffer a setback they'll go light candles at a ruble each and give to the poor. This is a great sin. A word about the poor. Don't waste money on them for nothing, don't give a lot. Why spoil them? You won't impress them. They'll spend it on drink and laugh at you. I know you have a soft heart; you'll probably start handing out silver coins. That's not at all necessary; God will provide. Will you go to church? Will you go to mass on Sundays?"

She sighed.

Alexander was silent. He remembered that when he was a university student and lived in the capital of the province, he hadn't attended church very faithfully, and in the country he had accompanied his mother to mass only to please her. It went against his conscience to deceive her. He was silent. His mother understood his silence and sighed again.

"Well, I shan't force you," she went on. "You're young. Where would you have found such zeal for God's church as we old people? Besides, perhaps your work will prevent you, or you'll stay late at society people's and sleep late. God will forgive your youth. Don't be sorry—you have a mother. She won't sleep late. As long as even a drop of blood remains in me, as long as the tears in my eyes have not dried and God suffers my sins, I will crawl, if I haven't the strength to walk, to the church door, and I will give my last sigh, weep my last tear for you, my dear. I'll pray that you'll find good health and advancement and medals and earthly and heavenly blessings. Surely the merciful father will not scorn a poor old woman's prayer. I need nothing for myself. Let him take everything from me: health, life; let him send me blindness—if only he gives you every joy, happiness and bliss..."

She did not finish speaking; tears fell from her eyes.

Alexander jumped up from his place.

"Mama dear," he said.

"Please, sit down, sit down!" she answered, quickly wiping her tears. "I still have a lot to say... What, indeed, did I want to say?—it's gone... Look, what a memory I have nowadays... Oh, yes! fast for Lent, my dear, that's important! God will forgive you for Wednesdays and Fridays, but the Lenten Fast—God forbid! Take Mikhailo Mikhailych, who thinks he's an intelligent person and what does he do? He eats the same way whether it's Passion Week or a season you can eat meat. Makes your hair stand on end! And he goes and helps the poor, as if his donations were acceptable to God. Listen, he once gave a ten-ruble bill to an old man who took it, then turned aside and spat. They all bow to him and say God knows what to his face, but behind his back they cross themselves when he's mentioned, as if he's some evil spirit."

Alexander listened with some impatience and looked out the window at the distant road.

She fell silent a moment.

"Take care of your health, above all," she continued. "If—God forbid—you fall dangerously ill, write... I'll gather up my forces and come. Who will take care of you there? Besides, they'll manage to cheat a sick person there. Don't walk in the streets late at night, keep away from people who look vicious. Watch your money... Oh, take care of it for a rainy day! Spend sensibly. Money, curses on it, is the root of all good and evil. Don't throw it away, don't acquire unnecessary tastes. You will get exactly two thousand five hundred rubles a year from me. Two thousand five hundred rubles is no joke! Don't start acquiring luxuries of any sort, nothing like that, but don't deny yourself what you can afford; if you feel like treating yourself, don't be miserly. Don't surrender to alcohol—alas, it's the greatest enemy of man! And one more thing" (here she lowered her voice) "beware of women! I know them! There are ones so shameless they'll hang themselves round the neck of someone like you on first sight..."

She looked lovingly at her son.

"Enough, Mama dear; might I have breakfast?" he said almost with vexation.

"Right away, right away... one more word..."

"Don't cast your eye upon a married woman," she hurried to finish, adding, "It's a great sin! 'Thou shalt not covet thy neighbor's wife,' it says in the Bible. If some woman there should try to catch you before there's a wedding—God prevent!—don't dare even think of it! They're ready to attach themselves to you as soon as they see you have money and are good-looking. Should your superior or some important person or rich nobleman set his sights on you and want to marry his daughter to you—well, that's possible, but you must write then; somehow I'll get there and have a look so they won't palm off some girl just to get rid of her— an old maid or a good-for-nothing. It's a plus for any one to catch a bachelor like you. Well, and if you fall in love yourself and a nice girl is willing, then in that case..."—here she spoke still more softly—"Sonya can be pushed aside." (Out of love for her son the old woman was ready to go against her conscience.) "What if Marya Karpovna has begun to dream of it! Her daughter's no match for you. A country girl! The likes of her needn't set their caps for you."

"Sofiya! No, Mama dear, I shall never forget her!" Alexander said.

"Come, come, my dear! calm down! I'm just talking. Do your work there, come back here, and then see what God wills. There will always be enough girls to marry! If you don't forget her, so be it... But..."

She wanted to say something, but hesitated, then bent down to his ear and asked softly, "But will you remember... your mother?"

"Look what we've talked ourselves around to," he interrupted. "Tell them to serve right away whatever there is for breakfast—fried eggs, did you say? Forget you! How could you think that? God will punish me..."

"Stop, stop, Sasha," she began hastily, "Don't bring that down on yourself! No, no! whatever comes, if such a sin takes place, let me alone suffer. You're young, just beginning to live, you'll make friends and marry—a young wife will take your mother's place, and all that... No! May God bless you, as I give you my blessing."

She kissed him on the forehead and with this concluded her admonitions.

"So why hasn't anyone come to say goodbye?" she said. "Aren't Marya Karpovna or Anton Ivanych or our priest coming? Communion is surely over by now! Oh, look, someone's driving up! It looks like Anton Ivanych... So it is, speak of the devil and he appears."

Who doesn't know Anton Ivanych? He's the Eternal Jew. He has existed always and everywhere, since the most ancient times, and he has never become extinct. He attended Greek and Roman banquets and ate, of course, of the fatted calf slaughtered by a happy father upon the return of his prodigal son.

Here in our Russia he takes on various shapes. The one we're talking about was this sort: he owned around twenty serfs who had been pawned and pawned again. He lived practically in a peasant's hut, or some kind of strange building that looked like a shed—the entrance somewhere in back across a plank alongside a wicker fence. Yet for twenty years he's been insisting he'll begin building a new house in the spring. He doesn't keep house. There isn't one of his acquaintances who has dined or supped or drunk tea at his house, but there isn't one either at whose house he hasn't done all that fifty times a year. Anton Ivanych used to wear wide, baggy pants and a short jacket; now on weekdays he goes about in a frock coat and trousers and on holidays he wears a cutaway of indescribable tailoring. He's stout in appearance because he doesn't have any grief, worries or trouble, though he pretends he has lived his whole life with the grief and worry of others. But, after all, everyone knows that the grief and worry of others don't make us lose weight—that's the way people are.

Properly speaking, Anton Ivanych is of no use to anyone for anything, but no ceremony—neither wedding nor funeral—takes place without him. He is present at every dinner and evening party and all family conferences; nobody takes a step without him. Some might perhaps think that he's very helpful, that he is carrying out some important mission here, giving good advice or concluding a piece of business there—no, not in the least! Nobody entrusts anything of the sort to him; he has no qualifications and knows nothing, neither how to appear in court, nor how to be an intermediary or an arbitrator—absolutely nothing.

But, for all that, they commission him, for instance, to drop by in passing to give a greeting from a certain lady to a certain gentleman and he'll take it there at an opportune time to have breakfast too. Or he'll be asked to inform a certain person that a certain document has been received, but which document isn't specified; or to take a tub of honey somewhere with the caution not to spill it, or a packet of seeds with the warning not to strew any; or to send remembrances when someone has a birthday. Anton Ivanych is also used for matters considered unsuitable to be entrusted to a servant. "We can't send Petrushka," they say. "Before you know it, he'll garble it. No, better have Anton Ivanych drive over!" Or: "It's awkward to send a servant; this or that lady or gentleman will be offended, and so it's better to send Anton Ivanych."

How it would astonish everyone if suddenly he failed to come to a dinner or a party!

"But where's Anton Ivanych?" everyone would be sure to ask in astonishment. "What's the matter with him? Why isn't he here?"

And without him the dinner isn't a dinner. Then they'll even send someone as a deputy to find out what's the matter, whether he's taken ill or gone away. And if he's sick, he'll get more sympathy than one of their own relatives.

Anton Ivanych kissed Anna Pavlovna's hand.

"Good day, dear Anna Pavlovna! I have the honor to congratulate you on your new acquisition."

"What new acquisition, Anton Ivanych?" asked Anna Pavlovna, looking herself over from head to toe.

"Why the little bridge at the gate! You can see you've just nailed it together, haven't you? I hear the boards don't dance under the wheels. I look, and it's new!"

Upon encountering acquaintances he almost always greets them with best wishes for some occasion—either for Lent or spring or autumn; if it gets cold after a thaw, then he congratulates them on the cold; if after a cold spell it thaws, then on its warming up...

This time there wasn't anything of the sort, but he thinks of something, of course.

"Alexandra Vasilievna, Matryona Mikhailovna, Pyotr Sergeich send you greetings," he said.

"My deepest thanks, Anton Ivanych! Are their children well?"

"Yes, thank God. I bring you God's blessing: the priest is on his way behind me. But have you heard, Madame, that our Semyon Arkhipych?..."

"What is it?"

"He's departed this life."

"What did you say! When?"

"Yesterday morning. I was informed toward evening. A young fellow galloped over, and I set off, indeed, I didn't sleep all night. Everyone's weeping and condolences must be offered and arrangements made—everyone there has lost heart. There are floods of tears—I alone..."

"Goodness, oh my goodness," said Anna Pavlovna, shaking her head. "This life of ours! Oh, how could this have happened? He sent his greetings with you just this week!"

"Yes, Madame! But then he's been unwell off and on for a long time, he's a very old man. It's a wonder he hasn't collapsed before now!"

"What do you mean old! He's only a year older than my dead husband. May his soul rest in Heaven!" said Anna Pavlovna, crossing herself. "I'm sorry for poor Fedosya Petrovna. She's left with small children on her hands. That's no laughing matter: five of them and almost all little girls! When is the funeral?"

"Tomorrow."

"Clearly everyone has his own sorrow, Anton Ivanych. I'm just sending off my son."

"What's to be done, Anna Pavlovna, we're all human! 'Endure,' it says in the Scriptures."

"Don't be angry that I've bothered you—sorrow should be shared with others. You love us like family."

"Oh, Madame Anna Pavlovna! Whom should I love, if not you? Are there many here like you? You don't know your own worth. I have my hands full—my new house is going around in my head now. Yesterday I fought the whole morning with the contractor, somehow we always disagree... but how, I thought, can I not go? What will she do alone there, I thought, without me? She's not young: perhaps she'll lose her head."

"God preserve you, Anton Ivanych, for not forgetting us! I really am not myself—there's such a vacuum in my head that I don't see anything! My throat is completely parched from crying. Please have a bite to eat. You're tired and you must be hungry."

"I humbly thank you. I admit I had a little something on the way at Pyotr Sergeich's; yes, I grabbed a bite. Well, but that won't interfere. The priest will be coming, let him give his blessing. Why, there he is at the entrance!"

The priest had arrived and Marya Karpovna, too, with her daughter, a plump and rosy-cheeked girl with a smile and tearful eyes. Sofiya's eyes and whole facial expression clearly said, "I shall love simply, without pretensions, I shall take care of my husband as a nanny would, obey him in everything and never appear more clever than he; indeed, how can you be more clever than your husband? That's a sin! I shall work diligently at housekeeping, bear him half a dozen children, feed them myself, dress them and do all the family sewing." The roundness and freshness of her cheeks and the fullness of her breasts confirmed her promise about the children. But at this moment the tears in her eyes and her sad smile gave her less conventional appeal.

First of all, morning prayers were held, for which Anton Ivanych called together the servants, lighted a candle, took the book from the priest when he had finished reading and passed it to the deacon, and then poured some holy water into a phial, hid it in his pocket, and said, "That's for Agafya Nikitishna." They sat down at the table. Except for Anton Ivanych and the priest, as usual nobody touched anything, but in their stead, Anton Ivanych did full honor to this Homeric breakfast. Anna Pavlovna cried the whole time and furtively wiped her tears.

"You've wasted enough of your tears, dear Anna Pavlovna!" said Anton Ivanych with pretended vexation, filling a small glass with liqueur. "Are you sending him to slaughter or something?" Then, having drunk half the glass, he smacked his lips.

"What a liqueur! What an aroma!" he said with a look of great pleasure. "You won't find the like of that in the whole province!"

"It's aged for three years," Anna Pavlovna burst out sobbing. "I just... now... opened it... for you."

"Ach, Anna Pavlovna, it's sickening to look at you," Anton Ivanych began again. "There's no one to punish you; if there were he'd beat and beat you!"

"Judge for yourself, Anton Ivanych, he's my only son and now he's going far away. If I die, there's no one to bury me."

"And what are we here for? Am I a stranger to you perhaps? And why are you hurrying to die? Watch out, you could be getting married! Then how I'd dance at the wedding! Enough weeping now!"

"I can't stop, Anton Ivanych, I just can't. I don't know myself where the tears come from."

"To keep such a fine fellow cooped up! Give him his freedom; he'll spread his wings and do Heaven knows what great deeds. He'll go far there!"

"Would it were so! Why have you taken so little of the pie? Have some more!"

"I shall, only let me finish this piece. To your health, Alexander Fyodorych! Bon voyage! Come back very soon; yes, and get married! Oh, Sofiya Vasilievna, why did you blush?"

"It's nothing... I only..."

"Oh, youth, youth! hee, hee, hee!"

"With you here, Anton Ivanych, one doesn't feel grief," said Anna Pavlovna. "You know how to comfort so well, God keep you! Do have more liqueur."

"I will, Madame, I will. How could I not drink to the departure?"

The breakfast ended. The driver had harnessed the carriage long ago. It was brought up to the entrance. People ran out, one after another. Someone carried the trunk, another a bundle, a third a sack. People swarmed about the carriage like flies around something sweet, and they all were thrusting their arms toward it.

"It's better to put the trunk here like this," said one, "and the basket of food there."

"But where will they put their legs?" another answered. "Better put the trunk in lengthwise, then you can put the basket on one side."

"That way the eiderdown will slide off, if the trunk is lengthwise. Better put it crosswise. What else? Did they pack the boots?"

"I don't know. Who packed?"

"I didn't. Wait, have a look—aren't they there on top?"

"You go look."

"And why don't you? I really have no time!"

"Here, this too, here don't forget this!" cried a maid, thrusting her hand with a bundle past the heads.

"Give it here!"

"Put it in the trunk somehow, they forgot it just now," said another, getting up on the coach step and handing in a brush and comb.

"Where are we to put it now?" a stout lackey cried out at her angrily. "Go away! you see the trunk's at the very bottom!"

"The mistress gave orders; what's it to me, throw it away, you devils!"

"Well, give it here all the same, but quick. We can put it here in the side pocket."

The shaft horse incessantly raised and shook his head. The little bell there-upon each time gave out a sharp sound signalling the departure, while the side horses stood thoughtfully, drooping their heads, as if they understood the whole delight of the journey ahead, and infrequently switching their tails or sticking out their lower lip toward the shaft horse. Finally the fateful moment came. One more prayer was said.

"Get in the carriage, get in everyone!" commanded Anton Ivanych. "Kindly get in, Alexander Fyodorych! And you, Evsei, get in. Get in, please, get in!" And he himself sat down sideways on a chair for just a second! "Now, then, god-speed!"

At this point Anna Pavlovna cried out and hung on Alexander's neck.

"Farewell, farewell, my dear!" was audible amid her sobs, "will I see you again?..."

That was all that could be understood. At that moment the sound of a differ-ent bell was heard: a cart drawn by a troika flew into the courtyard. Jumping down from the cart, a young man, covered with dust, ran into the room and threw himself upon Alexander's neck.

"Pospelov!" "Aduyev!" they exclaimed simultaneously, squeezing each other in an embrace.

"Where have you come from, how?"

"From home; I've galloped round the clock purposely to say goodbye to you."

"My friend! My friend! A true friend!" said Aduyev with tears in his eyes. "To gallop a hundred miles to say farewell! Oh, there is friendship in the world! Forever, isn't that so?" said Alexander fervently, pressing his friend's hand and springing toward him.

"To the grave!" answered the friend, pressing Alexander's hand harder and springing toward him.

"Write to me!"

"Yes, yes, and you to me!"

Anna Pavlovna didn't know how to welcome Pospelov enough. The depar-ture was delayed half an hour. Finally they were ready.

They all set off on foot as far as the orchard. At the moment they were passing through the dark entrance hall, Sophie and Alexander threw themselves at each other.

"Sasha! dear Sasha!..." "Dear Sonya!" they whispered, and the words died in a kiss.

"Will you forget me there?" she said tearfully.

"Oh, how little you know me! I shall return, believe me, and another girl will never..."

"Here, take this quickly; it's my hair and a little ring."

He skillfully hid both in his pocket.

Anna Pavlovna walked ahead with her son and Pospelov, then Marya Karpovna with her daughter, finally the priest with Anton Ivanych. The carriage followed them at some distance. The driver could hardly hold the horses. The ser-vants surrounded Evsei at the gate.

"Farewell, Evsei Ivanych, farewell, darling, don't forget us!" was heard on all sides.

"Farewell, friends; don't bear me any grudges!"

"Farewell, dear Evsei, farewell, my dearest!" said his mother, embracing him. "Here's a little icon; it's my blessing. Remember your faith, Evsei, don't abandon me and take up with the heathen there, or I'll curse you! Don't drink, don't steal; serve the master faithfully and truthfully. Farewell, farewell!"

She covered her face with her apron and went away.

"Farewell, Mother dear!" lazily mumbled Evsei.

A little girl about twelve years old threw herself toward him.

"Say goodbye to your little sister!" said one woman.

"And you go on back!" said Evsei, kissing her, "so, farewell! Farewell! Get going now, with your bare feet, back to the hut!"

Agrafena stood apart from everyone, the last one. Her face paled.

"Farewell, Agrafena Ivanovna!" Evsei said, drawing it out and raising his voice; he even held out his hands to her.

She let herself be embraced, but did not respond to the embrace. Only her face was distorted.

"It's for you!" she said, taking out a bag with something from under her apron and thrusting it at him. "So then, I guess you'll have your fun with the Petersburg girls!" she added, attentively observing him from the side. And in this glance all her sorrow and jealousy showed.

"Me have my fun, me?" Evsei began. "May God strike me dead on the spot, put out my eyes! May the earth swallow me, if I do anything of the kind there..."

"All right, all right!" Agrafena murmured distrustfully.

"Oh, I almost forgot!" said Evsei, and pulled a soiled pack of cards from his pocket. "They're for you, Agrafena Ivanovna, to remember me by; after all, there's no place for you to get them here."

He held out his hand.

"Give them to me, Evsei Ivanych," Proshka called out of the crowd.

"To you! I'd rather burn them than give them to you!" and he hid the cards in his pocket.

"So give them to me, you fool!" said Agrafena.

"No, Agrafena Ivanovna, do what you will, but I shan't give them to you; you'd start to play with him. Farewell!"

Not looking back, he waved his hand and lazily walked after the carriage, which, it seemed, he could have carried off on his shoulders, Alexander, driver, horses and all.

"Damn him!" said Agrafena, looking after him and wiping tears from her eyes with an end of her scarf.

They stopped at the orchard. While Anna Pavlovna sobbed and said goodbye to her son, Anton Ivanych patted one horse on the neck, then took it by the nostrils and shook it to both sides, which the horse seemed to resent greatly, for it bared its teeth and snorted.

"Tighten the breeching on the shaft horse," he said to the driver, "see, the strap on the side."

The driver looked at the strap, and seeing that it was in its proper place, didn't move off the box, but only straightened the breeching a little with the whip.

"Well, it's time, God be with you," said Anton Ivanych. "You've tortured yourself enough, Anna Pavlovna. And you, get in, Alexander Fyodorych. You must get to Shishko while it's light. Farewell, farewell, God give you happiness, promotion, medals, all things favorable and good, and property!!! Now, God be with you, start the horses, and mind you drive more easily there on the downgrade!" he added, turning to the driver.

Alexander got into the carriage, bathed in tears, and Evsei went up to the mistress, made a bow to her toes and kissed her hand. She gave him a five-ruble note.

"Look now, Evsei, remember: If you're a good servant, I'll marry you to Agrafena, but if not, then..."

She could not speak further. Evsei climbed up on the box. The driver, bored with the long wait, seemed to come alive. He pressed down his hat, straightened himself in his seat and picked up the reins; the horses moved first in a gentle trot. He flicked the side horses once, one after the other; they jumped, stretched, and the troika sped along the road into the forest. The crowd that saw them off was left behind in a cloud of dust, silent and motionless, until the carriage disappeared altogether from sight. Anton Ivanych came to first.

"Well, let us all go home now!" he said.

Alexander looked back from the carriage as long as possible, then fell face forward on the cushion.

Anna Pavlovna said, "Don't leave me when I'm so miserable, Anton Ivanych, stay for dinner here!"

"All right, dear lady, I'm ready! And for supper too, if you'd like."

"Yes, and you could stay the night too."

"Impossible, the funeral's tomorrow!"

"Oh, that's right! Well, I won't keep you. Give Fedosya Petrovna my greetings, say that I deeply sympathize with her grief and would have visited her myself, but that, God, tell her, sent sorrow to me too—I have said goodbye to my son."

"I'll tell her, I'll tell her, I shan't forget."

"My darling, dear Sasha," she whispered, looking around, "and now you've gone, vanished from my sight!"

Aduyeva sat silent a whole day, ate no dinner or supper. To make up, Anton Ivanych talked, dined and supped.

"Where is he now, my darling?" was all she would say at times.

"He should be in Neplyuev by now. No, what am I imagining? Not yet in Neplyuev, but getting there. He'll have tea there," Anton Ivanych replied.

"No, he never drinks tea at this hour."

And so in her thoughts Anna Pavlovna traveled with him. Then, when by her count he should have arrived in St. Petersburg, she prayed, told his fortune with cards, or talked about him with Marya Karpovna.

And he?

We'll meet him in St. Petersburg.

II

Our hero's uncle, Pyotr Ivanovich Aduyev, had, like him, been sent off at age twenty to St. Petersburg by his older brother, Alexander's father, and had lived there seventeen years without returning. After his brother's death he no longer corresponded with his relatives, and Anna Pavlovna knew nothing about him after he sold his modest estate not far from her village.

In Petersburg he was said to be wealthy and perhaps not inexplicably. He worked in the civil service under some important person or other and wore several honorary ribbons in his buttonhole. He lived on a big street, occupied a good apartment, kept three servants and as many horses. He was not old, but rather "a man in the best years" between thirty-five and forty. Incidentally he did not like going into the subject of his years, not out of petty self-love, but because of some considered calculation, as if he meant to insure his life for a higher fee. Yet in his manner of hiding his actual age, at least one could not discern any vain intentions to charm the fair sex.

He was a tall, well-proportioned man with large, regular features and a swarthy complexion; he had an even, pleasing gait and reserved, but pleasant manners. Such men are usually called *beaux hommes*.

Reserve appeared in his face also, that is, the ability to control himself, not to let his face be the mirror of his soul. He was of the opinion that this was awkward—both for himself and for others. That's how he was in society. His face couldn't be called wooden, though; no, it was merely calm. But sometimes traces of weariness were perceptible—doubtless from doubled efforts. He had the reputation of a busy and energetic man. He was always carefully, even stylishly dressed, not to any extreme, rather only with taste. He wore fine shirts; his hands were full and white, the nails long and transparent.

One day when he awoke in the morning and rang, his manservant brought three letters with his tea and a message that a young gentleman had come by, who had called himself Alexander Fyodorych Aduyev and called him, Pyotr Ivanych, his uncle, and he had promised to drop by around twelve.

Pyotr Ivanych listened calmly as usual to this news, pricking up his ears only a little and raising his eyebrows.

"Good, you may go," he told the servant.

Then he took one letter, started to open it, but stopped and thought a moment.

"A nephew from the country—that's a surprise!" he muttered. "And I'd hoped they'd forgotten me down there. Anyway, why bother with them! I'll get rid of him..."

He rang again.

"Tell that gentleman when he comes, that after I got up, I immediately left to go to the factory and will be back in three months."

"Very good, sir," answered the servant, "but what shall I do with the presents?"

"With what presents? "

"His servant brought them. The mistress, he said, sent presents from the country."

"Presents?"

"Yes, sir: a tub of honey, a bag of dried raspberries..."

Pyotr Ivanovich shrugged his shoulders.

"Two pieces of cloth, and jam..."

"I can imagine the cloth must be good..."

"Good cloth and sweet jam."

"Go on then, I'll have a look right away."

He picked up one letter, opened it and took in a page at a glance. It looked like an important Old Slavic document: the letter "v" was represented by two crossed strokes, one up, one down, while the letter "k" was simply two strokes; the whole thing was written without punctuation.

Aduyev began to read half-aloud:

Dear Mr. Pyotr Ivanovich! Having known your deceased father and been a friend, and I often comforted you yourself in childhood and broke bread in your home, for this reason I feel complete confidence in your zeal and favor, and that you have not forgotten me, an old man, Vasily Tikhonych, and we here esteem you and your parents most kindly, and pray God...

"What's this nonsense? From whom is this?" said Pyotr Ivanych, looking at the signature, "Vasily Zayezzhalov—strike me dead—I don't remember. What does he want of me?"
And he began to read further:

Now my most humble request and a bother for you—don't refuse, dear sir... for you in Petersburg it isn't the same as here, where, it seems, everything is known and everyone else's business. I have been caught up in a cursed lawsuit and for the seventh year now I can't get out of it. Do you remember the little wood a mile or so from my little village? The Registry Bureau made a mistake on the deed, and my adversary, Medvedev, is basing his suit on it. He says it's a forgery and that's that. Medvedev is the one who fished in your tracts without permission; your late father chased him out and shamed him, he wanted to complain to the governor about the man's highhandedness, but out of kindness, God rest his soul, he let it go, considering it unnecessary to act against such a villain. Help me, dear sir, Pyotr Ivanych; the affair is now in the Senate, I don't know in which department there and in whose hands, but surely they'll show you at once. Go see the secretaries and senators; get them on my side; tell them it's a mistake, that I'm truly suffering from a mistake in the deed: they'll do anything for you. By the way, while there get me patents for three ranks and send them to me. There's another little matter for you of great importance, dear sir, Pyotr Ivanych; show some sympathy to an innocently persecuted martyr and help us with advice and action. We have here in the provincial government a Councillor Drozhzhov, an angel, not a mere man; he'd die rather than betray his friends. I don't stay with anyone in town but him—as soon as I arrive, I go straight to his place; I live there for weeks and God forbid I should even think of staying with anyone else. He feeds me and gives me drink, and we play Boston from dinner till late at night. And now they've conspired against this man and are pressing him to retire. Go to see all the powerful people there—you're one of us—and persuade them what a fine man Afanasy Ivanych is. If there's something to be done, he speeds it on its way. Tell them the denunciation is surely false by connivance of the governor's secretary—they'll listen to you, and write me about it by return mail. And go see my former colleague Kostyakov. I heard from a traveler from your Petersburg who was passing through, one Studenitsyn—maybe you know him—that he lives in the outskirts, in Peski; any child there will show you the house. Write by return post, don't delay, whether he's alive, in good health, what he's doing, whether he remembers me. Make his acquaintance and become friends with him; he's a splendid fellow—open-hearted and a real joker. I'll finish my little note with one more tiny wish...

Aduyev stopped reading, slowly tore the letter in four and threw it under the table into the waste basket, then stretched and yawned.

He took the other letter and began reading half-aloud: "Dear Brother, Honored Sir, Pyotr Ivanych!"

"What sister!" said Aduyev, looking at the signature. "Marya Gorbatova..." He turned his face to the ceiling, half-remembering something...

"Whatever is this? Something familiar... oh, this is just great—my brother was married to a Gorbatova; this must be her sister, this is the girl... ah! I remember..."

He frowned and began to read. "Though destiny parted us, perhaps forever, and an abyss lies between us; years have passed..."

He skipped several lines and read further:

> Until the grave I shall remember how we walked together around our lake, and you at risk of life and health waded up to your knees in water to get a big yellow flower for me with your cane, how some kind of sap flowed from its stem and dirtied our hands, but you dipped up water with your cap so we could wash them, and then we laughed a lot about it. How happy I was then! That very flower is pressed today in a book...

Aduyev stopped. Obviously all this very much displeased him. He even shook his head in disbelief.

"And do you have that little ribbon," he continued reading, "that you pulled out of my bureau drawer despite all my cries and pleading..."

"I pulled out a little ribbon!" he said aloud with a deep frown. After a moment's silence he again skipped a few lines and read:

"But I sentenced myself never to marry and I feel quite happy; no one will forbid me to remember those blessed times."

"So, an old maid!" thought Pyotr Ivanych. "No wonder she still has yellow flowers on her mind! What else does she say?"

> Are you married, dearest Brother, and to whom? Who is that dear partner, embellishing your life's path by her presence; tell me her name. I shall love her like a real sister and join her image with yours in my dreams; I shall pray for you. But if you are not married, then for whatever reason— write openly. No one shall read your secrets; I will keep them on my breast, they will be torn out only along with my heart. Don't delay; I am burning to read your ineffable lines...

"No, yours are the ineffable lines!" thought Pyotr Ivanych, and read on:

> I did not know that our dear Sasha would suddenly want to visit the magnificent capital—the lucky fellow! He will see the splendid houses and stores, enjoy the luxury and embrace the uncle he worships—and I—I at the same time will shed tears, remembering a happy time. If I had known about his departure, I would have spent days and nights embroidering a pillow for you—an Arab with two dogs; you will not believe how I have cried many times looking at this pattern: what can be holier than friendship and faithfulness?... This one thought preoccupies me now; I shall devote my days to it, but I do not have any good wool here, and therefore most humbly beg you, most kind Brother, to send as quickly as pos-

sible from the best store whatever is the best English wool; use these samples I've enclosed. But what am I saying? A horrible thought stops my pen! Perhaps you have already forgotten us, and indeed, how could you remember a poor martyr who has retired from the world and now pours out her tears? But no! I cannot imagine that you could be a monster like all men—no! My heart tells me you have kept your former feelings for us, for us all, amid the luxury and pleasures of the magnificent capital. This thought acts as balsam for my heart. Forgive me, I cannot go on; my hand trembles.

I remain yours until the grave,
Marya Gorbatova

P. S. Do you have, dear friend, any good little books? Send them to me if you don't need them: I will remember you with every page and weep. Or buy some new ones in the store if they're not expensive. Mr. Zagoskin's books are said to be very good, and Mr. Marlinsky's—send them. And I also saw in the newspapers the title "Concerning Prejudices" by Mr. Puzini. Send it—I can't stand prejudices.

Having read this, Aduyev wanted to dispatch it after its fellow, but stopped.

"No," he thought, "I shall keep it: there are collectors of such letters; some compile whole collections. Perhaps by chance I can do someone a favor."

He tossed the letter in the beaded basket on the wall, then took the third letter and began to read:

Dearest Brother-in-law Pyotr Ivanych!
Do you remember how we gave you a send-off seventeen years ago? Now God has brought us to bless the departure of our own offspring on his long journey. Look at him closely, dear Brother, and remember the deceased, our beloved Fyodor Ivanych, for Sasha is quite the image of him. God alone knows what my maternal heart has suffered in sending him forth to a strange world. I send him, my friend, straight to you. I have urged him not to delay anywhere, but to go to you...

Aduyev again shook his head.
"Silly old woman!" he muttered and read:

In his inexperience, of course, he might have stayed at the posthouse inn, but I know how that might offend you, his own uncle, and I told him to go straight to you. Oh, what a joy it will be to see him! Don't deprive him of your advice, dear Brother-in-law, and take him under your wing. I pass him on from my care to yours.

Again Pyotr Ivanych stopped:

You see, you're all he has. Keep an eye on him, don't spoil him too much, but don't make very severe demands either. There'll be someone to make severe demands, others will see to that, but there will be no one to be caring to him but his own. He is himself such a loving fellow—you need only see him, then you won't turn away. And the superior under whom he will work—tell him to take care of my Sasha and go easy. Protect him from alcohol and cards. At night—for I imagine you likely will sleep in the same room—Sasha is accustomed to lie on his back. Because of this he moans pitifully and tosses; wake him gently and make the sign of the cross over him, the fit will pass. In the summer cover his mouth with a hankie; if he opens his mouth wide in his sleep, the wretched flies will crawl in toward morning. Also, don't abandon him in case of need and as for money...

Aduyev frowned, but his face cleared again quickly, as he continued reading:

I shall send him as much as he needs; indeed, I've now put in his hands a thousand rubles, but please don't let him waste them for nothing, or don't let hangers-on talk him out of them. For there in your capital, I understand, there are a lot of rascals and all kinds of people without conscience. Finally, forgive me, dear Brother-in-law, I've quite lost the habit of writing.
I remain your sincerely respectful sister-in-law,
A. Aduyeva

P. S. With this I send our country delights—raspberries from our garden, white honey—clear as a teardrop, Dutch cloth sufficient for two dozen shirts and homemade jam. Eat and wear with joy, and when they run out, I'll send more. Look out for Evsei; he's docile and doesn't drink, but if, indeed, he gets spoiled there in the capital, then you may give him a beating.

Pyotr Ivanych slowly laid the letter on the table, even more slowly fetched a cigar, and having rolled it in his hands, began to smoke. For a long time he thought about this trick, as he called it in thought, which his sister-in-law had played on him. He carefully went over in his mind both what they had done to him, and what he himself ought to do.

These are the assumptions on which he based the whole case. He didn't know his nephew and consequently did not love him; the matter had to be decided by the laws of reason and justice. His brother married and enjoyed the benefits of conjugal life—so why ought he, Pyotr Ivanych, to burden himself with the care of his brother's son, he who hadn't enjoyed the advantages of marriage? Of course, there was no reason for him to do it.

But looking at it from another point of view, he saw it thus: a mother had sent her son straight to him, into his hands, not knowing whether he was alive and in a position to do something for his nephew. Of course, this was stupid, but if the deed was already done and the nephew in Petersburg without help, without friends, even without letters of recommendation, young, without any experience... had he the right to leave him at the mercy of fate, throw him into the crowd without instructions, without advice, and if something bad happened—wouldn't he be responsible before his own conscience?...

At this moment Aduyev opportunely remembered how his dead brother and this same Anna Pavlovna had sent him on his way seventeen years before. Of course, they weren't able to do anything for him in Petersburg; he had found his own way... But he remembered her tears of farewell, her motherly blessings, her kindnesses, her meat pies, and finally, her last words: "Well, when little Sasha"—then a three-year-old child—"grows up, perhaps you will be kind to him, Brother..." At this point Pyotr Ivanych got up and quickly went into the hall...

"Vasily!" he said, "when my nephew comes, don't send him away. And go find out now whether the room upstairs here is taken, the one that was being rented a while ago, and if it isn't taken, say I'm keeping it for myself. Oh, and these delicacies! Well, what are we going to do with them?"

"Just now our storekeeper saw them being carried upstairs. He asked whether we wouldn't let him have the honey: 'I'll pay a good price, of course,' he said, and he'll take the raspberries..."

"Wonderful! Give them to him. Well, what can we do with the cloth? Might it not do for furniture covers? Hide the cloth and hide the jam. We can eat it: it seems rather good."

Just as Pyotr Ivanych was getting ready to shave, Alexander Fyodorych arrived. He was about to throw himself around his uncle's neck, but the latter, pressing Alexander's tender youthful hand in his own powerful one, held him back at some distance, as if to get a good look at him, but more, it seems, to stop this impulse and limit it to a handshake.

"Your mother tells the truth," he said, "you're the living picture of my late brother; I would have recognized you on the street. But you're more handsome than he. So, without ceremony I will go on shaving, and you sit down over here—opposite, so I can see you, and we can chat."

Pyotr Ivanych immediately began his shaving as if no one were there. He soaped his cheeks, tensing with his tongue now one, now the other. Alexander was puzzled by this reception and didn't know how to begin the conversation. He attributed his uncle's coldness to the fact that he hadn't stayed with him straight off.

"So, how is your mother? In good health? I imagine she has grown old?" his uncle asked, making various grimaces in front of the mirror.

"Mama is well, thank God; she sends her respects, and Aunt Marya Pavlovna too," said Alexander Fyodorych hesitantly. "Auntie told me to embrace you..." He stood and walked over to his uncle to kiss him on the cheek or the head or the shoulder or, finally, wherever he could.

"Your aunt should have become smarter with age, but I see she's still the same silly girl she was twenty years ago..."

Embarrassed, Alexander backed away to return to his seat.

"You received the letter, dear Uncle?" he asked.

"Yes, I got it!"

"Vasily Tikhonych Zayezzhalov," Alexander Fyodorych began, "urgently asks you to find out about his lawsuit and do something about it."

"Yes, he has written me... Aren't asses of his sort extinct yet in the country?"

Alexander didn't know what to think. These responses overwhelmed him.

"Pardon me, Uncle," he began, almost trembling.

"What?"

"Pardon me for staying overnight at the inn and not coming straight to your house. I didn't know your apartment..."

"Why ask my pardon for that? You did quite right. Heavens knows what your mother thought up. How could you come straight to my house, not knowing whether you could stay with me or not? My apartment, as you see, is a bachelor's for one person: hall, living room, dining room, study, another working room, cloakroom, dressing room—there is no extra room. I would bother you, you me. But I've found an apartment for you here in this house..."

"Oh, Uncle!" said Alexander, "how can I thank you for your trouble?"

And he again jumped up from his seat, intending by word and deed to show his gratitude.

"Easy, easy! Don't touch me!" his uncle said quickly, "the razor's sharp and before you know it, you'll get cut and so will I."

Alexander saw that despite all his efforts he would not succeed that day in even once embracing his adored uncle and pressing him to his heart, and so he postponed that intention to another time.

"It's a cheerful little room," Pyotr Ivanych began. "The windows look partly out onto a wall; but then, you see, you won't begin to sit at the window all the time; if you're at home, you'll be busy and won't have time to be yawning out the window. And it's not expensive—forty rubles a month. There's a front hall for your man. You'll have to learn to live alone from the very beginning without a nursemaid, and to run your own little household, that is, to eat at home, in a word, to have your own place—a *chez soi*, as the French say. You can be free to have anyone in you want... By the way, when I dine at home, I shall ask the pleasure of your company, and on other days—young people here usually dine out, but I advise you to have your dinner sent in: it's quieter at home and you don't risk encounters with God knows whom. Don't you think?"

"I'm very grateful, Uncle..."

"Why be grateful? You're my relative, aren't you? I'm only doing my duty. So now I'll get dressed and leave; I have both a government job and the factory..."

"I didn't know you had a factory, Uncle!"

"A glass and china factory. I'm not alone, though: there are three partners."

"Is it doing well?"

"Yes, very decently. We mostly visit the fairs in the interior provinces. The last two years—we've been everywhere! If it goes on like this for five years, we'll have made it... One partner, true, isn't very reliable; he squanders everything, but I can keep him in hand. Well, goodbye. Have a look at the city now, dine somewhere, and in the evening come have tea with me. I'll be at home—we'll have a talk then. Come here, Vasily! Show him the room and help him get settled there."

"So that's how it is here in Petersburg," Alexander thought, sitting in his new quarters. "If my own relative's like this, what are the others like?"

Young Aduyev walked back and forth in the room in deep thought, and Evsei talked to himself as he straightened up the room.

"What a life here," he muttered, "at Pyotr Ivanych's—hear?—they light the stove once a month; people eat dinner at other people's houses. Good Lord, they're strange people, you have to admit! And still they call themselves Petersburgers! Where we come from, even a dog laps from his own dish."

Alexander, it seems, shared Evsei's opinion, though he was silent. He went up to the window and saw only smokestacks and roofs and the black, dirty brick sides of houses... and he compared it with what he saw two weeks ago from the window of his house in the country. He felt sad.

He went out into the street—it was crazy. Everyone was running somewhere, preoccupied only with himself, hardly glancing at passersby, and if so, perhaps only so as not to bump into someone. He remembered his provincial city, where every encounter, no matter with whom, was somehow interesting. Ivan Ivanych is going to see Pyotr Petrovych and everyone in town knows why. Over there Marya Martynovna is driving home from a party, and Afanasy Savich is going fishing there. A policeman is galloping from the governor's at breakneck speed in order to fetch the doctor, and everybody knows that Her Excellency is to give birth, though in the opinion of various great aunts and grandmothers it is not proper to know about this in advance. Everybody wonders, is it a girl or a boy? The ladies get out their best hats. Here comes Matvei Matveich out of his house with his heavy walking stick at six o'clock in the evening, and everyone knows that he's going to take his evening constitutional, that without it his stomach does not digest, and that he will stop without fail at the window of the old councillor, who, as everybody knows, drinks tea at this time. You exchange a couple of words with whomever you meet, and whomever you bow to—you know who he is, where he's going and why, and you read in his eyes, I know who you are, where you're going and why. Finally, if people who are strangers meet, and they have never even seen each other before, then the faces of both are suddenly transformed into question marks. They stop, turn around to look back twice, and once they're home, describe the new person's dress and gait, and explanations and guesses go back and forth about who and from where and why. In Petersburg, though, people even push you off the sidewalk at a glance as if everybody there were an enemy.

At first Alexander looked with provincial curiosity at everyone he met and at every decently dressed person, taking some of them for government ministers or ambassadors, some for writers. "Isn't that he?" he thought, "isn't this the one?" But soon this bored him—ministers, writers, ambassadors came toward him at every step.

He looked at the houses—and found them even more boring. Sadness overwhelmed him when he saw these monotonous stone blockbusters, which dragged on like colossal mausoleums, one after the other, in a solid mass. "The street will end here, just another minute and the eyes will find freedom," he thought, "either a hill, or green, or a broken-down fence." But no, the same stone wall of identical houses with four rows of windows begins again. And when this street ends, it is obstructed by a street like it, with a new row of the same houses. Look to the right, to the left—everywhere you are surrounded as if by a troop of giants—houses, houses and houses, stone and stone, everything the same and alike... There's no open space and no escape for the eyes: closed in on all sides—and human thoughts and feelings are likewise closed in, it seems.

The first impressions of a provincial visitor in Petersburg weigh him down. He feels sad, disturbed; nobody notices him; he is lost here; neither novelty nor variety nor the crowd excites him. His provincial pride declares war on everything he sees here and didn't see at home. He falls into a reverie and is transported in thought to his home town. What a pleasing sight! One house with a peaked roof and a high fence with acacia. There's an added structure on the roof, a dovecote—the business man Izyumin hunts them, that's why he went and built a shelter for them on his roof, and mornings and evenings in nightcap and bathrobe he stands on the roof with a stick, to which a rag is fastened, and whistles, waving the stick. Another house looks exactly like a lantern: it's all windows on all four sides and with a flat roof. Built long ago, it looks as if it will collapse any minute or burn up in spontaneous combustion; the shingles have taken on a kind of light-gray color. How awful to live in such a house, but people live there. True, the owner sometimes looks at the sagging ceiling and shakes his head, mumbling, "Will it still be standing by spring? Perhaps!" he'll say then and go on living there, fearing not for himself, but for his pocketbook. Next to him the wild architecture of the surgeon's house basks coquettishly, spread out in a half-circle with two wings like sentry boxes, and the whole hidden in green; it has turned its back on the street, and its fence stretches for a mile; behind the fence red apples look out from the trees, the temptation of small boys. The houses have retreated to a respectful distance from the churches, which are surrounded by grass and grave-

stones. Government offices—it's obvious at once which ones they are: nobody
goes near them unless he has to. But here in the capital you can't tell them from
simple houses, and there are even little stores right in some houses, disgraceful to
say. In a provincial city after you've walked down two or three streets, you already
sense open space; woven-grass fences begin, then orchards, and then, indeed,
open fields with corn. And there is quiet, even stillness and boredom—and the
same beneficent paralysis is found on the street and among the people! Everyone
lives as he will, no one feels pressure; even the chickens and roosters wander
about the streets freely, the goats and cows crop the grass, the small boys set
snakes free.

But here... what sadness! The man from the provinces sighs at the wall opposite his window and the dusty, dirty street and the shaky bridge and the sign over
the pub. He hates to admit that St. Isaac's Cathedral is better and taller than the
church in his provincial city, that the hall of the Nobles' Assembly is bigger than
halls there. He keeps an angry silence at comparisons of the sort, but sometimes
he'll risk saying that there you can get a better such and such material or wine for
less, or that there they wouldn't even look at those overseas delicacies, the big
crabs and mollusks, or the red fish, or that, of course, you're free to buy various
materials and trinkets from foreigners here; they'll cheat you, but you'll be happy
to be made a fool of! Yet how he suddenly rejoices when he compares and sees
that the caviar in his home city is better, or there are better pears and sweet rolls.
"So you call that thing a pear?" he'll say. "Why at home even servants wouldn't eat
that!"

Still greater will be the provincial's sorrow when he enters one of these houses with a letter from afar. He thinks they'll throw open their arms to embrace
him, they won't know how to welcome him enough, where to seat him or how to
entertain him. They will slyly find out what is his favorite food. How uneasy he'll
feel at these kindnesses, how he'll finally cast ceremony aside, kiss his host and
hostess, begin to call them familiarly "thou", as if he'd known them for twenty
years. They'll all raise their glasses in a toast and perhaps strike up a song in cho-
rus.

Quite the contrary! They hardly look at him, frown, excuse themselves with
work. If you have a business matter, then they pick an hour when they won't be
dining, and they're ignorant of the "admirals' hour"—there's neither vodka nor
appetizers. The host backs away from embraces and looks somewhat strangely at
the guest. In the next room glasses and spoons may clink; they should invite you
then and there, but they try to show the provincial the door with clever hints...
Everything locked up, everywhere little alarm bells: isn't that wretched? And such
cold, unfriendly faces. But at home in the provinces you may enter boldly. If
they've finished dinner, they'll dine again for the guest's sake. The samovar is on
the table morning and evening, and there aren't any little bells in the stores.
People embrace and kiss all the time, every Tom, Dick, and Harry. A neighbor
there is a real neighbor; the two live hand in hand, one soul. A relative is a relative; he'll die for his own... Alas, how sad!

Alexander found his way to Admiralty Square and was transfixed. He stood
enraptured for an hour looking at the Bronze Horseman, but, unlike poor
Evgeny,[1] without any bitterness in his heart. He looked at the Neva River and
the buildings surrounding it—and his eyes sparkled. He was suddenly ashamed of
his partiality for shaky bridges, small front gardens and ruined fences. He felt
merry and lighthearted. The confusion and the crowd—everything he saw
acquired another meaning. His hopes which had been momentarily buried by

those initial sad impressions were renewed. A new life seemed to invite him into its embrace and beckon him to something unknown. His heart beat hard. He dreamed of noble work, high strivings, and he stepped out on Nevsky Prospect with an air of importance, considering himself a citizen of a new world. He returned home full of these dreams.

That evening at eleven o'clock his uncle sent for him to drink tea.

"I just got back from the theater," said his uncle, who was lying on the sofa.

"What a pity you didn't tell me a while ago, Uncle; I would have gone with you."

"I was in the orchestra, where would you have sat, on my knees?" said Pyotr Ivanych. "Go alone tomorrow by yourself."

"It's sad being alone in a crowd, Uncle; there's no one to share your impressions with..."

"And what for! You have to be able to feel and think, in a word, to live alone; in time you'll have to do that. Besides, you have to dress properly for the theater."

Alexander looked at his clothes and was amazed at his uncle's words. "In what way am I not properly dressed," he thought, "a dark-blue coat and dark-blue trousers..."

"Königstein has made a lot of clothes for me, Uncle," he said. "He works for the governor of our province."

"No matter, all the same the clothes aren't right. One of these days I'll take you to my tailor. But these are trifles. We have more important things to talk about. Tell me now, what have you come here for?"

"I have come... to live."

"Live? That is, if you mean by that eat, drink, and sleep, then it wasn't worth the trouble of traveling so far. You won't succeed either in eating or sleeping here as you would there at home. But if you were thinking of something else, then explain..."

"To enjoy life, I meant to say," Alexander added, turning quite red. "I was bored in the country. It was always the same..."

"So that's it. You thought you'd rent a first-floor apartment on Nevsky Prospect, have your own carriage, make a large circle of friends, hold open house on certain days?"

"But that's awfully expensive," Alexander remarked naively.

"Your mother writes that she gave you a thousand rubles; that's not enough," said Pyotr Ivanych. "One of my friends came here, who also was bored in the country. He wanted to enjoy life, so he brought fifty thousand with him and will receive that much annually. He will enjoy life in Petersburg, but you—no! you didn't come for that."

"According to what you say, Uncle, it turns out that I don't know myself why I came."

"Almost that; that's putting it better. There's truth in that; only it still isn't any good. Can it be, when you were getting ready to come here that you didn't ask yourself, 'Why am I coming?' That wouldn't have been out of order."

"Before I asked myself that question, I already had the answer!" replied Alexander with pride.

"So why don't you say? Come, why?"

"I was drawn by some irresistible striving, a thirst for ennobling activity. The wish surged in me to clarify and carry out..."

Pyotr Ivanych raised himself a little from the sofa, took the cigar from his mouth and pricked up his ears.

"To realize those hopes that crowded in..."

"Do you write poetry?" Pyotr Ivanich suddenly asked.

"And prose, Uncle; do you want me to bring you some?"

"No, no!... later. I was only asking!"

"So?"

"So, tell me then..."

"You mean that's wrong?"

"No—perhaps it's very good, only crazy."

"Our professor of aesthetics talked that way, and he was considered our most eloquent professor," said Alexander, becoming confused.

"About what did he talk that way?"

"About his subject."

"Ah!"

"How am I supposed to talk, Uncle?"

"Simpler, like everybody, and not like a professor of aesthetics. Besides, that can't be explained so quickly; you'll see yourself later. You're trying to say, it seems, inasmuch as I can remember university lectures and translate your words, that you came here to find a career and make your fortune—is that right?"

"Yes, Uncle, a career..."

"And a fortune," Pyotr Ivanych added. "What kind of career is there without a fortune? It's a good idea—only... You've come in vain."

"Why? I hope you're not saying that from your own experience?" said Alexander looking round him.

"A reply to the point. You're right, I've done well, and my business is doing not badly. But, as far as I can see, you and I are altogether different."

"I don't by any means dare compare myself with you..."

"That's not the point; you are perhaps ten times more intelligent and better than I... I mean you have, it seems, a character such that you do not easily submit to a new order, while the order where you come from—oh my! There you were coddled and spoiled by your mother. How are you to endure everything I endured? Probably you're a dreamer, but there's no time for dreams here. Our sort comes here to conduct business."

"Perhaps I am capable of accomplishing something like that if you don't deprive me of your advice and experience..."

"Advise you—I'm afraid. I can't take responsibility for the character you formed in the country. Nothing sensible will come of that—you'll begin to reproach me. But to tell you my opinion—if you will—I don't refuse. Listen or not, as you wish. Oh no! I don't hope to succeed. You have your view of life down there; how will you change it? You're obsessed with love, friendship, even with the delights of life, happiness; people think that's all there is to life—unfortunately! They weep, whimper, pay compliments, but don't do anything... How shall I wean you away from all that?—that's hard!"

"I'll try, Uncle, to adjust to contemporary notions. Already today, Uncle, looking at these enormous buildings, at the ships bringing us the gifts of distant countries, I thought about the achievements of contemporary mankind, I understood the excitement of this rationally busy crowd and was ready to merge with it..."

During this monologue Pyotr Ivanych raised his eyebrows meaningfully and looked fixedly at his nephew. Alexander stopped.

"It's a simple matter, it seems," said the uncle. "But they get God knows what into their heads... 'the rationally busy crowd'!! It truly would have been better for you to stay home. You would have lived your life in honor, would have been more intelligent than everybody, had the reputation of an author and eloquent speaker, you would have believed in eternal and unchanging friendship and love, in blood ties and happiness, and you would have married, imperceptibly lived to an old age and actually have been happy in your own way. But with the ways of this place you won't be happy; here you have to turn all these notions upside down."

"What do you mean, Uncle; can it be that friendship and love—these sacred and elevated feelings—after falling, as it were, by chance from the heavens into the mud of earth..."

"What?"

Alexander fell silent.

"'Love and friendship fell in the mud'! Why, what are you chattering about now?"

"Can you say they're not the same here as there?—that's what I mean."

"There are love and friendship here too—where are there not such values?—only they're not the same as they are there. In time you will see yourself. First of all, forget these *sacred*, even *heavenly* feelings, and see the thing more simply the way it is, and indeed better; then you'll speak more simply. However, that's not my affair. You've arrived here, there's no turning back; if you don't find what you were looking for, reproach yourself. I'll forewarn you of what is good in my opinion, what's bad, and then as you will... Let's try, perhaps we'll succeed in making something of you. Yes, your mother asked to keep you supplied with money. Do you know what I shall ask of you: Don't ask me for any; that always ruins a good relationship between decent people. However, don't think that I'm refusing you. No, if it becomes necessary so that there's no other way out, then it can't be helped, turn to me... It's better to borrow from your uncle than from a stranger, at least it'll be without interest. But, so as not to resort to this extreme, I shall find you a job as soon as possible, so that you can earn money. So, good-bye for now. Come to see me in the morning, we'll discuss what and how to begin."

Alexander Fyodorych started to go home.

"Listen, don't you want a bite of supper?" Pyotr Ivanych called after him.

"Yes, Uncle... I would, please..."

"I don't have anything."

Alexander was silent. "Why then that obligatory invitation?" he thought.

"I don't eat at home, and now the restaurants are closed," continued his uncle. "This will be a lesson to you at the very start—get used to it. In the country people get up and go to bed by the sun; they eat and drink when nature commands. If it's cold, they put on caps with ear-flaps and pay no attention. If it's light, then it's day; if dark, night. Your eyes are closing, but I shall sit down to work still: the books must be balanced at the end of the month. You breathe fresh air there all year round, but here that pleasure costs money—and everything is like that! The very opposite! Here people don't eat supper, especially at their own expense or mine either. This is even beneficial: you won't begin to moan and thrash about at night, and I have no time to make the sign of the cross over you."

"That's easy to become accustomed to, Uncle..."

"Good, if that's so. But at your home everything's still the old way. You can visit someone at night and they'll cook supper for you right away?"

"Why, Uncle, this custom can't possibly be condemned, I hope. Russian virtues..."

"Enough! What kind of virtue is that. Out of boredom they're glad to see any scoundrel. 'Welcome, eat as much as you want, just fill our emptiness somehow, help us kill time, and let us have a look at you. After all, you must know something new. And we don't begrudge food; that costs us absolutely nothing here...' Repulsive kindness!"

So Alexander went to bed and tried to guess what kind of man his uncle was. He called to mind their whole conversation. He didn't understand a lot, the rest he didn't wholly believe.

"Didn't I speak well?" he thought. "Aren't love and friendship eternal? Isn't Uncle making fun of me? Can it be that's the order of things here? What was it that Sofiya liked in me if not the gift of words? And is her love really not eternal? And do they really not eat supper here?"

He went on tossing in bed for a long time; his head was full of disturbing thoughts and his empty stomach kept him awake.

Two weeks passed.

Pyotr Ivanych grew ever more content with his nephew from day to day.

"He has tact," he said to one of his factory partners, "which I wouldn't have expected from a country boy. He doesn't attach himself to you, doesn't intrude without invitation, and when he notices his presence is superfluous, leaves at once; and he doesn't ask for money. He's a quiet fellow. There are strange things... he creeps up to embrace you, talks like a theology student... Oh well, he'll get out of the habit of that. And it's good he hasn't hung himself round my neck."

"Does he have a fortune?" the partner asked.

"No, around a hundred serfs."

"So what! If he has ability, he'll go far here... Look at you; starting from small beginnings, and now, thank Heaven..."

"No! Nonsense! He won't get anywhere. This stupid exaltation is no good for anything; unfortunately he won't get used to the order of things here. How can he have a successful career! He's come here in vain... Oh well, that's his affair."

Alexander thought it his duty to love his uncle, but found no way to get used to his character and manner of thinking.

"My uncle is a good man, it seems," he wrote one morning to Pospelov, "very intelligent, only altogether prosaic, always deep in business and calculation... His spirit seems to be fastened to the earth and unable ever to rise to the pure contemplation of man's spiritual nature, isolated from earthly brawls. In his mind Heaven is inseparably connected to earth, and he and I shall never, it seems, shall never be wholly of one soul. On the way here I thought that, as my uncle, he would give me a place in his heart, would warm me in the cold crowd here by the affectionate embraces of his friendship. But friendship, you know, is a *second Heaven!* However, he too is nothing other than a product of this crowd. I thought he and I would share time together, be inseparable every minute, and what have I encountered?—cold bits of advice which he calls practical. I'd rather they were, instead, impractical, but full of warm sympathy from the heart. Not that he's very proud, but he's the enemy of every kind of sincere outpouring. We don't dine, don't sup together, don't go anywhere. When he gets home, he never tells where he was, what he did, and likewise he never says where he's going and why, who are his friends, whether he likes or not the way he spends his time. He's never especially angry or affectionate or sad or merry. All impulses of love, friendship, all strivings toward the beautiful are strange to his heart. Often you speak and speak like an inspired prophet, almost like our great, unforgettable Ivan Semyonych when, you remember, he thundered from the lectern and we trembled with rapture at his fiery glance and speech. But Uncle?—he listens, raising his eyebrows, and gives me a strange look, or begins to laugh somehow in his unique way with a laugh that freezes my blood—and farewell inspiration! I often fancy I see Pushkin's Demon in him... He doesn't believe in *love*, and so on. He says there is no happiness and no one ever promised it; there's simply life which is equally divided between good and evil, between pleasure, success, health, quiet, on the one hand, and discontent, failure, anxiety, illnesses and so on, on the other; that one must look at all this simply, not get useless questions into one's head—useless, hear, hear!—questions about why we were created and to what end we strive—that this is not our worry, and that because of this we don't see what is before our nose, and don't do what is to be done—that's all you hear about: doing! You can't tell the difference with him whether he's thinking of some pleasure or of a prosaic business deal. Whether he's at his business accounts or at the theater, it makes no difference, he's a stranger to strong impressions and, it seems, doesn't love anything elegant. That's alien to his soul; I think he hasn't even read Pushkin..."

Pyotr Ivanych unexpectedly appeared in his nephew's room and found him writing this letter.

"I came to see how you've settled in here," the uncle said, "and to talk about business."

Alexander jumped up and hastily covered something with his hand.

"Hide it, hide your secret," said Pyotr Ivanych, "I'll turn my back. So, have you hidden it? But what's this that's fallen out? What's this thing?"

"This is nothing, Uncle...," Alexander was about to begin, but became confused and fell silent.

"Hair, it seems! Truly nothing! Now that I've seen one thing, show me now that other you're hiding in your hand."

Like a schoolboy caught in the act, Alexander unwillingly opened up his hand and showed a ring.

"What's this? Where did this come from?" asked Pyotr Ivanych.

"These are material tokens, Uncle, of spiritual relationships."

"What? What? Give these tokens here."

"These are pledges..."

"You no doubt brought them from the country?"

"From Sofiya, Uncle, to remember her by... when we said goodbye..."

"So that's it. So you brought them nine hundred miles." The uncle shook his head. "You'd better have brought one more bag of dried raspberries. That we could at least have sold at the store, but these pledges..."

He inspected first the hair, then the ring, sniffed the hair and weighed the ring in his hand. Then he took a slip of paper from the table, wrapped both tokens in it, pressed the whole into a compact ball and—bang, out the window.

"Uncle!" cried Alexander, furious, seizing him by the hand, but too late. The paper ball flew over the corner of the neighboring roof, fell in the canal on to the edge of a barge full of bricks, rebounded and bounced into the water.

Alexander looked in silence with an expression of bitter reproach at his uncle.

"Uncle!" he repeated.

"What?"

"What's a name for what you've done?"

"Ejection of non-material tokens out the window and into the canal—all kinds of junk and trifles which need not be kept in one's room..."

"Trifles, you call those trifles!"

"And what did you think—half of your heart?... I come to see him on business, and this is what he's doing—sitting thinking about junk!"

"Does that really hurt your business, Uncle?"

"Very much. Time is passing and till now you haven't yet said a word about your intentions: whether you want to enter the civil service, or have chosen another occupation—not a word! And all this because you have Sofiya and her tokens on your mind. Here you are, it seems, writing a letter to her? Are you?"

"Yes... I was about to begin..."

"And have you written your mother?"

"Not yet, I wanted to tomorrow."

"Why tomorrow? To your mother tomorrow, but to Sofiya, whom you'll inevitably forget in a month, you're writing today."

"Sofiya? Could I forget her?"

"Probably. If I hadn't thrown away your pledges, then indeed you'd have remembered her a month longer. I did you a double favor. In a few years these tokens would have reminded you of a stupidity to make you blush."

"Blush for such a pure, sacred recollection? That means not to believe in poetry..."

"What poetry is there in what's stupid? The poetry in your aunt's letter, for example! A yellow flower, the lake, some secret or other... When I began to read—I began to feel inexpressibly ill! I almost blushed when I thought I couldn't blush any more."

"That's awful, awful, Uncle! Can it be you have never loved?"

"I can't stand tokens."

"What a wooden life that is!" said Alexander, strongly aroused. "That's vegetating but not living! Vegetating *without inspiration, without tears, without life, without love...*"[2]

"And without hair!" the uncle added.

"Uncle, how can you so coldly make fun of what is best on earth? Why, that's a crime... Love... sacred emotions!"

"I know this sacred love. At your age you need only see a curl, a tiny shoe, a garter, or touch a hand—and sacred elevated love begins to run through your whole body, and if you give it reign, then it... Your love, unfortunately, lies in the future; you won't escape it in any case, but doing—accomplishing—will escape you, if you don't set to work at it."

"But do you mean loving isn't doing?"

"No, it's a pleasant distraction. Only you mustn't yield to it too much, or the result will be foolishness. That's what I'm afraid of for you." The uncle shook his head. "I've almost found you a job; you do want to be a civil servant, don't you?" he said.

"Oh, Uncle, how glad I am!"

Alexander pounced upon his uncle and kissed him on the cheek.

"You managed it!" said his uncle, wiping his cheek, "however much I was on my guard! Well, then, listen. Tell me what you know, what you feel yourself capable of?"

"I know theology, civil, criminal, natural and common law, diplomacy, political economy, philosophy, aesthetics, archeology..."

"Stop, stop! But can you write decently in Russian? For now that's the most needed of all."

"What a question, Uncle: can I write Russian!" said Alexander and ran to the bureau, from which he began to take out various papers, and his uncle meanwhile took from the desk some letter or other and began to read.

Alexander came over to the desk with the papers and saw that his uncle was reading his letter. The papers fell from his hands.

"What's this you're reading, Uncle?" he said, alarmed.

"Why, a letter was lying here, to a friend, it must be. Pardon, I wanted to see how you write."

"And you've read it all?"

"Yes, almost—look, only two lines are left—I'll be finished right away. Why look, there are no secrets here; otherwise it wouldn't have been lying around like this..."

"What do you think of me now?"

"I think you write decently, correctly, smoothly..."

"Therefore, you haven't finished reading what I wrote?" asked Alexander eagerly.

"No, apparently that's all," said Pyotr Ivanych, looking at both pages. "First you describe Petersburg, your impressions, and then me."

"Heavens!" exclaimed Alexander and covered his face with his hands.

"What is it? What is the matter with you?"

"And you say this calmly? You're not angry, don't hate me?"

"No! Why should I fly into a rage?"

"Tell me again, reassure me."

"No, no, no."

"I still can't believe it; prove it, Uncle..."

"How do you want me to do that?"

"Embrace me."

"Excuse me, I can't."

"Why?"

"Because in that action there's no reason, that is, mind, or speaking in the words of your professor, my consciousness does not impel me to do that. Now if you were a woman—that's something else, then—it's done mindlessly from a different impulse."

"Feeling, Uncle, will out, demands expression, outpourings..."

"It doesn't require anything of me, and if it did, I would restrain myself—and advise you to do the same."

"What for?"

"Why, so that later, when you look more closely at the man you embraced, you don't have to blush for your embraces."

"Does it not happen then, Uncle, that you repulse a man and regret it later?"

"It happens; that's why I also never repulse anyone."

"You won't repulse me either for what I've done, won't call me a monster?"

"According to you, whoever writes nonsense is a monster. In that case the count would be incalculably many."

"But to read such bitter truths about oneself—and from whom?—from one's own nephew!"

"You imagine you wrote the truth?"

"Oh, Uncle!... of course, I was mistaken... I'll correct it... forgive me..."

"If you want, I'll dictate the truth to you."

"Oh, please do."

"Sit down and write."

Alexander took out a sheet of paper and a pen, and Pyotr Ivanych, looking at the letter he'd just read, dictated: "'Dear Friend.' Do you have that?"

"I do."

"'I won't describe Petersburg and my impressions to you.'"

"'I won't describe,'" said Alexander, writing.

"'Petersburg has long since been described, and what hasn't been, you must see for yourself; my impressions won't be of any value to you. No need to waste time and paper for nothing. Better that I describe my uncle because that relates to me personally.'"

"'... my uncle,'" said Alexander.

"Here you write that I'm very good and intelligent—maybe that's true too, and maybe it isn't. We'd better take the middle ground; write: 'My uncle isn't stupid and not mean, he wishes me well...'"

"Uncle! I can judge and feel..." said Alexander and reached out to kiss him.

"'Though he doesn't hang himself round my neck!'" Pyotr Ivanych continued dictating. Alexander, not having reached far enough, quickly sat down in his chair, "'and he wishes me well because he has no reason or occasion to wish evil upon me and because my mother wrote in my favor; long ago she had been good to him. He says he doesn't love me—and quite with good reason. It's impossible in two weeks to love, and I don't yet love him, though I assure him of the contrary.'"

"How can you say that?" said Alexander.

"Write, write: 'But we're beginning to get used to each other. He even says it's possible to get along together without love. He doesn't sit with me, embracing from morning to night because he says it's not at all necessary, and besides he doesn't have time.'"

"'An enemy of sincere outpourings'—we can leave that; it's good. Have you got it down?"

"I've got it."

"So, what else is in your letter? 'A prosaic spirit, a demon...' Write that."

While Alexander was writing, Pyotr Ivanych took some other paper from the desk, rolled it, put fire to it and lit his cigar, then threw down the paper and stomped on it.

"'My uncle is neither a demon nor an angel but the same kind of human being as everybody,'" he dictated, "'only not quite like you and me. He thinks and feels in an earthly manner, assumes that if we live on earth, then it isn't necessary to fly away to Heaven, where they don't ask us to be now for the time being. Rather we should busy ourselves with the human affairs to which we are called. For this reason he enters into all earthly affairs, and by the way, into life as it is, and not as we would wish it to be. He believes in the good and in evil along with it, in the beautiful and the horrible. He believes in love and friendship too, only he doesn't think that they've fallen from Heaven into the mud, but assumes that they were created along with people and for people, that we must understand and in general, look at things steadily from their real side, and not be carried away, God knows where. Between honest people he admits the possibility of amicable relations, which, thanks to frequent encounters and habit, are transformed into friendship. But he also assumes that habit loses its force when people are separated, and that people forget one another and that this is by no means a crime. He therefore assures me that I will forget you and you me. To me and probably to you too, this seems absurd, but he advises me to think about it as little as possible, and I so advise you. This, he says, will come of itself—without effort. He says that life doesn't consist only in this one thing, that there's a right time for it as for everything else, and dreaming a whole lifetime about love alone is stupid.

Those who seek it and cannot manage even a minute without it—they live by the heart and still worse, at the expense of their heads. Uncle likes to be busy with an enterprise and advises me to do the same, and I pass on the advice to you. We belong to society, he says, which needs us. In being busy, he doesn't forget himself either. An enterprise brings in money, and money, comfort, of which he's very fond. Besides, perhaps he has intentions which will make it likely I won't be his heir. Uncle is always thinking about his government job and his factory; he knows by heart not just Pushkin'"...

"You, Uncle?" said the astonished Alexander.

"Yes, sometime you'll see. Write: 'He reads in two langages everything excellent that is published in all branches of human knowledge, loves art, has a fine collection of pictures of the Flemish school—that's his taste—goes to the theater often, but doesn't make a fuss about it, throw his arms about, cry ah! and oh!, as he thinks that's childish. He believes in restraining oneself, not foisting one's impressions, which nobody needs, on others. He also doesn't speak in a wild language, which he advises me not to do, and I you. Farewell, write me less often and don't waste time in an empty way. Your friend So-and-so. And the month and day.'"

"How can I send a letter like that?" said Alexander. "'Don't write so often'—send that to a person who purposely drove eighty miles to say a last farewell! 'I advise this, that and a third thing...' He's no stupider than I am. He graduated in second place."

"You don't have to; all the same, send it. Maybe he'll be the wiser for it; it'll put him on to some new ideas. Though you two have graduated, your schooling is only just beginning."

"I can't bring myself to do it, Uncle..."

"I never interfere in other people's affairs, but you yourself asked me to do something for you. I'm trying to put you on the right track and make the first step easy, but you're being stubborn. Well, as you wish. I'm only telling you my opinion but I won't force you; I'm not your nanny."

"Pardon me, Uncle. I'm ready to obey," said Alexander and at once sealed the letter.

After sealing one, he began to look for the other to Sophie. He looked on the desk—it wasn't there, under the desk—not there either, in the drawer—not there.

"What are you looking for?" said his uncle.

"I'm looking for the other letter... to Sofiya."

His uncle began to look too.

"Where is it?" said Pyotr Ivanych. "Indeed I didn't throw it out the window."

"Uncle! what a thing to do—look, you lit your cigar with it!'" said Alexander aggrieved, and picked up the charred remains of the letter.

"Did I really?" exclaimed the uncle, "now how did I do that?—and didn't notice; indeed, look, I burned up such a treasure... But, by the way, do you know? It may from one point of view even be a good thing..."

"Oh, Uncle, Heaven knows, it isn't good from any point of view..." remarked Alexander in desperation.

"Really, it is a good thing. You can't make it to write her with this post, and by the next you'll already, doubtless, have changed your mind. You'll be busy with your government job; you won't have the inclination, and so you'll commit one stupidity less."

"What will she think of me?"

"Whatever she wants. Yes, I think it's good for her too. Look, you're not going to marry her? She'll think you've forgotten her, will forget you herself and will blush less before her future fiancé when she begins to assure him she's never loved anyone but him."

"Uncle, you're an amazing man! For you constancy doesn't exist, promises aren't sacred... Life is so good, so full of delight, leisure; it's like a smooth, beautiful lake..."

"On which yellow flowers grow, isn't it?" interrupted his uncle.

"Like a lake," Alexander continued. "It's full of mysterious, alluring things, so much hiding within it..."

"Sludge, dear fellow."

"Why bring up sludge, Uncle; why destroy and annihilate all joys, hopes, bliss... Why do you take the dark view?"

"I take a realistic view—and advise you too to do the same. You won't be made a fool of. According to your concepts life is good in the country where they don't know about sludge—angels live there, not people. Take Zayezzhalov, a holy man; your auntie, an exalted sensitive soul; Sofiya, I imagine, the same foolish sort as Auntie, and also..."

"Enough, Uncle!" said Alexander, furious.

"Then also such dreamers as you. They search with their nose to the wind for a scent from somewhere of inalterable friendship and love... For the hundredth time I say: You came here in vain!"

"Is she going to assure her fiancé that she hasn't loved anyone!" Alexander said, almost speaking to himself.

"And you your own!"

"No, I'm convinced that she will at once with noble frankness give him my letters and..."

"And tokens," said Pyotr Ivanych.

"Yes, and pledges of our relationship... and will say, 'See, here is the first man to awaken the strings of my heart to music; this is the man at whose name they first began to sing...'"

The uncle's brows were raised and his eyes widened. Alexander fell silent.

"And why have you stopped playing on your heart strings? Well, dear fellow, your Sofiya is truly stupid if she does a thing like that. I hope she has a mother or someone who can stop her?"

"You, Uncle, have decided to call stupid this most sacred impulse of the soul, this noble outpouring of the heart; what is one to think of you?"

"However you judge best. She will force her fiancé to suspect God knows what Perhaps the engagement will be broken, and for what? Because you picked yellow flowers together in the country. No, things are not done that way. Well, so you can write Russian. Tomorrow we'll go to a government department. I've already spoken to my former colleague, the head of the department, about you. He said there is a vacancy. We mustn't lose any time... What is this pile of papers you pulled out?"

"Those are my university notes. Here, let me read you a few pages from Ivan Semyonych's lectures on art in Greece."

He was already beginning quickly to turn the pages.

"Oh, have mercy, spare me!" said Pyotr Ivanych frowning. "And what are these?"

"These are my term papers. I would like to show them to my superior. There's one project here especially that I worked on..."

"Ah! One of those projects which was carried out a thousand years ago, or which it is impossible or unnecessary to carry out."

"What do you mean, Uncle! Why, this project was proposed to a certain person, a sponsor of enlightenment. Because of it he invited me to dinner once with the rector of the university. Here's the beginning of another project."

"Dine with me twice, as long as you don't finish writing up this second project."

"Why then?"

"For the reason that you won't write anything well now, and it'll take up our time."

"What, after hearing the lectures?..."

"They'll be useful to you in time, but for now look, read, study and do what they ask."

"How will my superior find out my abilities then?"

"He'll see in a flash; he's a master at finding out. Oh, what job would you like to have?"

"I don't know, Uncle, whatever would..."

"There are the ministers' jobs," said Pyotr Ivanych, "their deputies, directors, vice-directors, heads of departments, head clerks, their assistants, civil servants with special portfolio, to name but a few!"

Alexander reflected. He was lost in thought and didn't know which to choose.

"Perhaps for the start the job of head clerk would be good," he said.

"Yes, good!" Pyotr Ivanych repeated.

"I would watch carefully what they do, Uncle, and after a couple of months there I'd be promoted to head of the department..."

His uncle pricked up his ears.

"Of course, of course!" he said, "then three months later director, well, and after a year there, even minister, don't you think?"

Alexander blushed and fell silent.

"The head of the department probably told you what kind of vacancy there is," he said then.

"No," his uncle answered, "he didn't say, so we'd better rely on him; we'll have trouble choosing ourselves, while he of course knows where to place you. Don't tell him about your trouble in choosing; yes, and not a word about the projects either. You see, he might even be offended that we don't trust him and might even frighten you with the rules; he's a stickler. I would not advise you to mention *the material tokens* to young ladies here; they won't understand, why should they! That's too elevated for them; I hardly followed you, but they will look puzzled."

While his uncle was speaking, Alexander was turning over some kind of rolled-up papers in his hand.

"What else do you have there?"

Alexander had been waiting for this question with impatience.

"These are... I've long wanted to show you... poems. You once said you were interested."

"Somehow I don't remember; it seems I wasn't interested..."

"But you see, Uncle, I think the civil service is a dry occupation in which the soul has no part, but the soul thirsts to express itself, to share with its neighbors the superfluity of feelings and ideas overflowing within..."

"What, how's that?" his uncle asked with impatience. "That is, beside the government job you want to work at something else—say, perhaps translation? Well, very laudable. Translating what? Literature?"

"Yes, Uncle, I wanted to ask you, whether you are able to get something published...?"

"Are you convinced that you have talent?—without that, you see, you'll be an outsider in art—what good's that? Talent is another matter. You can work, accomplish much that's good, and besides, this is capital—it's worth your hundred serfs."

"You measure that too in money?"

"What measurement do you recommend? The more they read you, the more they pay you money."

"And the glory? Glory is the true reward of the poet..."

"Glory is tired of nursing poets; there are too many pretenders. In former times that glory, like a woman, would take care of any and everyone, but now, haven't you noticed, it seems she doesn't exist at all or has gone into hiding—yes! There's fame, but somehow glory goes unmentioned, or she's thought up another way to manifest herself. Whoever writes the best is best paid, who's a worse writer needn't complain. For all that, a decent writer also lives decently nowadays, doesn't suffer cold and hunger in an attic, even if they don't run after him in the streets and point at him with their fingers as if at a clown. It's understood that a poet doesn't live in Heaven, but is a human being, looks the same, walks about, thinks and makes stupid mistakes like others; what's to stare at in that?..."

"Like others—how can you, Uncle! how can you say that! The poet is marked with a special brand; in him the presence of a higher force is concealed."

"Just as it sometimes is in others—in the mathematician, the watchmaker and the likes of us, the factory owner. Newton, Gutenberg, Watt were just as much gifted with a higher power as Shakespeare, Dante and the rest. If by some process I can make from our Pargolovo clay a porcelain that is better than that from Dresden or Sèvres, then don't you think a higher force would be present in that?"

"You're confusing craft with art, Uncle."

"Heaven forbid! Art is one thing, handicraft another, and creativity can be involved in both one and the other, just as indeed it may not be present at all. If it isn't, then the craftsman is called a craftsman and not a creator, and a poet without creativity is also not a poet, but a writer. Why didn't they give lectures on that at the university! What did you learn there?..."

The uncle was annoyed that he had gotten launched on such explanations of what he considered commonly known truths. "This is like sincere outpourings," he thought. "Let me see, what have you there?" he asked—"poems!"

He took the roll and began to read the first page.

> From where at times do grief and sadness
> Fly down in a sudden cloud
> And, embroiling the heart in a quarrel with life...

"Give me a light, Alexander," and lighting his cigar, he continued:

> Replace the flock of wishes there?
> Why suddenly in gray bad weather
> Does a gloomy dream fall upon the soul,
> And disturb it suddenly
> With vague unhappiness...

"You've said the same thing in the first four verses, and the result is water," remarked Pyotr Ivanych, and continued reading:

Who can say why
The brow, gone pale,
Breaks out in icy tears...

"How's that? A brow breaks out in sweat, but in tears—I've never seen that."

And what is happening to us then?
The stillness of distant heavens,
At that moment horrible and terrible...

"Horrible and terrible—two of the same."

I look up to Heaven; the moon...

"Inevitably the moon; you can't do without it! If you have *dream* and *maiden*—
that's the end. I'm disassociating myself from you."

I look up to Heaven; the moon
Floats, wordless, shining,
And it seems, buried within it
Lies the fateful secret of our time.

"Not bad! Give me another light... my cigar's gone out. Where was I—oh yes!"

Hiding in the ether
Stars tremble in unsteady gleaming,
And, as if in mutual accord,
Keep a strict silence.
So in the world everything threatens misfortune,
Everything savagely forewarns of evil,
As if a deceptive calm securely
Cradles us here;
And there is no name for that sorrow...

The uncle yawned markedly and continued:

It will pass, whirling every trace away,
As the fleeting wind of the steppes
Blows the trace of beasts from the sands.

"Well, the beasts are unbelievably awful here! What are they here for? Ah!
This was about sorrow, but now about joy..."
And he began to read at a rapid rate, almost to himself:

For all this, it sometimes happens
That some demon steals inside us,
Then in a living stream rapture
Powerfully forces its way into our soul...
And begins sweetly to agitate the breast... and so on.

"Not bad, not good!" he said, finishing. "By the way, others have begun worse.

Keep on trying, write, study if you want; perhaps your talent will be revealed; when is another matter."

Alexander grew sad. He hadn't at all expected such a criticism. It was some comfort to him that he considered his uncle a cold person, almost without a soul.

"Here's a translation from Schiller," he said.

"That's enough; I see. So you know languages too?"

"I know French, German and a little Euglish."

"I congratulate you. You should have said that long ago—you can go far. You told me a while back about political economics, philosophy, archeology, God knows what besides, but said not a word about the most important thing—an inappropriate modesty. I'll find you a literary job at once."

"Really, Uncle? Then you will do me a great favor!—let me embrace you."

"Wait till I've found it."

"Won't you show my future superior some of my writings to give him an idea?"

"No, it's not necessary; if it is, you show them yourself, but perhaps it won't even be necessary. Make me a gift of your projects and writings!"

"Give them to you? With pleasure, Uncle," said Alexander, flattered by his uncle's request. "Would you like me to make you a table of contents of all the articles in chronological order?"

"No, that's not necessary... Thank you for the gift. Evsei! Take these papers to Vasily."

"Why to Vasily? Rather to your study."

"He asked me for paper to glue on something. "

"What, Uncle?" asked Alexander, horrified, and snatched back the pile.

"Look, you made the gift, so what do you care about the use I make of your gift?..."

"You spare nothing... nothing!" Alexander groaned in despair, hugging the papers with both hands to his breast.

"Listen to me, Alexander," said his uncle, snatching the papers from him, "later you won't blush and will thank me."

Alexander let go his hold on the papers.

"So, take them away, Evsei," said Pyotr Ivanych. "Now, you see, it's nice and clean in your room, no waste papers. It will depend on you whether you fill it with trash or something useful. Let's go to the factory, take a drive, enjoy ourselves, get a breath of fresh air and have a look at people working."

In the morning Pyotr Ivanych drove his nephew to the government office, and while he spoke with his friend, the head of the department, Alexander became acquainted with a world that was new to him. He was still dreaming of projects and racking his brains about what problem of state they would ask him to solve; meanwhile he stood and looked.

"Exactly like my uncle's factory!" he decided finally. "Just as there a master takes a piece of clay, throws it in the machine, revolves it once, twice, three times and as you look a cone, oval, then a semi-circle emerges; next he hands it over to another; that man dries it by fire; a third gilds it; a fourth does the painting; and the result is a cup or vase or saucer. Here, too, an outsider comes in with a petition, hands in his paper, makes a deep bow with a pitiful smile—a master takes it, hardly touches it with his pen, and hands it over to another; that man throws it into a pile of a thousand other papers—but it won't be lost. Stamped with a number and a date, it will pass unhurt through twenty hands, multiplying and producing the likes of itself. A third man will take it and climb up after something or other in a cabinet, look either in a book or at another paper, say a few magic words to a fourth—who will go scratch with his pen. Having scratched a bit, he'll hand over the parent paper with its new offspring to a fifth man—who, in turn, scratches with a pen and one more fruit is born; the fifth pretties it up and passes it on further, and so the paper goes ever on its way—never gets lost. Its producers will die, but it continues to exist for whole centuries. When century-old dust finally covers it, even then they'll be disturbing it and consulting it. And every day, every hour, today, and tomorrow, and for a whole century, the bureaucratic machine works smoothly without pause, without rest, as if there were no people, only wheels and springs...

"Where's the intelligence animating and moving the paper factory?" Alexander thought "In the books, in the papers themselves or in the heads of these people?"

And what faces he saw there! On the street you don't encounter their likes—they don't go out into the light of day. Here, it seems, is where they were born, grew up, grew into their jobs and will die. Aduyev focussed his gaze for a while on the head of the section: he was the image of Jupiter the Thunderer: he opens his mouth—and there is Mercury with his bronze breastplate; he stretches out his hand with a paper and ten hands reach out to take it.

"Ivan Ivanych!" the head said.

Ivan Ivanych jumped up from behind his desk, half-ran to Jupiter and stood before him like a leaf before grass. Even Alexander felt shy without knowing why.

"Give me a bit of tobacco!"

With servility the fellow offered his open tobacco box with both hands.

"You test this man!" said the superior, pointing to Aduyev.

"So he's the one who will test me!" thought Aduyev, looking at the yellow figure of Ivan Ivanych with the worn elbows. "Does this man really resolve problems of state?"

"Do you have a good hand?" asked Ivan Ivanych.

"Hand?"

"Yes, sir, handwriting. Here, try to copy this little document."

Alexander was surprised at this request, but fulfilled it. Ivan Ivanych frowned after a look at his work.

"He writes badly," he said to the head of the section. The head looked.

"Yes, not good. He can't write the final copy. But let him copy leaves of absence for the time being, and then when he's gotten accustomed a bit, use him for the execution of documents; maybe he can do that. He's studied at the university."

Soon Aduyev also became one of the cogs in the machine. He wrote, wrote, and wrote endlessly and was even surprised mornings to see that it was possible to do something different. And when he remembered his projects, color rushed to his face.

"Uncle!" he thought, "you're right in one thing, mercilessly right; can you be right in everything? Can I have been wrong in my intimate, inspired thoughts and my warm beliefs in love, friendship... and in people... and in myself?... What is life?" He bent over his paper and scratched more strongly with his pen, and as for himself, tears sparkled under his lashes.

"Fortune decidedly smiles on you," said Pyotr Ivanych to his nephew. "In the beginning I worked a whole year without pay, but you entered at once into the senior category; see, that's 750 rubles and with a bonus it'll be a thousand. Excellent on the first try! The head of the section praises you; only, he says you're absentminded. Sometimes you don't put in the commas, other times you forget to write down the content of the document. Please get out of that habit. The main thing—pay attention to what's before your eyes and don't get carried away to Heaven knows where."

The uncle pointed upward. From then on he became more friendly toward his nephew.

"What a fine man, my subdivision head, Uncle!" Alexander once said.

"How do you know?"

"We've made friends. Such an exalted soul, such an honest, noble tendency in his ideas! And with his assistant too: he seems to be a man of firm will with a character of iron..."

"You've already managed to make friends with them?"

"Yes, and how!..."

"Didn't your subdivision head invite you to his house on Thursdays?"

"Oh, indeed, every Thursday. It seems he feels a special attraction for me."

"And his assistant asked to borrow money?"

"Yes, Uncle, a mere trifle... I gave him twenty-five rubles, which I had with me; he asked for fifty more."

"You've already given them! Oh dear!" said the uncle, vexed. "I'm partly to blame for not forewarning you. Indeed, I didn't think you so naive as to lend money after two weeks of acquaintance. It can't be helped; we'll halve the loss. Count me in for twelve-fifty."

"What, Uncle, surely he'll pay back?"

"Nonsense! I know him. I lost a hundred rubles to him during the time I worked there. He borrows from everyone. If he asks again, tell him I'd like him to remember his little debt to me—he'll leave you alone! And don't go to the subdivision head's house."

"Why, Uncle?"

"He's a cardplayer. He'll have you sit down with two of the boys like him, and they'll conspire to leave you without a penny!"

"A cardplayer!" said Alexander in astonishment, "is it possible? He seems so inclined to sincere outpourings..."

"And tell him also in conversation that I have all your money in safekeeping, and you'll see whether he's inclined to 'sincere outpourings,' and whether he'll ever invite you to his house on Thursday."

Alexander was plunged in thought. His uncle shook his head.

"And you thought angels were sitting around you there! 'Sincere outpourings,' 'a special attraction'! Why not, indeed, first assume that they are some sort of scoundrels? You've come here in vain!" he said, "truly in vain!"

Once Alexander had just awakened when Evsei brought him a big package with a note from his uncle.

"At last here's a literary job for you," the note said. "Yesterday I met a journalist friend of mine; he sent you work on trial."

Alexander's hands trembled with joy as he opened the package. In it was a German manuscript.

"What is this—prose?" he said, "and what about?"

And he read what was written at the top in pencil: "On manure, an article for the agriculture section. Kindly translate as quickly as possible."

For a long time he sat pensively, looking at the article, then slowly with a sigh he readied a pen and began to translate. Two days later the article was finished and had been sent off.

"Excellent, excellent!" Pyotr Ivanych said to him several days later. The editor is very pleased, only he finds the style not sufficiently severe. Well, you can't demand everything the first time. He wants to make your acquaintance. Go to see him tomorrow around seven in the evening; he's already got another article ready for you."

"Again on the same subject, Uncle?"

"No, about something else; he told me, but I've forgotten... Oh, yes; about potato molasses. You must have been born lucky, Alexander. At last I'm beginning to hope you'll get somewhere. Soon perhaps I won't be saying, why did you come. It's not been even a month and everything's already coming your way from all directions. A thousand rubles there, and the editor has promised a hundred rubles a month for four printed pages; that makes two thousand two hundred rubles! No, I didn't start out like that!" he said, contracting his brows a little. "Write to your mother that you've found jobs and of what sort. I, too, will answer her letter. I'll write that for her kindness to me I have done all I could for you."

"Mama will be very grateful to you... Uncle, and I am too..." said Alexander with a sigh, but by now he did not rush to embrace his uncle.

III

More than two years passed. Who would have recognized our country boy in this young man with elegant manners in a fashionable suit? He had changed and grown up a great deal. The softness of lines in his youthful face, the transparency and delicacy of skin, the tuft of hair on his chin—all that had gone. His shy timidity and the awkward grace of his movements were no longer there. The features of his face had matured and formed a face—and a face of character. The lilies and roses had disappeared as if under a light sunburn. The tuft of beard had been replaced by slight sideburns. The light and uncertain gait had become an even and firm one. A few bass notes had been added to his voice. The sketched-in picture had yielded a finished portrait. The youth was transformed into a man. Self-confidence and daring shone in his eyes—not that daring which, visible half a mile away, gazes at everything arrogantly and with aggressive look and gestures says: "See, watch out, don't touch me, don't tread on me, and if you do—do you understand?—you'll get it back fast!" No, the expression of the daring I mean does not repel, but attracts. It is expressed in a striving for the good, for success, in a wish to overcome the obstacles that bar the way. The former enthusiasm in Alexander's face was tempered by a slight shade of thoughtfulness, the first sign of the uncertainty that had infiltrated his soul and perhaps the only consequence of the lessons and unsparing analysis to which his uncle had subjected everything Alexander saw and felt. Alexander had at last acquired tact, that is, the ability to get on with people. He did not throw himself upon everyone's neck, especially since the man inclined to *sincere outpourings* had twice, despite his uncle's warnings, cleaned him out at cards, and the man of firm character and iron will had borrowed no small amount of his money. Other people and events had greatly contributed to this too. At one place he noticed how people secretly laughed at his youthful enthusiasm and nicknamed him a Romantic. At another he was hardly given any attention because he treated the others neither warmly nor coldly. He did not give dinner parties, did not keep a carriage, did not play for high

stakes. At first Alexander's heart ached from these conflicts between his rosy
dreams and reality. It did not enter his mind to ask himself: What remarkable
things have I done, how have I distinguished myself from the crowd? Where are
my achievements and what should people notice me for? Meanwhile his pride
suffered.

Then he began gradually to admit the idea that clearly not everything in life is
roses, that there are also thorns which prick sometimes, though only lightly and
not the way his uncle said. At this point he began to learn to control himself; he
did not express his impulses and emotions and he less frequently spoke wildly, at
least before strangers.

But still to the considerable grief of Pyotr Ivanych he was far from making a
cold analysis of the simple basics of everything that excites and agitates a man's
soul. He would not even hear of rendering intelligible all of the heart's mysteries
and puzzles.

Pyotr Ivanych would give him a regular lesson in the morning. Alexander
would listen, look disturbed or deeply thoughtful and then go somewhere that
evening and return walking on clouds; for three days he'd go about as if in seventh heaven—and to the devil with Uncle's theory. The magic and intoxication of
society balls, the resonance of the music, the bare shoulders, the fire of glances,
the smile of rosy lips would keep him awake all night. He was haunted sometimes by the waist his hands had touched, sometimes by a languishing, prolonged
look thrown him in parting, sometimes by the warm breath which had melted
him in the waltz or a conversation in low voices at the window to the roar of the
mazurka, when the glances so sparkled and the tongue spoke God knows what.
His heart would beat and he embraced the pillow in cramplike agitation and for
a long time turned from one side to another.

"Where is love? Oh, I thirst for love!" he would say, "and will it come soon?
When will those heavenly minutes begin, those sweet sufferings, the agitation of
bliss, the tears..." and so on.

The next day he appeared before his uncle.

"What an evening I spent yesterday at the Zaraiskys!" he said, sinking into recollections of the ball.

"A good time!"

"Oh, heavenly!"

"Was there a decent late-night supper?"

"I didn't have supper."

"What? Not to have any supper at your age, how could you! So, I see you're
getting used in earnest to the life here, even, indeed, too well. So, they gave a
good party? The clothes, the lights..."

"Yes, sir."

"And proper guests?"

"Oh, yes! Very proper. What eyes, shoulders!"

"Shoulders? Whose?"

"Are you asking about them?"

"About whom?"

"Why, about the girls?"

"No, I didn't ask about them, but it doesn't matter—were there many pretty
ones?"

"Oh, very pretty... but unfortunately they are all alike. Whatever one will say
and do in a certain situation, another will repeat, as if they'd learned it by rote.
There was one not quite like the others... but still without either independence or

character. All movements and glances are the same. You won't hear an original thought or feel a spark of feeling—the same surface has concealed and embellished everything. It seems nothing will open them up... Will they really be like that forever, closed up and never able to reveal themselves to anyone? Will some corset always inhibit their sigh of love and the cry of a tormented heart? Will it really never allow any feeling?..."

"Everything will be revealed in front of their husbands, although if they discuss things as you do, that is, aloud, then, if you will, many will spend their lives as virgins. There are some fools who prematurely reveal what they should hide and repress, and then later make up for it with tears and tears—there's no counting them!"

"Is this a matter for calculation, Uncle?"

"Like everywhere, my dear fellow; and whoever doesn't calculate is, in plain Russian, uneconomical and a fool. To put it bluntly."

"To hold back within your breast a noble burst of feeling!..."

"Oh, I know you're not going to hold back; you're ready on the street, in the theater, to throw yourself upon a friend's neck and sob."

"So what's bad about that, Uncle? People would only say that there's a man with strong feelings, that a man of such feeling is capable of everything beautiful and not capable..."

"Not capable of calculating, that is, thinking. A fine figure—a man with strong feelings, immense passions! Aren't there enough of such temperaments? Enthusiasms, exaltations; they make a man even less like a man and are nothing to boast of. The question should be whether a man can rule his feelings; if he can, then indeed he's a man..."

"In your opinion you have to control even feeling like steam," remarked Alexander, "now let it out a little, now suddenly stop, open the valve, shut it off..."

"Yes, nature gave man that valve for a purpose—it's his reason, though you don't always use it—too bad! Still, you're a decent fellow!"

"Really, Uncle. I'm sad when I listen to you! You might better introduce me to the lady who just arrived..."

"Which one? To Mrs. Lyubetsky? Was she there yesterday?"

"She was; she talked with me a long time about you, she asked about her piece of business."

"Oh, yes! By the way..." The uncle took a document out of the drawer. "Take her this document; say that the Chamber released it only yesterday, and then under pressure. Explain the affair to her clearly; you did hear me talk to the official, didn't you?"

"Yes, I know, I know; I'll be sure to explain it."

Alexander seized the paper with both hands and hid it in his pocket. Pyotr Ivanych looked at him.

"But why have you got it in your head to be introduced to her? She seems rather unattractive—there's a wart on her nose."

"A wart? I don't remember. How did you notice that, Uncle?"

"It's on her nose, how could I have missed it! What do you like about her?"

"She's so kind and respected..."

"How is it you didn't notice the wart on her nose, but saw that she's kind and respected? That's strange. Oh, wait a minute... she has a daughter—the small brunette. Ah! now I'm not surprised. So that's why you didn't notice the wart on her nose!"

They both laughed.

"But I'm surprised though, Uncle," said Alexander, "that you noticed the wart sooner than the daughter."

"Give me back the document. You'll probably let out all your feelings there and will altogether forget to close the valve; you'll do something foolish and the devil knows how you'd explain..."

"No, I won't, Uncle. And I won't give back the paper as you wish; I'm off right now..." And he disappeared from the room.

Until this time things had been on course. At the office Alexander's abilities had been noted and he was given a decent job. Ivan Ivanych began to offer his tobacco box to Alexander too, sensing that he, like a number of others would, as he put it, get ahead of him in no time at all, climb on his shoulders and make a leap to office head and then, who knows, to vice director, as the former head had, or to director like the former vice director, and they had started learning the civil service along with many others under Ivan Ivanych's guidance. "But now I work for them!" he would add. Alexander also became an important person at the magazine's editorial office. His work was choosing, translating and correcting other people's articles, while he himself wrote up various theoretical views on agriculture. In his opinion he had more than enough money, although in his uncle's opinion, not yet enough. But he didn't always work for money. He hadn't renounced the rewarding idea of a higher calling. He was staking his youthful energies on everything. He stole time from sleep and from the office and wrote verse and stories and historical essays and biographies. His uncle was no longer papering screens with his works, but read them in silence, then whistled and said, "Yes, that's better than before!" Some of the articles appeared under another name. Alexander listened with joyous excitement to the favorable opinion of friends, of whom there were many—at the office, at the baker's and in private homes. He had fulfilled his best dream, next to love. The future promised him much glory, triumphs. A not altogether ordinary fate awaited him, when suddenly...

A few months passed. Alexander began no longer to be seen anywhere, as if he had disappeared from society. He visited his uncle less often. The latter thought his several occupations were to blame and did not interfere. But one day, upon meeting Pyotr Ivanych, the magazine editor complained that Alexander had been delaying articles. His uncle promised to have it out with his nephew as soon as he saw him. He did see him three days later. Alexander ran into his uncle's rooms in the morning like a madman. In his walk and movements he showed a joyous haste.

"Good morning Uncle. Oh, how glad I am to see you again!" he said and wanted to embrace him, but the latter managed to escape behind his desk.

"Good morning, good morning, Alexander! How is it I haven't seen you for a long time?"

"I've... been busy, Uncle. I was doing abstracts from German economists..."

"Oh, so the editor is lying. Day before yesterday he told me you weren't doing a thing—like a real journalist! I'll tell him off when I see him..."

"No, don't tell him anything," Alexander interrupted. "I haven't sent him my work yet, that's why he told you that..."

"Yes, so what's the matter?—you have such a festive look! Have they promoted you to assessor perhaps, or awarded you a medal?"

Alexander shook his head.

"So, money?"

"No."

"Then why do you have the look of a commanding general? If it isn't money, don't bother me. Here, better sit down and write a letter to the business man Dubasov in Moscow, and tell him to send me the rest of the money at once. Read his letter: Where is it? Here."

Both fell silent and began to write.

"I've finished," said Alexander in a few minutes.

"Well done; you're wonderful! Let me see. What's this? You've written it to me. 'Honored Sir, Pyotr Ivanych.' His name's Timofei Nikonych. What do you mean five hundred twenty rubles!—five thousand two hundred! What's the matter with you, Alexander?"

Pyotr Ivanych put down his pen and looked at his nephew. The latter blushed.

"Don't you notice anything in my face?" he asked.

"A kind of silly look... Wait... You're in love?" said Pyotr Ivanych.

Alexander was silent.

"You are, aren't you? I guessed it?"

With a solemn smile and a beaming glance Alexander nodded his head yes.

"So that's it! Why didn't I guess it right off? So that's why you've gone lazy and are nowhere to be found. The Zaraiskys and Scacinis keep asking me, 'Why, where in Heaven is Alexander Fyodorych?' and that's where he is—in seventh Heaven!"

Pyotr Ivanych resumed writing.

"In love with Nadenka Lyubetskaya! " Alexander said.

"I didn't ask," his uncle answered. "Whoever it is, they're all the same kind of silly fool. Which Lyubetskaya? The one with the wart?"

"Oh, Uncle!" interrupted Alexander with irritation. "What wart?"

"Right by the nose. You still haven't seen it?"

"You're still confusing things. It's the mother, you mean, who has a wart near her nose."

"Well, no matter."

"No matter! Nadenka! That angel! You really didn't notice her? To see her once—and not notice!"

"Well, what's so special about her? What's there to notice? She doesn't have a wart, you say?..."

"Haven't you talked enough about that wart! Tell the truth, Uncle: How can you say that she resembles those wooden affected debutantes? Look carefully at her face: what quiet, deep thoughts repose there! This is a young woman who not only feels, but also thinks, a character of depth..."

His uncle started scratching away with his pen on a document, but Alexander continued: "You won't hear any vulgar commonplaces in her conversation. What a bright mind illumines her judgments! What fire in her feelings! With what depth she understands life! You poison life with your views, but Nadenka reconciles me to it with hers."

Alexander was silent for a moment and immersed himself altogether for a while in his dream of Nadenka. Then he began again: "And when she raises her eyes, you see at once what a fiery and tender heart shines in them! And her voice, her voice! What a melody, what languor in it! But when this voice sounds in confession... There is no higher bliss on earth! Uncle, how beautiful life is! How happy I am!"

Tears came to his eyes. He threw himself forward and vigorously embraced his uncle.

"Alexander!" Pyotr Ivanych cried out, jumping up from his chair, "close the valve at once—you've let all the steam escape! You're mad! Look what you've done! In one second two stupid things: messed up my hair and spotted the letter with ink. I thought you'd given up your old habits. You haven't been like this for a long time. Look, look at yourself in the mirror for God's sake. Well, can there be a stupider face? And you're not stupid."

"Ha, ha, ha! I'm happy, Uncle!"

"That's obvious!"

"Isn't it? Pride gleams, I know, in my gaze. I look at the crowd as only a hero, a poet and a man in love—happy that his love is returned—can look..."

"The way madmen look, or still worse... So what shall I do now with my letter?"

"Allow me, I'll scrape off the spots—and it won't be noticeable," said Alexander. He threw himself at the desk with the same tense agitation, began to scrape, clean up, rub and rubbed through, leaving a hole in the letter. The desk began to wobble from the rubbing and pushed against the étagère. A little bust of Italian alabaster stood on the étagère—Sophocles or Aeschylus. The venerated tragic author first wobbled three times from the blow, then was overthrown from his high place and fell, shattered in fragments.

"Third stupidity, Alexander!" said Pyotr Ivanych, picking up the pieces, "and this is worth fifty rubles."

"I'll pay for it, Uncle, I'll pay. But don't curse my impulse; it is pure and noble. I am happy, happy! Heavens! How good life is!"

His uncle frowned and shook his head. "When will you get smarter, Alexander? God knows what he's saying!"

Meanwhile his uncle, crushed, looked at the broken bust. "'I'll pay', he said, 'I'll pay.' That would be the fourth stupidity. I see you want to tell about your happiness. Well, it can't be helped. If, after all, uncles are condemned to sympathize with every foolishness of their nephews, so be it. I'll give you a quarter of an hour. Sit quietly, don't commit some fifth stupidity, and tell your story. And then, after this further stupidity, leave—I have no time. So... you're happy... what about it... tell me as quickly as possible."

"If that's the way it is, Uncle, then these things can't be told," Alexander noted with a modest smile.

"I was just preparing you, but I see you want nevertheless to begin with the usual preludes. That means the telling will go on for a whole hour. I have no time; the mail won't wait. Stop, it'll be better if I tell it myself."

"You? Now that's amusing!"

"Well, listen, it's very amusing! Yesterday you had some time alone with your beauty..."

"And how do you know?" Alexander began heatedly. "Did you have me followed?"

"What's this—you think I keep spies in my pay to watch for you. Where did you get the idea I worry that much about you? What's it to me?" These words were accompanied by an icy look.

"So how do you know?" asked Alexander stepping closer to his uncle.

"Sit down, sit down, for God's sake, and don't come near my desk—you'll break something. Everything's written on your face. I'll read from that. So, you made a declaration of your love," he said.

Alexander was silent. Obviously his uncle had again guessed right.

"You both were very silly, as is the custom," said Pyotr Ivanych.

His nephew made an impatient gesture.

"It began from some little thing when you were left alone, from some embroidery border," the uncle continued. "You asked for whom she was embroidering. She answered, 'For dear Mama or Auntie,' or something like that, and for your part you trembled as if you had a fever..."

"This time no, Uncle; you didn't guess right. Not with embroidery. We were in the garden..." Alexander blurted out and stopped.

"Well, with a flower then," said Pyotr Ivanych, "maybe a yellow one, it doesn't matter. Anything that meets the eye, only so as to start the conversation. Otherwise the words won't come. You asked whether she liked this flower; she answered yes. Probably you asked why. 'I don't know,' she said, and you were both silent because you wanted to say something quite different and the conversation didn't get going. Then you looked at each other, smiled and blushed."

"Oh, Uncle, Uncle, how can you!..." said Alexander, with great embarrassment.

"Then," continued his relentless uncle, "you began to talk indirectly about how, well, a new world had opened up before you. She suddenly looked at you as if she'd heard unexpected news. You, I imagine, stopped dead, became confused, then spoke again, hardly audible, saying that not until now had you realized the value of life, that even before you had seen her... What's her name? Mary, is it?"

"Nadenka."

"You saw as if in a dream, that is, had a presentiment of meeting her, that your feeling had brought you together and probably you said that now you would dedicate to her alone your poetry and prose... And how you were waving your arms! You probably knocked something over or broke something."

"Uncle! You were spying on us!" cried Alexander beside himself.

"Yes, I was sitting behind a bush there. You see, I have nothing else to do but run after you and eavesdrop on all kinds of nonsense."

"How do you know everything?" asked Alexander in amazement.

"Simple! Since Adam and Eve it's been the same old story for everyone, with slight variations. Know the character of the actors, and you'll know the variants. This astonishes you, yet you're a writer! So now you'll jump and gallop for three days like a madman, hang onto everyone's neck—only, for God's sake, not to mine. I would advise you to lock yourself in your room for this period, let off all that steam and go through all your tricks with Evsei so no one sees you. Then you'll come to your senses a little and you'll achieve something more, a kiss, for example..."

"Nadenka's kiss! Oh, what a high, heavenly reward!" almost howled Alexander.

"Heavenly!"

"What do you mean—is it an earthly, material reward in your opinion?"

"No doubt about it, the effect of electricity. Lovers are the equivalent of two Leyden jars. Both are highly charged; the electricity is released by kisses and when it has been completely discharged—goodbye, love; cooling follows..."

"Uncle..."

"Yes! And what did you think?"

"What a notion! What ideas!"

"Oh, I forgot. 'Material tokens' will come into play again for you. Once more you'll dredge up all kinds of junk and you'll ponder and analyze, and put work aside."

Alexander suddenly felt for his pocket.

"What, it's already happened? You'll do all the things people have been doing since the creation of the world."

"Therefore, the same things you too did, Uncle?"

"Yes, only more stupidly."

"More stupidly! Aren't you calling it stupid that I shall love more deeply, more powerfully than you, not lash out at feeling, not coldly joke and play with it like you... and not draw away the veil from sacred mysteries..."

"You will love like others do, neither more deeply nor more powerfully; you will even draw the veil from mysteries... Only you'll believe in the eternity and immutability of love, indeed think only of that, and that's precisely what is stupid. You'll make more grief for yourself than there ought to be."

"Oh, that's awful, awful, Uncle, what you're saying! How many times have I vowed to myself to keep what goes on in my heart a secret from you."

"Why didn't you keep your vow? Here you've come and bothered me..."

"But you're the only one I have, Uncle, who is close to me. With whom can I share this overflow of feelings? And you mercilessly plunge your dissecting knife into the most secret corners of my heart."

"I don't do it for my pleasure. You asked my advice. How many stupidities I've saved you from!..."

"No, Uncle, let me be forever stupid in your eyes, but I cannot live with your notions of life and people. That hurts and depresses me! If they're true, I don't want to live. I don't want to live under such conditions—do you hear? I don't want it."

"I'm listening, but what am I to do? After all, I can't deprive you of life."

"No," said Alexander, "despite your predictions I shall be happy, shall love once and forever."

"Oh dear! I have the feeling you'll still break a lot more of my things. But it really doesn't matter: Love is love; no one's keeping you from it. It's not our custom that at your age one should be so preoccupied with love, still, it shouldn't be done to such a degree that you abandon work. Love is one thing, work another..."

"Yes, I'm working at abstracts from the German..."

"Enough said, you're not working on abstracts, you're giving yourself only to *sweet languor,* and the editor will refuse you..."

"Let him! I'm not in need. How can I think now about contemptible usefulness when..."

"*About contemptible usefulness!* Contemptible! You'd better build a shack in the mountains and live on bread and water:

> My poor hut
> Will be your paradise...

But when you run out of 'contemptible metal' don't ask me for it—I won't give it to you..."

"I don't think I've bothered you for it often."

"Till now, thank God, no, but it can happen if you quit work. Love also takes money—for extra elegance and various other expenses... Oh my, what I think of love at age twenty! That's when it's contemptible, so contemptible it gets you nothing!"

"What love, then, is good for something, Uncle? Love at forty?"

"I don't know how love is at forty, but at thirty-nine..."

"Like yours?"

"If you will, like mine."

"That is, no love.

"How do you know?"

"As if you could love?"

"Why not? Do you think I'm not human, or I'm eighty years old? Only if I love, then it's with reason. I keep my head, don't hit or knock anything over."

"Reasonable love! That's a fine love that keeps its head!" said Alexander with ridicule, "which never forgets itself for a moment..."

"Wild animal love," interrupted Pyotr Ivanych, "loses its head, but a reasonable love must keep it; otherwise it isn't love..."

"What is it then?"

"Then it's something vile, as you say."

"You... love!" said Alexander, as he looked, unbelievingly, at his uncle, "ha, ha, ha!"

Pyotr Ivanych wrote in silence,

"Whom, Uncle?" asked Alexander.

"You'd like to know?"

"I would,"

"My fiancée,"

"Not... your fiancée!" Alexander hardly got the words out as he jumped up and went toward his uncle.

"Not too close, not too close, Alexander, close the valve!" Pyotr Ivanych began, seeing what big eyes his nephew had, and he quickly surrounded himself with various small objects, little busts, figures, a clock and the inkwell.

"That means you're getting married?" asked Alexander with the same astonishment.

"So I am."

"And you're so calm! You write letters to Moscow, chat about unrelated matters, go to the factory and still reason about love with such hellish coldness!"

"'Hellish coldness'—that's new! People say it's hot in hell. Well, why are you looking at me so wildly?"

"You're—getting married!"

"What's so astonishing about that?" asked Pyotr Ivanych, putting down his pen.

"What do you mean? You're getting married—and didn't say a word to me!"

"Pardon me, I forgot to ask your permission."

"You didn't have to ask permission, Uncle, but I should know. My own uncle is getting married, and I know nothing about it; nobody tells me!..."

"Well, now I've told you."

"You told me because it happened to come up."

"I try whenever possible to do everything as it comes up."

"No, you should have told me first of your joy. You know how I love you and how I share..."

"I avoid sharing in general and in marriage all the more."

"Do you know what, Uncle," said Alexander animatedly, "perhaps... No, I can't keep a secret from you... I'm not that sort, I tell everything..."

"Oh dear, Alexander, I have no time, If this is a new story, can't you tell me tomorrow?"

"I only want to say that perhaps... I'm close to the same happiness..."

"What?" asked Pyotr Ivanych, pricking up his ears a bit, "this is something curious."

"Ah! Curious? So I'll torment you a while: I won't say."

Pyotr Ivanych picked up the letter packet with indifference, put in his letter and began to seal it.

"I, too, perhaps am getting married!" said Alexander in his uncle's ear.
Pyotr Ivanych did not finish sealing the letter and looked at him very seriously.
"Close the valve, Alexander," he said.

"Go on joking, go on joking, Uncle, but I'm not joking. I shall ask permission of Mama."

"Ought you to be marrying?"

"What do you mean?"

"At your age!"

"I'm twenty-three years old."

"A fine time! At that age only peasants marry when they need a woman to work in the house."

"But if I'm in love with a girl and there's a possibility of getting married, then you think I shouldn't..."

"By no means do I advise you to marry a woman you're in love with."

"What do you mean, Uncle? This is something new—I've never heard that."

"There are a lot of things you've never heard of!"

"I've always thought there should be no marriage without love."

"Marriage is one thing, and love is another," said Pyotr Ivanych.

"How should one marry... by calculation?"

"With calculation, though not by calculation. One should not calculate in money alone, however. A man is made to live in companionship with a woman; you'll begin to calculate how you should marry, begin to look, to choose among women..."

"Look, choose!" said Alexander, amazed.

"Yes, choose. That's the reason I don't advise you to marry when you fall in love. You see, love passes—that's the horrid truth."

"That's the rudest lie and slander."

"Well, one can't persuade you now. In time you'll see yourself, but for now just mark my words: Love will pass, I repeat, and then the woman who seemed the ideal of perfection to you will seem very imperfect perhaps, and then there's nothing you can do. Love prevents you from seeing that she lacks various qualities necessary in a wife. In time you'll judge coolheadedly while making your choice: Does this or that woman have the qualities you'd like to see in a wife—that's the most important calculation. And if you find such a woman, she will please you all the time without fail because she corresponds to your wishes. That will give rise to close relations between you, which then form..."

"Love?" asked Alexander.

"Yes, well... habit."

"To get married without being carried away, without the poetry of love, without passion; to judge like a case in court—what's the good of that!!"

"Yet you would marry without judging and asking yourself what for? Just as when you came here you also didn't ask yourself what for."

"So you're getting married by calculation?" asked Alexander.

"With calculation," Pyotr Ivanych corrected him.

"It's all the same."

"No. By calculation—that means to marry for money. That's ignoble. But to marry without calculation—that's stupid!... And you shouldn't get married at all now."

"When should I marry? When I've gotten old? Why am I to follow silly examples."

"Mine among them? Thanks!"

"I'm not speaking of you, Uncle, but about people in general. You hear about a wedding, you go to have a look—and what do you see? A beautiful, delicate being, almost a child, who has been awaiting only the touch of love to unfold into luxuriant flower, and suddenly they are tearing her away from her dolls, her nurse, her child's games, dances, and Heaven be thanked, if only from that; and often they don't look into her heart, which perhaps already no longer belongs to her. They dress her in gauze and lace and adorn her with flowers, and disregarding her tears and her pallor, drag her like a sacrificial victim and stand her up beside—whom?—an elderly man, usually unattractive, who has lost the glow of youth. He either throws her glances of offensive desires, or looks her over from head to toe while apparently thinking: 'Oh, you're pretty, all right, with those blissful notions of love and roses in your head—I'll cure you of this foolishness, these stupidities! I've had enough of sighs and dreams; just conduct yourself with dignity.' Or, worse yet—he dreams about her estate. The youngest is at least thirty years old. Often he's bald; though, true, he's been awarded a cross, or sometimes, a star. And they tell her: 'Here's the man to whom the treasures of your youth have been consigned; your first heartthrobs are for him as are your confessions of love, and glances, and words and maidenly caresses, and your whole life.' And around them presses a crowd of men who are her equal in youth and good looks, and who should be standing beside the bride. They devour the poor sacrifice with their glances, as if saying: 'See, when we have exhausted our freshness and health, when we're bald, we too will marry and just as luxuriant a flower will be provided us too.' It's horrible!"

"It's wild, it's not good, Alexander! You've been writing for two years now," Pyotr Ivanych said, "about fertilizer and potatoes and other serious subjects that require a severe, compressed style, and your style is still wild. For Heaven's sake, don't yield to ecstasy, or at least when this craziness comes over you, be still and let it pass; you won't say or do anything sensible—it's bound to result in foolishness."

"How so, Uncle, isn't it true that the thoughts of a poet are born in ecstasy?"

"I don't know how they're born, but I know they come out of the head quite finished, that is, after they have been worked over by thinking; only then are they indeed good. So, to whom in your opinion," began Pyotr Ivanych after a moment's silence, "should one marry off these wonderful creatures?"

"To those they love, those who haven't yet lost the glow of youthful good looks, in whom life is noticeably present everywhere—in both head and heart—to those in whose eyes the glow hasn't yet died out, on whose cheeks the red hasn't paled or the freshness—signs of health—been lost; to someone who would not lead his beautiful companion on the road of life with a weary hand, but would offer her the gift of his heart, full of love for her and capable of understanding and sharing her feelings when the rights of nature..."

"Enough! That is, to such young braves as you. If we lived *amid the fields and slumbering forests*, all right. But otherwise there's no point for such a young brave as you to marry! The first year a husband will go crazy, then he'll go looking backstage, or give his wife a rival in her maid, because those rights of nature you speak of demand change, novelty—a marvelous system! And then the wife, who will have noticed the tricks of the male, will also suddenly fall in love—with a helmet or a masquerade costume—and will do unto him the same thing... And without wealth it's even worse! 'The cupboard is bare,' he'll say."

Pyotr Ivanych put on a sour look. He continued: "'I'm married,' he'll say. 'I already have three children. Help me, I can't feed my family. I'm poor...' Poor, what a nasty business! No, I hope you won't fall into either the one or the other category."

"I shall fall into the category of happy husbands, Uncle, and Nadenka will be a happy wife. I don't want to marry the way most people do. They intone a single song: 'Youth has passed, living alone has begun to bore me, so it's time to marry!' I'm not that kind!"

"You're raving, my dear fellow."

"So how do you know?"

"Because you're just the same as others, and I have known the others for a long while. So tell me now, why are you getting married?"

"What do you mean why? Nadenka is... my wife!" Alexander exclaimed, covering his face with his hands.

"Well, see, you don't know yourself."

"Ooh! my heart stops beating at the very thought. You don't know how I love her, Uncle! I love as no one has ever loved—with all the strength of my soul—it's all for her..."

"You might better thunder back at me, or embrace me, if you must, than keep repeating that silliest phrase! How dare you say, 'As no one has ever loved!'" Pyotr Ivanych shrugged his shoulders.

"Are you saying that can't be?"

"Perhaps not; looking at your love, I think that it's quite possible—no one could love more foolishly!"

"But she says we must wait a year, that we are young and must test ourselves... for a whole year. .. and then..."

"A year! Ah! You should have said that long ago!" interrupted Pyotr Ivanych. "She's the one who suggested it? What an intelligent young woman! How old is she?"

"Eighteen."

"And you're twenty-three. Well, my boy, she's twenty-three times more intelligent than you. She knows what she's doing: She's having fun with you, flirting, passing the time merrily and then... Some of these wenches are very intelligent! Well, so you're not getting married. I thought you wanted somehow as quickly as possible to accomplish it, even secretly. At your age these stupidities are carried out so skillfully that one doesn't manage to intervene. But a year from now! By then she'll already deceive you!..."

"Nadenka—cheat and flirt! A wench! My Nadenka, Uncle! With whom have you lived your whole life, with whom had relations, whom loved, that you harbor such dark suspicions?..."

"I have lived with people, loved a woman."

"Nadenka deceive! This angel, this sincerity incarnate, this woman such as God first created in all her purity and glory..."

"But a woman all the same, so probably she'll deceive."

"And now you'll say that I will cheat on her too?"

"In time—you, you too."

"I! You can conclude anything you like about someone you don't know. But me—isn't it a sin that you should suspect me of such foul play. Who do you think I am?"

"A human being."

"They're not all alike. You should know that in earnest I gave her my sincere promise to love her all my life. I'm ready to confirm this with an oath..."

"I know, I know! A decent person doesn't doubt the sincerity of an oath when he gives it to a woman, but then he betrays her, or grows cold toward her and doesn't know why himself. This does not happen by intent, and there's nothing vile about it, no one to blame: nature hasn't allowed us to love forever. And believers in eternal and immutable love do the same thing as non-believers, only they don't notice or want to admit it. If you say that you and I are above it, aren't people but angels—that's stupid!"

"Why are there loving married people who eternally love each other and live together all their lives?..."

"Eternally! They call someone who loves for two weeks flighty, but two or three years—even that's eternal! The liveliness, fire, feverishness of this feeling doesn't permit it to be drawn out. It's true that loving spouses live their whole lives together! But do they really love each other their whole lives? Does their initial love bind them forever? Do they go on forever searching for each other and looking at each other every minute and never tiring of it? Where do the little favors eventually go, the constant attentiveness, the yearning to be together, the tears, the enthusiasms—all these foolishnesses? The coldness and clumsiness of husbands has become proverbial. 'Their love is transformed into friendship!' everyone says meaningfully: so there, it's no longer love! Friendship! But what kind of friendship is it? Husband and wife are bound by common interests, circumstances, a single fate—for they live together; and if they aren't, they separate and they love others, first one and, later, the other. That's what is called infidelity!... But living together, they come to live by habit, which is stronger among us than any love; not for nothing is it called second nature!... Otherwise people wouldn't stop torturing each other all their lives after parting, or after the death of the loved one, but they do resign themselves, you see. Otherwise they would repeat: forever, forever!... They wouldn't look at it reasonably, they would just carry on."

"Why is it that you're not afraid for yourself, Uncle? According to this, won't your bride too... pardon me... cheat on you?..."

"I don't think so."

"What self-esteem!"

"That isn't self-esteem, but calculation."

"Again calculation!"

"Well, reasoning, if you will."

"But if she falls in love with someone?"

"One mustn't let it come to that. But if such a sin were to be committed, the affair can be cooled down adroitly."

"Is that possible, is it really in your power?..."

"Quite."

"Then all betrayed husbands would act," said Alexander, "if there were a means..."

"Not all husbands are alike, my dear fellow. Some are quite indifferent to their wives, pay no attention to what goes on around them and don't want to notice; others would like to out of self-esteem, but aren't good at it, they don't know how to begin."

"How will you do it?"

"That's my secret. You wouldn't understand—you're too impassioned."

"I'm happy now and thank God. And I don't want to know what lies ahead."

"The first half of your sentence is so reasonable that a man in love shouldn't perhaps say it. It shows a capacity to take advantage of the present. But the second half, pardon me, won't get you anywhere. 'I don't want to know what lies

ahead'; that is, 'I don't want to think about what was yesterday and what is today.
I shan't either consider or reason, I shan't prepare or watch for which way the
wind will blow!' I beg you, does that make sense?"

"So what do you advise, Uncle? When a moment of bliss arrives, must one
take a magnifying glass and examine..."

"No, the opposite; reduce it so as not to make a fool of yourself for joy, so as
not to hang on everyone's neck."

"And if a moment of sorrow comes," Alexander continued, "should that also
be examined in your miniaturizing glass?"

"No, put sorrow under the magnifying glass; it's easier to overcome when you
imagine the unpleasantness twice as large as it is."

"Why," continued Alexander ruefully, "am I to kill every joy at the start with
cold reasoning and before drinking it to the full, think that it will betray me, it will
pass. Why shall I torment myself in advance with grief before it occurs?"

"Because when it does come," his uncle interrupted, "then you'll think: the
grief will pass too, as it did at such a time and such a time with me and with that
man and with that one too. I hope this isn't foolish, and it is worth thinking
about. If you do, you won't torment yourself when you realize the inconstancy of
all eventualities in life. You'll be cold and calm as much as a human being can be
calm."

"So this is the secret of your tranquillity," said Alexander thoughtfully.

Pyotr Ivanych was silent and wrote.

"But what kind of life is it!" Alexander began, "not to forget yourself, but
always be thinking, thinking... No, I feel things are different. I want to live without your cold analysis, not think whether misfortune and danger lie ahead or
not—I don't care! Why should I think about it in advance and poison..."

"I've been saying why, but he sticks to his opinion! Don't force me to make
some insulting comparison at your expense. The reason is that when you foresee
the danger, the obstacle, the misfortune, then it's easier to fight or endure it.
You'll neither go crazy nor die. And when joy comes, you won't gallop and over-
turn busts—do you see? He's told: this is the beginning; look at it, on this basis
consider the end. But he closes his eyes, wags his head, as if he saw some scarecrow, and lives like a child. Live day by day, according to you, as it comes; sit at
the door of your hut. Measure life by dinners, dances, love, and immutable
friendship. People have always desired Heaven on earth! I've already told you
that with your ideas you'd be best off in the village with your woman and half a
dozen children, but here you have work to do; hence you must constantly think
and remember what you did yesterday and what you're doing today, so as to
know what must be done tomorrow, that is, live with a constant evaluation of
yourself and what you're doing. In this way one progresses to something worth
doing; otherwise... But what's the use of explaining to you; you're delirious just
now. Oh dear! it's almost one o'clock. Not another word, Alexander; go away... I
won't listen. Dine with me tomorrow; there will be someone else."

"Your friends?"

"Yes... Konev, Smirnov, Fyodorov—you know them, and someone else too..."

"Konev, Smirnov, Fyodorov! Of course, the same people you do business
with."

"Correct. Useful people."

"And they're your friends? In truth, I haven't seen you receive anyone with
especial warmth."

"I've told you that what I call friends are those I see most often who bring me either profit or pleasure. For God's sake, why feed people for nothing?"

"But I thought before your wedding you were saying goodbye to real friends whom you loved with all your soul, with whom you'd remember your merry youth for the last time over a goblet of wine, and that perhaps at parting you'd press them warmly to your heart."

"Well, your word or two expresses everything that doesn't exist in life or shouldn't. With what rapture your auntie would have thrown herself upon your neck! There are *true friends* there, when there are simply friends; a *goblet*, when people actually drink from wine or water glasses; and embraces *at parting*, when there are no final partings. Oh, Alexander!"

"And aren't you sorry to take leave of these friends, or at least see them less often?" said Alexander.

"No! I have never gotten close with anyone to the point of being sorry, and I advise you not to."

"But perhaps they're not like that; perhaps they feel sorry to lose a good companion and someone to talk to?"

"That isn't my worry, it's theirs. I've also lost such companions more than once, and see, I haven't died of it. So you'll come tomorrow?"

"Tomorrow, Uncle, I..."

"What?"

"I've been invited to the country."

"Probably to the Lyubetskys?"

"Yes."

"Well, as you wish. Remember about your work, Alexander. I'll tell the editor what you're busy with..."

"Oh, Uncle, how can you! I'll finish the abstracts for the German economists without fail."

"You'd best begin them if you're to finish. Look, remember, don't ask for any *contemptible metal*, once you've wholly surrendered to *sweet languor.*"

IV

Alexander's life was divided in two. His government job swallowed up the mornings. He was buried under by tedious business, had to weigh circumstances that were of absolutely no importance to him and count the money of others on paper by the millions. But sometimes his mind rebelled against thinking for others, the pen fell from his hand, and he was overcome by that *sweet languor* which so infuriated Pyotr Ivanych.

At those times Alexander leaned back against his chair and was carried away in thought to a golden place, a place of calm where there is no ink and no papers, there are no strange faces, no civil service uniforms, tranquillity, languor and coolness prevail, there are fragrant flowers in an elegantly furnished hall, the sound of a piano is heard, a parrot jumps in its cage and the birch branches and lilac bushes sway in the garden. And reigning over all... is she.

While sitting in the office in the mornings, Alexander was invisibly present on one of the islands at the Lyubetskys' country place. And in the afternoons he was really there in person. Let's have an indiscreet look at his bliss.

It was a hot day, one of those rare days in St. Petersburg. The sun blessed the fields with life, but burned the city streets; its rays heated the granite, bounced off the stone, and baked everyone. People walked slowly with drooping heads; dogs walked with their tongues hanging out. The town resembled one of those fairy-tale cities where everything has suddenly been turned to stone by a magician's enchantment. Coaches did not thunder over the pavement; awnings covered the windows like closed eyelids; the wooden sidewalks gleamed like parquet floor-ing, hot to the step. Boredom and sleep prevailed everywhere.

A pedestrian, wiping the sweat from his face, sought the shade. A rented car-riage with six passengers slowly dragged on its way out of town, hardly raising any dust in its wake. At four o'clock the civil servants took off from work and slowly made their way home.

Alexander ran out as if the ceiling had collapsed. He looked at his watch. It was late, not enough time for dinner. He rushed to the restaurant.

"What is on today's menu? Quick!"

"*Soupe julienne* and *à la reine*. Dressing *à la provençale à la maître d'hôtel*. Roast turkey, game. Soufflé, cake."

"Well, *provençale* soup, *julienne* sauce, and roasted soufflé, but hurry!"

The waiter looked at him.

"Well, what's the matter? " said Alexander impatiently.

The waiter rushed out and brought whatever entered his head. Aduyev was very happy with it. He didn't wait for the dessert, but ran to the Neva embank-ment. There a boat with two oarsmen was waiting.

An hour later he caught sight of the promised land, stood up in the boat and strained his gaze into the distance. At first his eyes clouded over with fear and an anxiety which turned to doubt. Then suddenly his face lighted up with joy as with the glow of sunlight. He made out the familiar dress at the garden gate. Look, they had recognized him, a handkerchief fluttered. He had been awaited, per-haps for a long time. The soles of his feet seemed almost to burn with impa-tience.

"Oh, if only one could walk on the water!" thought Alexander. "All sorts of crazy things are being invented, but this is the kind of thing they don't invent!"

The oarsmen moved their oars slowly, measuredly like a machine. Sweat streamed down their sunburned faces. Little they cared that Alexander's heart had begun pounding in his breast, that without turning an eye from that single spot he had twice now unconsciously put first one, then the other leg over the edge of the boat, but they paid no attention. They rowed at their own speed and with the same sluggishness, wiping their faces at times with their sleeve.

"Faster!" he said, "a half-ruble tip."

How they started to work, how they began to rise in their places! Where had their weariness gone? Where did they get their strength? The oars began truly whipping through the water. The boat would glide, then traverse dozens of feet at a time. They made ten or so sweeps, and the stern described a curve; the boat gracefully approached the bank and tipped toward it. Alexander and Nadenka smiled at each other from a distance and did not take their eyes off each other. Aduyev put one leg down in the water instead of on the bank. Nadenka began to smile.

"Not so fast, Sir, wait, here, take my arm," said one oarsman after Alexander was already on the bank. Nadenka began to laugh.

"Wait for me here," Aduyev told them and started running toward Nadenka.

She tenderly smiled at Alexander from afar. With each movement of the boat toward the bank she had been breathing harder.

"Nadezhda Alexandrovna!" said Aduyev, hardly catching his breath for joy.

"Alexander Fyodorych ..." she answered.

They instinctively rushed toward each other, then stopped and looked at each other with a smile and wet eyes, unable to say anything. Several minutes passed this way.

Pyotr Ivanych could not be blamed for not having noticed Nadenka at first. She was not a beauty and didn't catch your attention at once.

But whoever studied her features could not look away for some time. Her expression seldom stayed the same for two minutes. The thoughts and varied feelings of her extremely impressionable and sensitive soul were constantly changing, and the nuances of these feelings flowed together in amazing play, bringing a new and unexpected look to her face every minute. Her eyes, for example, would suddenly seem to flash like lightning, burn, and then immediately hide under her long lashes. Her face would become lifeless and immobile, and you'd see a marble statue before you. After that you'd expect another penetrating ray—not a chance! Her eyes would open quietly, slowly—the gentle glow of her gaze would shine upon you as if the moon had slowly floated out from behind the clouds. Your heart would surely respond to her glance by beating slightly faster.

Nadya's movements were of the same essence. They had a lot of grace, though not the grace of sylphs. Much of her gracefulness was wild and impulsive, of the sort nature gives to everyone but which art will then take away completely rather than just tone down. Traces of such wildness and impulsiveness often broke through in Nadenka's movements. She sometimes sat in a picturesque pose, but suddenly God knows what inner impulse would break that picturesque pose with a wholly unexpected and again enchanting gesture. In conversation the same unexpected reverses; she would display true judgment, then dreaminess, then sharp condemnation, followed by a childish prank or subtle pretense. Everything in her revealed a fiery mind, a willful and inconstant heart. And why wouldn't Alexander fall madly in love with her; only Pyotr Ivanych came away scotfree—but are there many like him?

"You were waiting for me! Heavens, how happy I am!" said Alexander.

"I waiting? I wouldn't dream of it!" answered Nadenka, tossing her head. "You know I'm always in the garden."

"Are you angry?" he asked shyly.

"What for? That's a funny idea!"

"Let me kiss your hand."

She gave him her hand, but as soon as he touched it, she snatched it away—and suddenly her mood changed. Her smile disappeared, her face showed something like vexation.

"What's this, you're drinking milk?" he asked.

Nadenka had a cup in her hands and a piece of dry toast.

"This is my dinner," she answered.

"Having dinner at six o'clock and dining on milk!"

"Of course you think milk is strange after your luxurious dinner at your uncle's? But we're in the country here; we live modestly."

With her front teeth she broke off some crumbs of toast and took a drink of milk, curling her lips in a charming pout.

"I didn't dine with Uncle. I told him no yesterday," Aduyev answered.

"You just have no conscience. How can you lie like that? Where have you been till now?"

"I sat through the day at the office until four o'clock..."

"But it's six now. Don't lie; admit you were tempted by dinner, by the pleasant company? It was very amusing there."

"Word of honor, I didn't go to Uncle's..." Alexander began to defend himself heatedly. "If I had, then how could I have gotten here by now?"

"What! Do you think this is early? You should have been here some two hours ago!" said Nadenka and quickly turned on her heel away from him and set off on the path to the house, Alexander after her.

"Don't come near me, don't come near me," she began, waving her hand, "I can't bear to look at you."

"Enough of playing games, Nadezhda Alexandrovna!"

"I'm not playing games at all. Tell me, where were you till now?"

"I left the office at four o'clock," Aduyev began, "and spent an hour on the way here..."

"So it should be five then, but it's six by now. Where did you spend the extra hour? You see how you lie!"

"I ate a quick dinner in a restaurant..."

"A quick dinner! Only an hour!" she said, "poor thing! You must be hungry. Don't you want some milk?"

"Oh, give me, do give me your cup..." Alexander began and reached out his hand.

But she suddenly stopped and turned the cup upside down; ignoring Alexander, she watched with curiosity the last drops drip from the cup onto the sand.

"You're without pity!" he said. "How can you torment me so?"

"Look, look, Alexander Fyodorych," Nadenka suddenly interrupted him, absorbed in her own pursuit. "Shall I hit this bug with a drop, see, that one crawling along the path?... Oh dear, I hit her, the poor thing! She'll die!" she said. Then she anxiously picked up the bug, put it on the palm of her hand and began to breathe on it.

"How taken you are with the bug!" he said, annoyed.

"Poor thing! Look, she'll die," said Nadenka with sorrow. "What have I done?"

She carried the bug for a while on her hand and when it began to wiggle and crawl back and forth on her hand, Nadenka shuddered, quickly threw it to the ground and crushed it with her foot, saying, "Nasty bug!"

"Where were you?" she asked then.

"I told you..."

"Oh, yes! At your uncle's. Were there many guests? Did you drink champagne? I can smell the champagne from here."

"I told you no, not at Uncle's!" Alexander interrupted in desperation. "Who told you I was?"

"You did."

"Why, they're just now sitting down to table at Uncle's, I imagine. You don't know these dinners. Do you think a dinner like that is over in an hour?"

"You took two for yours—from four to six."

"Then when did I have time for the trip here?"

She didn't answer, jumped and caught a branch of acacia, then ran off along the path.

Aduyev ran after her.

"Where are you going?" he asked.

"Where, where indeed! To Mama."

"Why? Perhaps we'll bother her."

"No, we won't."

Marya Mikhailovna, Nadezhda Alexandrovna's mama, was one of those kind and naive mothers who find whatever their dear children do admirable. Marya Mikhailovna, for example, would order the carriage harnessed.

"Where are you going, Mama?" Nadenka would ask.

"Let's go for a drive, the weather's so beautiful," her mother would say.

"How can you, Alexander Fyodorych wanted to come."

And the carriage would be put away.

Another time Marya Mikhailovna would sit down to work on her endless scarf and begin sighing, taking snuff and clicking her bone needles or getting deep into a French novel.

"Mama, why don't you get dressed?" Nadenka would ask with severity.

"Why, where are we going?"

"We're going for a drive."

"A drive?"

"Yes. Alexander Fyodorych is coming for us. Had you really forgotten!"

"But I didn't even know."

"How could you not know!" Nadenka would say, displeased.

Her mother would leave both scarf and book and go to get dressed. Thus Nadenka enjoyed full freedom, organized her own and her mother's day and activities as she wished. She was, by the way, a kind and affectionate daughter, one couldn't say otherwise—obedient only because not she, but her mother did the obeying. Therefore, one could say she had an obedient mother.

"Go to see Mama," said Nadenka when they got to the living room doors.

"And you?"

"I'll come later."

"Well, then I'll come later too."

"No, you go first."

Alexander went in and immediately came back again.

"She's dozing in her armchair," he said in a whisper.

"No matter, we'll go in. Mama, oh Mama!"

"Ah!"

"Alexander Fyodorych has come."

"Ah!"

"Mr. Aduyev wants to see you."

"Ah!"

"You see how soundly she's fallen asleep. Don't wake her!" Alexander restrained her.

"No, I'm going to wake her. Mama !"

"Ah!"

"Wake up, Alexander Fyodorych is here."

"Where is Alexander Fyodorych?" said Marya Mikhailovna, looking right at him and straightening her bonnet, which had slipped to one side. "Oh! Is that you, Alexander Fyodorych? Do come in! I just sat down here and dozed off, I don't know why myself, apparently the weather. My corn is starting to hurt—it must be going to rain. While dozing I dreamt that Ignaty announced guests, only I didn't understand who. I heard him say they've come, but I didn't catch who. Then Nadenka called and I woke up at once. I am a light sleeper: the slightest squeak and my eyes are wide open. Sit down, Alexander Fyodorych. Are you well?"

"Yes, thank you."

"And Pyotr Ivanych too?"

"Thank God, he is too, thank you."

"Why doesn't he ever come to see us? Just yesterday I was thinking perhaps he'd drop by some time, I thought, but no—he's probably busy, isn't he?"

"Very busy," said Alexander.

"You didn't come yesterday either!" Marya Mikhailovna went on. "The other day I woke up and asked, how's Nadenka? 'She's still asleep,' they said. 'Well, let her sleep,' I said. 'She's outdoors all day—in the garden, the weather is good, she gets tired.' At her age one sleeps soundly, not like me at mine. I have such trouble sleeping, would you believe it? I even get depressed, perhaps it's nerves—I don't know. So they brought my coffee, I always have breakfast in bed. As I drank it, I thought, 'Why is it we don't see Alexander Fyodorych? Perhaps he isn't well?' Then I got up, and looked: it was past eleven. I ask you, why wouldn't the servants tell me! I looked in on Nadenka—she wasn't awake yet either. I woke her. 'It's time to get up, my dear. It's almost noon, what's the matter with you?' You see, I'm after her all day long like a nursemaid. I purposely let the governness go so there'd be no strangers. Entrust yourself to strangers and Heaven knows what they'll do. No! I take care of her upbringing myself. I keep strict watch, don't allow her a step away from me, and I may say, Nadenka appreciates this. She never keeps any thoughts secret from me. It's as if I saw right through her... At this point the cook came. I spent about an hour talking to him. Then I read *Les Mémoires du diable*... Oh, Soulié[3] is such an agreeable author! How charmingly he describes things! Then my neighbor Marya Ivanovna and her husband came to call. So the morning was gone before I knew it. I looked and it was already going on four and time for dinner! Oh yes, why didn't you come for dinner? We waited for you till five."

"Until five?" said Alexander. "I just couldn't make it, Marya Mikhailovna; I was held up at the office. I beg you never to wait for me after four o'clock."

"That's what I said, but Nadenka kept saying, 'Let's wait till he comes, once we're waiting.'"

"I! Oh dear, oh dear Mama, what do you mean! Wasn't it I who said, 'It's time for dinner, Mama,' but you said, 'No, we must wait a bit. Alexander Fyodorych hasn't been here for a long time, probably he'll come to dinner.'"

"Hear, hear!" Marya Mikhailovna began, shaking her head. "Oh, how can she say that! Her very words, only she pretends I said them!"

Nadenka turned away, walked among the flowers and began to tease the parrot.

"I say, 'Wherever can Alexander Fyodorych be now,'" Marya Mikhailovna went on. "'It's already four-thirty.' 'No,' she says, 'We must wait, Mama, we must wait—he'll come.' I look, it's quarter-to-five. 'As you wish, Nadenka,' I say. 'Alexander Fyodorych has probably been invited out and isn't coming. I'm terribly hungry.' 'No,' she says, 'we must wait a bit longer till five.' That's how you were starving me to death. Isn't that so, Mademoiselle?"

"Polly parrot!" came a voice from behind the flowers, "where did you have dinner today, at your uncle's?"

"What? Are you hiding!" said her mother. "You obviously are ashamed to look us in the face!"

"Not at all," Nadenka answered, coming out of the bushes and sitting down at the window.

"So she didn't come to table!" said Marya Mikhailovna. "She asked for a cup of milk and went into the garden. And she hasn't had dinner. Right? Look me straight in the eyes, Mademoiselle."

Alexander melted on hearing this. He looked at Nadenka, but she turned her back to him and plucked at a leaf of ivy.

"Nadezhda Alexandrovna!" he said. "Am I so fortunate that you were thinking of me?"

"Don't come near me!" she cried, annoyed that her tricks had been exposed. "Mamma's joking and you're ready to believe her!"

"So, where are the berries you fixed for Alexander Fyodorych?" asked her mother.

"Berries?"

"Yes, berries."

"Why, you ate them for dinner..." answered Nadenka.

"I! I remember, my dear, you hid them and didn't give them to me. 'Look,' she says, 'Alexander Fyodorych will come, then I'll give them to you.' Isn't that so?"

Alexander glanced tenderly and slyly at Nadenka. She blushed.

"She cleaned them herself, Alexander Fyodorych," her mother added.

"What's this you're imagining, Mama? I cleaned two or three little berries and you yourself ate them, or maybe Vasilisa..."

"Don't believe her, Alexander Fyodorych. Vasilisa was sent to town this morning. Why keep it a secret? Probably it would make Alexander Fyodorych happier that you cleaned them and not Vasilisa."

Nadenka smiled, then disappeared again amid the flowers and reappeared with a whole plate of berries. She stretched out her hand to Aduyev with the plate. He kissed her hand and received the berries as a marshal of the army receives the staff of authority.

"You don't deserve it! Making people wait for you so long! " said Nadenka. "I stood two hours at the gate, imagine! When someone came along, I thought it was you and waved my handkerchief. Then I realized I didn't know him, some officer. And he waved back, so impudent!..."

That evening guests came and went. It began getting dark. The Lyubetskys and Aduyev again numbered three. Gradually this trio too separated. Nadenka went into the garden. Marya Mikhailovna and Aduyev formed an awkward duet. She sang him at length her litany of what she did yesterday, and today, and what she would do tomorrow. A dreary boredom and unrest seized him. Evening came on quickly and he still hadn't managed to say a single word to Nadenka alone. The cook rescued him; this savior came to ask what to prepare for supper, and Aduyev was taken over by a greater impatience than before in the boat. Hardly had they begun talking of chops and clotted milk when Alexander artfully began to withdraw. How many maneuvers he used just to get away from Marya Mikhailovna's chair! At first he went up to the window and looked out at the yard while his legs seemed to pull him out the open door. Then with slow steps, barely keeping himself from rushing off in a flash, he walked slowly over to the piano, hit a note here and there on the keyboard, took the music off the rack with feverish palpitation, looked at it and put it back, even had the strength of mind to smell two flowers and wake up the parrot. Then he reached the highest level of impatience; the door was beside him, but to leave was somehow still awkward—he would have to stand there a couple of minutes and walk out as if by accident. Now the cook took two steps backward, a word more—and he'd be gone; then Mrs. Lyubetsky surely would turn again to him. Alexander could stand it no longer and, like a snake, slithered out the door and, leaping off the porch without counting the steps, reached the end of the allée in a few paces—to find himself on the embankment beside Nadenka.

"He finally remembered me!" she said, this time with gentle reproach.

"Oh, what torment I've suffered," answered Alexander, "and you didn't help!"

Nadenka showed him a book. "Here's what I would have gotten you out with if you hadn't come in another minute," she said. "Sit down. By now Mama won't come any more; she's afraid of dampness. I have so many, so many things I must tell you... Oh my!"

"And I you too... Oh my!"

Then they said nothing, or almost nothing, that is, what they had already spoken of ten times before: ordinary things, dreams, the sky, the stars, what they liked, happiness. They carried on their conversations mostly in the language of looks, smiles and exclamations. The book fell on the grass.

Night set in... no, what do you mean, night! Can you say there are nights in Petersburg in the summer? This isn't night, but... Really you'd have to invent another name—say, half-light... Everything was quiet all around. The river Neva slept; sometimes, as if half-waking, it lapped against the bank with a slight ripple and fell silent. Then a late breeze came from somewhere and swept over the sleepy waters, but could not wake them, it only made ripples on the surface and blew a bit of coolness on Nadenka and Alexander, or brought them the sound of a distant song—and then everything was silent again, and again the Neva was still like a sleeping human who will open his eyes for a minute at a slight noise and close them again at once; and sleep will weigh down his heavy lids all the more. Then from the direction of the bridge something like distant thunder was heard and afterwards the bark of the watchdog from the nearest fishery and again everything was quiet. The trees formed a dark vault, and shook their branches just a bit, without a sound. In the cottages along the banks little lights flickered.

What special thing does the warm air carry at these times? What secret runs through the flowers, trees and grass, and breathes with ineffable languor upon the soul. Why does it give birth to thoughts and feelings so different from those that arise amid din and crowds? What an environment there is for love in this sleep of nature, this twilight, these silent trees, these flowers and this solitude! How powerfully everything attunes the mind to dreams and the heart to rare feelings which seem such useless, out-of-place and ridiculous aberrations in the everyday, proper and disciplined life... Yes! useless, but meanwhile at these moments the soul but dimly comprehends the possibility of the happiness it so diligently seeks at other times and does not find.

Alexander and Nadenka went up to the river and leaned on the gate. For a long time Nadenka looked pensively at the Neva and into the distance; Alexander looked at Nadenka. Their souls were overflowing with happiness; together their hearts yearned sweetly and somehow painfully, but they did not speak.

Now Alexander quietly touched her waist. With her elbow she quietly pushed his hand away. He put it back and she pushed it away more gently without taking her eyes off the Neva. The third time she did not push it away.

He took her by the hand—she did not take her hand away. He pressed her hand; her hand returned the pressure. So they stood in silence, but what they felt!

"Nadenka!" he said quietly.

She was silent.

With his heart standing still Alexander bent toward her. She felt his warm breath on her cheek, trembled, turned around—but did not step away in noble indignation, did not cry out—she hadn't the strength to resist and step away. The enchantment of love forced her reason to silence, and when Alexander's lips clung to hers, she responded to his kiss, though weakly, hardly perceptibly.

"Not proper!" the strict mamas will say. "Alone in the garden without her mother she kisses a young man!" What's to be done! It wasn't proper, but she responded to his kiss.

"Oh, how happy a person can be!" said Alexander to himself and again bent down to her lips and remained thus for several seconds.

She stood pale, motionless; tears glistened on her lashes. She breathed heavily, unevenly.

"Like a dream!" whispered Alexander.

Suddenly Nadenka started; the moment of forgetfulness had passed.

"What has happened? You forget yourself!" she said suddenly and threw herself several paces away from him. "I shall tell Mama!"

Alexander fell from the clouds.

"Nadezhda Alexandrovna! Don't destroy my bliss with reproach," he began, "don't be like..."

She looked at him and suddenly began to laugh loudly, merrily; again she came over to him, again stood at the gate and trustingly leaned her head and hand on his shoulder.

"Do you love me very much?" she asked, wiping away the tear that rolled down her cheek.

Alexander moved his shoulders in an indescribable gesture. "A most stupid expression," Pyotr Ivanych would have said, appeared on his face, and perhaps this was true, but at the same time how much happiness there was in this stupid expression!

They looked again in silence at the water and the sky and into the distance, as if nothing had happened between them. Only they were afraid to look at each other. Finally they did, smiled and immediately turned away again.

"Can there be sorrow in the world?" asked Nadenka after a silence.

"It's said there is..." Aduyev answered thoughtfully, "but I don't believe it..."

"What sorrow can there be?"

"Uncle says poverty. "

"Poverty! Can the poor possibly not feel what we felt just now? So then they're not poor."

"Uncle says they don't care about that—they need to eat and drink..."

"Pah! Eat! Your uncle doesn't speak the truth. You can be happy without it too. I had no dinner today, and how happy I am!"

He laughed.

"Yes, at this minute I would give everything to the poor, everything, everything!" Nadenka went on. "Let the poor come. Oh! why can't I comfort and make them all glad with some joy?"

"Angel! Angel!" solemnly declared Alexander, pressing her hand.

"Ouch, you're squeezing so hard it hurts!" Nadenka suddenly interrupted, frowning and taking her hand away.

But he seized her hand again and heatedly began to kiss it.

"How I shall say prayers," she continued, "today, tomorrow, always for this evening! How happy I am! And you?..."

Suddenly she stopped to think; a look of alarm came into her eyes.

"Do you know," she said, "people say that what happens once can never happen again! Therefore will this moment too never be repeated?"

"Oh, no!" answered Alexander, "that's not so: It will happen again. There will be better moments; yes, I feel it!..."

She shook her head in doubt. And for him his uncle's lessons came to mind and he suddenly stopped.

"No," he said to himself. "No, that can't be! Uncle has never known such happiness. That's why he's so severe and skeptical with people. Poor man! I'm sorry for his cold, callous heart. He hasn't known the intoxication of love. That explains his jaundiced cynicism about life. God forgive him. If he saw my bliss, he would bless it, not deprecate it with doubt. I'm sorry for him..."

"No, Nadenka, no, we shall be happy!" he continued aloud. "Look around you. Isn't everything here rejoicing at the sight of our love? Even God blesses it. How merrily we shall go through life, hand in hand! How proud we shall be, great in our mutual love!"

"Oh, stop, stop guessing! " she interrupted. "Don't prophesy. I get frightened when you talk like that. Even now I feel sad..."

"What is there to be afraid of? You don't mean we mustn't believe in ourselves?"

"We mustn't, we mustn't!" she said, shaking her head. He looked at her and stopped to think.

"Why? What, indeed," he then began, "can destroy this world of our happiness? Who will tell us what to do? We shall be alone always, shall begin to get away from others; what do we need them for, and they us? They won't remember us, will forget us, and then even rumors about grief and misfortunes won't disturb us, just as now here in the garden no sound disturbs this solemn silence..."

"Nadenka! Alexander Fyodorych!" was suddenly heard from the porch, "where are you?"

"Do you hear!" said Nadenka in a prophetic tone. "That's a sign from fate. This minute will never come again—I feel it..."

She seized his hand, pressed it, looked at him somehow strangely, sadly and suddenly dashed off into a dark path.

He remained alone in thoughts.

"Alexander Fyodorych!" came the cry again from the porch, "the clotted milk has been on the table for a long time."

He shrugged his shoulders and went inside.

"After a moment of inexpressible bliss suddenly clotted milk!" he said to Nadenka. "Is it always like that in life?"

"If only it's no worse," she answered merrily. "And clotted milk is awfully good, especially for someone who had no dinner."

Happiness lent her animation. Her cheeks were aflame, her eyes burned with an unusual gleam. How busily she played the hostess, how merrily she chatted! There wasn't the slightest sign of her momentarily passing sorrow; joy absorbed her.

Dawn had already taken over half the sky when Aduyev boarded the boat. In expectation of the promised reward the oarsmen rowed full strength and were about to begin standing up in their places as before, pulling on the oars for all they were worth.

"Go slow!" said Alexander, "one more half-ruble tip!"

They looked at him, then at each other. One scratched his chest, the other his back, and they hardly rippled their oars, hardly touched the water. The boat glided like a swan.

"And Uncle wants to assure me that happiness is an illusion, that one must not believe anything unconditionally, that life is... without conscience! Why did he want to deceive me so cruelly? No, this is life!"

A fresh morning breeze just barely blew from the north. Alexander gave a slight shudder both from the breeze and his recollection, then yawned and wrapping himself in his cloak, plunged into dreams.

V

Aduyev reached the peak of his happiness. He had nothing more to wish for. His work at the office, his journalistic efforts were all cast aside and forgotten. He was passed by for promotion, but he hardly noticed it and only then because his uncle remarked on it. Pyotr Ivanych advised him to quit this silly nonsense, but Alexander shrugged his shoulders at the word "silly nonsense," smiled regretfully and was silent. Realizing the futility of his admonitions, his uncle also shrugged, smiled regretfully and fell silent; he only said, "As you wish; it's your business. But see that you don't ask for any of the contemptible metal."

"Don't be afraid, Uncle," Alexander replied. "It is bad when one doesn't have much money. I don't need much, but I have enough."

"Well, I congratulate you," Pyotr Ivanych added.

Apparently Alexander was avoiding him. He had lost all faith in his uncle's sorry predictions and feared his cold view of love in general and his offensive remarks about Alexander's relationship to Nadenka in particular.

He found it offensive to hear his uncle analyze his love according to general laws, as if it was the same as everyone's, and thereby simply profane this noble and, in Alexander's opinion, sacred matter. He kept secret his joys and the whole prospect of rosy bliss, feeling that at the slightest contact with his uncle's analysis, before he knew it the roses would scatter in ashes or be changed to dirt. At first his uncle avoided him because, look, he thought, the boy will get lazy, run out of cash, come to him for money, or be a weight around his neck.

In Alexander's walk, look, and whole bearing there was something solemn, mysterious. He conducted himself with others as a rich capitalist on the stock exchange would act with small business men, that is modestly and with dignity, while thinking to himself, "Poor things! Who of you has such a treasure at his disposal as I? Who knows how to feel as I do? Whose powerful soul..." and the like.

He was convinced that he alone in the world loved in this way and was so loved.

Moreover, he not only avoided his uncle, but *crowds* too, as he called them. He either paid court to his deity or sat at home in his study, drinking in bliss while analyzing it, breaking it down into endlessly small atoms. He called this *creating a special world*, and sitting in his isolation, he actually did create such a world for himself out of nothing and made himself more at home there, and rarely and unwillingly went to work, calling that *a bitter necessity, a necessary evil* or *dreary prose*. In general, he had many variants on this theme. He didn't go to see the editor and his friends at all.

Chatting with his *self* was his greatest pleasure. "Alone with only himself, " he wrote in some kind of story, "a man sees himself as in a mirror. Only then does he learn to believe in human greatness and dignity. How beautiful he is in con-

versation with his spiritual powers! Like a military leader he inspects them strict-
ly, disposes them according to a wisely considered plan, and pushes forward to
take charge; and he takes action and shapes things. How pitiful, on the contrary,
is the man who is unable to be alone, who flees himself and everywhere seeks
society, other people's reasoning and inspiration..." You might imagine a thinker
like this is discovering new laws about the world's structure or human existence,
but here he's simply a man in love!

He is sitting in a winged armchair now. Before him lies a sheet of paper on
which a few verses are jotted down. He bends over the sheet and makes some cor-
rection or adds two or three verses, then throws himself against the back of the
chair and thinks. A smile moves on his lips; it is obvious that he has only just
removed them from the brimming *goblet* of happiness. His eyes close languorously
like a dozing cat, or flash suddenly with the fire of an inner excitement.

All around is quiet. Only the roll of carriages is heard from afar on the big
street, and at times Evsei, tired of polishing boots, will say aloud: "I must remember: just now at the shop I bought a penny's worth of vinegar and ten pennies'
worth of cabbage; I must pay tomorrow, or the storekeeper likely won't give me
credit again—the dog! He weighs bread in pounds as if in a famine year—a dis-
grace! At Grachi they'll have long been asleep—it's not like here. Sometime the
good Lord will bring me to see it again..."

Here he sighed loudly, blew on the boot and began once more to run the
brush back and forth. He considered this task his chief and almost his only duty,
and generally he measured the worth of a servant, and even of a man, by his ability to polish boots; he himself polished with a kind of passion.

"Stop it, Evsei! You keep me from doing my business with your silly nonsense!" cried Aduyev.

"Silly nonsense," muttered Evsei to himself. "Not at all nonsense! You may
think this is nonsense, but I'm doing my business. Just look how you dirtied your
boots; it's hard to get them clean." He put the boot on the table and gazed with
love at the mirror-like shine of the leather.

"Let somebody else get a polish like that!" he said. "Nonsense, indeed!"

Alexander sank ever deeper in his dreams of Nadenka, then in his creative
dreams.

The top of desk was empty. Everything that reminded him of his former business, his job, his journalistic work, lay under the desk, or in the closet or under
the bed. "Just the sight of that *dirt*," he said, "frightens away creative thought,
and it takes flight like a nightingale that flies from the orchard at the sudden
creak of ungreased wheels on the road."

Often dawn found him still at some elegy. All the hours he didn't spend at the
Lyubetskys were dedicated to his creative work. He would write a poem and read
it to Nadenka. She would copy it on good paper and learn it by heart, and he
would know *the highest bliss of the poet—to hear his work from beloved lips.*

"You are my Muse," he told her. "Be the Bearer of that holy flame that burns
in my breast; if you abandon it, it will go out forever." Then he sent his verses
under a pseudonym to a magazine. They published them because they weren't
bad, some passages had energy and they all were replete with ardor and fluently
written.

Nadenka was proud of his love and called him "my poet."

"Yes, yours, eternally yours," he added. In his future fame smiled on him, and
Nadenka, he thought, would weave the wreath of myrtle and bind it on his brow,
and then... "Life, oh life, how beautiful you are!" he exclaimed. "But, Uncle? Why

has he disturbed my peace of soul? Is he a demon sent me by fate? Why does he poison all my well-being with bile? Isn't it from envy because his heart does not know these pure joys, or perhaps it's a dark urge to do harm... Oh, stay away, away from him!... He'll crush my loving soul, infect it with his hatred, pervert it..."

And he fled his uncle, did not see him for whole weeks, months. But if the conversation turned to feeling when they met, he remained silent with a sneer or listened like a man whose convictions cannot be shaken by any proofs. He considered his own judgments unerring, his opinions and feelings unalterable and decided in future to be guided only by them, saying that he was not a boy any more and that *there was no reason to hold only other people's opinions sacred,* and the like.

But his uncle stayed the same. He didn't ask his nephew about anything, did not notice or want to notice his tomfoolery. Seeing that Alexander's situation hadn't changed, that he led his former way of life and asked no money of him, he was as friendly with him as before and gently reproached Alexander for coming so rarely to see him.

"My wife is angry with you," he said. "She became accustomed to considering you a relative. We dine at home every day. Come to see us."

And that was all. But Alexander rarely made visits, indeed there was no time for them. Mornings at the office, afternoons and evenings at the Lyubetskys. There remained the night, but at night he went off into the special *world* of his own creation and went on creating. And with all this, true, it didn't hurt to get a little sleep.

He was less fortunate with his prose pieces. He wrote a comedy, two stories, an essay of sorts and an account of his travels to somewhere. His productivity was astonishing; the paper simply burned under his pen. He first showed the comedy and one story to his uncle and asked him to say whether they were any good. His uncle spot-checked several pages and sent them back after writing at the top: "Good for... papering screens!"

Alexander was furious and sent them off to a magazine, but both were returned. At two places on the margins of the comedy the comment "Not bad" was pencilled in—and that was all. In the story comments like these were often encountered: "Weak, false, immature, flabby, not developed" and the like; the final comment read: "On the whole, this shows ignorance of the human heart, superfluous fervor, unnaturalness, all high rhetoric; nowhere does one see a human being... the hero's monstrous... there are no such people... unsuited for publication! However, the author, it seems, is not without talent, he needs to work!..."

"'There are no such people!'" thought Alexander, distressed and surprised. "How so, there are no such? Why I myself am that hero. Am I supposed to describe these low-life heroes whom one encounters at every turn, who think and feel like the crowd, who do what everyone does—these pitiful characters of everyday comedies and tragedies, not distinguished by any special mark... am I to lower art to that?..."

To confirm the truth of his ideas on literature he evoked the shade of Byron, cited Goethe and Schiller. He conceived the only possible hero of a drama or story to be some corsair or great poet or actor and had them do and feel as he would himself.

In one story he chose America as the place of action; the environment was luxurious—American nature, mountains and amid all this an exile who had carried off his beloved. The whole world forgot them, they adored each other and nature, and when news came of forgiveness and the possibility of returning home, they refused. Some twenty years later a certain European traveled there, went hunting, accompanied by Indians, and on a certain mountain found a hut and in it a skeleton. The European was the rival of the hero. How good this story seemed to Alexander! With what enthusiasm he read it to Nadenka on winter evenings! How eagerly she listened to him! And not to accept this story!

He said not even a half-word to Nadenka about this failure, but swallowed the affront in silence—and that was the end of it. "What happened to the story?" she asked, "did they publish it?" "No!" he said, "they can't; there's a lot in it that would seem wild and strange in this country..."

If he had known how truly he spoke, while thinking he was speaking in a quite different sense.

To work seemed strange to him too. "What is talent for?" he said. "An untalented laborer works; talent creates easily and freely." Still, remembering that his articles about agriculture, yes, and his verses too, had been at first quite unremarkable, but then gradually were perfected and attracted some special attention from the public, he reconsidered, understood the stupidity of his conclusion and with a sigh postponed belles-lettres to another time when his heart would beat more evenly and his thoughts fall into place; then he promised himself to set to work properly.

One day followed another, days of uninterrupted enjoyment for Alexander. He was happy when he would kiss the tip of Nadenka's finger or sit opposite her for an hour or two in a picturesque pose, without taking his eyes off her and in the grip of tender emotions, sighing or declaiming verses pertinent to the moment.

In all fairness it must be said that she sometimes responded to the sighs and verses with a yawn. And that's not hard to understand: her heart was busy, but her mind remained idle. Alexander did not try to feed it. The year designated by Nadenka as a trial period passed. She and her mother were again living at their country place. Alexander brought up her promise, asked permission to speak to her mother. Nadenka was for postponing it until their move to the city, but Alexander insisted.

Finally, one evening while taking leave, she gave Alexander permission to speak of it to her mother the next day.

Alexander did not sleep the whole night, did not go to the office. The next day went round and round in his head. He kept thinking how to talk with Marya Mikhailovna; he was going to compose a speech, he prepared for it, but hardly remembered that Nadenka's hand was at issue, lost himself in dreams and again forgot everything. So he arrived that evening at their country place not prepared for anything. Indeed, it wasn't necessary. Nadenka met him as usual in the garden, but with a shade of slight thoughtfulness in her eyes and without a smile, yet somehow absentminded.

"You can't talk to Mama," she said, "that nasty Count is sitting with her!"

"Count! What Count?"

"You don't know what Count! Count Novinsky, you know, our neighbor. His country home is here; how many times you yourself have praised his garden!"

"Count Novinsky at your house!" said Alexander, surprised. "What has he come for?"

"I really don't know yet myself," answered Nadenka. "I was sitting here reading your book and Mama wasn't home; she'd gone to see Marya Ivanovna. It had just begun raining a little. I came inside and suddenly a coach drives up to the entrance, blue with white upholstery, that same one that used to drive past us—you praised it, too. I look, Mama gets out with some man. They come in, Mama says, 'This is my daughter, Count; please do us the honor.' He bowed and I, too. I was embarrassed, blushed, and ran off to my room. But Mama—she's so unbearable—I heard her say, 'Pardon, Count, she's such a wild thing...' Then I guessed this must be our neighbor, Count Novinsky. Probably he brought Mama in his coach from Marya Ivanovna's because of the rain."

"Is he... an old man?" asked Alexander.

"An old man! What are you talking about! He's young and handsome!..."

"You've already managed to notice he's handsome!" said Alexander, vexed.

"That's nice! Does it take long to notice that? I've already talked with him. He's very charming. He asked what I do, he talked about music, asked me to sing something, but I knew almost nothing. This winter without fail I'll ask Mama to get me a good singing teacher. The Count says that's very much in fashion just now—singing."

All this was said with unusual liveliness.

"I thought, Nadezhda Alexandrovna," remarked Aduyev, "that this winter you would have an occupation beside singing..."

"What?"

"What!" said Alexander reproachfully

"Oh! yes... so you came here by boat?"

He looked at her in silence. She turned away and set off for the house.

Aduyev entered the living room, not altogether at ease. What kind of count was this? How should one conduct oneself with him? What sort of manner would he display? Proud? Casual? Alexander entered. The Count rose first and bowed politely. Alexander responded with a constrained and awkward bow. Their hostess introduced them to each other. For some reason Alexander did not like the Count, who was a handsome man, tall, well-built, blond with large expressive eyes and an agreeable smile. His manners showed simplicity, elegance, a kind of gentleness. He seemed a man able to win over anyone, but he didn't win over Aduyev.

Despite Marya Mikhailovna's invitation to join them, Alexander sat down in a corner and began to look at a book, which was very unsociable, awkward and out of place. Nadenka stood behind her mother's chair, looked at the Count with curiosity and listened to what he said and how he spoke; he was a novelty for her.

Aduyev was unable to conceal his dislike of the Count. The Count, it seemed, did not notice his rudeness. He was attentive and turned to Aduyev, trying to make the conversation general. All in vain. The latter was silent or answered yes and no.

When Mrs. Lyubetsky by chance repeated Alexander's last name, the Count asked, wasn't Pyotr Ivanych related to him.

"My uncle!" answered Alexander abruptly.

"I often see him in society," said the Count.

"You might. What's strange about that?" answered Aduyev with a shrug.

The Count concealed a smile, biting his lower lip a little. Nadenka exchanged glances with her mother, blushed and lowered her eyes.

"Your uncle is an intelligent and pleasant man!" remarked the Count in a tone of slight irony.

Aduyev was silent.

Nadenka could bear it no longer and went up to Alexander, and while the Count was talking with her mother, whispered to him, "Aren't you ashamed! The Count is so friendly to you, but you?..."

"Friendly!" Alexander almost aloud with vexation, "I don't need his friendly gestures; don't repeat that word..."

Nadenka started back from him and from a distance, motionless, looked at him with amazement, then again stood behind her mother's chair and quite ignored Alexander.

But Aduyev went on waiting for the Count to leave and for the opportunity to speak at last with Nadenka's mother. But ten, eleven o'clock passed and the Count didn't go away and talked on.

All subjects usually covered in conversation at the beginning of an acquaintance had been covered. The Count began to jest. He did so intelligently—in his jokes there was not the least strain nor pretension to wit, but still something absorbing, some special ability to tell amusingly not just a funny story, but even a bit of news, or an event, or he could turn a serious matter into a laughing one thanks to a single unexpected word.

Both the mother and daughter submitted altogether to the spell of his humor, and Alexander himself more than once half concealed an involuntary smile with his book. But he raged inwardly.

The Count spoke uniformly well and with tact about everything, about music and people and foreign places. The conversation touched on men, on women; he rebuked men, himself too among them, skillfully praised women in general and paid several compliments to his hostesses in particular.

Aduyev thought of his own literary work, of his verse. "I'd put him at a loss there," he thought. The conversation turned to literature. Mother and daughter recommended Alexander as a writer.

"Now he'll be embarrassed," thought Aduyev.

Not at all. The Count talked about literature as if he'd never devoted himself to anything else. He made a few fleeting and true remarks about contemporary Russian and French big names. In addition to all this, it turned out that he was friends with first-class Russian writers and in Paris had made the acquaintance of several French ones too. He rated some with respect, sketched others with slight caricature.

He said he didn't know Alexander's verse and hadn't heard of it.

Nadenka gave Alexander a somewhat strange look, as if to ask, "What about it, Sir? You haven't gotten very far..."

Alexander began to feel shy. His impudent, rude attitude yielded to depression He resembled a rooster with a wet tail hiding from inclement weather under a shed.

In the serving room glasses and spoons clinked; they were setting the table, but the Count didn't leave. Every hope vanished. The Count even accepted Mrs. Lyubetsky's invitation to stay for their supper of clotted milk.

"A count, but he eats clotted milk!" whispered Aduyev, looking with hatred at the Count.

The Count ate supper with appetite, went on jesting as if he were at home.

"He's at a house for the first time, yet shamelessly, eats enough for three!" whispered Alexander to Nadenka.

"So what! He's hungry!" she answered naively.

The Count finally left, but it was late to talk about a serious matter. Aduyev took his hat and ran. Nadenka overtook him and succeeded in calming him.

"Till tomorrow?" asked Alexander.

"We won't be at home tomorrow."

"Well, the day after tomorrow."

They parted.

On the day after tomorrow Alexander arrived early. Even in the garden unfamiliar sounds carried to him from indoors... A violincello, or perhaps not... He drew nearer... A man's voice was singing and what a voice!—resonant, fresh, such as, it seems, goes to a woman's heart. It went even to Aduyev's heart, but differently. His heart sank, began to ache from sadness, envy, hate, from a vague and heavy presentiment. Alexander went into the entry hall from the courtyard.

"Who's here?" he asked the servant.

"Count Novinsky."

"Has he been here long?"

"Since six o'clock."

"Tell the young lady quietly that I came and will come back later."

"Yes, Sir."

Alexander left and went walking around the country houses, hardly noticing where he went. About two hours later he returned.

"What, is he still here? " he asked.

"He's here and will stay for a meal. The mistress ordered partridge to be roasted for supper."

"And you told the young lady about me?"

"I did."

"And what did she say?"

"She gave no orders."

Alexander went home and didn't come again for two days. Heaven knows what he imagined and suffered; finally he set out.

At last he saw the house, stood up in the boat, and shading his eyes from the sun with his hand, looked ahead. There among the trees flashed the blue dress so becoming to Nadenka; the blue color suited her so. She always put on this dress when she particularly wanted to please Alexander. He was greatly relieved.

"Oh! she wants to reward me for her temporary involuntary neglect," he thought. "Not she, but I am to blame; how could I act so unforgivably? You only arm people against you by such conduct. A stranger, a new acquaintance... It's very natural that as hostess... Oh, see there, she's coming out of the shrubbery from the narrow path, going to the gate, there she'll stop and wait..."

Indeed she did come out upon the large allée... but who else was turning with her out of the path?

"The Count!" Alexander exclaimed aloud in distress and did not believe his eyes.

"Huh?" asked one oarsman.

"She's alone in the garden with him..." whispered Alexander, "as with me..."

The Count and Nadenka went up to the gate, and not looking at the river, turned and slowly started back along the allée. He bent down to her and said something to her quietly. She walked with her head bent down.

Aduyev still stood open-mouthed in the boat without moving, his arms outstretched to the shore. Then he let them down and sat down. The oarsmen continued to row.

"Where are you going?" cried Alexander in a rage, coming to. "Back!"

"We're to go back?" repeated one, looking at him and opening his mouth.

"Back! Are you deaf perhaps, you!"

"So, there's no need to go there?"

Without a word the other oarsman began pulling on the left with one oar, then struck out with two, and the boat moved in the opposite direction. Alexander banged his hat down almost to his shoulders and plunged into tormenting thoughts.

After that he didn't make the trip to the Lyubetskys for two weeks.

Two weeks—what a long time for a man in love! But he kept waiting: Look, they'll send a servant to see what's the matter? Isn't he ill?—as they had always done when he took sick, or got some crazy idea this way. Formerly Nadenka would *pro forma* in her mother's name at first inquire, then what might she not write in her own? What affectionate reproaches, what tender concern! And such impatience!

"No, this time I won't surrender quickly," thought Alexander. "I'll torment her a while. I'll teach her how she should treat a casual male acquaintance. Our reconciliation won't be easy!"

And he thought up a cruel plan of revenge, dreamed of her repentance, how he would magnanimously forgive and teach her a lesson. But they didn't send a servant, and no note of confession was delivered; it was as if he no longer existed for them.

He lost weight, grew pale. Jealousy causes more suffering than any disease, especially jealousy based on suspicions and without proofs. When proof comes to light, then there's an end to jealousy, for the most part even to love itself; then at least one knows what to do, but until then—torment! And Alexander experienced it to the full.

Finally he resolved to go in the morning, thinking to find Nadenka alone and have it out with her.

He arrived. There was no one in the garden, no one in the living and dining room either. He went out into the hall, opened the door onto the courtyard...

What a scene met his eye! Two riders in the Count's livery held two riding horses. The Count and his servant were mounting Nadenka on one of the horses; the other was ready for the Count himself. Marya Mikhailovna stood on the porch of the carriage entrance. Frowning, she anxiously watched this scene.

"Sit tighter, Nadenka," she said. "Look after her, Count, for Heaven's sake! Oh! I'm afraid, Heaven knows, I'm afraid. Hold on to the horse's ear, Nadenka. You see, she's absolutely a devil—see how restless she is."

"Don't worry, Mama," said Nadenka merrily. "Look, I can already ride; look."

With her crop she touched the horse; it leapt forward and began to jump and rear in place.

"Oh, oh! Hold her in!" cried Marya Mikhailovna, waving her arm. "Stop, she'll kill you! "

But Nadenka pulled the reins and the horse stood.

"You see how she obeys me!" said Nadenka and patted the horse on the neck.

Nobody even noticed Aduyev. Pale and silent, he looked at Nadenka, and she, as if to mock him, never seemed so pretty as now. How the side-saddle riding habit suited her with its hat and green veil! How it showed off her waist! Her face was enlivened by a shameful pride and the luxury of a new experience. A flush of pleasure now vanished, now reappeared on her cheeks. The horse pranced slightly and compelled the shapely rider to bend forward and lean backward gracefully. Her figure rocked in the saddle like the stem of a flower cradled by the wind. Then the groom led a horse up for the Count.

"Count! Shall we ride around the grove again?" asked Nadenka.

"Again!" thought Aduyev.

"Very well," answered the Count.

The horses set off.

"Nadezhda Alexandrovna!" Aduyev suddenly cried out in a kind of wild voice.

Everyone stood still, as if nailed to the spot or turned to stone, and looked, perplexed at Alexander. This lasted a minute.

"Oh, it's Alexander Fyodorych!" the mother said, the first to come to.

The Count bowed in greeting. Nadenka skillfully tossed back the veil from her face, turned and looked at Alexander in fear, opened her little mouth a bit, then quickly turned away, spurred her horse, who tore forward and in two leaps disappeared out the gate. The Count sped after her.

"Slow down, slow down for Heaven's sake, slow down," the mother cried after them. "Hold on to the horse's ear. Oh, Lord in Heaven, before you know it, she'll fall; what strange hobbies these!"

And all vanished, only the horses' hoofbeats were audible and the dust rose in a cloud from the road. Alexander remained behind with Mrs. Lyubetsky. He looked at her in silence as if asking with his eyes, "What does this mean?" She did not keep him waiting long for an answer.

"They've gone," she said. "Even their trail has gone cold! Well let the young people have their fun, but you and I will chat for a while, Alexander Fyodorych. Now what does this mean that for two weeks we haven't seen hide nor hair of you? Have you stopped loving us?"

"I was ill, Marya Mikhailovna," he answered sullenly.

"Yes, that's obvious. You've grown thin and you're so pale! Sit down at once and rest. Wouldn't you like some soft-boiled eggs cooked for you? It's a long while till dinner."

"Thank you, I don't want any."

"Why not? They'll be ready right away, and the eggs are wonderful. The Finnish peasant brought them today."

"No, no, please."

"What is the matter with you? I've been waiting and waiting, thinking what does it mean? He doesn't come over himself or bring any French books. You remember you promised something—Balzac's *Peau de chagrin,* wasn't it? I waited and waited—Nothing! He's stopped loving us, I thought, Alexander Fyodorych has surely stopped loving us."

"I fear something else, Marya Mikhailovna. Haven't you stopped loving me?"

"It's a sin for you to fear that, Alexander Fyodorych! I love you as if you were family. Now I don't know about Nadenka. Why, she's still a child. What sense has she? How does she know how to value people! Every day I repeat to her, 'What does it mean that we don't see Alexander Fyodorych; why doesn't he come? I keep expecting him.' Would you believe it? For days we haven't sat down to dinner before five o'clock; I kept thinking, he'll arrive soon. Though Nadenka would say sometimes, 'What is it, Mama, whom are we waiting for? I'm hungry and the Count too...'"

"So the Count... visits often?" asked Alexander.

"Yes, almost every day and sometimes twice on a single day. He's so kind, has taken such a liking to us... 'Well, then,' Nadenka would say, 'I'm hungry and that's that—it's time to sit down.' 'But what about Alexander Fyodorych?' I'd say. 'He's not coming,' she'd say, 'want to bet he won't come? It's no use waiting...'" With these words Mrs. Lyubetsky cut Alexander as if with a knife.

"She... really spoke like that?" he asked, trying to smile.

"Yes she spoke like that and hurried things. I'm strict, you see, though I look so soft-hearted. I even scolded her. 'One time,' I said, 'you wait till five for him and don't have dinner; another time you absolutely won't wait—you don't make sense! I don't like it! Alexander Fyodorych is our old friend, he's loves us and his uncle Pyotr Ivanych has shown great fondness for us. I don't like your uncaring attitude! He'll surely resent it and won't come any more!...'"

"And what did she say?" asked Alexander.

"Why, nothing, you know how lively she is—she'll jump up, begin to sing and run off, or say 'He'll come if he wants to!' She's so playful! So then I'd think he'll come! But another day passes—and no! I'd begin again, 'What is this, Nadenka, is Alexander Fyodorych well?' 'I don't know, Mama,' she'd say, 'how should I know?' 'Let's send a note and find out what's the matter with him?' But thinking's one thing, doing another. I forgot, I counted on her, but she's no better than the wind. Here now, she's taken up with this riding. One day she saw the Count on horseback from the window and began pestering me with one thing only, 'I want to ride!' I tried to talk her out of it; but no, 'I want to.' She's a crazy girl! In my time what was horseback riding! We were not brought up like that at all. But now, it's terrible to say, ladies have even started to smoke. Over there, across from us, lives a young widow; she sits on the balcony the whole day with a straw in her mouth and smokes. People walk and ride past—and she doesn't mind! It used to be in our time that even if a man smelled of tobacco in the living room..."

"Did this begin a long time ago?" asked Alexander.

"Why, I don't know. They say it became the fashion about five years ago. It's all from the French, you know..."

"Not that; I mean, has Nadezhda Alexandrovna been riding for long?"

"About a week and a half. The Count is so kind, so obliging. What, indeed, doesn't he do for us; how he spoils her. Look at all these flowers—all from his garden! Sometimes I get worried. 'How's this, Count,' I'll say, 'you're spoiling her. She'll be altogether insufferable!'—and I'll scold her. Marya Ivanovna, Nadenka and I were in his riding ring—you know that I watch out for her myself; who better than a mother to look out for a daughter? I have taken care of her upbringing and without boasting, I'll say: May God give everyone such a daughter! Nadenka took lessons right there in our presence. Then we had lunch in his garden, and now they ride there every day. Why, what a wealthy house he has! We took a look—everything was so tasteful and luxurious!"

"Every day!" said Alexander almost to himself.

"Yes, why not have fun! I too was young myself... we used..."

"And they ride for long?"

"About three hours. But what is it has made you feel ill?"

"I don't know... Something hurts in my chest..." he said, pressing his hand to his heart.

"You don't take anything for it?"

"No."

"That's the way with you young people! Everything's always all right for the time being, but then you suddenly realize that time is up. What is it, does it ache, gnaw, or stab?"

"Indeed, it aches, gnaws, and stabs!" said Alexander, distraught.

"It's a cold, Heaven preserve us! You must not neglect it, you'll wear yourself out that way... it can turn into pneumonia, and there are no medicines! Do you know what? Take some liniment, and rub your chest hard at night, rub till it's red, then instead of tea, drink herb tea, I'll give you the recipe."

Nadenka returned, pale from weariness. She threw herself on the sofa, hardly breathing.

"Just look!" said Marya Mikhailovna, putting her hand on Nadenka's head, "how you've tired yourself out; you can hardly breathe. Drink a little water and go change your clothes, loosen the laces. This riding will do you no good!"

Alexander and the Count stayed the whole day. The Count was unfailingly polite and attentive to Alexander, invited him to his house to see the garden, suggested he share the horseback ride, offered him a horse.

"I don't know how to ride," said Aduyev coldly.

"You don't know how?" asked Nadenka, "but how much fun it is! We're going again tomorrow, Count?"

The Count bowed.

"That's enough from you, Nadenka," remarked her mother. "You're bothering the Count."

But nothing showed that there were any special relations between Nadenka and the Count. He was uniformly charming with mother and daughter, sought no occasion to speak with Nadenka alone, didn't run after her into the garden, looked at her exactly the same way as at her mother. Her free contact with him and their horseback rides were explained on her part by the wildness and changeability of her character, her naiveté, perhaps too by her lack of proper upbringing and ignorance of the conditions of society, and on her mother's part—by weakness and shortsightedness. The attentiveness and complacency of the Count and his daily visits could be attributed to the proximity of their country places and the cordial reception he always found at the Lyubetskys.

It seemed natural enough if you looked at things with an impartial eye. But Alexander looked through a magnifying glass and saw a lot... a lot... that you wouldn't see with the naked eye.

"Why had Nadenka changed toward him?" he asked himself. She no longer waited for him in the garden, did not meet him with a smile, but with fear, and dressed much more carefully lately. There was no carelessness in her manner. She was more considered in her actions as if she had become more reasonable. Sometimes her eyes and words concealed something like a secret... Where were her lovable caprices, her wildness and pranks? All gone. She had become serious, thoughtful, silent. It was as if something was tormenting her. She was now very like all the girls—the same kind of hypocrite, telling the same lies, asking about one's health with the same concern... just as constantly attentive, charming in clichés... to him Alexander! Who?... oh Heavens! And his heart sank.

"It's no use, no use," he insisted to himself. "Something's hidden here! But I'll find out whatever it costs, and then bear the grief.

> "I'll not permit the shameless schemer
> With sighs and praise and sultry art
> To tempt the inexperienced heart,
> That noisome gnawing worm shan't slither
> Near the young lily's tender stem
> Oozing his poison, to condemn
> The yet half-open bud to wither."[4]

And that day after the Count had gone, Alexander tried to seize the moment to talk with Nadenka alone. What did he not try? He took a book with which she used to call him into the garden away from her mother, showed it to her and

went to the bank, thinking she'd run after him at once. He waited and waited—
she didn't come. He returned to the house. She was reading a book and did not
look at him. He sat down next to her. She did not raise her eyes, then asked fleet-
ingly in passing whether he was busy with his writing, had he finished something
new? Not a word about the past.

He began talking with her mother. Nadenka went out into the garden. Her
mother left the room and Aduyev rushed into the garden. Nadenka, seeing him,
got up from the bench and set off, not to meet him, but by the circular path quietly towards home, as if running away from him. He quickened his pace, she likewise.

"Nadezhda Alexandrovna!" he called from a distance, "I'd like to say two
words to you."

"Let's go into the house; it's damp here," she answered.

Returning, she again sat down next her mother. Alexander almost felt ill.

"And you too now fear dampness?" he said pointedly.

"Yes, the evenings are so dark now and cold," she answered, yawning.

"Soon we're moving back to the city," remarked her mother. "Try to look in at
our apartment, Alexander Fyodorych, and remind the landlord to repair the two
locks on the doors and to the shutter in Nadenka's bedroom. He promised—he'll
forget for sure. They're all like that; they only want to get your money."

Aduyev began to say goodbye.

"See that it's not for long!" said Marya Mikhailovna.

Nadenka was silent.

He had already reached the door and turned to her. She took three steps to
him. His heart skipped a beat.

"At last!" he thought.

"Will you come to see us tomorrow?" she asked coldly, but her eyes were fixed
on him with greedy curiosity.

"I don't know, why?"

"I'm only asking, will you?"

"You'd like me to?"

"Will you come to see us tomorrow?" she repeated in the same cold tone, but
with greater impatience.

"No," he answered vexedly.

"And the day after?"

"No. I'm not coming for a whole week, maybe two... not for a long time." And
he fixed on her a searching glance, trying to read in her eyes what impression this
answer would make.

She was silent, but upon his answer her eyes instantly dropped, and what was
in them? Did sorrow cloud them or had the lightning of joy illumined them? It
was impossible to read anything on this beautiful marble face.

Alexander squeezed his hat in his hand and left.

"Don't forget to rub your chest with liniment!" Marya Mikhailovna called after
him. And now Alexander had another task—to find out the purpose of Nadenka's
question. What did she mean by it: did she want to see him or was she afraid?

"Oh, what torment! What torment!" he said in despair.

Poor Alexander didn't hold out; he came again three days later. Nadenka was
at the garden gate when he rowed close to the shore, she turned as if she did not
see him, and after taking a few aimless steps along the path, as if she were just
walking without purpose, started off home.

He found her with her mother. A couple of people from town were there, the neighbor Marya Ivanovna and the unavoidable Count. Alexander's torments were unendurable. Again a whole day passed in empty, petty conversation. How the guests bored him! They talked calmly about all kinds of nonsense, passed judgment, joked, laughed.

"They laugh!" said Alexander, "they can laugh when... Nadenka has changed toward me! They don't care! Pitiful, empty people; they rejoice at everything!"

Nadenka went off into the garden; the Count did not go with her. For some time both he and Nadenka seemed to avoid each other in Alexander's presence. He sometimes would find them in the garden or the house alone, but then they would separate and—in his presence—not come together any more. It was a new terrible discovery for Alexander—a sign that they were conspiring together.

The guests departed. The Count left too. Nadenka did not know this and did not hurry home. Aduyev took leave of Marya Mikhailovna without ceremony and went into the garden. Nadenka stood with her back to Alexander, holding on to the gate with her hand and resting her head on her hand as on that unforgettable evening. She did not see and did not hear his approach.

How his heart beat as he crept up to her on tip-toe. His breathing ceased. "Nadezhda Alexandrovna!" he began, hardly audible in his excitement.

She started as if a shot had been fired at her side, turned and took a step back from him.

"Tell me, please, what's that smoke over there?" she began in embarrassment, pointing in a lively manner to the opposite side of the river, "a fire or one of those factory furnaces?..."

He looked at her in silence.

"Indeed, I thought it was a fire... Why do you look at me that way, you don't think so?..."

She fell silent.

"And you," he began, shaking his head, "you too are like the others, like all of them! Who would have expected this... two months ago?..."

"What do you mean? I don't understand you," she said and tried to leave.

"Stop, Nadezhda Alexandrovna, I haven't the strength to bear this torture any longer."

"What torture? Really, I don't know..."

"Don't pretend; tell me, is this you? Are you the same person you were?"

"I'm the same!" she said firmly.

"What! You haven't changed toward me?"

"No. I'm just as friendly with you, I think; I receive you just as cheerfully..."

"Just as cheerfully! So why do you run away from the gate?..."

"I, run away? See what have you invented. I stand at the gate, but you say—I run away."

She began to laugh in a constrained manner.

"Nadezhda Alexandrovna, stop dodging!" Aduyev continued.

"What dodging? Why have you fastened on me?"

"Is this you? Heavens! A month and a half ago right here..."

"What smoke is that on the other shore, I would like to know."

"It's terrible! terrible!" said Alexander.

"And what have I done to you? You stopped coming to see us yourself—as you wish... to keep you against your will..." Nadenka began.

"You're pretending! As if you didn't know why I stopped coming?"

Looking to one side, she shook her head.

"And the Count?" he said almost threateningly.

"What Count?"

She put on a face as if she were hearing about the Count for the first time.

"What Count! Will you also say," he said, looking her straight in the eyes, "that you don't care about him?"

"You're mad!" she answered, stepping back from him.

"Yes, you're right!" he went on, "my reason is failing with each passing day... How can you act with such cunning, such ingratitude toward a person who loved you more than anything in the world, who forgot everything for you, everything, who imagined all along he'd soon be happy forever, but you..."

"What have I done?" she said, retreating further.

"What do you mean?" he answered, infuriated by her coolness. "You have forgotten! I remind you that here on this very spot you swore a hundred times to belong to me. 'God hears our vows!' you said. Yes, he heard them! You ought to blush before Heaven and before these trees, before every blade of grass... It all bears witness to our happiness, every grain of sand here speaks of our happiness. Look, glance around you!... You've committed perjury!!!"

She looked at him with horror. His eyes flashed, his lips had gone white.

"Ooh! How angry you are!" she said timidly. "Why are you angry? I did not refuse you. You had not yet spoken to Mama... How do you know?..."

"Speak to her after what you've done?..."

"What have I done? I don't know..."

"What? I'll tell you. What do these meetings with the Count mean, these horseback rides?"

"I can't run away from him when Mama leaves the room! And the horseback riding means... that I love to ride... It's so pleasant: you gallop... Oh, that horse Lucy is such a darling! Did you see her?... She already knows me..."

"But the change in your treatment of me?" he continued. "Why is the Count at your house every day from morning till evening?"

"Oh! Heavens! How do I know! How ridiculous you are! It's Mama's wish!"

"That's not so! Your mama wants what you want. For whom all these presents, music scores, the album, the flowers?—all for Mama?"

"Yes, Mama is very fond of flowers. Yesterday she bought some from the gardener."

"But what do you talk to him about in a low voice?" Alexander continued, not paying attention to what she said. "See, you're turning pale. You feel your guilt yourself. To destroy a person's happiness, forget, ruin everything so quickly, easily—it's hypocrisy, ingratitude, a lie, betrayal!...—yes, a betrayal! How could you stoop to that? A rich count, a society lion, condescended to cast a kindly glance on you—and you melted, fell on your knees before this tinsel sun. Where's your sense of shame!!! Don't let me find the Count here!" he said in a choking voice, "do you hear? Give him up, cease all relations with him, let him forget the way to your house!... I don't want him around..."

He seized her hand in a fury.

"Mama, Mama! Come here!" Nadenka cried in a shrill voice, tearing herself away from Alexander, and once free, dashing off headlong to the house.

He sat down slowly on the bench and seized his head with his hands.

She ran into the house, pale, frightened, and fell upon a chair.

"What has happened to you? What is the matter? Why did you cry out?" asked her mother, alarmed as she went to meet her.

"Alexander Fyodorych... isn't well!" her daughter barely managed to say.

"But what is there to be so frightened about?"

"He's so terrifying... Mama, don't let him come near me, for Heaven's sake."

"What a fright you gave me, you crazy girl! Being sick is not so bad. I know his chest hurts. What's so terrible about that? It's not consumption! Let him rub it with liniment—it will all go away. Clearly he didn't listen, he didn't rub it in."

Alexander came to himself. His delirium passed, but his torment doubled. He hadn't cleared up any doubts, and he'd terrified Nadenka, and now, of course, would get no answer from her. He'd gone about it all the wrong way. Suddenly it occurred to him, as it might to any man in love, "Suppose she's not to blame? Perhaps she doesn't really care for the Count. Her silly mother invites him every day; what is she to do? As a man of the world, he is charming; Nadenka is a pretty girl; perhaps he does want her to like him, but that doesn't necessarily mean that she already does. Maybe she likes the flowers, the horseback riding, their innocent amusements, but not the Count himself. Let's even suppose there is a bit of flirtation in this. Isn't that forgivable? Other girls, even older ones, do Heaven knows what."

He sighed; a ray of joy flashed in his soul. People in love are all this way, first quite blind, then too clairvoyant. Besides it's so pleasant to justify the object of our affections!

"But why the change in her treatment of me?" he suddenly asked himself, and went pale again. "Why does she avoid me, fall silent, seem to be ashamed? Why did she dress up so yesterday on an ordinary day! There were no guests beside him. Why did she ask whether the ballets will begin soon?" A simple question, but it recalled the Count's casual promise always to put a box at their disposal, no matter what the difficulties; therefore he would be with them. "Why did she leave the garden yesterday? Why didn't she come into the garden? Why did she ask one thing, why not another?..."

And again he was overcome by serious doubts and again he cruelly tortured himself and even concluded that Nadenka had never loved him at all.

"God! Oh, God!" he said in despair. "How hard, how bitter it is to live! Give me that dead calm, that sleep of the soul..."

A quarter hour later he walked into the house, dejected and fearful.

"Farewell, Nadezhda Alexandrovna," he said timidly.

"Farewell," she answered abruptly without raising her eyes.

"When will you let me come to see you?"

"When it suits you. By the way... we're moving to the city this week. We'll let you know then..."

He went away. More than two weeks passed. Everyone had moved back from their summer places. The salons of the nobility began to shine again. Even a civil servant would light two wall lamps in the living room, buy half a pound of tallow candles and put out two card tables in expectation of Stepan Ivanych and Ivan Stepanych, declaring to his wife that Tuesdays would be their day at home.

But Aduyev had still not received an invitation from the Lyubetskys. He came across both their cook and their maid. The maid, catching a glimpse of him, precipitately dashed away. Obviously she was acting in the spirit of her young mistress. The cook stopped.

"What's happened with you, sir; have you forgotten us?" he said. "Why, we've been moved back a week and a half."

"Yes, but perhaps you... haven't gotten settled, perhaps you aren't receiving visitors?"

"What's this, sir, not receiving—everybody's already been to see us—except you; the mistress is surprised. His Excellency now deigns to come by every day...

such a kind gentleman. I recently went to his house with some notebook, a reddish one, from the young mistress."

"What a fool you are!" said Aduyev and rushed away from this chatterbox. In the evening he walked past the Lyubetskys' apartment. A light was burning. There was a carriage at the entry.

"Whose carriage?" he asked.

"Count Novinsky's."

The next day and the day after that—the same thing. At last one day he went in. The mother received him warmly with reproaches for his absence and scolded him for not rubbing his chest with liniment; Nadenka was calm, the Count polite. The conversation failed to get started.

He called a couple of times with the same result. In vain he looked meaningfully at Nadenka. She acted as if she didn't notice his glances, yet how she had noticed them before! When he had talked with her mother then, she used to stand behind Marya Mikhailovna and make faces at him, play jokes, and make him laugh.

An unbearable sadness came over him. He thought only about how to cast down this cross he'd voluntarily taken up. He wanted to get an explanation. "Whatever the answer," he thought, "it doesn't matter if only I turn doubt into certainty."

For a long while he pondered how to go about it; finally he thought up something and went to see the Lyubetskys.

Everything was in his favor. There was no carriage at the entry. He went quietly through the reception room and stopped for a moment in front of the living room door to catch his breath. Inside Nadenka was playing the piano. Further across the room Mrs. Lyubetsky herself was sitting on the sofa and knitting a scarf. Nadenka, hearing steps in the outer room, went on playing more quietly and stretched her head forward. She awaited the appearance of a guest with a smile. The guest appeared and her smile at once disappeared; fright took its place. She changed her expression a little and rose from her chair. This was not the guest she had expected.

Alexander bowed in silence and like a shadow walked past her to her mother. He walked quietly without his former assurance with bowed head. Nadenka sat down and went on playing, looking round behind her nervously from time to time.

Half an hour later for some reason the mother was called out of the room. Alexander came in to Nadenka. She got up and wanted to go.

"Nadezhda Alexandrovna!" he said dejectedly, "wait, allow me five minutes, no more."

"I can't listen to you!" she said and was about to go away; "the last time you were..."

"I was to blame then. I shall speak differently now, I give you my word. You won't hear a single reproach. Don't refuse me perhaps for the last time. An explanation is unavoidable. You did, after all, give me permission to ask your mama for your hand. Since then a lot has happened... that... in a word—I must repeat the question. Sit down and go on playing; better your mother doesn't hear; this isn't, after all, the first time."

She obeyed mechanically; blushing slightly she began picking out chords and in agitated expectation fixed her gaze on him.

"Where have you gone, Alexander Fyodorych?" asked her mother as she returned to her place.

"I wanted to talk a while with Nadezhda Alexandrovna about... literature," he answered.

"Well, have your talk, do; in truth you haven't talked for a long time."

"Answer only one question for me briefly and sincerely," Alexander began half aloud, "and our explanation will be over right away!... Don't you love me any more?"

"*Quelle idée!*" she answered, taken aback. "You know how Mama and I have always valued your friendship... have always been glad to see you..."

Aduyev looked at her and thought, "Is this you, the capricious, but sincere child? The mischievous prankster? How quickly she learned to dissemble! How quickly female instincts developed in her! Were the lovable caprices but hypocrisy and cunning in germ?... And even without Uncle's method! But how swiftly the girl was transformed into a woman! And all under the Count's tutelage, and in some two or three months! Oh Uncle, Uncle! you are relentlessly right about this too!"

"Listen," he said in such a tone that the dissembler suddenly dropped her mask. "Leave Mama out of this. For a minute be that old Nadenka when you loved me a little bit... and answer directly. I need to know this, for Heaven's sake I do."

She was silent, only changed the sheet music, and began reading closely and playing through some difficult passage.

"Well, good, I'll change the question," Aduyev went on. "Tell me, didn't someone—I won't say who—just say, didn't someone replace me in your heart?"

She corrected the lamp for a long time, but said nothing.

"Answer, Nadezhda Alexandrovna. A single word will free me from torment and you from this unpleasant explanation."

"Oh, Heavens, stop! What shall I say to you! I have nothing to say!" she answered, turning away from him.

Another man would have been content with such an answer and realized there was no need to insist further. He would have understood everything from the wordless, tormented sorrow painted on her face, showing through even her movements. But it wasn't enough for Aduyev. Like an executioner, he tormented his victim and was impelled by a wild desperate desire to empty the cup at one draught and to the bottom.

"No!" he said, "finish this torture today; doubts, one blacker than the other, agitate my mind, and tear my heart to pieces. I have worn myself out. I think my chest will burst from the tension... There's nothing for me to be sure of in my suspicions. You yourself must resolve them; otherwise I'll never find peace."

He looked at her and waited for an answer. She was silent.

"Take pity on me!" he began again. "Look at me; do I look like myself? Everyone is afraid of me, doesn't recognize me... Everyone pities me, except you."

It was quite true; his eyes burned with a wild gleam. He was thin and pale; large beads of sweat appeared on his forehead.

She threw him a furtive glance, and something like pity flashed in her look. She even took him by the hand, but immediately let it go with a sigh and still was silent.

"What is it?" he asked.

"Oh, leave me alone!" she said sadly. "You torment me with questions..."

"I implore you, for God's sake!" he said. "Finish it all with a word... What use is concealment to you? A stupid hope will remain for me, I won't give up, I'll come every day to see you, pale, distraught... I'll make you sad. Refuse to see me—I'll begin walking under your windows, meeting you at the theater, on the street, everywhere like an apparition, a memento mori. All this is stupid, perhaps laughable, if you feel like laughing—but I feel pain! You don't know what passion is, where it leads! God spare you from ever knowing!... What's the use? Isn't it better to say at once?"

"What are you asking me about?" said Nadenka, flinging herself against the back of her chair. "I'm quite lost... my head is truly in a fog..."

With a shiver she pressed her hand against her forehead and immediately took it away again.

"I'm asking: Has someone replaced me in your heart? One word—yes or no—decides everything. Does it take long to say!"

She wanted to say something, but couldn't, and lowering her eyes, began tapping one piano key with her finger. It was obvious that she was powerfully struggling with herself. "Oh dear!" she finally brought out with sadness. Aduyev wiped his forehead with his handkerchief.

"Yes or no?" he repeated, holding his breath.

Several seconds passed.

"Yes!" Nadenka got out in a barely audible whisper and began to strike big chords as if unaware of what she was doing.

This yes, though hardly audible like a sigh, deafened Aduyev. His heart had been all but torn out, his legs gave way under him. He sank upon a chair beside the piano and was silent.

Nadenka looked at him fearfully. He looked at her inanely.

"Alexander Fyodorych!" called her mother suddenly. "In which ear do you hear a ringing?"

He did not answer.

"Mama is asking you a question," said Nadenka.

"What?"

"In which ear do you hear a ringing?" cried her mother. "Come quickly!"

"In both!" Aduyev managed to say gloomily.

"Why, which—in the left! I've been guessing whether the Count would come today."

"The Count!" said Aduyev.

"Forgive me!" said Nadenka in an imploring voice, rushing toward him. "I don't understand it myself... It all happened unexpectedly, against my will... I don't know how... I could not deceive you..."

"I shall keep my word, Nadezhda Alexandrovna," he answered. "I shall not speak a word of reproach. I thank you for your sincerity. You have helped a lot, a lot... today... it was hard for me to hear that yes... but it was harder for you to say it... Farewell; you won't see me any more, a reward for your sincerity... But the Count, the Count!"

He clenched his teeth and started toward the door.

"Yes," he said, turning. "What will it lead to? The Count will not marry you. What are his intentions?..."

"I don't know!" answered Nadenka, sadly shaking her head.

"Heavens! How blind you are!" exclaimed Alexander, taken aback.

"He can't have bad intentions..." she answered in a weak voice.

"Be careful, Nadezhda Alexandrovna!"

He took her hand, kissed it and left the room with uneven steps. It was frightening to look at him. Nadenka remained motionless in her seat.

"Why aren't you playing, Nadenka?" asked her mother some moments later. Nadenka awoke as if from a deep sleep and sighed.

"Right away, Mama!" she answered and thoughtfully inclining her head a little to one side, shyly began to pick out notes. Her fingers shook. Apparently she was suffering from pangs of conscience and the doubt which the words "Be careful!" had bred in her mind. When the Count arrived, she was uncommunicative, boring; there was something forced in her manner. Under pretense of a headache she went to her room early, and that evening it seemed bitter to her to live in this world.

Aduyev had just reached the bottom of the stairs when his strength abandoned him. He sat down on the last step, covered his eyes with a handkerchief and began to sob loudly, but without tears. At that moment the doorman was passing the entrance. He stopped and listened.

"Marfa, oh Marfa!" he cried as he came up to his dirty entryway. "Come here, listen there's somebody howling just like a beast. I wonder, isn't it perhaps the black dog—who's gotten loose from its chain, but no that's not it."

"No, it's not our black dog!" Marfa repeated after listening. "What strange thing is it?"

"Come, bring the lantern; it's hanging there behind the stove."

Marfa brought the lantern.

"Is it still howling?" she asked.

"It still is. Perhaps some rascal's broken in?"

"Who's there?" asked the doorman.

No answer.

"Who's there?" repeated Marfa.

Still the same howling. They both entered suddenly. Aduyev rushed away.

"Oh, it was some gentleman," Marfa said, looking after him. "And you thought it was a rascal. Now, see what a crazy idea! Would a rascal be howling in other people's doorways!"

"Well, then, he must have been drunk!"

"Come on," Marfa answered. "You think everybody's like you. Not everybody howls like you when they're drunk."

"Then out of hunger, do you think?" remarked the doorman, annoyed.

"What!" said Marfa, looking at him and not knowing what to say. "How should I know; perhaps he lost something—money..."

They both stooped at once and with the help of the lantern began to scrape every corner of the floor.

"Lost!" objected the doorman, lighting the floor. "Where could you lose something here? The stairs are clean, made of stone; you'd see a needle here. You'd hear it if you dropped it; it would ring against the stone; of course, you'd pick it up! Where could you drop something here? There's no place you could. Drop indeed. No, his likes wouldn't have dropped anything. Before he'd lose anything a man like that would manage to put it in his own pocket before you know it, he wouldn't drop it! We know them, the rascals! Dropped, you say! Where?"

And they kept on crawling around the floor for a long while yet, looking for lost money.

"No, there's nothing!" the doorman said at last with a sigh, then blew out the candle, and after squeezing the wick with two fingers, wiped them off on his sheepskin coat.

VI

That very evening around midnight when Pyotr Ivanych was on his way from his study to his bedroom to go to bed, carrying a candle and a book in one hand and holding on to the bottom of his dressing gown with the other, his valet reported that Alexander Fyodorych wanted to see him.

Pyotr Ivanych frowned slightly, thought a bit, then said calmly, "Ask him into my study, I'll be there right away."

"How are you, Alexander," he greeted his nephew upon returning there. "We haven't met for a long time. You haven't taken time during the day and then—bang! in the middle of the night! Why so late? Why, what's the matter with you? You don't look well."

Without answering a word Alexander sat down in the armchair in utmost exhaustion. Pyotr Ivanych looked at him with curiosity.

Alexander sighed.

"Are you well?" asked Pyotr Ivanych, concerned.

"Yes," Alexander answered in a weak voice. "I move, eat, and drink; therefore I'm well."

"But don't toy with your health; go see a doctor."

"Others have already told me that, but no doctor or medicine will help. My illness is not of the body..."

"What's wrong with you? You haven't gambled away everything or lost money?" quickly asked Pyotr Ivanych.

"You just can't imagine any grief not connected with money!" answered Alexander, trying to smile.

"What kind of grief is it, then, if it's not worth a red cent, as is sometimes the case with you?..."

"Yes... like now, for example. Do you know about my present grief?"

"What grief? Everything's fine at home. I know this from the letters your dear mama favors me with monthly. At the office nothing can be worse than it's been; they've put your subordinate over you—that's the latest. You say you're healthy, haven't lost money or lost at cards... These are the important things, and with all the rest it's easy to cope. So, therefore, it's nonsense, love, I guess..."

"Yes, love. But do you know what happened? When you do, perhaps you'll stop taking it so lightly and be horrified..."

"Tell me; I haven't been horrified for a long time," said his uncle, settling down with a smile, "though, by the way, it isn't hard to guess. No doubt someone's done you wrong."

Alexander jumped up, wanted to say something, but said nothing and sat down again.

"So, that's what it is? You see, I told you so, but you said, 'No, how could that be!'"

"Could anyone have foretold it?..." said Alexander, "after all that..."

"You had not to foretell it, but to foresee it, that is, know it could happen—that's more like it—yes, and act accordingly."

"You can reason about it so calmly, Uncle, while I..." said Alexander.

"Why, what's it to me?"

"Yes, I forgot. You wouldn't even care if the whole town burned to the ground or fell apart."

"Please! And my factory?"

"You're joking, and I'm suffering in earnest. I'm so miserable, I'm as good as ill!"

"Have you really lost so much weight from love? How shameful! No, you were ill, but now you're beginning to get well, yes, and high time! It's no joke that this stupidity has been dragging on a year and a half. A little bit more, really, and I'd believe in unchanging and eternal love."

"Uncle, spare me!" said Alexander. "There is poison in my soul right now..."

"Yes! And so what?"

Alexander moved his chair toward the table, and his uncle began to move inkwell, paperweight, and so on, out of his nephew's reach.

"He's come at night," thought his uncle, "with poison in his soul. He'll surely break something again."

"I won't get any comfort from you, nor do I ask it," began Alexander. "I'm asking your help as an uncle, a relative... I seem stupid to you—don't I?"

"Yes, if you weren't pitiable."

"So you're sorry for me?"

"Very. Do you think I'm made of wood? A nice chap, intelligent, well brought up, and his life is ruined for nothing—and why? For trifles!"

"Show me, then, that you're sorry for me."

"How? You don't need money, you say..."

"Money, money! Oh, if my unhappiness were only lack of money, I'd bless my fate."

"Don't say that," warned Pyotr Ivanych in all seriousness. "You're young—so you curse instead of blessing fate! Time was, I cursed mine more than once—I!"

"Listen to me patiently..."

"Are you staying long, Alexander?" asked his uncle.

"Yes, I need all your attention; why?"

"Well, look here, I'd like some supper then. I was about to go to bed without supper, but now if we'll be sitting here for a while, let's have supper and drink a bottle of wine while you tell me everything."

"You're able to eat supper?" asked Alexander with surprise.

"Yes, and very much so... Aren't you really going to eat?"

"Eat! Why you won't choke down a bite either when you learn that this is a matter of life and death."

"Of life and death?... his uncle repeated. "Yes, then that is indeed very important, but well... let's try; perhaps we'll manage to swallow something."

He rang.

"Ask what there is for supper," he told the valet who entered, and tell them to get a bottle of Lafitte with the green seal.

The valet went away.

"Uncle! You're not in the right mood to listen to the sad tale of my grief," said Alexander, taking his hat. "I'd better come tomorrow..."

"No, no, no matter," quickly said Pyotr Ivanych, holding his nephew back by the hand. "I'm always in the same mood. Tomorrow too for sure you'll find me eating lunch or still worse—working. Better, let's finish it all at once. Supper won't spoil this piece of business. I'll listen and understand the better. On an empty stomach, you know, it's awkward..."

Supper was brought in.

"Come, Alexander, won't you..." said Pyotr Ivanych.

"But, Uncle, I don't want anything to eat!" said Alexander with impatience and shrugged his shoulders, watching as his uncle fussed over the supper.

"At least, do drink a glass of wine; it's not a bad wine!"

Alexander shook his head no.

"Well, so take a cigar and tell your story while I listen with both ears," said Pyotr Ivanych and set about eating.

"Do you know Count Novinsky?" asked Alexander after a moment's silence.

"Count Platon?"

"Yes."

"We're acquaintances. Why?"

"I congratulate you on such a friend! He's a scoundrel!"

Pyotr Ivanych suddenly stopped chewing and looked with astonishment at his nephew.

"Now that's blunt!" he said. "Do you really know him?"

"Very well."

"You've known him long?"

"For three months."

"How so then? I've known him for five years and always considered him a decent fellow; yes, and no matter whom you listen to, everyone praises him; and yet all of a sudden you have demolished him completely."

"Since when have you begun defending people, Uncle? Before, you used..."

"Before I also defended decent people. And since when have you begun to berate them and stopped calling them angels?"

"I didn't know then, but now... Oh, people, people! *A pitiful species, deserving of tears and laughter!*[6] I admit I'm completely to blame that I didn't listen to you when you advised me to beware of everybody..."

"I'd advise it again: It doesn't hurt to beware. If the person proves to be a scoundrel, you won't be deceived, but if he's a decent fellow, you'll be pleased to have made a mistake."

"Show me where there are any decent people," said Alexander contemptuously.

"Take you and me, for example—aren't we decent? The Count, since we've already mentioned him, he's a decent person too; so isn't that a start? Everybody has faults... but they're not entirely bad, and not everyone is bad."

"Everyone, everyone!" said Alexander emphatically.

"And you?"

"I? At least I shall walk away from the crowd with a heart that, though broken, is free of meanness, a soul that is wounded but beyond the reproach of lying, hypocrisy, betrayal; I shan't succumb to that..."

"Well, good, let's see. But what has the Count done to you?"

"What has he done? He's robbed me of everything."

"Be more precise. Under the word *everything* one can mean Heaven knows what, say, money. But the Count wouldn't do that..."

"I mean what is dearer to me than all the treasures of the world," said Alexander.

"And what would that be?"

"Everything—happiness, life."

"Look, you're alive!"

"Unfortunately, yes! But this life is worse than a hundred deaths."

"Tell me exactly what happened?"

"It's terrible!" exclaimed Alexander. "Oh God! God!"

"I see! He's taken your girl, hasn't he, this... what's her name? Yes, he's good at that; it's hard for you to compete with him. A charmer! a charmer!" said Pyotr Ivanych, putting a piece of turkey in his mouth.

"He'll pay dearly for his mastery of the art!" said Alexander, flaring up. "I won't yield without a fight. Death will decide which of us is to have Nadenka. I'll destroy that wretched womanizer! He shan't live, shan't enjoy his stolen treasure... I'll wipe him from the face of the earth..."

Pyotr Ivanych burst into laughter.

"How provincial!" he said. "A propos the Count, Alexander, did he say whether he'd gotten his china from abroad? This spring he ordered a set; I would have liked to have a look..."

"We're not talking about china, Uncle; did you hear what I said?" Alexander interrupted threateningly.

"Mm-m!" assented his uncle, as he gnawed a little bone clean.

"What did you say?"

"Why, nothing. I'm listening to what you say."

"Listen attentively at least once in your life. I came on business. I want to set my mind at rest, resolve a million tormenting questions that agitate me... I'm lost... out of my mind, help me..."

"Excuse me, I'm at your service, just say what I should do... I'm even ready with money... if only not for trifles..."

"Trifles! No, not trifles, when in a few hours perhaps I'll have departed this world, or else I shall have become a murderer... but you're laughing, calmly eating supper."

"I beg you! You've had your supper, I believe, yet you disapprove my eating!"

"For forty-eight hours I haven't known what it is to eat."

"Oh, is it really something important?"

"Give me a single word: will you do me a very great service?"

"What service?"

"Will you agree to be my witness?..."

"The cutlets are quite cold!" remarked Pyotr Ivanych with displeasure, pushing the dish away.

"You're laughing, Uncle?"

"Judge for yourself; how can one listen seriously to such nonsense, asking someone to be his second in a duel!"

"What do you mean?"

"It's obvious: I won't do it."

"Good. I'll find someone else, a stranger who'll feel for the bitter insult I've suffered. Just take upon yourself the task of talking to the Count to learn his conditions..."

"I can't. My tongue won't twist itself into putting such a stupid thing to him."

"Then, farewell!" said Alexander, picking up his hat.

"What, you're leaving already? You won't drink any wine?..."

Alexander was headed for the door, but at the door he sat down in deepest dejection.

"Whom shall I turn to, to whom shall I look for sympathy?..." he said quietly.

"Listen, Alexander!" Pyotr Ivanych began, wiping his mouth with his napkin and pushing an armchair toward his nephew. "I see I must really talk to you a bit without joking. Let's talk. You've come to me for help. I shall help you, but not the way you imagine and under the condition that you obey. Don't ask anyone to be your witness; there's no use in that. You'll make a big thing out of nothing; the story will spread everywhere. People will laugh at you, or worse, make trouble.

Nobody will back you up, or if some madman finally is found, it'll be no use; the Count is not going to fight; I know him."

"He won't! Then there's not a drop of noble blood in him!" remarked Alexander hatefully. "I didn't suppose he was so base!"

"He's not base, but only intelligent."

"So that makes me stupid in your view?"

"N... no, in love," said Pyotr Ivanych, hesitating.

"Uncle, if you intend to convince me of the senselessness of a duel by calling it premature judgment, then I warn you, the effort's in vain: I shall remain firm."

"No. It was proven long ago that in general duelling is a stupidity; yet everybody fights duels—there are many asses in the world, aren't there? You won't bring them to reason. I only want to prove to you that fighting a duel is not the right thing for you in particular."

"I'm curious how you'll persuade me."

"Well, listen. Let's say you're especially angry at somebody, at the Count or at her... what's her name... Anyuta, is it?"

"I hate him, disdain her," said Alexander.

"Let's begin with the Count. Let's assume he accepts your challenge, let's even assume that you find some fool of a second—what will be the result? The Count will kill you like a fly and afterwards everybody will laugh at you; a fine revenge! But, see, that's not what you want. You'd like to blot out the Count."

"We don't know who'll kill whom," said Alexander.

"Probably he'll kill you. Look, apparently you don't even know how to shoot, but according to the rules the first shot is his."

"Divine Judgment will decide the matter."

"Well, as you like—but He'll decide in the Count's favor. It's said that the Count puts bullet after bullet on the mark at fifteen paces, yet for your sake he'll miss on purpose! Suppose that Divine Judgment permits such awkwardness and injustice: you somehow even kill him by accident—what's the sense in that? Do you think you'll get your beauty's love back that way? No, she'd truly begin to hate you, and you'd be drafted into the army for this... And the main thing, the very next day you'd start tearing your hair in desperation and at the same time cool off toward your love..."

Alexander shrugged his shoulders contemptuously.

"You reason so cleverly about this, Uncle," he said. Give me your reasoning on what I should do in my situation."

"Nothing! Leave it as it is. Everything's already ruined."

"Leave happiness in his hands. Leave him the proud possessor... oh! can some threat or other stop me? You don't know my tortures! You've never loved if you thought you'd prevent me with cold moralizing... milk flows in your veins, not blood..."

"Stop talking nonsense, Alexander! Don't you think there are lots of girls in the world like your Marya—or Sofiya, what's her name?"

"Her name is Nadezhda."

"Nadezhda? And who was Sofiya then?"

"Sofiya... that was in the country," said Alexander unwillingly.

"Do you see?" his uncle went on. "There Sofiya, here Nadezhda, somewhere else Marya. The heart is a deep well; you probe for a long while to reach bottom. The heart keeps on loving till old age..."

"No, the heart loves once..."

"And you're repeating what you've heard from others. The heart keeps on loving until it loses its strength. It lives its own life and like everything in the human being has its youth and old age. If one love fails, it is only quiescent, it remains silent until the next. If this next is thwarted, if the lovers are parted—the capacity to love remains unfulfilled till the third, till the fourth time, until finally the heart puts all its strength into one happy encounter which no one prevents, and then it slowly and gradually cools. Some love happily that first time; they're the ones who shout that it's possible to love only once. As long as a man isn't old, is healthy..."

"You keep talking about youth, Uncle, therefore about physical, material love..."

"I talk about youth because in old age love is a mistake, an aberration. And what sort of thing is material love? There isn't any such love, or it isn't love, just as there isn't any uniquely ideal love. Both soul and body play equal parts in love; if not, love is incomplete; we are not spirits and not beasts. You say yourself, 'Milk, not blood, flows in the veins.' Well, do you see then: on the one hand, take the blood in the veins—that's the physical part; on the other hand, self-love, habit—that's the non-physical; and there you have love! Where did I leave off... yes, drafted into the army! Besides, after this scandal the girl won't let you come near her. You will have done harm both to her and to yourself, you see. I hope we've gone over this question in depth from one point of view. Now..."

Pyotr Ivanych poured himself some wine and drank.

"That idiot!" he said, "served us chilled Lafitte."

Alexander was silent, his head bowed.

"Now, tell me," he said, warming the glass of wine in both hands, "why did you want to wipe the Count off the face of the earth?"

"I've already told you why! Isn't he the one who destroyed my happiness? Like a wild beast he burst in..."

"Into the sheepfold!" interrupted his uncle.

"Carried off everything," Alexander continued.

"He didn't carry her off, but came and took her. Was he obliged to inquire whether your girl was taken by someone else? I don't understand this stupidity, which, true, the majority of lovers have been committing since the creation of the world up to our time—getting angry at their rivals! Can there be anything more nonsensical—*to wipe him off the face of the earth!* What for? Because she liked him! As if he were to blame, and as if for this reason things would be better if we punish him! And your girl... what's her name?—Katenka, isn't it?—did she resist him perhaps? Make some effort to avoid the danger? She yielded on her own, she stopped loving you; there's no use fighting—you won't bring her back! To insist would be egoism! To require faithfulness of a wife makes sense. An obligation has been undertaken on which the material welfare of the family often depends. Of course, it's impossible to demand that she not love anyone else, and you can only demand that she... the man... Yes, and you yourself, didn't you hand her over to the Count with both hands? Did you contend for her?..."

"That's what I want, indeed to contend," said Alexander, jumping up from his place, "and you're stopping my noble impulse..."

"Contend with an oak club in your hands!" interrupted his uncle. "We're not in the Kirghizian steppes. In the educated world there's another way of fighting. For that you would have had to go about it at the proper time and differently, fight a different kind of duel with the Count in the presence of your girl."

Alexander looked at his uncle in amazement.

"What duel?" he asked.

"I'll tell you now. What has been your course of action thus far?"

With numerous jibes, extenuations, dodges, and grimaces somehow Alexander recounted the whole course of events.

"You see? You're guilty on all counts," Pyotr Ivanych concluded, with a frown after hearing him out. "How many stupidities were committed! Oh, Alexander! Was it worth coming to St. Petersburg for this? You could have had this whole escapade at home on the lake with your aunt. Why, how could you be so childish, make scenes... lose your temper so? For shame! Who does that nowadays? What if your girl... what's her name? Yuliya?... tells the Count everything? Not really, no fear of that, thank Heaven! Probably she's clever enough to have answered his question about your relations by saying..."

"Saying what?" Alexander asked eagerly.

"That she fooled you, that you fell in love, you were obnoxious, you bored her... that's what they always do..."

"You think she really said that?" asked Alexander, turning pale.

"Without any doubt. You don't imagine she'd be likely to tell about gathering yellow flowers there in the garden with you? What naiveté!"

"What duel with the Count do you mean? asked Alexander impatiently.

"One like this. You shouldn't have been rude, avoided him, made sour faces, but on the contrary, responded to his charm with two, three, ten times as much. And this—Nadenka? I've got it right it seems—you shouldn't have irritated her with reproaches, but deferred to her caprices, pretended you noticed nothing, that you harbored no notion of betrayal, as if that were impossible. You shouldn't have let them get close to the point of intimacy, but artfully broken it up as if unintentionally, prevented their meeting, just the two of them together, been everywhere with them, even ridden horseback with them and meanwhile quietly challenged your rival in her presence to competition, and then and there loaded and brought to bear all the forces of your mind, set up an artillery of wit, cunning and the like... discovered and struck down the weaknesses of your rival as if unintentionally, without forethought, good-naturedly, even unwillingly, with regret, and little by little stripped him of that finery in which a young man strikes a pose in front of a pretty girl. You should have noticed what impressed and dazzled her most in him and then artfully attacked those sides of him, simply exposed them, showed them up as ordinary, demonstrated that the new hero is secondrate... and has put on Sunday clothes only for her... But all must be done coolly, patiently and skillfully—that is what a real duel means in our time!"

Pyotr Ivanych had finished a glass the while and at once poured another.

"Contemptible trickery! Resorting to cunning to win a woman's heart!..." indignantly remarked Alexander.

"Do you think it's better to resort to a heavy club? It's possible to keep someone's affection by trickery, but by force—I don't think so. I understand the wish to get rid of a rival. Taking steps to keep a beloved for oneself, preventing or averting danger—that's very natural! But to club your rival because he has inspired love—that's like bruising yourself and then banging the place where you did it, as children do. Have your way, but the Count is not to blame! As I see it, you don't understand anything about the mysteries of the heart, and that's the reason your love affairs and your stories are so bad."

"My love concerns!" said Alexander shaking his head contemptuously. "Do you really think love inspired by trickery can be fulfilling or lasting?"

"I don't know whether it's fulfilling, that depends on how you look at it, it's all the same to me. In general, I don't think highly of love—you know that. To my mind, we don't need it at all... but what's more lasting is truth. To work on the heart directly is impossible. It's a complex instrument; if you don't know which spring to touch, it'll start playing Heaven knows what. Awaken love by whatever means, but maintain it by intelligence; there's nothing contemptible in that. No need to run your rival down and resort to character smears. That way you'll only get your girl up in arms against you... You need only strip him of those blandishments with which he's blinded your beloved, make him a simple, ordinary man in her eyes and not a hero... I think it's pardonable to defend your own with noble trickery; that's not disdained in military affairs. Look, you wanted to get married; it would be all right for a husband to make a scene over his wife, but threaten one's rivals with a club—that would be..."

Pyotr Ivanych implied madness by pointing at his forehead.

"Your Varyenka was twenty percent more intelligent than you when she suggested waiting a year."

"But could I have practiced cunning even if I'd known how? To do that you couldn't love as I do! Some pretend to be cold at times, stay away for several days by cool calculation—and it works... But I can't pretend or calculate! When I see her I stop breathing and my knees tremble and bend beneath me, I am ready for every torture if only to see her... No! say what you will, but for me the rapture is greater—to love with all the forces of my soul, even though I suffer, rather than be loved without loving, or love somehow half-heartedly for sport, or use some repulsive system and play with a woman as with a lap-dog, only to push her away..."

Pyotr Ivanych shrugged his shoulders.

"Well then, suffer if you enjoy it," he said. "Oh, unspoiled country life! Oh, Asia! You should live in the Orient; there they still command women whom to love, and if they don't obey, they drown them. No, here," he continued, as if to himself, "to be happy with a woman, that is, not as you think, like a madman, but reasonably, requires a lot... You must know how to make a woman of a girl according to a well-thought-out plan, a method, if you will, so that she comes to know and fulfill her destiny. You draw a magic circle round her, not very narrow, so that she feels no limits and does not overstep them; you cunningly rule not only her heart—what's that!—that's a slippery and uncertain power—but her mind and will, subordinate her taste and habits to yours so that she sees things through you, is of the same mind as you..."

"That is, make her into a doll or a wordless slave of her husband," Alexander interrupted.

"Why? Arrange things so that she does not play her feminine character and value false in any way. Give her freedom of action in her sphere, but let your penetrating intelligence watch over her every movement, sigh, act, so that each momentary excitement, flare-up, germ of feeling should always and everywhere meet the outwardly calm, but ever watchful eye of her husband. Organize constant checks without any tyranny, artfully even, imperceptibly to her, and lead her the way you want... Oh, a complex and difficult schooling is necessary, and that schooling is an intelligent and experienced man—that's what's needed."

He cleared his throat significantly and tossed down a glass of wine in one gulp.

"Then," he went on, "a husband can sleep peacefully even when his wife is not at his side, or sit without worry in his study when she sleeps..."

"Ah, so this is the famous secret of conjugal happiness!" remarked Alexander. "By deception you chain a woman's mind, heart and will to yourself—and take comfort in this, act proud of it... this is happiness! And how will she perceive it?"

"Why act proud?" added his uncle. "That's not necessary!"

"It follows, Uncle," Alexander continued, "that since you sit without worry in your study while my aunt sleeps, this man, I would guess, is..."

"Sh! sh!.. Be quiet," began his uncle, waving his hand, "it's good my wife is asleep, for otherwise..."

At this moment the door to the study opened quietly, but no one was to be seen.

"And the wife," began a woman's voice from the corridor, "must not show that she understands the great schooling of her husband and must institute a little of her own, but not gossip about it over a bottle of wine..."

Both Aduyevs rushed to the door; rapid steps sounded in the corridor, the rustle of a dress—and all became quiet.

Uncle and nephew looked at each other.

"Well, Uncle?" asked the nephew after a moment's silence.

"Well! Nothing!" said Pyotr Ivanych, frowning. "I boasted too soon. Learn from this, Alexander: Better not get married or else choose a fool. You won't manage with an intelligent woman—that's a difficult school!"

He thought it over, then struck himself on the forehead.

"How did I fail to consider that she knew of your late visit?" he said, annoyed, "and that a woman won't go to sleep when there's a secret between two men in the next room. Without fail she'll either send her maid or come herself... and not to foresee it! How stupid! It's all you and this cursed Lafitte here. I shot off my mouth! Such a lesson from a twenty-year-old woman..."

"You're afraid, Uncle!"

"Why should I be afraid? Not at all! I made a mistake. I mustn't lose my cool-headedness, I must get myself out of this."

He thought it over again.

"She bragged," he began. "What kind of schooling does she have! She can't have any school; she's young! She only talked that way... out of annoyance! But now she's aware of the magic circle, she'll become cunning herself... Oh, I know a woman's nature! But we shall see..."

He smiled proudly and merrily; the wrinkles on his forehead smoothed out.

"Only things must be done differently," he added. "The former method's devilishly bad. Now we must..."

He suddenly caught himself and was silent, looking fearfully at the door.

"But that's all in the future," he continued. "Now let's look at your business, Alexander. What were we talking about? Yes! It seems you wanted to kill, didn't you, your... what's her name?"

"I despise her too deeply," said Alexander, sighing deeply.

"So, you see? You're already half cured. Only, isn't it true?—you're apparently still angry. However, despise, despise; that's best in your situation. I wanted to say something... better not..."

"Oh, speak, for Heaven's sake, speak!" said Alexander. "Right now I haven't a spark of reasonable judgment. I'm suffering, I shall perish... Give me some of your cold reasonableness. Say everything that can relieve and calm my sick heart..."

"Yes, I'll tell you—but perhaps you'll return there again..."

"What an idea! After what..."

"People return after even more! Your word of honor—you won't go?"

"I'll swear it, if you insist."

"No, give your word of honor; that's better."

"Word of honor."

"Well, do you see? We've decided that the Count is not to blame..."

"Let's suppose that's so; then what?"

"Then, what's your—whatever her name—guilty of..."

"What is Nadenka guilty of!" Alexander objected with amazement. "She's not guilty!"

"No! So, not guilty of anything? Then there's nothing to despise her for."

"Nothing! No, Uncle, that's going too far! Let's suppose the Count... that he, too... didn't know. .. and then, but no! And she? After that, who then is to blame? I?"

"Yes, almost that way, but in actual fact nobody. Tell me now, what do you despise her for?"

"For a dastardly deed."

"Consisting of what?"

"She repaid a high-minded, unlimited passion with ingratitude..."

"What was there to be grateful for? Do you mean you loved for her sake, to be nice to her? Wanted to do her a favor perhaps? Then, in that case you'd have loved better than a mother."

Alexander looked at him and didn't know what to say.

"You shouldn't have shown her the depth of your feelings; a woman cools when a man completely declares himself. You should have come to know her character and then acted accordingly and not lain like a pet dog at her feet. How can one not study a partner with whom there is business of any kind? Then you would have seen that you could expect nothing more of her. She had acted out her romance with you to the end; you'd have seen that she would play it to the end the same way with the Count and maybe with someone else as well... You can't ask more of her. She can't go higher and further! She isn't that kind of person, but you imagined Heaven knows what..."

"But why did she fall in love with someone else?" interrupted Alexander bitterly.

"Still looking for causes; the reasonable question! Oh, you, barbarian! And why did you fall in love with her? Well, fall out of love right away!"

"You think that depends on me?"

"But you think her falling in love with the Count depended on her? You yourself affirmed that one mustn't compel emotional impulses, but when it is your turn, you reason why she fell in love! Why did a certain man die, a certain woman go crazy? How should we answer such questions? Love must end some time; it can't last a century."

"Yes, it can. I feel in myself that strength of heart. I would have loved with an eternal love."

"Yes! But if her love for you were really strong, you'd take off... go back on your word. Everyone's like that, I know!"

"Granted her love was over," said Alexander, "but why did it end like that?..."

"Does it matter? Look, you had love, enjoyed it and that's enough!"

"She went to another!" said Alexander, going pale.

"And you'd have wished her to love another on the sly and go on assuring you of her love? Now, you yourself decide: what was she to do? Is she to blame?"

"Oh, I'll avenge myself on her!" said Alexander.

"You're ungrateful," Pyotr Ivanych went on. "That's not nice! Whatever a woman has done to you, betrayed you, grown cold, acted, as the poets say, in a *wily* manner—blame nature, devote yourself, please, to philosophical reflection on

the event, scold the world, life, what you will, but never impugn a woman's character by word or deed. The weapon against a woman is condescension; in the
end the most cruel tactic is to forget her. This is the only weapon permitted a
decent man. Remember, for a year and a half you've hung on everyone's neck
out of joy, not known what to do with yourself for happiness! A year and a half of
uninterrupted pleasure! Say what you will, you're ungrateful!"

"Alas, Uncle, for me there was nothing on earth more sacred than love; without it life is not life..."

"Oh! it's sickening to listen to such nonsense!" interrupted Pyotr Ivanych with
irritation.

"I would have worshipped Nadenka," continued Alexander, "and not been
envious of any happiness in the world. I dreamed of spending my whole life with
Nadenka. And what now? Where is that noble, gigantic passion of which I
dreamed? It's lost in some stupid, pigmy comedy of sighs, ugly scenes, jealousy,
lying, hypocrisy—oh God! God!"

"Why did you imagine what doesn't exist? Didn't I keep telling you that till
now you wanted to lead a kind of life not found on earth. You think a man is sole-
ly concerned with being a lover, husband, father... and you don't even want to
know about anything else. A man is also a citizen, has some kind of profession,
occupation—a writer, perhaps, a landowner, soldier, civil servant, factory owner...
But in your mind everything is subordinated to love and friendship—what a paradise! You've read too many novels, listened too much to your auntie there in the
sticks, and brought these ideas here. In addition, you've dreamed up *noble passion!*"

"Noble, yes!"

"Enough, I beg you! You think there actually are noble passions!"

"There are!"

"Well, listen. Passion, after all, means the moment when feeling, attraction,
devotion or things like that have reached a point where the mind ceases to function. So what's noble about that? I don't understand; it's sheer madness—that's
not human. And why do you only see one side of the coin? I'm speaking of love—
just look at the other side too, and you'll see that love isn't bad. Remember the
happy moments. You buzzed my ears full of it..."

"Oh, don't remind me, don't remind me!" said Alexander with a gesture of
rejection. "It's easy for you to reason thus because you can trust the woman you
love. I would like to see what you would do in my place..."

"What I would do?... I would distract myself... go to my factory. Do you want
to come along tomorrow?"

"No, you and I will never be of the same mind," Alexander declared sadly.
"Your view of life does not comfort but repels me. I am sad, cold chills my soul.
Until now love saved me from this cold; now it's gone, and now there's sorrow in
my heart. I'm frightened, bored..."

"Get busy with something."

"All that's true, Uncle. You and your likes can think thus. You're by nature
cold... with a soul incapable of agitation..."

"And you imagine that you're endowed with a powerful soul? Yesterday you
were in seventh heaven for joy and just a bit later... and you can't endure your
grief."

Alexander spoke weakly, hardly defending himself: "Steam, steam! Just like a
locomotive gliding over the rails, you think, feel, and talk evenly, smoothly, calmly."

"I hope that isn't bad, better than jumping the track, bouncing down the embankment like you are now, and not being able to get up again. Steam! Steam! Yes, steam indeed, and you see, this is to a man's credit. This metaphor embodies the essence of what makes you and me human, while even an animal can die of grief. There have been cases where dogs have died on their masters' grave, or suffocated from joy after a long separation. What's the achievement in that? But you thought you were a special creature of a higher order, an extraordinary man..."

Pyotr Ivanych glanced at his nephew and suddenly stopped.

"What's this? You're not crying, are you?" he asked, and his face darkened, that is, he blushed.

Alexander said nothing. The last argument had quite overwhelmed him. There was nothing to retort, yet he remained under the influence of his feelings, feelings of the moment. He remembered his lost happiness, that now another... And tears streamed down his cheeks.

"Uncle! Remember the years of your youth," said Alexander, sobbing. "Could you really have endured with calm and indifference the most bitter insult fate ever delivers to a human being? To live such a full life for a year and a half and then suddenly there's nothing! Emptiness... After such sincerity this hypocrisy, concealment, and coldness—toward me! God! Is there a stronger torture? It's easy to say, of someone else, 'he was betrayed,' but to suffer it?... How she changed! How she began to dress up for the Count! It got so, I'd come and she would turn pale, could hardly speak... lies... Oh, no..."

The tears gushed harder.

"If I had the consolation," he went on, "that I had lost her by force of circumstances, if she had been compelled against her will, say even that she died—then it would be easier to endure... but this way, no, no... Another man! That's terrible, unendurable! And there's no way to snatch her away from her abductor. You've disarmed me... What am I to do? Teach me! I can't breathe, I feel sick... Grief, torment! I shall die... shoot myself..."

He leaned his elbows on the desk, covered his head with his hands and began to sob loudly...

Pyotr Ivanych was at a loss. He walked back and forth a couple of times, then stopped opposite Alexander and scratched his head, not knowing what to do.

"Have some wine," said Pyotr Ivanych as gently as he could, "perhaps that..."

Alexander did not respond, but his head and shoulders jerked convulsively; he went on sobbing. Pyotr Ivanych frowned, gestured with his hand and left the room.

"What am I to do with Alexander?" he said to his wife. "He's sobbing his heart out so in my study that I've had to leave. I've quite worn myself out with him."

"And you've left him thus?" she asked. "Poor fellow! Let me try, I'll go to him."

"You won't get anywhere either; it's simply his nature. He quite takes after his aunt; she's just such a crybaby. I've already been reasoning with him for some time."

"You reasoned?"

"And I convinced him; he agreed with me."

"Oh, I don't doubt it. You're very reasonable and... cunning!" she added.

"Thank Heaven, if that's so. Well, it seems I've done all that can be done."

"It seems you have, but he's still crying."

"I'm not to blame; I've done everything to comfort him."

"What did you do?"

"Too little, you think? I talked to him a whole hour... My throat has even gone dry... I exposed the whole theory of love as if spread out on my palm, and I offered him money... and supper... even did my best with the wine..."

"And he's still crying?..."

"He's absolutely howling! Ever worse at the end."

"Amazing! Let me try. I'll see what I can do, and you meanwhile think over your new method..."

"What, what do you mean?"

But like a ghost, she had slipped out of the room.

Alexander was still sitting, resting his head on his hands. Someone touched him on the shoulders. He raised his head: a young, beautiful woman stood before him in her dressing gown and a boudoir cap in the Finnish style.

"Dear Aunt," he said.

She sat down beside him, looked at him fixedly as only women can sometimes look, then quietly dried his eyes with a handkerchief and kissed him on the forehead; then he pressed his lips to her hand. They talked for a long while.

An hour later he left, thoughtful but with a smile, and fell calmly asleep for the first time after many sleepless nights. She returned to her bedroom with tearstained eyes. Pyotr Ivanych had been snoring for a very long time.

Part Two

I

A year had passed since the scenes and events described in the last chapter of Part One.

Little by little Alexander's mood turned from gloomy despair to cold dejection. He had stopped thundering curses at the Count and Nadenka and grinding his teeth thereafter, but he displayed deep contempt towards them.

Lizaveta Alexandrovna, his aunt, comforted him with all the tenderness of a friend and sister. He gladly yielded to her kind concern. All such natures as his love to hand over responsibility to another. They need a nanny.

At last passion subsided in him; his true sadness passed, though he was sorry to part with it; he forced it to continue, created an artificial melancholy, played and showed off with it, and drowned in it.

Somehow he liked playing the role of a martyr. He was quiet, important, gloomy like a man who, in his words, has sustained a *blow of fate*. He spoke of noble sufferings, of sacred, elevated feelings, trampled upon and ground under foot in the mud—"and by whom?" he would add, "by a minx and coquette and a contemptible rake and tawdry dandy. Did fate really send me into the world in order that everything noble in me be sacrificed on the altar of insignificance?"

No man would have forgiven a fellowman this pose, nor a woman another woman, they would have pulled the other person from his pedestal right away. But what don't young people of different sexes forgive each other?

Lizaveta Alexandrovna listened to his Jeremiads sympathetically and comforted as best she could. This in no way went against the grain with her, perhaps because she found in her nephew, after all, sympathy with her own emotions; she heard in his accusations against love a suffering not foreign to her own.

She eagerly lent an ear to the groans of his heart and responded to them with imperceptible sighs and tears which no one noticed. Even for her nephew's simulated and high-flown outpourings of grief she found comforting words in a like tone and spirit, but Alexander wouldn't even listen.

"Oh, don't talk to me, dear Aunt," he objected, "I don't want to shame the sacred name of love by so calling my relationship with that..."

Here he made a contemptuous face and was ready, like Pyotr Ivanych, to ask, what's her name?

"She's excusable, however," he would add with still greater contempt. I was too far above her and the Count and all that pitiful and trivial ambiance; no wonder I remained a puzzle to her."

And after these words he would keep his look of contempt for a long time.

"Uncle insists I should be grateful to Nadenka," he went on, "for what? What was notable about this love? It was completely base and commonplace. Was there anything about it that transcended the ordinary circle of everyday squabbles?

Was there any bit of heroism and self-denial in this love? No, she almost always acted with the knowledge of her mother! Did she depart even once from the rules of society, of duty for my benefit?—never! And this was love!!! The girl was not even able to put poetry in this emotion!"

"What kind of love would you ask of a woman?" asked Lizaveta Alexandrovna.

"What kind?" answered Alexander. "I would ask for the first place in her heart. The woman I love should not notice, should not see other men beside me; they should all seem unbearable to her. Only I am higher, handsomer"—here he straightened up—"better, nobler than all of them. Every moment she endures without me is a lost moment. She is to find bliss in my eyes and in my conversation, and to know no other..."

Lizaveta Alexandrovna tried to hide a smile. Alexander didn't notice.

"For me," he went on with flashing eyes," she must sacrifice everything, all contemptible advantages and calculations, she must throw off the tyrannical yoke of her mother, her husband, run away, if necessary, to the end of the world, energetically bear all deprivations, finally disdain death itself—that is love! But this..."

"And how would you reward this love?" asked his aunt.

"I? Oh!" Alexander began, raising his eyes to Heaven, "I'd dedicate my whole life to her. I'd lie at her feet. To look into her eyes would be my greatest happiness. Her every word would be law to me. I would celebrate in song her beauty, our love, nature:

> And in her arms my lips will strain
> For Petrarch's and for love's refrain...[6]

But would you say I didn't show Nadenka how I can love?"

"So you altogether doubt a feeling which isn't displayed as you'd like? Powerful feeling is concealed..."

"Aren't you trying to assure me, dear Aunt, that such a feeling as Uncle's, for example, is concealed?"

Lizaveta Alexandrovna suddenly blushed. Inwardly she couldn't but agree with her nephew that a feeling without any outward show is somehow suspicious, that perhaps it isn't even there, that, if it were, it would break out and be seen, that alongside love itself, its ambiance embodies an inexplicable charm. At this point she ran through in thought the whole period of her married life and remained deep in thought. The overweening comment of her nephew stirred up a secret in her heart which she kept deeply hidden and it brought her to the question, was she happy?

She had no right to complain. She had been provided with all the external conditions of that happiness which the common herd pursues, as if according to a schedule. Great plenty, even luxury in the present, security in the future—all this rid her of those trivial bitter worries which eat at the heart and drain the breast of most poor people.

Her husband had worked untiringly and continued to work. But what was the chief goal of his labors? Was he working for a general human cause, fulfilling a task assigned him by fate, or was he working only for trivial reasons, so as to gain rank and financial importance among his fellows, so that in the end he need not bend to the yoke of need or circumstance? Heaven knows. He didn't like to talk about higher goals and called such talk delirium; instead he spoke dryly and simply of *doing a job*.

Lizaveta Alexandrovna only came to the sad conclusion that the unique goal of his zeal and striving was not she or a love for her. He had worked before his marriage when he did not yet know his wife. He never spoke to her of love or asked her about it; he turned aside her questions about it with a joke, a witticism or sleepiness. Soon after he met her, he began to speak of marriage as if giving notice that love went without saying and there was no need to talk much about it...

He was opposed to any kind of grand gesture—well and good. But he didn't like even sincere manifestations of feeling and didn't believe in other people's need for such. Meanwhile, with a single glance, a single word he could have aroused in her a deep passion for him, but he said nothing, didn't want it. It didn't even flatter his vanity.

She tried to make him jealous, thinking then that his love would show itself without fail... Nothing came of it. He hardly noticed that she singled out some young man in society; he'd hurry to invite him to their house, be friendly to him, himself couldn't say enough in his praise and wouldn't fear leaving him alone with his wife.

Lizaveta Alexandrovna sometimes pretended to herself, dreaming that Pyotr Ivanych was perhaps acting strategically, as if this were his secret method so as to keep her love alive by keeping doubt constantly alive in her. But her husband's first comment about love immediately disillusioned her.

If he had also been rude, rough, unfeeling, slow-witted, one of those husbands whose name is legion, whom it is so innocuous, so necessary, so delightful to deceive for their and one's own happiness—husbands, it seems, created in order that a woman should look around her and love another diametrically opposite—then that would have been different. She would perhaps have acted differently, as a majority of women act in such a case. But Pyotr Ivanych was a man of reason and tact such as is seldom encountered. He was subtle, perceptive, adroit. He understood all the agitations of the heart, all storms of the emotions; he understood—and that was all. The whole book of affairs of the heart was in his head, and not in his heart. In his judgments about such it was obvious that he said things he had heard, things that were accepted but that he had by no means experienced. He made fair judgments about the passions but did not acknowledge their power over him, even laughed at them, considering them mistakes, ugly transgressions against reality, something like sicknesses for which in time the proper medicine would turn up.

Lizaveta Alexandrovna felt his intellectual superiority over everything around him and was tormented by it. "If he weren't so intelligent, I would be spared...," she thought. He revered positive goals—that was clear, and he requested his wife not to lead a dreamer's life.

"But, Heavens!" thought Lizaveta Alexandrovna, "could he have married only to have a hostess, to give his bachelor apartment the fullness and dignity of a family home, to have more prestige in society? A hostess, a wife—in the most prosaic sense of these words! With all his intellect could he possibly not comprehend that love is inevitably one of a woman's positive goals...? Family obligations—these are her duties, but can she possibly fulfill them without love? Nannies, wet nurses and the like idolize the child they care for; how much more so a wife and mother! Oh, let me pay for my feeling with torments, let me endure all the sufferings which passion requires, if only I live a full life, feel my existence and don't wither away!..."

She looked at the luxurious furniture and all the baubles and expensive trifles in her dressing room—all the comforts with which the beloved is provided by the caring hand of a loving man in other homes seemed to her a cold mockery of true happiness. She bore witness to two terrible extremes—in her nephew and her husband. The one was exalted to the point of folly, the other icy to the point of cruelty.

"How little they both—yes, and the majority of men—understand genuine feeling! And how I understand it!" she thought. "But what use is that? What for? Oh, if only..."

She closed her eyes and remained that way for several minutes, then she opened them, looked about her, gave a deep sigh and immediately put on her ordinary calm look. Poor thing! Nobody knew about this, no one saw it. They would have regarded these unseen, intangible, nameless sufferings as a crime without wounds or blood, and covered not with rags but velvet. But with heroic self-denial she kept her sadness secret; moreover, she found sufficient strength to comfort others.

Soon Alexander stopped talking of noble sufferings and misunderstood and unappreciated love. He moved on to a more general theme. He complained of the boredom of life, the emptiness of his soul and wearisome melancholy.

> "I have outlasted all desire,
> My dreams and I have grown apart;"[7]

"And now a black demon pursues me. Oh, dear Aunt, he's with me everywhere: at night and when I chat with friends or have a drink with them and during moments of deep thought!"

Several weeks passed this way. It seems another two weeks and this strange fellow might perhaps have calmed down and become quite a regular person, simple and ordinary like others. But no! The particularity of his strange nature found occasion to show itself everywhere.

One day he came to his aunt in a fit of resentful anger directed at the whole race of man. His every word was a jibe, every opinion an epigram aimed at those one ought to respect. No one was spared. Even Pyotr Ivanych and she were targets. Lizaveta Alexandrovna began to seek the causes.

"You want to know," he began quietly and solemnly, "what *disturbs, enrages* me. Listen, you remember I had a friend whom I did not see for several years, but for whom I always reserved a corner in my heart. When I first came here, Uncle made me write a strange letter to him which contained Uncle's favorite rules and way of thinking, but I tore that one up and sent another; therefore, my friend had no reason to change. After this letter our correspondence ceased, and I lost touch with my friend. What happened? Three days ago walking along the Nevsky Prospect, I suddenly saw him and could not say a word for joy; my breath failed me. He took one hand and squeezed it. 'Hello, Aduyev!' he said in a tone as if he'd parted from me only the night before. 'Have you been here long?' He expressed surprise we hadn't met till now, casually asked what I was doing, where I worked, felt himself obliged to inform me he had a wonderful job, liked his work, his bosses and comrades and everyone, and his luck... then said he had no time, that he was hurrying to a dinner invitation—do you hear, dear Aunt? On meeting a friend after a long separation, he couldn't postpone dinner..."

"But perhaps they'd wait dinner for him," remarked Alexander's aunt. "Good manners didn't allow..."

"Good manners and friendship? Yes, there's another thing; I'll tell you a better one. He shoved his address into my hand, said that he'd expect me the next evening at his place—and disappeared. This is my childhood friend, the friend of my youth!—a fine friend! But then I thought again, that perhaps he had put off everything till the evening and would then devote time to a sincere, soulful conversation. 'Well and good,' I thought; 'I'll go.' I appeared. Ten people were there. He held out his hand more cordially than the day before—true. But for all that, without a word he then gestured for me to sit down and play cards. I said I didn't play and sat down alone on the sofa, assuming he'd quit the game and come over to me. 'You don't play?' he said with surprise. 'How do you spend your time?' A fine question! So I wait an hour, two hours; he doesn't come near me; I lose patience. He offers me a cigar, then a pipe, regrets that I don't play, am having a boring time, tries to interest me—guess how!—by constantly talking to me about his every successful and unsuccessful move. Finally, I'd had enough and went up to him and asked whether he intended to spare any time that evening for me. And my heart was in such turmoil that my voice trembled. This apparently surprised him. He looked at me strangely. 'Good,' he said, 'just let us finish this rubber.' As soon as he told me that, I picked up my hat and wanted to leave, but he noticed this and stopped me. 'The rubber is ending,' he said. 'We'll have supper right away.' At last they finished. He sat down beside me and yawned; that's how our friendly chat began. 'You wanted to say something to me?' he asked. This was uttered in such a monotone and so without feeling that I only looked at him with a sad smile and said nothing. Thereupon he suddenly came alive, so to speak, and began to shower me with questions. 'How goes it with you? Do you need anything? Perhaps I can be of use to you at the office?...' and so on. I shook my head and told him I wanted to talk to him not about the office, not about material advantages, but about what was closer to his heart, about the golden days of childhood, about our pranks... Oh, imagine! He didn't even let me finish. 'You're still,' he said, 'the same dreamer!' Then he suddenly changed the subject, as if he thought it empty and began seriously to question me about my affairs, my hopes for the future, my career, like Uncle. I was surprised, I didn't believe a man's heart could coarsen so. I wanted to test it one last time, and taking up his question about my affairs, I began to tell how they had treated me. 'Listen to what *people* did to me...' I was about to begin. 'What?' he interrupted at once, frightened, 'really, you were robbed?' He thought I was talking about the lackeys. Like Uncle, he knows no other sorrow; a man can turn to stone to such a degree! 'Yes,' I said, 'people plundered my soul...' Here I started to speak of my love, my sufferings, my emotional emptiness... I began to dare being carried away and thought the story of my sufferings would melt his icy sheath, that the tears in his eyes had not quite dried... When suddenly—he burst out laughing. I look—he is holding a handkerchief in his hands. He had restrained himself during my account and finally could not stand it... In horror I stopped.

"'Enough, enough,' he said. 'Better have a drink of vodka; yes, and we'll have supper... there's some splendid roast... ha, ha, ha!... roast beef...'

"He was going to take my arm, but I pulled loose and fled from this monster. That's the way people are, Aunt!" concluded Alexander, then waved his arm and left.

Lizaveta Alexandrovna began to be sorry for Alexander, sorry for his fiery but misdirected heart. She saw that with a different upbringing and proper outlook on life he could be happy and could make someone else happy. But now he was the victim of his own blindness and his heart's most tormenting delusions. He had made his life a martyrdom. How could she point his heart in the right direction? Where was the compass of salvation? She felt that only a tender, friendly hand could care for this flower.

She had already succeeded once in taming the agitated impulses of her nephew's heart, but that was in a matter of love. In that case she knew how to handle a wounded heart. Like an artful diplomat, she first heaped reproaches on Nadenka, presented her behavior in the worst light, debased her in Alexander's eyes and successfully proved her unworthy of his love. Thus she tore the tormenting pain out of Alexander's heart, replacing it with a calm, though not altogether justified feeling—contempt. Pyotr Ivanych, on the contrary, tried to justify Nadenka and in so doing not only did not calm Alexander but further agitated his torment, making him think that his successor had been more worthy.

But friendship is another matter. Lizaveta Alexandrovna saw that Alexander's friend was in the wrong in his eyes and right in the eyes of the crowd. Try to explain that to Alexander! She hadn't the courage to attempt this herself and resorted to her husband, assuming not without reason that he would not lack for arguments against friendship.

"Pyotr Ivanych!" she said to him once in a caressing tone, "I've come to ask a favor."

"What is it?"

"Guess."

"Just say what; you know there's no refusing you a favor. As for the summer place in Peterhof, it's still early for that, you know..."

"Not that!" said Lizaveta Alexandrovna.

"What then? You said you're afraid of our horses, wanted some quieter ones..."

"No!"

"So, new furniture?..."

She shook her head.

"I give up, I don't know," said Pyotr Ivanych. "Here, take instead this I.O.U. and use it for whatever you need; I won it last night at cards..."

He was about to pull out his wallet.

"No, don't bother, put the money back," said Lizaveta Alexandrovna. "This favor will not cost you a penny."

"Not to take money when it's offered!" said Pyotr Ivanych, putting away his wallet. "It's unbelievable! What do you want then?"

"I want only a little good will..."

"As much as you wish."

"Well, you see, the day before yesterday Alexander came to see me..."

"Oh, I fear the worst!" interrupted Pyotr Ivanych. "So?"

"He's so gloomy," Lizaveta Alexandrovna went on. "I'm afraid all this may lead Alexander to a point where..."

"So what's the matter with him now? Has he been betrayed in love again perhaps?"

"No, in friendship."

"In friendship! From bad to worse! How in friendship? That's curious; tell me, please."

"Here's how."

Lizaveta Alexandrovna then told him everything she had heard from her nephew. Pyotr Ivanych shrugged his shoulders expressively.

"What do you want me to do? You see what sort he is!"

"Show him some sympathy; ask him how he feels..."

"No, it's better you ask."

"Talk to him a bit... how shall I say?... more gently and not as you always talk...

don't laugh at his feeling..."

"You're not demanding that I cry, are you?"

"It wouldn't hurt."

"What's the good of that for him?"

"A lot... and not only for him..." remarked Lizaveta Alexandrovna half-aloud.

"What?" asked Pyotr Ivanych.

She was silent.

"Oh, this Alexander really; I've had him up to here!" said Pyotr Ivanych, pointing to his neck.

"What makes you think he's such a burden to you?"

"How can you ask! I've been fussing over him for six years. Sometimes he'll burst into tears and I have to comfort him, and then I correspond with his mother too.

"Indeed, you poor thing. How could this burden fall upon you! What a terrible chore—once a month you get a letter from an old lady and throw it, unread, into the waste basket, and you must have talks with your nephew. 'But,' you say, 'it distracts me from my game of whist!' Men, men! If there's a good dinner, a bottle of gold-label Lafitte and cards—that's enough; they don't need any further contact. And if, in addition, they have occasion to act important and show off their wisdom—then they're really happy."

"Just as you women need to play the coquette," remarked Pyotr Ivanych. "To each his own, my dear! What more do you want?"

"What more! Have a heart! But we never even mention that."

"That again!"

"We women are very wise; why should we busy ourselves with such trifles? We spin the fates of men. They look to see what a man has in his pocket or what awards in his buttonhole and don't care about the rest. And they want everyone to be like that. If a single feeling man turns up among them, capable of loving and making others love him..."

"He did a marvelous job of making this girl... what's her name?... love him. Verochka, was it?" remarked Pyotr Ivanych.

"He found someone to treat as an equal! It's fate's cruel joke. Fate, as if on purpose, always puts a tender, feeling person together with some cold creature! Poor Alexander! His mind doesn't run an even race with his heart, so he's faulted by those for whom mind has too much taken the lead, who would be ruled by reason alone in all things..."

"Agree, though, that it's the important thing; otherwise..."

"I don't agree, not for anything will I agree; it's the important thing there at the factory maybe, but you forget that a person also has feelings..."

"Five of them," said Aduyev. "I learned that with the alphabet way back."

"That's both vexing and sad!" whispered Lizaveta Alexandrovna.

"Come, come, don't be angry. I'll do everything you say, just tell me how!" said Pyotr Ivanych.

"Then please give him an easy lesson..."

"Scold him?—fine, I'm good at that."

"Well, a reprimand if you must. Explain to him very affectionately what one may ask and expect of friends today; tell him his friend is not so much to blame as he thinks... But is it for me to instruct you? You're so wise... you dissemble so well..." added Lizaveta Alexandrovna.

At her last word Pyotr Ivanych frowned a little.

"Didn't you two have enough sincere outpourings," he said angrily. "They

whispered and whispered to each other, whispering and still didn't whisper everything about friendship and love; now they're involving me..."

"But then it'll be the last time," said Lizaveta Alexandrovna. "I hope that after
this he'll be comforted for good."

Pyotr Ivanych shook his head skeptically.

"Does he have money?" he asked, "maybe not and for that reason he..."

"You have only money on your mind. He was ready to give away all his money
for one cordial word from his friend."

"Some day he may indeed do that. Once he gave money away to a colleague in
his department because of the man's sincere outpourings... There, someone
rang. Isn't it he? What must I do? Tell me again. I'm to give him a scolding...
What else? Money?"

"What scolding! You'll only make it worse. I asked you to talk to him a bit
about friendship, about the heart and be very affectionate, very attentive."

Alexander bowed in silence and in silence ate a great deal at dinner, and in
the pauses rolled little balls of his bread and looked, frowning, at the wine bottle
and the water caraffe. After dinner he was about to look for his hat.

"Where are you going?" asked Pyotr Ivanych. "Sit for a while with us."

Alexander obeyed in silence. Pyotr Ivanych thought about how to approach
his task the more affectionately and skillfully and suddenly stated quite rapidly:
"Alexander, I heard your friend somehow behaved meanly toward you."

At these unexpected words Alexander jerked his head as if wounded and gave
a look full of reproach at his aunt She, too, did not expect so abrupt an approach
to the matter and at first bowed her head to her work, and then she too looked
reproachfully at her husband. But he was under the double influence of digestion
and sleepiness and therefore did not notice the rebound of these glances.

Alexander answered his uncle's question with a barely audible sigh.

"Indeed, how insidious," Pyotr Ivanych continued. "What a friend! He hasn't
seen you for five years and has grown so cold that upon meeting you he didn't
smother his friend in embraces, but invited him to his house to a party, tried to
sit him down to play cards... and fed him... But then—treacherous fellow!—noticed
the sour look on his friend's face and started asking about his affairs, circumstances, needs—what odious curiosity! And further—oh ! height of treachery—
dared offer his services... help... perhaps money! And no sincere outpourings!
Horrible, horrible! Show me this monster, please; bring him to dinner Friday!...
What card game does he play?"

"I don't know," Alexander said, angrily. "Have your laugh, Uncle; you're right,
it's all my fault. To trust people, seek sympathy—from whom? Strew pearls—
before whom? All around baseness, lack of courage, pettiness, while I've still kept
my youthful belief in goodness, heroism, constancy..."

Pyotr Ivanych began repeatedly and regularly to nod his head.

"Pyotr Ivanych!" said Lizaveta Alexandrovna in a whisper, pulling at his sleeve,
"Are you asleep?"

"What!" said Pyotr Ivanych, waking up. "I heard everything: 'heroism, constancy'; what do you mean 'sleep'?"

"Don't bother Uncle, dear Aunt!" reproved Alexander. "If he didn't fall
asleep, his digestion would be disturbed and Heaven knows what would come of
it. Man is the master of this earth, but he's also the slave of his stomach."

With this he wanted, it seems, to smile bitterly, but the smile was somehow
sour.

"Tell me what you wanted from your friend? Sacrifice of some sort perhaps, that he climb a wall or throw himself out a window? How do you understand friendship, what do you mean by it?" asked Pyotr Ivanych.

"By now I don't ask any sacrifice—don't worry. Thanks to people I've settled on a pitiful understanding of friendship too, as of love... I was always carrying with me those lines which seemed to me the truest definition of those two feelings as I understand them and as they ought to be, but now I see that it's a lie, a slander of people or a pitiful ignorance of their heart... People aren't capable of such feelings. Away with these treacherous words!..."

He took his wallet out of his pocket and out of the wallet two octavo pages covered with writing.

"What's that?" asked his uncle. "Let us see."

"It's not worth it!" said Alexander, wanting to tear up the pieces of paper.

"Read it aloud, read it aloud!" Lizaveta Alexandrovna began to request.

"This is how two of the latest French novelists define true friendship and love, and I agreed with them, thinking I'd meet such creatures in life and find in them... Find what!" He contemptuously waved his hand and began to read. "'To love, not with that false half-hearted friendship to be found in our gilded halls of government, which does not withstand a handful of gold and fears any ambiguity, but to love with that powerful friendship which gives blood for blood, proves itself in battle and bloodshed, to the cannons' roar, beneath the howl of storms when friends kiss with mouths blackened by gunpowder and embrace with bloodied arms. And if Pylades is fatally wounded, Orestes, while energetically bidding him farewell, will end his tortures with a sure blow of his dagger, will swear a terrible oath of vengeance and keep it, then wipe away a tear and be at peace...'"

Pyotr Ivanych began to laugh in his measured quiet way.

"Whom are you laughing at, Uncle?" asked Alexander.

"At the author, if he says that sincerely and not as a joke, and then at you if you have truly understood friendship in this way."

"Is this really only laughable?" asked Lizaveta Alexandrovna.

"Only that. No, I'm wrong; it's laughable and pitiful. Moreover, Alexander agrees with this too and made bold to laugh. He just now admitted that such a friendship is a lie and a slander against people. That's already an important step forward."

"It's a lie because people are incapable of rising to this conception of friendship as it ought to be..."

"If people are incapable of it, then it oughtn't to be such..." said Pyotr Ivanych.

"But there have been examples..."

"Those are exceptions and exceptions are almost always no good. 'Bloodied embraces, a terrible oath, a blow of the dagger!...'" and he laughed again. "Please read the page about love. My sleepiness is gone."

"If this can give you occasion to laugh again—gladly!" said Alexander and began to read the following: "'To love means not to belong to oneself, to stop living for oneself, to enter into the existence of another, to concentrate on one object all human feelings, hopes, fears, sorrows, enjoyments. To love means to live in the infinite...'"

"The devil knows what that is!" interrupted Pyotr Ivanych. "What verbiage!"

"No, it's very good! I like it," remarked Lizaveta Alexandrovna. "Go on, Alexander."

"'To know no limit to feeling, to devote oneself to a single being,'" Alexander went on reading, "'and live and think only for his happiness, find greatness in humiliation, enjoyment in melancholy and melancholy in enjoyment, surrender to all sorts of contradictions, except love and hate. To love means to live in an ideal world...'"

Pyotr Ivanych shook his head during this.

"'In the ideal world,'" Alexander continued, "'all splendor and magnificence is superb splendor and magnificence. In that world the sky seems purer and nature more luxurious. Life and time are divided into two parts—presence and absence, into two times of year—spring and winter. Spring corresponds to presence, winter to absence, because, no matter how beautiful the flowers and pure the azure of the sky, the charm of both is darkened by absence; to love is to see only one being and the universe is contained in this being... Finally, to love means to watch every glance of the beloved, as a Bedouin guards every drop of dew in order to refresh his lips which are parched by the desert heat; it means to be overcome by a swarm of thoughts in the absence of the beloved, but to be unable to express a single one in his presence; it means striving to outdo the other in sacrifices...'"

"Enough, for Heaven's sake, enough!" interrupted Pyotr Ivanych, "My patience is gone! You wanted to tear these up; tear away, tear them up quickly! That's right!"

Pyotr Ivanych even got up from his chair and began to walk back and forth in the room.

"Was there really a time when people seriously thought that way and went through all those silly motions," he said. "Is not all that is written about knights and shepherdesses really an offensive invention about them? How does one acquire the desire to stir up and analyze in such detail these pitiful effusions of the human soul... love! To give such importance to it!"

He shrugged his shoulders.

"Why go so far, Uncle?" said Alexander. "I myself feel this force of love in me and I am proud of it. It's my misfortune only that I have not met a being worthy of this love and endowed with the same power..."

"The power of love!" repeated Pyotr Ivanych. "That's the same thing as saying the power of weakness."

"It's not a matter for you, Pyotr Ivanych," remarked Lizaveta Alexandrovna. "You don't want to believe in the existence of such love even in others..."

"But you? Do you really believe in it?" asked Pyotr Ivanych, walking up to her. "No, really, you're joking! He's still a child and does not know either himself or others, but it would be shameful for you! Could you really respect a man if he loved that way?... Do people love like that?..."

Lizaveta Alexandrovna let go her work. "How?" she asked quietly, taking him by the hands and drawing him to her.

Pyotr Ivanych quietly freed his hands from hers and unobtrusively pointed to Alexander, who stood at the window with his back to them, and he again began to pace about in the room. "How!" he said, "as if you'd never heard how people love!..."

"They do love!" she repeated thoughtfully, and slowly set about her work again.

The silence lasted about a quarter of an hour. Pyotr Ivanych broke it first.

"What are you doing now?" he asked his nephew.

"Why... nothing."

"Too little. Well, do you read at least?"

"Yes..."

"What, then?"

"Krylov's fables."[8]

"A good book; but not just that?"

"Only that now. Heavens, what portraits of people! How true to life!"

"You're somehow angry at people. Could your love for that—what's her name?—have made you this way?..."

"Oh! I'd even forgotten about that stupidity. I recently passed through those places where I was so happy and suffered so much, I thought the recollections would cause my heart to burst."

"Well, did it?"

"I saw the villa, the garden and the garden gate, but my heart didn't even beat faster."

"Well, see; I told you so. Then why do you dislike people so?"

"Why! For their baseness, their smallness of spirit... My God! When you think what base deeds are perpetuated, where nature sowed such wonderful seed..."

"What does it matter to you? Do you want to reform people!"

"What does it matter! Do you think I don't get splashed with that dirt in which people bathe? You know what happened to me—and after all that how can I not hate, not disdain people!"

"What happened to you?"

"Betrayal in love, a kind of coarse, cold forgetfulness in friendship... Yes, and in general, it's disgusting, repulsive to look at people and live with them. All their thoughts, words, doings—everything is founded on sand. Today they're running toward one goal, hurrying, knocking each other over, doing mean tricks, flattering, abasing themselves, plotting intrigues, but tomorrow they've forgotten about yesterday and are running after something else. Today they're enthusiastic about one thing, tomorrow they rail against it; today they're warm and tender, tomorrow cold... Yes, however you look at it, life is terrible, repulsive! And people!..."

Pyotr Ivanych, sitting in his armchair, was about to doze off again.

"Pyotr Ivanych!" said Lizaveta Alexandrovna, giving him a quiet push.

"You're disheartened, that's all! You need to be busy with something," said Pyotr Ivanych, wiping his eyes, "then you won't inveigh against people for nothing. In what way are your friends bad? There are always decent people."

"Yes! Whomever you take, you've got hold of some animal out of Krylov's fables," said Alexander.

"The Khozarovs, for example?"

"A whole family of animals!" interrupted Alexander. "One will heap flattery upon you to your face, he'll caress you, but behind your back... I heard what he says about me... Another will sob with you today over your injury, but tomorrow he'll begin sobbing with the offender. Today he'll laugh with you at somebody else, but tomorrow will laugh at you with that somebody... it's disgusting!"

"And the Lunins?"

"They are fine specimens also. He is the very image of the ass the nightingale flew away from to the ends of the earth. And she looks at you like a kind fox..."

"What would you say about the Sonins?"

"Well, there's nothing good to say. Sonin will always give good advice when you've escaped misfortune, but try to get his help in time of need... Then he'll let you go home without supper, as the fox did the wolf. Do you remember how he played up to you when he was looking for a job under your protection? But now listen to what he says about you..."

"You don't like Volochkov?"

"A contemptible and, in addition, mean animal..." Alexander even spit.

"Well, you've dispatched them all!" Pyotr Ivayych remarked.

"What have I to expect from people?" continued Alexander.

"Altogether, friendship and love and a field-marshal's rank and money... So, now finish this portrait gallery with ours: what kind of beasts are my wife and I?"

Alexander said nothing in response, but an expression of subtle, hardly noticeable irony flickered on his face. He smiled. Neither the expression nor the smile escaped Pyotr Ivanych. He exchanged glances with his wife, who lowered her gaze.

"Well, and what kind of beast are you yourself?" asked Pyotr Ivanych.

"I haven't done harm to people!" Alexander pronounced judgment with dignity. "I did everything I should in relation to them... I had a loving heart. I opened my arms in wide embrace to people and what did they do?"

"Hear how ridiculously he talks!" remarked Pyotr Ivanych, turning to his wife.

"Everything's ridiculous to you!" she answered.

"And I myself did not ask of people," Alexander continued, "either heroic good deeds or magnanimity or self-sacrifice... I asked only what was due, owed me by all rights..."

"So you're right! You came out of the water quite dry. Wait, I'll take you out into fresh water..."

Lizaveta Alexandrovna noticed that her husband had begun speaking in a severe tone and was alarmed.

"Pyotr Ivanych!" she whispered, "stop..."

"No, let him listen to the truth. I'll be finished in a minute. Tell me, please, Alexander, when you branded your friends just now as ne'er-do-wells and fools, was there no slight ripple in your heart of something like a pang of conscience?"

"For what, Uncle?"

"For the reason that you were cordially welcomed for several years running at the houses of these beasts. Let's assume that they acted slyly, and plotted intrigue against those from whom they could get something. But they had nothing to gain from you. Why did they constantly invite you to their house, why were they friendly to you?... It's not kind of you, Alexander!" Pyotr Ivanych added seriously. "Another man would be silent for that alone, even if he knew they were guilty of certain peccadillos!"

Alexander turned completely red.

"I would attribute their attentions to me to your recommendation," he answered, but added now without his pose of dignity and quite humbly, "Besides, that is good social manners..."

"All right, let's take manners outside high society... I was trying to prove to you, only I don't know whether I really proved it, that you were unjust to your Sashenka, was it?... whatever her name. For a year and a half you were at their house as if it were your own, you lived there from morning to night, and, besides, you were loved by this *contemptible slut*, as you call her. It seems she doesn't deserve contempt..."

"But why did she betray me?"

"You mean, fall in love with somebody else? We've gone over that enough. Do you really think that if she had gone on loving you, you wouldn't have fallen out of love with her?"

"I? Never."

"Why then you don't understand anything. Let's go on. You say you have no friends, but I've always thought you have three!"

"Three?" exclaimed Alexander. "Once I had one, but he..."

"Three," persistently repeated Pyotr Ivanych. "The first, let's begin by seniority, that *one*. A different friend who hadn't seen you for several years would have turned away from you when he met you. But he invited you to his house. And when you came with a sour look, he kept asking sympathetically if you didn't need something and began offering you his services and help, and, I'm convinced, would have given you even money—yes! And in our time money is the touchstone to test more than feeling... Introduce me to him; I see him as a decent fellow... But according to you, he's a villain."

Alexander stood with lowered head.

"So, what do you think, who's your second friend?" asked Pyotr Ivanych.

"Who?" said Alexander, amazed. "Why no one..."

"Have you no conscience!" interrupted Pyotr Ivanych. "Huh? Liza, he doesn't even blush! And I, how do I rate with you, may I ask!"

"You... you're a relative."

"A fine title! I thought I was more. Not kind, Alexander. That's a character trait which even in grade-school copy books is called *vile*, and such as you don't find even in Krylov."

"But you always pushed me away..." Alexander said shyly, not raising his eyes.

"Yes, when you wanted to embrace."

"You laughed at me, at feeling..."

"And why, to what end?" asked Pyotr Ivanych.

"You watched my every step."

"Ah! I agree! I kept my eye on you! Find yourself such a tutor! Why did I bother? I could even add a bit more, but that would seem like a vulgar reproach..."

"Uncle!" said Alexander, going toward him and extending both hands.

"Stay where you are; I haven't finished yet!" Pyotr Ivanych said coldly. "Your third and best friend I hope you'll name yourself..."

Alexander again looked at him and appeared to ask, "So where is he?" Pyotr Ivanych pointed to his wife. "There she is!"

"Pyotr Ivanych," interrupted Lizaveta Alexandrovna. "Don't try to be clever, for Heaven's sake, let him be..."

"No, don't interfere."

"I can appreciate my aunt's friendship," mumbled Alexander inaudibly.

"No, you can't; if you could, you wouldn't be looking at the ceiling to find a friend, but would point to her. If you truly felt her friendship, out of respect for her merits you wouldn't think ill of people. She alone should redeem in your eyes the faults of others. Who dried your tears and whimpered along with you? Who sympathized with your every bit of nonsense, and what sympathy! You may well think only a mother could take to heart so warmly everything related to you, and even a mother couldn't have. If you had felt her sympathy, you wouldn't have smiled ironically just now; you would have seen that she is no fox, or wolf, but that here is a woman who loves you like your own sister..."

"Oh, dear Aunt!" said Alexander, confounded and completely disconcerted by this reproach, "You don't think, I hope, that I don't value you and consider you a shining exception to the crowd? Goodness, goodness! I swear..."

"I believe you, I believe you, Alexander!" she answered. "Don't listen to Pyotr Ivanych. He's making mountains out of molehills—glad of a chance to show off his intelligence. For Heaven's sake, stop, Pyotr Ivanych."

"Right away, I'll finish right away—*just one last word!* You said you fulfill everything demanded of you by your obligations to others?"

Alexander couldn't say a word and did not raise his eyes.

"So, tell me do you love your mother?"

Alexander suddenly came alive. "What a question? " he said. "Whom am I to love after this? I adore her, I'd give my life for her..."

"Good. Therefore you know that she lives, breathes only through you, that every joy and grief of yours is a joy and grief for her. She counts time now not by months, not weeks, but by news about you and from you... Tell me, how long is it since you wrote to her?"

Alexander started. "Around three weeks," he muttered.

"No. Four months! What name should I call such conduct by? Well, what kind of beast are you? Perhaps you don't name it because Krylov doesn't have one."

"And has something happened?" Alexander suddenly asked with fear.

"Why this, the old woman is sick with grief."

"Really? Oh, Heavens! Heavens!"

"Not so! It's not so!" said Lizaveta Alexandrovna, and immediately ran to the desk and pulled out a letter, which she gave to Alexander. "She's not sick, but much grieved."

"You spoil him, Liza," said Pyotr Ivanych.

"And you are immoderately severe. There were certain difficulties which distracted Alexander for a time..."

"To forget his mother for some girl—a fine difficulty!"

"Enough, for Heaven's sake!" she said persuasively and pointed to her nephew.

After reading his mother's letter, Alexander covered his face with it. "Don't interrupt Uncle, dear Aunt. Let him thunder his reproaches. I've deserved worse. I'm a monster!" he said, making faces of desperation.

"Come, don't worry, Alexander!" said Pyotr Ivanych, there are lots of such monsters. You got carried away by some stupidity and forgot about your mother. That's natural; love for one's mother is a calm feeling. You're all she has in the world—that's why it's natural for her to be distressed. There's nothing here worth putting you to death for yet. I'll only say in the words of your favorite author:

> Rather than trying to evaluate others,
> Better turn your fox eye on yourself!

And better be lenient toward the weaknesses of others. That's the kind of rule without which there's no living either for oneself or others. That's all. Now I shall go take a nap."

"Uncle! Are you angry?" said Alexander in a voice of deep repentance.

"Where did you get that idea? Why would I roil up my blood? I only wanted to play the part of the bear in the fable of the martin and the mirror. I played it artfully, didn't I? Didn't I, Liza?"

He wanted to kiss her in passing, but she turned away.

"It seems I've done exactly what you asked," added Pyotr Ivanych, "don't you think? Oh! I forgot one thing... In what state is your heart Alexander?" he asked.

Alexander remained silent.

"Do you need money?" again asked Pyotr Ivanych.

"No, Uncle..."

"He'll never ask!" said Pyotr Ivanych, closing the door after him.

"What will Uncle think of me?" asked Alexander after a moment's silence.

"The same as before," answered Lizaveta Alexandrovna. "Do you think he told you all that sincerely from the heart?"

"What do you mean?"

"No! Believe me, he wanted to show off. Do you see now he did all that according to plan? Arranged his argument in order: first the weak ones, then stronger ones; at first he brought out the reason for your bad opinion of people... and then... all planned! Now he's quite forgotten, I think."

"What intelligence! What a knowledge of life, of people, self-control!"

"Yes, much intelligence and too much self-control," said Lizaveta Alexandrovna thoughtfully "but..."

"But you, dear Aunt, will you stop respecting me? Be sure, only such shattering experiences as I've been through could distract me... Heavens, poor dear Mama!"

Lizaveta Alexandrovna gave him her hand.

"I, Alexander, shall not cease respecting the heart in you," she said. "It's feeling that lures you even into your errors, and so I always pardon them."

"Oh, dear Aunt! you're an ideal woman!"

"Simply a woman."

His uncle's scolding had quite a strong effect on Alexander. Then and there, sitting with his aunt, he plunged into tormenting thoughts. It seemed that the calm she had so artfully labored to instil in his heart suddenly deserted him. She waited in vain for some mean diatribe or other, she herself invited him to acid remarks and diligently exposed Pyotr Ivanych to epigrams, but Alexander was deaf and dumb. It was as if a tub of cold water had been poured on him.

"What is the matter? Why are you like this?" his aunt asked him.

"It's just, dear Aunt, that my spirits are low. Uncle helped me to understand myself; he explained things very well!"

"Don't listen to him; he sometimes says what isn't so."

"No, don't comfort me. I am disgusted with myself. I scorned and hated people, and now myself too. You can hide from people, but where do you run away from yourself? So everything, is worthless: all these blessings, all the little things of life, and people and oneself..."

"Alas, this Pyotr Ivanych!" exclaimed Lizaveta Alexandrovna with a deep sigh. "He would bring melancholy to whomever you will!"

"Only one negative comfort indeed is left me, that I did not deceive or betray anyone in love or friendship..."

"They weren't capable of esteeming you," said his aunt, "but be sure, you'll find a heart that will; I'll guarantee you. You're still so young. Forget all this, get back to work—you have talent; write... Are you writing anything now?"

"No."

"Write something."

"I'm afraid, dear Aunt..."

"Don't listen to Pyotr Ivanych. Discuss politics, agronomics, whatever you will with him, only not poetry. He'll never tell you the truth about that. The public will esteem you—you'll see... So you will write?"

"All right."

"You'll begin soon?"

"As soon as I can. This is the only hope left me now."

Pyotr Ivanych, quite rested, joined them, fully dressed with his hat in his hands. He too advised Alexander to get back to his civil service work and his articles on agriculture for the magazine

"I shall try, Uncle," answered Alexander, "but, look, I promised Aunt..."

Lizaveta Alexandrovna signaled to him not to tell, but Pyotr Ivanych noticed.

"What? What did you promise?" he asked.

"To bring some new music," she answered.

"No, not so. What is it, Alexander?"

"To write a story, or something like that..."

"You haven't yet given up belles-lettres?" said Pyotr Ivanych, picking lint from his clothes. "And you, Liza, are leading him astray—to no purpose!"

"I don't have the right to give it up," remarked Alexander.

"And who forbids you?"

"Why should I arbitrarily and ungratefully cast aside the honorable destiny to which I've been called? One bright hope has remained for me in life and should I destroy that too? If I annihilate what is given to me from on high, then I annihilate myself as well..."

"So what sort of thing has been given to you; explain, please?"

"That, Uncle, I can't explain to you. You have to understand yourself. Has the hair of your head been made to stand on end by anything but a comb?"

"No!" said Pyotr Ivanych.

"Well, so you see. Have passions raged in you, has your imagination stormed and created elegant spirits who begged to be incarnate? Has your heart beat in a special rhythm?"

"Barbarous, barbarous! So, what then?" asked Pyotr Ivanych.

"Why this, that it's impossible to explain to someone to whom this has never happened why one wants to write when some restless spirit insists both day and night, both sleeping and waking: write, write..."

"But look, you're not able to write."

"Enough, Pyotr Ivanych. You can't write, but why prevent others?" said Lizaveta Alexandrovna.

"Pardon me, Uncle, if I remark that you're no judge of this matter."

"Who is a judge? She?" Pyotr Ivanych pointed to his wife. "Her advice is slanted toward a purpose, and you believe her," he added.

"Yes, and you yourself, when I first came here, advised me to write, to try out my potential..."

"So, what then. You tried—since nothing came of it, you should give it up."

"You mean you never found in my work either a viable idea or a successful verse?"

"Of course I found some! You're not stupid. How is one not to find a successful idea in several pounds of work by a person who is not stupid? That's not talent, though, that's intelligence."

"Oh, dear!" said Lizaveta Alexandrovna, vexedly turning around on her chair.

"But the beating of the heart, the storm, the sweet languor and other experiences of the sort—who hasn't had them?"

"Yes, first of all, not you, I think!" remarked his wife.

"Well, indeed! Don't you remember, I formerly used to be enthusiastic..."

"About what? I don't remember."

"Everyone experiences these things," Pyotr Ivanych continued, turning to his nephew. "Who is not touched by the quiet or then by the darkness of the night, or perhaps the rustle of leaves in a grove, by a garden, a pond, the sea? If only artists felt this, then there'd be no one to understand them. But to express all these sensations in one's work—that's another business. Talent is needed and that, it seems, you don't have. One doesn't hide that; it shines in every line, in every stroke of the brush..."

"Pyotr Ivanych! It's time for you to be on your way," said Lizaveta Alexandrovna.

"Right away... You want to distinguish yourself," he continued. "You have what it takes to distinguish yourself. The magazine editor praises you, says your articles on agriculture are excellently worked up; there is thought in them—everything shows, he says, the learned creator, not the mere craftsman. I was glad; 'Indeed!' I thought, 'all Aduyevs apparently are not without a good head!'—you see, I too have my self-esteem! You can distinguish yourself in the civil service and acquire the renown of a writer..."

"Fine renown, a writer about manure."

"Everyone to his own taste. One is destined to soar in space, and another to dig in manure and find treasure there. I don't understand why one should neglect a modest destiny? It too has its poetry. If you had completed your term of service, you'd have acquired money by your labor, have married advantageously like most people... I don't understand, what more do you want? One's duty done, one's life lived with honor, industriously—here's the stuff of happiness, in my opinion, that is. Here am I a privy councillor by rank, a factory owner by craft; if you were to offer me in exchange the title of poet laureate, by God, I wouldn't take it!"

"Listen, Pyotr Ivanych, really you'll be late! " interrupted Lizaveta Alexandrovna, "it's almost ten o'clock."

"Indeed, it's time. Well, goodbye. And so they consider themselves, God knows why, unusual people," muttered Pyotr Ivanych in parting.

II

When Alexander got back home from his uncle's, he sat down in an armchair and began to think. He recalled the whole conversation with his uncle and aunt and held a strict accounting with himself.

How had he let himself at his age hate and scorn people, how had he examined and condemned their worthlessness, triviality, weakness, picked over each and every one of his friends, yet forgotten to go over himself. What blindness! And his uncle had given him a lesson like a schoolboy, gone over him with a fine-tooth comb—and in front of a woman as well—so that he might take a thorough look at himself! How his uncle must have grown that evening in his wife's eyes! That's nothing, perhaps, that's the way it should be; only he had gained at Alexander's expense. His uncle indisputably had the upper hand over him everywhere and in everything.

"What good, then," he thought, "is superiority of youth, freshness, fire of mind and feelings, when a man of only a bit of experience, with a hard heart and without energy, destroys you at every turn—so effortlessly, in passing. When would the contest be equal and when would the advantage finally be on his side? Yet on his side, it seems, he had both talent and a superfluity of spiritual strength... still his uncle appeared a giant alongside him. With what assurance he argues, how easily he pushes aside every counterargument, and makes his point, joking, with a yawn, laughing at feeling, at heartfelt outpourings of friendship and love, laughing, in a word, at everything which the elderly are accustomed to envy in the young."

Going over all this in his mind, Alexander blushed for shame. He vowed to watch himself severely and at the first chance, destroy his uncle, prove to him that no experience can replace gifts from above, that, however he, Pyotr Ivanych, might predict, from this minute on not one of his cold methodical prophecies would come true. Alexander himself would find his way and walk it, no longer with hesitant, but with firm and measured steps. He was not the same as he had been three years ago. He had penetrated at a glance hidden secrets of the heart, analyzed the play of passions, acquired for himself the secret of life, of course, not without sufferings, but in return he had steeled himself forever against their recurrence. The future was clear to him. He got up, inspired to move boldly ahead—he wasn't a child but a grown man! His uncle would see and consequently take his turn in the role of pitiful schoolboy before Alexander, the experienced master. He would realize to his surprise that there is another life, other distinctions, another happiness beside the pitiful career he had chosen for himself and which he was foisting on Alexander, perhaps out of envy! Just one more, one more noble effort—and an end to their contest!

Alexander brightened. He began again to create a special world, a little more mature than the first. His aunt supported this inclination in him, but in secret, when Pyotr Ivanych slept, or was away at his factory or the English Club.

She questioned Alexander about his work. And how even this pleased him. He told her the plan of his literary efforts and sometimes, as if requesting advice, asked her approval.

She often argued with him, but more often agreed.

Alexander clung to this work as to a last hope. "Beyond this," he said to his aunt, "there is, you see, nothing; then there's the naked steppe without water or green, only darkness, desert—what will life be then? Nothing but to lie down in the grave!" And he worked untiringly.

Sometimes he recalled his dead love; he would get excited—reach for his pen and write a touching elegy. Another time bile would flood his heart and raise from the depths the hatred and contempt for people which had of late raged there—lo, and some energetic verse would be born. At the same time he was planning and writing a story. He expended on it much thought, feeling, material labor and about half a year's time. Then at last the story was ready, proofread, and the final copy made. His aunt was enthusiastic.

The action in this story did not occur in America this time, but somewhere in a small town in Tambov. The characters were ordinary people: gossips, liars, and all kinds of tyrants in dress coats—and traitresses in corsets and hats. Everything was correct and proper.

"I think, dear Aunt, I can show this to Uncle, don't you?"

"Yes, yes, of course," she replied. "But, then again... wouldn't it be better to send it to be published now without showing it to him? He's always against these things, he'll say something... You know, it will seem childish to him."

"No, it's better to show him!" answered Alexander. "With your favorable opinion and my own confidence I fear no one, and meanwhile let him see..."

They showed it. Upon seeing the copybook, Pyotr Ivanych frowned a little and shook his head. "What's this, did you both write it?" he asked. "There's certainly a lot here. And in such a small hand, why do you write so much!"

"Wait with your headshaking," his wife answered, "and listen first. Read it to us, Alexander. And you listen attentively, don't doze off and then give us your condemnation. It's easy to find blemishes everywhere if you want to look for them. Be considerate."

"No, what for? Only be just," interrupted Alexander.

"There's nothing else to do, I'll hear you out," said Pyotr Ivanych with a sigh.

"Only on the condition, first, that you don't read right after dinner, in which case I don't guarantee I won't fall asleep. Don't take that to be your fault, Alexander; no matter what might be read after dinner, I'm always sleepy. My second condition is that if it's something viable, I shall speak my mind, and if not, I shall only be silent, and you do then as you wish."

The reading began. Pyotr Ivanych didn't doze even once, but listened without averting his gaze from Alexander, he even hardly blinked and twice nodded his head approvingly.

"You see!" his wife said half-aloud to her husband, "I told you so."

He nodded to her too.

They read on two successive evenings. The first evening after the reading Pyotr Ivanych to his wife's amazement foretold how everything in the story would develop.

"How do you know?" she asked.

"That's easy! The idea isn't new—it's been done a thousand times. No need to read further, but let's see how it's developed in his version."

The next evening when Alexander was reading the last page, Pyotr Ivanych rang and the servant entered.

"Help me dress," he said. "Pardon me for interrupting, Alexander. I'm in a hurry. I shall be late for whist at the club."

Alexander finished. Pyotr Ivanych quickly got up to go.

"Well, goodbye!" he said to his wife and Alexander. "I shan't come back here before going out."

"Stop! Stop!" called his wife. "Won't you say anything about the story?"

"By agreement I mustn't!" he answered and wanted to go.

"That's obstinacy," she said. "Oh, he's obstinate—I know him. Pay no attention, Alexander."

"This is ill will! " thought Alexander. "He wants to trample me in the mud, drag me down into his world. All the same, he's an intelligent civil servant and industrialist, but nothing more, while I'm a poet..."

"This is too much, Pyotr Ivanych!" his wife began, almost in tears. Please say something. I saw you nodding your head in approval; therefore you liked it. You don't want to admit it only out of obstinacy. How hard it is to admit that you like the story! We're too intelligent for that. Admit that it's good."

"I nodded my head because from this story too you can see that Alexander is intelligent, but he didn't act intelligently in writing it."

"But, Uncle, a judgment of this sort..."

"Listen, you won't believe me, no use arguing. Let's choose an intermediary. Look what I'll even do so as to finish this between us once and for all. I'll name myself the author of this story and send it off to my friend, editor of a magazine; let us see what he'll say. You know him and doubtless will trust his judgment. He's an experienced person."

Pyotr Ivanych sat down at the table and quickly wrote several lines, then handed the letter over to Alexander: "In my old age I'm having a try at being an author," he wrote. "What's to be done; the desire to be famous comes over you—and there you are—you've gone crazy! So I've turned out the story herewith enclosed. Look through it, and if it's any good, then publish it in your magazine, of course for money; you know I don't like to work for nothing. You'll be surprised and not believe me, but I'm allowing you even to sign it with my last name; therefore, I'm not lying."

Confident of a favorable reaction to the story, Alexander calmly awaited the answer. He was even glad his uncle had mentioned money in his note. "Very, very wise," he thought. "Mama complains that grain is selling cheap; I daresay she won't be sending money soon. So it will be nice to get a thousand or so."

Nonetheless, some three weeks passed, all the time without an answer. Then finally one morning a big package and a letter came for Pyotr Ivanych.

"Ah! They've sent it back!" he said, slyly glancing at his wife.

He did not open the note and did not show it to his wife, no matter how she begged. That same day in the evening before going to the club, he set off for his nephew's. The door was not closed. He entered. Evsei was snoring, stretched out diagonally on the floor in the vestibule. The wick was in terrible need of snuffing; it hung down from the candléholder. He looked into the other room; it was dark.

"Oh, country life!" muttered Pyotr Ivanych.

He poked Evsei awake, pointed to the door and the candle and threatened with his stick. In the third room Alexander was sitting at his desk, his arms on the desk, his head on his arms and he, too, asleep. A piece of paper lay in front of him. Pyotr Ivanych glanced at it—verse. He took the paper and read:

> "Beautiful springtime has passed.
> The magic moment of love is gone forever.
> In the sleep of the grave love slumbers
> And does not race like flame through the blood!
> On its orphaned altar
> I long ago raised up another idol,
> To him I pray... but..."

"And he's gone to sleep himself. Pray, dear fellow, don't be lazy!" Pyotr Ivanych said aloud. "Have your own verses worn you out! Why do you want another opinion? You have pronounced judgment on yourself."

"Ah!" said Alexander, stretching, "You're still against my writings! Tell me frankly, Uncle, what makes you so persistently persecute talent when you can't help admitting..."

"Yes, it's envy, Alexander. Judge for yourself: You will acquire fame, honor, even immortality, but I shall remain an obscure fellow and will have to be content with the name of a useful, hardworking person. But, look, I too am an Aduyev! Say what you will, it's hard to take! What am I? I've lived my life quietly, inconspicuously, only done my duty and have been, indeed, proud and happy with that. Isn't that a pitiful fate? When I die, that is, when I stop feeling and knowing, the *prophetic strings of the bards* will not tell of me; *distant centuries, posterity, the world* will not be filled with my name, people won't know that there once lived in the world the State Councillor Pyotr Ivanych Aduyev, and I will not be comforted by this in my coffin, if the coffin and I somehow come down to posterity intact. How different for you, when, *spreading your whirring wings,* you will fly to *the clouds,* and I'll have to comfort myself only with the knowledge that in the mass of human labors there is *a drop of my mead too,* as your favorite author says."

"Leave him out of this for Heaven's sake—what do you mean favorite author! He only ridicules his neighbors."

"Ah! ridicules! Isn't it since you found your own portrait in Krylov that you've stopped loving him? By the way! Do you know that your future fame and immortality is in my pocket? But I'd wish rather your money were there; that's more like it."

"What fame? "

"Why the answer to my note."

"Oh dear! Let me have it right away for Heaven's sake. What does he say?"

"I haven't read it; read it yourself and aloud."

"And you could bear it?"

"Why, what difference is it to me?"

"How's that! Am I not your nephew by blood? How could you not be curious? What frigidity! This is egoism, Uncle!"

"Perhaps; I don't rule it out. But then, I know what's in it. So read it!"

Alexander began to read loudly, and Pyotr Ivanych beat time with his cane against his boots. The note contained the following:

"What kind of mystification is this, my dearest Pyotr Ivanych? You writing stories! Now who will believe that of you? And you meant to hoodwink me, old coot, you! If it's even true—which God forbid—if you had snatched your pen away for a time from writing the literally precious business letters, each line of which is worth, of course, many a gold coin, and if giving up your respected rendering of accounts, you had produced the story I have before me, then I would tell you that the fragile products of your china factory are much more solid than this piece of work."

The volume of Alexander's voice suddenly grew less. "But I reject such an offensive suspicion of you," he continued shyly and quietly.

"I can't hear you, Alexander; speak louder!" said Pyotr Ivanych.

Alexander continued in a quiet voice: "Out of sympathy with the author of the story you probably want to know my opinion. Here it is: The author must be a young man. He's not stupid, but somehow pathologically angry at the whole world. In what an enraged, furious mood he writes! Probably he's disappointed. What a pity that by reason of a false view of life many talents in this country are lost in fruitless dreams, vain strivings toward goals for which they lack the gifts."

Alexander stopped and took a deep breath. Pyotr Ivanych lit a cigar and blew a smoke ring. His face, as usual, expressed complete calm.

In a hollow, hardly audible voice Alexander went on reading: "Pride, day-dreaming, the immature development of emotional tendencies, the stultification of the mind with the inevitable consequence—indolence—these are the causes of this evil. Learning, labor, a practical job—these are the remedies which can sober up our idle, sick young people."

"The whole thing could have been explained in three lines," said Pyotr Ivanych, looking at his watch, "but he has written a whole dissertation in a friendly letter. Isn't he the pedant, though? Should we read further, Alexander? Let it be, it's boring. I have something to talk to you about..."

"No, Uncle, allow me, I had better empty the cup altogether; I'll read it to the end."

"Read on to your heart's content!"

"This unfortunate direction of mental capacities," Alexander read, "shows in every line of the story you've sent me. Tell your protégé that, first of all, a writer only writes sensibly when he's not under the influence of personal enthusiasms and preferences. He must view life and people in general with a calm and bright eye—otherwise he'll express only his own *ego*, which interests no one. This failing strongly predominates in the story. The second and main condition—please don't tell this to the author out of pity for his youth and an author's pride, the most unruly of all forms of pride, as everyone knows—talent is essential and there isn't even a trace of it here. True, the language is everywhere correct and pure; the author even writes with style..." Alexander finished with difficulty.

"Well, it's none too soon!" said Pyotr Ivanych, "God knows he's talked our heads off! About the rest you and I shall decide without him."

Alexander's hands dropped to his sides. Silent, like a man stunned by an unexpected blow, he looked with troubled eyes straight at the wall. Pyotr Ivanych took the letter from him and read the following P.S.: "If you nevertheless want to get this story into our magazine—all right, for your sake I'll put it in in the summer when few people read, but it's impossible even to think of remuneration."

"Well, Alexander, how do you feel?" asked Pyotr Ivanych.

"Calmer than one might expect," answered Alexander with effort. "I feel like someone who's been deceived in everything."

"No, like a person who has deceived himself and further wanted to deceive others too..."

Alexander did not hear this objection.

"Is this really a dream?... and has this too betrayed me?..." he whispered. "A bitter loss! How am I to avoid the habit of beginning new self-deceptions! But I don't understand why all these insuperable impulses to creativity were given to me?..."

"That's it! You were given the impulses, but clearly they forgot to give you the creativity itself," said Pyotr Ivanych. "I told you!"

Alexander answered with a sigh and thought for a moment. Then suddenly with great energy he hurriedly opened all the desk drawers. He pulled out several notebooks, little sheets of paper and scraps and began bitterly throwing them into the fire.

"Don't forget this one!" said Pyotr Ivanych, pushing toward him a sheet of unfinished verses that lay on the desk.

"Give me that too!" said Alexander with despair, throwing the verses into the fireplace.

"Isn't there something more? Search well," asked Pyotr Ivanych, looking around. "For once you'd be doing the wise thing. What's that bundle on the cabinet?"

"That too into the fire!" said Alexander, seizing it. "Those are articles about agriculture."

"Don't, don't burn them! Give them to me!" said Pyotr Ivanych, reaching out his hand. "Those are not nonsense."

Alexander didn't listen. "No," he said with anger. "If I have lost my noble creativity in the field of literature, I don't want hack work. Fate won't crush me with that!" The bundle too flew into the fireplace.

"Too bad!" remarked Pyotr Ivanych and meanwhile poked with his cane in the basket under the desk to see whether there was something more to throw into the fire.

"So what shall we do with the story, Alexander? It's in my apartment."

"Don't you need to paper any screens?"

"No, not now. Shouldn't I send for it? Evsei! He's fallen asleep again. Watch out, or they'll steal my overcoat under your nose! Go down quickly to my place, ask Vasily there for the thick notebook that's in the cabinet on the desk and bring it here."

Alexander sat, leaning on his arm and looked into the fireplace. The notebook was brought in. Alexander stared a while at the fruit of a halfyear's work and was plunged in thought. Pyotr Ivanych noticed this.

"Come, have done, Alexander," he said, "then let's talk of something else."

"This goes there too!" cried Alexander, flinging the notebook into the stove.

Both began watching it ignite, Pyotr Ivanych apparently with pleasure, Alexander with sadness, almost with tears. Now the uppermost sheet rustled and rose, as if an unseen hand were turning the page; its edges curled, it blackened, then curled and suddenly burst into flame. After it another, a third quickly caught fire and then suddenly several arose and a bunch took fire, but the next page under them still shone white, then two seconds later it too began to blacken at the edges.

Alexander, however, managed to read the words "Chapter III." He remembered what was in that chapter and began to feel sorry about it. He got up from his chair and seized the tongs so as to save the remains of his work. "Maybe, still..." whispered hope...

"Wait, I'll do better with my cane," said Pyotr Ivanych, "you'll burn yourself with the tongs."

He moved the notebook into the depths of the fireplace directly onto the hot coals. Alexander stopped, undecided. The notebook was thick and did not at once yield to the action of the fire. Thick smoke rolled out from under it at first, from time to time a flame erupted from below, licked the side, left a black spot and hid again. The book could still be saved. Alexander was stretching out his hand, but at that very moment the flame lit up both his chair and Pyotr Ivanych's face, as well as the desk. The whole notebook burst into flame and a minute later went out, leaving behind it a pile of black ash, along which in certain places ran little snakes of fire. Alexander dropped the tongs.

"It's all over!" he said.

"All over!" repeated Pyotr Ivanych.

"Ooh!" Alexander uttered, "I'm free!"

"This is by now the second time I've helped you clean up the apartment," said Pyotr Ivanych. "I hope this time..."

"It's irrevocable, Uncle."

"Amen!" said his uncle, putting his hands on his shoulders. "So, Alexander, I advise you not to delay. Write at once to Ivan Ivanych and ask him to send you work in the field of agriculture. After all your stupidities you're on a hot trail; now you'll write a very intelligent piece. He's always broaching the subject: 'What about your nephew?...' he says."

Sadly Alexander shook his head. "I can't," he said. "No, I can't; it's all over."

"What are you going to do now?"

"What?" he asked and thought about it. "Now, for the time being, nothing."

"It's only in the country that they somehow manage to do nothing, but here... Why did you come here? It's incomprehensible!... Well, for the time being, enough about that. I have a favor to ask of you."

Alexander slowly raised his head a bit and looked at his uncle questioningly.

"Look, you know my partner Surkov?" Pyotr Ivanych began, moving his chair toward Alexander.

Alexander nodded.

"Yes, you sometimes dined with him at my house; but, did you manage to get an idea of what sort he is? He's a good fellow, but very shallow. His greatest weakness is women. To his misfortune, as you see, he's not bad-looking—he's blond, sleek, tall; his hair is always curled, he's heavily perfumed and dresses like a fashion plate. So he imagines that all women are mad about him—in short, a dandy! The Devil take him with all that, I wouldn't have paid any attention, but here's the trouble. He's no sooner fallen for a woman then he goes and throws money around. He dreams up surprises and presents and pretty pleasures; he launches into dandyism, begins to change his coach and horses... pure financial ruin! He's even tried courting my wife. It used to be that if I hadn't taken care of sending our servant for a theater ticket, Surkov would bring it without fail. If you had to exchange horses, get hold of something rare, get through a crowd, take a trip to look over a country place, wherever you needed to send someone for something—Surkov was as good as gold. How useful he was; you couldn't hire his like for money. Too bad! I purposely haven't interfered with him, though when he very much bothered my wife, I drove him off. So, whenever he has gone on a spending spree, his percentage hasn't been sufficient. He begins asking me for money—if he's refused, he starts talking about withdrawing from the capital. 'What do I care about your factory?' he says. 'You never have cash on hand!' If only he'd take on some floozy... But no; he's always looking for connections in society. 'I need a *high-society affair*; I can't live without love!'—isn't he an ass? He's pushing forty and can't live without love!"

Alexander remembered about himself and sadly smiled.

"He's always lying," Pyotr Ivanych went on. "I've lately investigated why he bustles about. He only wants to brag so that people talk about him, say that he has a relationship with such and such a lady, that he's been seen in the box of another lady or at the country place of another till late evening—they sat on the balcony, just the two of them—or went for a ride, let's say, with her somewhere in a solitary place in the country in a carriage, or on horseback. And meanwhile it turns out that these so-called *high-society affairs*—Devil take 'em—cost a lot more than others. So that's what he's up against, the fool!"

"What's all this leading to, Uncle?" asked Alexander "I don't see how I can help."

"Wait, you'll see. Recently a young widow returned here from abroad. Yuliya Pavlovna Tafayeva. She's quite good-looking herself. Surkov and I were friends of her husband. Tafayev died in foreign parts. Well, have you guessed?"

"I'll guess—Surkov fell in love with the widow."

"Right, he's quite mad about her! And what else?"

"What else... I don't know..."

"You're a fine one! Well, listen: Surkov has twice let it be known that he'll soon need money. I guessed right away what that meant; only I couldn't guess the wind's direction. I questioned him, what's the money for? He squirmed and squirmed, finally said he wanted to rent an apartment in the Liteiny section of the city. I tried to remember what was there—and then remembered that Tafayeva lives there, straight across from the place he had chosen. He already made a deposit. Unavoidable disaster threatens unless you help. Have you guessed?"

Alexander raised his head a bit, ran his gaze along the wall, across the ceiling, then blinked twice and began to look at his uncle, but remained silent.

Pyotr Ivanych looked at him with a smile. He terribly loved to note a lack of intelligence or intuition in someone, and then let them feel it.

"What's the matter with you, Alexander? And you even write stories!" he said.

"Oh, I've guessed, Uncle!"

"Well, thank God!"

"Surkov's asking for money, you don't have any and you want me to..." He stopped speaking.

Pyotr Ivanych began to laugh. Alexander didn't finish the sentence and looked at his uncle in amazement.

"No, not that!" said Pyotr Ivanych. "Have you really ever known me to be short of money? Just try asking when you want it; you'll see! No, it's this: through him Tafayeva reminded me of my acquaintance with her husband. I went to see her. She asked me to come often. I promised to, and said I'd bring you; so now, I hope, you've got it?"

"Me?" he repeated, staring wide-eyed at his uncle. "Yes, of course... now I've got it..." he added hastily, but hesitated on the last word.

"And what have you got?" asked Pyotr Ivanych.

"Strike me dead, Uncle, I don't understand anything! Excuse me... Maybe she has a nice house... You want me to be entertained... since I'm bored..."

"Oh, splendid! For that purpose I should start taking you around to people's houses! And thereafter I need only cover your mouth with a handkerchief to keep off the flies at night! No, it's all wrong. Here's what I mean! Get Tafayeva to fall in love with you."

Alexander suddenly raised his eyebrows and looked at his uncle, "You're joking, Uncle? That's absurd!" he said.

"When there are indeed absurdities, you make them very important, and when something is simple and natural—you call it absurd. What's absurd about it? Look closely at how absurd love itself is, a game of blood and pride... But what's the use of reasoning with you? You still believe that lovers are destined to meet, you believe in the harmony of souls!"

"Excuse me, I don't believe in anything now. But do you think you can make someone fall in love and fall in love yourself by force of will?"

"It's possible, but not for you. Never fear; I won't give you such a complicated assignment. Only here's what you do. Pay court to Tafayeva, be attentive, don't let Surkov be alone with her... In short, make him furious. Stand in his way! If he says one word, you say two; if he expresses an opinion, you refute it. Constantly keep confusing him, destroy him at every turn..."

"What for?"

"You still don't understand. Why, so that in the beginning, dear fellow, he'll go mad from jealousy and vexation, and then he'll cool down. With him the one quickly follows the other. He's conceited to the point of stupidity. Then he won't need the apartment, our capital will remain whole, our factory business will go on as usual... Well, do you understand. This will be the fifth time I've played a joke on him. Earlier when I was a bachelor and younger, I used to do it myself, or otherwise send one of my friends."

"But I don't even know her," said Alexander.

"That's the very reason that I'll take you to call on her on Wednesday. On Wednesdays some of her old acquaintances gather at her house."

"But if she reciprocates Surkov's love, then you'll agree that my favors and attentions will not just enrage him."

"Enough of that! A proper woman, having seen through a fool, will stop having anything to do with him, especially before witnesses. Her self-respect won't allow it. She'll have another man at hand, a handsomer, more intelligent man; she'll be ashamed and quickly drop the first. That's why, indeed, I chose you."

Alexander made a bow.

"Surkov isn't dangerous," his uncle continued, "but Tafayeva sees very few people, so that he can, indeed, in her small circle have the reputation of a lion and intelligent fellow. Appearance makes a big impression on women. He's good at pleasing, so they suffer him. Maybe she'll flirt with him, and he'll do the same with her... And intelligent women love having silly things done for them, especially expensive ones. But most of the time in such cases they don't love the one who loves them, but someone else. A lot of men don't want to understand this, among them Surkov—so you'll teach him this lesson."

"But Surkov probably doesn't come Wednesdays; I won't get in his way on Wednesday, and on other days how am I to do it?"

"I'm always instructing you! You flatter her, pretend to be in love a little—after the second time she'll invite you not on a Wednesday, but on Thursday or Friday. You double your attentions, and then I'll put her in the mood a little, hint as if, indeed, you'd fallen... As far as I can tell, it seems she's... the emotional sort... probably with weak nerves... I think she's also not averse to sympathy... outpourings..."

"How is it possible?" Alexander asked pensively. "If I could fall in love again—then yes. But I can't... it won't work."

"On the contrary, this way it will. If you fell in love you couldn't pretend. She'd notice at once and would start making fools of you both. But this way... just so you make Surkov furious. For sure, I know him like my five fingers. As soon as he sees he's having no luck, he won't start wasting money for nothing, and that's all I need, indeed... Listen, Alexander, it's very important for me. If you accomplish it, do you remember the two vases you liked at the factory?—they're yours. Only you buy the pedestal for them yourself."

"Oh, Uncle, do you really imagine that I..."

"Well, why, indeed, would you trouble yourself for nothing, waste your time? Fine! Never mind! The vases are very beautiful. In our time people don't do anything for free. When I do something for you, offer me a present—I'll take it."

"It's a strange assignment!" said Alexander indecisively.

"I hope you won't refuse to do this for me. I too am ready to do what I can for you. When you need money, turn to me... So, on Wednesday! This business will take a month, two at the most. I'll tell you when it's no longer necessary; then you'll quit."

"Pardon, Uncle. I'm willing, only it's strange... I don't guarantee success... If I could fall in love myself, then... but this way, no..."

"And it's a very good thing you can't, or else you'd spoil the whole thing. I myself guarantee success. Goodbye!"

He left, and Alexander still sat for a long time at the fireplace near the beloved ashes.

When Pyotr Ivanych returned home, his wife asked: "What about Alexander, what about his story, will he be writing?"

"No, I've cured him for good."

Aduyev told her the content of the letter he had received with the story and about their burning everything.

"You are without pity, Pyotr Ivanych!" said Lizaveta Alexandrovna, "or else you can't do anything properly, no matter what you undertake."

"Did you do well by constraining him to muck up paper! Do you think he has talent?"

"No."

Pyotr Ivanych looked at her with amazement. "So, why did you..."

"And you still haven't understood, haven't guessed?"

He was silent and couldn't help remembering his scene with Alexander. "What didn't I understand? It's very clear!" he said, looking straight at her.

"Tell me, then."

"That... that... you wanted to teach him a lesson... only another way, more gently in your own way..."

"He doesn't understand, though he's an intelligent person... Why all this time has he been cheerful, healthy, almost happy? Because he had hope. So I supported this hope. Now do you see?"

"So that means you were slyly deceiving him the whole time?"

"I think that's allowable. And what did you do to him? You're not at all sorry for him; you took away his last hope."

"That's enough! What last hope—a lot more stupidities still lay ahead."

"What will he do now? Will he go around hanging his head again?"

"No, he won't, he won't get to that; I've assigned him a task."

"What? Again some translation or other about potatoes? Do you think that can absorb a young person and especially a fiery and exalted one? Under your care only the mind would be busy."

"No, my dear, not about potatoes, but something to do with the factory."

III

Wednesday came round. In Yuliya Pavlovna's drawing room some twelve or fifteen guests assembled. Four young ladies, two foreigners with beards, the hostess' friends from abroad and one officer formed a small circle.

An old man sat apart from them in an armchair, a retired army man, apparently, with two tufts of gray hair under his nose and numerous ribbons in his buttonhole. He was discussing the forthcoming land leases with an elderly man.

In another room an old lady and two men were playing cards. A very young lady sat at the piano while another was chatting there with a student.

The Aduyevs arrived. Not many people could enter a room with such ease and dignity as Pyotr Ivanych. Alexander followed him with a kind of reluctance.

What a difference between them: one a whole head taller, well-built, robust, a man of a strong healthy nature with self-assurance in his eyes and manners. But no one could guess Pyotr Ivanych's thoughts or character either from a single glance or movement or word—everything within him was so concealed by his manners and the art of self-control. His gestures and his glances both seemed calculated. His pale, calm expression showed that the slightest outburst of passion in this man came under the despotic rule of his mind, that his heart beat or didn't beat by dictate of his head.

On the other hand, everything in Alexander pointed to a weak and gentle constitution, that is, the changeable expression of his face, and a kind of laziness or slowness and unevenness of movement and the cloudy glance which would at once show what feeling troubled his heart or what thought flickered in his head. He was of medium height, but thin and pale—not by nature like Pyotr Ivanych, but as a result of his constant emotional agitation. The hair on his head and cheeks had not grown thick like his uncle's, but drooped down over his temples and the back of his neck in long, thin, but unusually soft, silky and light locks with a beautiful wave.

The uncle introduced his nephew. "But isn't my friend Surkov here?" Pyotr Ivanych asked, looking about with surprise. "He's forgotten you."

"Oh, no! I'm very grateful to him," the hostess answered. "He comes to call on me. You know, except for friends of my late husband, I see almost no one."

"But where is he?"

"He'll be here shortly. Imagine, he gave his word to get me and my cousin

without fail a box for tomorrow at the theater when, they say, none is to be had...
He went for them just now."

"And he'll get them. I'll guarantee he will; he's a genius at that. He always gets
them for me when neither friends nor influence helps. Where he gets them and
for how much money—that's his secret."

Surkov, indeed, arrived. His dress was in the latest style, but every pleat and
every detail sharply expressed his ambition to be fashionable, to surpass all
dandys, and even fashion itself. If, for example, open frockcoats were in style,
then his frockcoat was opened up to the point of resembling a bird's spread
wings. If turned-back collars were being worn, he ordered himself such a collar
that in his frockcoat he looked like a criminal seized from behind who's trying to
escape. He gave his tailor his own directions on how to make his clothes. When
he arrived at Tafayeva's, this time his necktie was pinned to his shirt with a tie pin
so enormous that it looked like a club.

"Well, did you get them?" came the question from all sides.

Surkov was just about ready to answer, but, seeing Aduyev and his nephew,
suddenly stopped and looked at them with surprise.

"He has a presentiment!" Pyotr Ivanych said quietly to his nephew. "Ah! and
he's got a cane. What does that mean?"

"What's that?" he asked Surkov, pointing to the cane.

"I was getting out of the carriage recently... I stumbled and am a little lame,"
he answered, coughing.

"Nonsense!" whispered Pyotr Ivanych to Alexander. "Notice the head of the
cane; do you see the gold lion's head? Day before yesterday he bragged to me
that he paid Barbier six hundred rubles for it, and now he's showing it off. That's
an example for you of the means by which he works. Do battle with him and
drive him out of the field."

Pyotr Ivanych pointed through the window at the house across the street.
"Remember the vases will be yours, and be inspired," he added.

"Do you have a ticket for tomorrow's play?" Surkov asked Tafayeva, going up
to her triumphantly.

"No."

"Allow me to present these!" he continued and finished by reciting
Zagoretsky's whole speech from *Woe from Wit.*[9]

The officer's whiskers moved slightly in a smile. Pyotr Ivanych cast a sideward
glance at his nephew, and Yuliya Pavlovna blushed. She started to invite Pyotr
Ivanych to her box.

"Thank you very much," he answered, "but tomorrow I am engaged to be at
the theater with my wife. But here, let me present a young man to you in
exchange..." He pointed to Alexander.

"I wanted to ask him too; there are but three of us: I, my cousin and..."

"He'll take my place," said Pyotr Ivanych, "and, in case of need, he'll replace
this fellow too." He pointed to Surkov and began to tell her something in a low
voice. While he spoke, she looked furtively twice at Alexander and smiled.

"I thank you," answered Surkov, "only it would have been better to propose
this replacement earlier, before there was a ticket; then I would have seen how I
would be replaced."

"Oh dear! I'm very grateful for your kindness," the hostess said spiritedly to
Surkov, "but I didn't invite you to sit in the box because you have an orchestra
seat. Surely you prefer to face the stage directly... especially for the ballet..."

"No, no, you're being sly, you don't think that: Exchange a place beside you—

not for anything!"

"But it's already promised..."

"How? To whom?"

"To M. René." She pointed to one of the bearded foreigners.

"Oui, Madame m'a fait cet honneur..." he quickly began to mutter.

Surkov looked at him, opening his mouth wide, then back at Tafayeva. "I'll change with him: I'll offer him my orchestra seat," he said.

"You can ask him his preference."

The bearded man answered with both hands and feet.

"I'm deeply obliged to you," said Surkov to Pyotr Ivanych, nodding toward Alexander, "this I owe to you."

"No need to be grateful. But won't you sit in my box? We're only two, my wife and I. You haven't seen her for a long time, you could pay her court."

Surkov turned away in vexation. Pyotr Ivanych quietly left the party. Yuliya seated Alexander next her and talked with him a whole hour. Surkov intruded in the conversation several times, but somehow inopportunely. He started saying something about the ballet and got yes for an answer when it should have been no and vice versa. It was clear they weren't listening. Then suddenly he got off on oysters, insisting he had swallowed a hundred eighteen of them that morning— and he didn't receive even a glance. He made several more commonplace remarks, and not seeing any sense in all this, he seized his hat and hovered around Yuliya, letting her notice that he was discontent and getting ready to leave. But she didn't notice.

"I'm leaving!" he finally said with emphasis. "Goodbye!" His badly concealed vexation was obvious in his words.

"So soon!" she answered calmly. "Will you come tomorrow to see us in the box if only for a minute?"

"How sly of you! One minute, when you know that for a place beside you I'd give up a place in paradise."

"If it's theatrical paradise, I believe you!"

By now he didn't want to leave. His vexation had disappeared, thanks to the friendly word Yuliya had tossed him in farewell. But everyone had seen him taking his leave; now he would have to go whether he wanted to or not, so he left, looking back like a little dog who would like to follow his master, but instead is chased back.

Yuliya Pavlovna was twenty-three or twenty-four years old. Pyotr Ivanych rightly guessed she was, indeed, a bundle of nerves, but this did not prevent her being at the same time a very pretty, intelligent and graceful woman. She was shy, however, dreamy and emotional like the majority of nervous women. She had a gentle, refined face, a sensitive and always thoughtful look, partly sad—for no reason, or, if you will, by reason of her nerves.

Her outlook on the world and life was not altogether kindly and when she thought about the question of her existence, she found she was superfluous here. But if, Heaven prevent, anyone, even by chance, should blurt out anything about the grave, about death in her presence—she grew pale. The bright side of her life slipped from her view. She chose the dark overgrown path for her walk in the garden and in the grove and looked with indifference at the smiling countryside. At the theater she always saw drama, rarely a comedy and never a farce. She covered her ears when the sounds of a merry song reached her by chance and she never laughed at a joke.

At other times her face expressed weariness, though not of a martyred or sick person, but the weariness as if of leisure. Clearly she struggled inwardly with some kind of fascinating dream—and weakened. After such a struggle she became silent, sad, then suddenly fell into an infinitely merry mood without being false to her character, however—what cheered her would not have amused another. All nerves! But to listen to the words of these ladies—what they won't say!—*fate, sympathy, infinite attraction, unprecedented melancholy, vague desires*—so they reason about one thing and another, and it ends, nevertheless, with a sigh, the word "nerves," and the little flask of smelling salts.

"How you have understood me!" said Tafayeva to Alexander at parting. "No man, even my husband, has altogether understood my character!"

And the fact of the matter was that Alexander came close to being that man. It was a liberation for him!

"Goodbye."

She gave him her hand. "I hope that now you'll find the way to my house without your uncle?" she added.

Winter came. Alexander usually dined at his uncle's on Friday. But four Fridays had now passed and he hadn't appeared, nor had he come on other days. Lizaveta Alexandrovna was angry; Pyotr Ivanych muttered that he had made them wait extra half-hours in vain.

But meanwhile Alexander was not unoccupied; he was fulfilling his uncle's command. Surkov had long since ceased going to see Tafayeva and he declared everywhere that everything was finished between them and that he had *broken off the relationship with her.* One evening—it was on a Thursday—upon returning home, Alexander found two vases and a note from his uncle on the desk in his room. Pyotr Ivanych thanked him for his friendly diligence and invited him to dinner the next day as usual. Alexander pondered it, as if this invitation interfered with his plans. The next day, however, he went to Pyotr Ivanych's an hour before dinner.

"What have you been doing? Aren't we to see you at all? Have you forgotten us?" both aunt and uncle pelted him with questions.

"Well! You did me a favor," Pyotr Ivanych continued, "beyond expectation!— and you were so modest: 'I can't,' he says, 'I don't know how!'—doesn't know how indeed! I've wanted to see you for a long time, but it was impossible to catch you. Well, I'm very grateful! Did you receive the vases undamaged?"

"I did. But I shall send them back."

"Why? No, no, they're yours by all rights."

"No," said Alexander decisively, "I shan't take this present."

"Well, as you please! My wife fancies them; she'll take them."

"I didn't know, Alexander," said Lizaveta Alexandrovna with a sly smile, "that you were so artful in these things... you said not a word to me..."

"It was Uncle's idea," answered Alexander, embarrassed. "I counted for nothing in this; it was he taught me..."

"Yes, yes, listen to him; he himself doesn't know how. Yet he so wrapped up this little deal... I'm very, very grateful! But my silly Surkov almost went crazy. He made me laugh. Two weeks ago he ran in to my office quite beside himself; I at once knew why, only gave no sign. I went on writing as if I knew nothing. 'Oh, it's you,' I say, 'what's the good news?' He smiled, wanted to pretend he was calm... but in reality he almost had tears in his eyes. 'Nothing good,' he says, 'I've come to you with bad news.' I looked at him as if with surprise. 'What's this?' I ask. 'Yes,' he says, 'about your nephew!' 'Why what? You frighten me; tell me right away!' I ask. Now his calm broke; he began to shout, to rage. I rolled my chair back from him—it was impossible to talk, he was spitting so. 'You yourself complained,' he says, 'that he wasn't working much, but you're the one who's taught him idleness.' 'I?' 'Yes, you. Who introduced him to *Julie?*' I have to tell you that since the second day of their acquaintance Surkov had begun calling her by her nickname. 'What's the misfortune in that?' I say. 'Why this misfortune,' he says, 'is that he now sits at her house from morning till night...'"

Alexander immediately blushed.

"You see how he lies out of rage, I thought," Pyotr Ivanych went on, looking at his nephew. "Would Alexander be sitting there from morning till night! I didn't ask him to do that, did I?"

The gaze Pyotr Ivanych fixed on Alexander was cold and calm, but it seemed simply fiery to Alexander.

"Yes... I sometimes... go to see..." muttered Alexander.

"Sometimes—that's different," continued his uncle. "I did ask that, but not every day. I knew he was lying. What is there to do there every day? You'd be bored with it!"

"No! She's a very intelligent woman... excellently brought up... loves music..." said Alexander indistinctly with pauses, and scratched one eye, though it didn't itch, stroked his left temple, then got out his handkerchief and wiped his lips.

Lizaveta Alexandrovna, unnoticed, looked fixedly at him, turned away to the window and smiled.

"Ah! well, all the better!" said Pyotr Ivanych, "if you weren't bored. And I feared all the time I had burdened you with an unpleasant task. So I told Surkov, 'Thanks, dear fellow, for taking an interest in my nephew. I'm very, very grateful to you... Only, don't you exaggerate things? The misfortune isn't yet that bad?...' 'How isn't it a misfortune!' he shouted. 'He doesn't do anything,' he says. 'A young man ought to work...' 'That, too, is not a misfortune,' I say. 'What's it to you?' 'What's it to me,' he says. 'He's got it in his head to act against me in cunning ways...' 'So that's where the misfortune is!' I began to tease. 'He insinuates Heaven knows what to Yuliya,' he says, 'about me... She's now quite changed toward me. I'll teach him, the brash puppy.' Pardon me, I'm repeating his words. 'What reason has he,' he says, 'to fight with me? He passed on gossip about me. I hope you'll set him straight.' 'I'll scold him,' I say, 'without fail.' But, enough, is it true what he's said about you? Have you given her flowers?...' Pyotr Ivanych stopped again as if waiting for an answer. Alexander was silent. Pyotr Ivanych continued. 'How do you mean,' he says, 'untrue? Why does he take her a bouquet of flowers every day? It's winter now,' he says. 'What does that cost... I know,' he says, 'what those bouquets cost.' Here, I thought to myself, he's one of our family; really, I see blood's no empty matter. So, would you take so much trouble for someone else but me? 'Why, is that true, every day?' I say. 'Stop, I'll ask him. You, no doubt, have lied.' And in truth, he did lie, didn't he? It can't be that you..."

Alexander would have liked to sink through the earth. But Pyotr Ivanych pitilessly looked him straight in the eye and awaited an answer. "Sometimes... true... I did bring..." said Alexander, lowering his eyes.

"So again—sometimes. Not every day. That's indeed superfluous. Moreover, tell me what all this cost you. I don't want you spending your money for me; it's enough that you're taking trouble. Give me the bill. So, for a long time Surkov talked nonsense. 'They're always,' he says, 'the two of them, either on foot or in the carriage, taking the air together where there are the fewest people.'"

At these words Alexander was a bit bent out of shape: he stretched out his legs under the desk and suddenly drew them in close again.

"I shook my head in doubt," his uncle continued. "'Would he be taking walks every day!' I say. 'Ask people...' he says. 'I'll do better to ask him himself,' I say... It isn't true, is it?"

"I did several times... walk with her... it's true..."

"So, not every day. I didn't ask you to do that. I knew he was lying. 'So,' I tell him, 'What's the importance of that? She's a widow, has no men close to her. Alexander's a modest fellow—not like you, you man-about-town. So, she takes him along; she can't go about alone.' He won't buy that. 'No,' he says, 'you won't fool me! I know. He's always with her at the theater. I'm the one,' he says, 'who'll get her a box, sometimes, Heaven knows with how much trouble and he'll sit in it!' Here I couldn't stand it and burst out laughing. 'That's the way you'd have it,' I think, 'idiot!' Oh, my, Alexander! You're a real nephew! Only I feel bad that you've gone to so much trouble for me."

Alexander felt he was undergoing torture. Large drops of sweat fell from his brow. He barely heard what his uncle was saying and didn't look at him or his aunt.

Lizaveta Alexandrovna was sorry for him. She shook her head at her husband, reproaching him for torturing his nephew. But Pyotr Ivanych didn't stop.

"Out of jealousy Surkov took it into his head to assure me that you were up to your ears in love with Tafayeva. 'No,' I tell him, 'look, that's not true. After all that happened to him, he won't fall in love. He knows women too well and scorns them.' Isn't that so?"

Alexander, without raising his eyes, nodded his head.

Lizaveta Alexandrovna suffered for him. "Pyotr Ivanych!" she said, so as somehow to change the subject.

"Well? What?"

"Just now a servant came with a letter from the Lukyanovs."

"I know, good. Where was I?"

"Pyotr Ivanych, you've started dropping cigar ash on my flowers again. What is this?"

"No matter, dear. They say ash furthers growth. So, I wanted to say..."

"So, isn't it time we dined, Pyotr Ivanych?"

"Good, tell them to serve! You've rightly mentioned dinner. Surkov says that you, Alexander, dine there almost every day, and that's the reason, he says, you're not at home lately on Fridays. He pretends you spend whole days together, just you two... The Devil knows what lies he told, I got fed up; I finally got rid of him. So, the result is, he lied. Today's Friday and here you are!"

Alexander shifted from one foot to the other and bent his head to the left shoulder.

"I'm extremely, extremely grateful to you. This is—the service of both a friend and a relative!" concluded Pyotr Ivanyoh. "Surkov is convinced he has nothing to gain and has withdrawn. 'She imagines,' he says, 'I shall be pining for her—she's mistaken! And I even wanted,' he says, 'to renovate an apartment completely from scratch and Heaven knows what intentions I had,' he says. 'She perhaps didn't even dream of such happiness as was being prepared for her. I would even,' he says, 'not have been averse to marrying her, had she been able to hook me. Now it's all over. You gave me the right advice, Pyotr Ivanych,' he says. 'I shall save both money and time!' And now the fellow plays the part of Byron, he walks around in such gloom and doesn't ask for money! I, too, shall say it's all over! Your mission's accomplished, Alexander, and well done!... Pardon me, please... I'll make it up to you somehow. When you need money, ask me. Liza! Have a good wine served us for dinner; we'll drink to the success of this business."

Pyotr Ivanych left the room. Lizaveta Alexandrovna, unnoticed, looked at Alexander twice and seeing that he was not saying a word, also left to give some orders to the servants.

Alexander sat as if unconscious and kept staring at his knees. At last he raised his head, looked around—no one was there. He took a deep breath, looked at his watch—four o'clock. He hastily seized his hat, waved his hand in the direction his uncle had gone, and quietly, on tiptoe and looking round in all directions, made it to the vestibule, where he took his overcoat in hand, rushed headlong down the stairs and drove off to Tafayeva's.

Surkov didn't lie; Alexander did love Yuliya. He experienced the first attacks of this love almost with horror, as if it was some kind of infection. Both fear and shame tormented him: fear of again being subject to all the whims of his own and another person's heart, shame before others, above all before his uncle. He would have paid dearly to hide it from him. It wasn't long ago, three months before, that he had so proudly and decisively renounced love, he'd even written an epitaph in verse to this restless emotion and read it to his uncle, he'd at last openly scorned women—and suddenly again was at a woman's feet! Once more a proof of childish impetuosity. Heavens! When would he be free of his uncle's inescapable influence? Was his life never to take on its own special unexpected shape, but always to go according to Pyotr Ivanych's predictions?

This thought drove him to despair. He would have been glad to run away from any new love. But how escape? What was the difference between love for Nadenka and love for Yuliya? First love is nothing but an unfortunate error of the heart which demands food, and the heart in those years is so undiscriminating that it accepts whatever first comes its way. But Yuliya! She was, indeed, no capricious girl who didn't understand him, or herself, or love. She was a woman in full maturity, weak in body but with energy of spirit—for love; she was all love! She recognized no other conditions for happiness and life. Is love but an idle act?—it's also a gift, and Yuliya was a genius at it. This was the love he had dreamt of, a conscious, reasonable, but at the same time powerful love which knew nothing beyond its own sphere.

"I don't sigh for joy like an animal," he told himself. "My spirit does not die, but a more important process, a higher one, occurs in me: I am aware of my happiness, I reason about it, and it is fuller, though perhaps quieter. How nobly, unaffectedly, completely without pretense Yuliya gave herself to her feeling! It was as if she'd been waiting for someone to understand love deeply—and the someone came. He, like a legal owner, proudly entered into ownership of inherited wealth and was obediently acknowledged. What comfort, what bliss, thought Alexander on the way to her from his uncle's, to know that there is a being in the world who, wherever she might be, whatever doing, remembers him, directs all thoughts, occupations, actions—everything toward one point and one idea, the beloved! It's like the man with a double. Whatever he hears, whatever he sees, whatever he goes past or is passed by, everything is verified as an impression of the other, the double. The impression is known to both, both have learned each other by heart—and then the verified impression is accepted and confirmed in indelible lines in the soul. The double rejects his own sensations if they cannot be shared or accepted by the other. One loves what the other loves and hates what the other hates. They live inseparably in one thought, one feeling; they have one spiritual eye, one ear, one mind, one soul..."

"Sir, which place is it in Liteiny?" asked the cab driver.

Yuliya loved Alexander more than he her. She was not even conscious of the whole strength of her love and did not muse on it. She loved for the first time—that wouldn't have been anything—it's impossible to fall in love straight away for the second time. But the misfortune was that her heart was developed to the utmost, formed by novels and prepared not for a first love, but for that romantic love which exists in certain novels, but not in nature, and which is always unhappy because it is impossible in reality. Meanwhile Yuliya's mind did not find any healthy food in her reading of certain novels and so it lagged behind her heart. She could not at all imagine a simple quiet love without stormy outbursts and immoderate tenderness. She would at once have stopped loving anyone who *did not fall at her feet* at a suitable moment, who didn't swear loyalty to her *with all the powers of his soul,* who dared not *to burn her up and reduce her to ash in his embraces,* or presumed to work at another occupation beside love, who did not drink drop by drop from the *chalice of life* in her tears and kisses alone.

This was the source of the dreaminess that created a special world for her. No sooner did something in the normal world take place not in accord with the laws of her special world than her heart was disturbed and she suffered. Her woman's organism, weak even without this, was subject to shock, often a quite powerful one. Frequent excitements irritated her nerves and finally caused them to break down completely. This is why many women have a pensiveness and sadness without reason, a gloomy view of life; this is why a harmonious and wisely constructed order of human existence created on the basis of immutable law seems to them a heavy chain; this is why, in a word, reality frightens them, compelling them to construct a fata morgana world.

Who had tried prematurely and so wrongly to cultivate Yuliya's heart and leave her mind alone?... Who? Why that classical triumvirate of pedagogues whom the parents had invited to come to take a young mind into their care, open it to the *movements and causes of all things,* raise the curtain of the past and show what is under us, over us, and in our very selves—a difficult assignment! But then three nations were called upon for this important undertaking. The parents themselves abstained from educating their child, assuming that their whole task would end when, on the recommendation of good friends, they hired a Frenchman, Poulet, to teach French literature and other subjects; then a German, Schmidt, because it was the custom to begin, though by no means to complete, German studies; and finally, a Russian teacher, Ivan Ivanych.

"Indeed, they're all so unkempt," the mother said, "always dressed so badly, looking worse than a lackey, even smelling sometimes of wine..."

"How can we do without a Russian teacher?—that's impossible!" decided the father. "Don't worry; I'll find a cleaner one."

So the Frenchman took up his task. Both mother and father paid him special attention. They invited him into the house as a guest, treated him very respectfully; he was a very expensive Frenchman.

It was easy for him to teach Yuliya. Thanks to a governess, she chattered in French, read and wrote almost without errors. It remained for M. Poulet only to busy her with compositions. He assigned her various subjects, now to describe the sunrise, now to define love and friendship, again to write a congratulatory letter to her parents or pour out her sorrow at separating from her girlfriend.

But from her window Yuliya could only see the sun set behind the house of the merchant Girin, she had never separated from her friends, and friendship and love... so here for the first time an idea of these feelings flashed through her mind. One must learn about them some time.

After exhausting his whole supply of these subjects, Poulet at last resolved to start with that sacred slender notebook on whose title page was printed in bold letters *Cours de littérature française*. Who of us does not remember this notebook? Two months later Yuliya knew French literature by heart, that is, the content of the slender notebook, and three months after that, she had forgotten it, though fatal traces remained. She knew there had been Voltaire and sometimes charged him with *Les Martyres*, but attributed *Le Dictionnaire philosophique* to Chateaubriand. She called Montaigne M-r Mountain and mentioned him alongside Hugo. She said of Molière that he *writes* for the theater. Of Racine she learned by heart the famous speech: "A peine nous sortions des portes de Trézènes."[10]

In mythology she very much liked the comedy played out by Vulcan, Mars and Venus. She was about to defend Vulcan, but after learning he was crippled and clumsy and a blacksmith besides, she defected right away to side with Mars. She fell in love too with the myth about Semele and Jupiter and about Apollo's exile and his pranks on earth, taking it all just as it is written and not suspecting any other meaning in these tales. Did the Frenchman himself suspect any— Heaven knows! To her questions about the religion of the ancients he would answer, wrinkling his brow, with importance: "Stupidities. But that beast of a Vulcan must have looked pretty peculiar... don't you think?" He added then, winking an eye and stroking her hand, "What would you have done in Venus' place?" She didn't answer, but blushed for the first time in her life without knowing why.

The Frenchman finally perfected Yuliya's education by acquainting her not theoretically but practically with the new school of French literature. He gave her *Le manuscrit vert, Les sept péchés capitaux*, and *L'âne mort*[11] along with a whole army of books which were then overrunning France and Europe.

The poor girl eagerly threw herself into this limitless flood. What geniuses these writers, Janin, Balzac, Drouineau, seemed to her—along with a whole string of heroes! What was the pitiful tale about Vulcan compared to their marvelous portrayals? Venus was pure innocence compared to these new characters! Yuliya eagerly read the new school and is probably still reading them now.

Meanwhile, just as the Frenchman only got so far, the thorough German did not manage even to get through the grammar. He very pompously set up tables of declensions and conjugations and thought up various intricate means of memorizing case endings; he explained that sometimes the prefix *zu-* is placed at the end, and so forth.

But when he was asked to teach literature, the poor fellow was taken with fright. They showed him the Frenchman's notebook. He shook his head and said you couldn't teach that in German; but there was Aller's anthology, in which all writers were represented with excerpts of their works. He didn't get off so easily, though; they kept at him to acquaint Yuliya with various writers, as had M. Poulet.

Finally the German promised and went home in deep thought. He opened, or, rather, uncovered a cupboard, removed one door altogether and leaned it against the wall because for a long time the cupboard had had neither latch nor lock—from it he took some old boots, half a block of sugar, a bottle of snuff, a carafe of vodka and a crust of black bread, then a broken coffee grinder, further a razor with a piece of soap and a brush in a tin of pomade, old suspenders, a whetstone for his penkife and still more junk of the sort. Finally, behind all this a book appeared, then another, a third and a fourth—yes, five by count—all there. He clapped them, one against the other—dust rose in a cloud, like smoke, and solemnly shrouded the pedagogue's head.

The first book was Gessner's *Idylls*. "*Gut!*" said the German and read through the idyll about the broken pitcher with enjoyment. He turned over the second book: *The Gotha Almanac* for 1804. He leafed through: in it were the dynasties of European rulers, pictures of various castles, waterfalls. "*Sehr gut,*" said the German. The third was the Bible; he laid it aside, piously muttering, "*Nein!*" The fourth was Jung's "Nights"[12]; he shook his head and muttered, "*Nein!*" The last was Weisse.[13] And the German smiled triumphantly: "*Da habe ich's!*"[14] When they mentioned the existence of Schiller, Goethe and others, he shook his head and stubbornly insisted, "*Nein!*"

Yuliya yawned as soon as the German translated the first page from Weisse for her and then she stopped listening. Thus, only one thing from the German stayed in her memory, that the prefix *zu* is sometimes placed at the end.

And her Russian teacher? He did his duty even more conscientiously than the German. Almost to the point of tears he assured Yuliya that a *substantive* or a *verb* are a so-called part of speech, and a *preposition* is one too, and he finally got her to accept this and learn by heart definitions of all the parts of speech. She could even enumerate in one breath all the prepositions, conjunctions and adverbs, and when the teacher solemnly interrogated her, "And what are the exclamations of fear or surprise?" she at once without drawing in breath blurted out, "Ach, och, ech, alas, oh, ah, well, oh my!" Her instructor was in ecstasy.

She recognized certain truths even of syntax, but could never apply them in practice and kept making grammatical mistakes for the rest of her life.

As for history, she knew that Alexander the Great had existed, that he fought a lot of wars, was super brave... and, of course, very handsome... but what he or his age had meant in addition neither her teacher nor she thought to ask. Indeed, even Kaidanov doesn't go into that very much in his history books.

When literature was requested of her teacher, he dragged in a pile of old, worn books. Among them were Kantemir and Sumarokov, then Lomonosov, Derzhavin and Ozerov. Her family were amazed. They carefully turned over one book, sniffed it, then tossed it out and asked for something newer. The teacher brought Karamzin. But to read Karamzin after the new French school! Yuliya read *Poor Liza* and a few pages from *Letters of a Russian Traveller* and gave them back.

The poor pupil had lots of breaks between these studies without any high-minded healthy nourishment for thought! Her mind began to fall asleep and her heart to sound an alarm. But at this point an obliging cousin turned up and at the right moment brought her several chapters of Pushkin's *Eugene Onegin, The Caucasian Prisoner,* and so on. And the young girl experienced the sweetness of Russian verse. She learned *Onegin* by heart and it never left her night table. Even her cousin, like her other instructors, didn't know how to explain to her the meaning and merits of this work. She took Tatyana as her role model and in her thoughts she repeated to her ideal hero the flaming lines from Tatyana's letter, and her heart ached and throbbed. Yuliya's imagination at times sought Onegin, at times one of the pale, sad, and disillusioned heroes of the new school of writers.

An Italian and another Frenchman completed her education, giving harmonious measure to her voice and movements, that is, they taught her to dance, sing, play or, more precisely, perform on the piano until her marriage, but they didn't teach her music. And so, at eighteen, she appeared in the salons on show

to society, with a constantly thoughtful look, despite her age, an interesting pallor, slight waist, and tiny foot.

Tafayev noticed her, a man with all the attributes of a suitor—an honorable
rank, considerable wealth, a medal round his neck, in a word, with a career and
a fortune. It couldn't be said that he was just a simple and kind man. Oh, no! He
was able to stick up for himself and made perfectly sensible judgments about the
present state of Russia and what was wrong with its finances and production, and
in his world he was considered a practical man.

Because of the strange contrast with his own solid nature the pale, thoughtful
girl made a strong impression on him. At evening parties he left the card game
and plunged into unaccustomed thought, watching this half-ethereal apparition
hovering before him. When, by chance, of course, her languid gaze fell upon
him he, dashing gladiator that he was in social conversation, lost countenance
before the shy young girl; sometimes he wanted to say something to her, and
couldn't. This annoyed him and he resolved to act more positively with the help
of various elderly ladies.

Information about the dowry proved satisfactory. "So, it's a match!" he concluded to himself. "I'm only forty-five, she's eighteen. On both our fortunes more
than two could make out very well. Looks? She's more than ordinarily pretty,
and I am what is called an imposing... man. They say she's well-educated, but so
what? I was once a student. I remember I was taught both Latin and Roman history. Even now I remember that at that time there was a—what was his name?...
well, Devil take him! I remember we read about the Reformation too... and those
verses: 'Beatus ille...'[15] How does it go? *puer, pueri, puero*? No, that's not right, the
Devil knows—I've clean forgotten everything. But, then, that's why they teach
you, so that you'll forget. Well, you can shoot me dead, but I say that you can take
that one there and this one here, all of them high-ranking intelligent people, but
no one will say what consul was in power... or in what year the Olympic games
took place, that's the way we're taught... because that's the system—it's just so
that you can see from his eyes that a person has studied. And how can you keep
from forgetting; after all, nothing is ever said about it later in society, and if anyone started talking that way, he'd simply be shown the door. No, we're a match."

Thus, when Yuliya left childhood, at her first step she was met by the sorriest
reality, an ordinary husband. How far he was from those heroes conjured up by
her imagination and the poets!

She spent five years in a boring stupor, her word for marriage without love,
then suddenly freedom and love appeared. She smiled, extended her ardent
embraces to them and surrendered to her passion, like a person who yields to a
horse's fast gallop. You rush off with the powerful animal and forget space. Your
breath is taken away, objects speed past, fresh air blows on your face, your heart
can hardly bear the sensation of bliss... Or like a person in a boat who yields to the
flow of the current: the sun warms you, green banks flash before your eyes, a playful wave caresses the stern and whispers so sweetly, running ahead and beckoning
on, on, pointing the way in an unending stream... And you're lured on. There's
no time to look and think of how the course will end, whether your steed is speed-
ing toward the abyss or the wave toward a cliff... The wind carries away all thoughts,
your eyes close, the fascination is insurmountable... And, indeed, she did not sur-
mount it, but was lured on, on... At last the poetic moments of her life had set in;
she fell in love with this now sweet, now disturbing agitation of the soul, she sought
excitement, invented both torment and happiness for herself. She gave herself up
to her love as people surrender to opium and greedily drank love's poison.

Yuliya was already aroused by expectation. She stood at the window and her impatience grew with each minute. She was fingering a Chinese rose and throwing the petals on the floor with vexation, and her heart was standing still; this was a moment of torture. She was playing a mental game of question and answer: will he come or won't he? All of her mind's energy was focused on the resolution of this simple problem. If the result was positive, she smiled, if not—she turned pale.

When Alexander drove up, she sank into a chair, pale from exhaustion—so powerfully had her nerves been at work. When he entered... it's impossible to describe the look with which she met him, the joy which instantly poured over all her features, as if they had not seen each other for a year, whereas they had met the evening before. In silence she pointed to the clock on the wall, but he had hardly cleared his throat to explain when, without hearing him out, she believed him, forgave him, forgot all the pain of her impatience, gave him her hand to kiss, and they both sat down on the sofa and talked at length, sat silent at length and at length looked at each other. If a servant hadn't reminded them, they would surely have forgotten to have dinner.

How many pleasures! Alexander would never have dreamed of such an abundance of *sincere heartfelt outpourings*. In the summer there were excursions for two outside the city; if music or fireworks drew a crowd, they were glimpsed in the distance between the trees, walking arm in arm. In the winter Alexander came to dinner, and afterward they sat side by side before the fire till night time. Sometimes they had the horse sleigh harnessed and they rushed through the dark streets, then hastened to continue their unending conversation at the samovar. Everything in the world around them, every momentary shift of thought and feeling—everything was remarked on and shared by both.

Alexander feared meetings with his uncle like a fire. He sometimes came to see Lizaveta Alexandrovna, but she was never successful in encouraging any candid revelations on his part. He was always worried his uncle would find him there and act out another scene, and therefore he always cut short his visits.

Was he happy? About others one can say in such a case both *yes* and *no*, but about him *no*; in his case love began with suffering. For moments, when he succeeded in forgetting the past, he believed in the possibility of happiness, in Yuliya and her love. At other times he would suddenly grow distressed in the heat of the most *sincere outpourings*, listen with fear to Yuliya's passionate, exalted ravings. It seemed to him that she could change in the turn of a hand or that some other unexpected *blow of fate* would in a flash destroy their marvelous world of bliss. Savoring the moment of joy, he knew that it must be bought with sufferings, and melancholy would again overtake him.

Still, the winter passed, summer came, and love did not cease. Yuliya became more and more attached to him. There was no change and no *blow of fate*. Something quite different happened. The outlook brightened. He made his peace with the notion of a possible lasting attachment. "This love is not so fiery now," he thought once, looking at Yuliya, "but on the other hand, it's solid, perhaps eternal! Yes, there's no doubt. Ah! At last I understand you, Fate! You want to reward me for past sufferings and after long wanderings bring me to a peaceful haven. This is the shelter of happiness... Yuliya!" he exclaimed aloud.

She started. "What is it?" she asked.

"Oh, nothing!..."

"No, tell me, you had some thought?"

Alexander resisted. She insisted.

"I thought that for the completion of our happiness we lack..."

"What?" she asked, worried.

"Oh, nothing! I had a strange idea."

Yuliya became agitated. "Oh dear! don't torment me, tell me right away!" she said.

Alexander thought and said under his breath, as if to himself, "To acquire the right not to be apart from her for a minute, not to leave for home. To be the lawful master... She would call me out loud without blushing or turning pale, her... and so for life! and be proud of it eternally..."

Speaking in this high style, word for word, he arrived at the word *marriage*. Yuliya was shaken, then began to cry. She gave him her hand to kiss with a feeling of inexpressible tenderness and gratitude, and both became animated; both began to speak at once. It was agreed that Alexander would talk with his aunt and ask her help in this complicated business.

In their joy they didn't know what to do. It was a beautiful evening. They set out for somewhere in the country, in the woods, and having with great trouble discovered a hill somewhere, they purposely passed the whole evening there, looking at the setting sun, dreaming about their future way of life. They decided to limit themselves to a narrow circle of friends, not to have "at homes" and not to make empty "calls."

Then they returned home and began to discuss the future order in their house, the arrangement of the rooms, and so on. Alexander proposed turning her dressing room into his study so that it would be alongside their bedroom.

"What kind of furniture do you want in your study?" she asked.

"I'd like walnut with dark-blue velvet upholstery."

"That's very nice and not easily soiled. For a man's study you have to choose dark colors without fail because the light ones are soon ruined by the smoke. And right here in the little passageway from your future study into the bedroom I'll arrange an 'environment' of plants—don't you think it will be beautiful? I'll put an armchair there so that I can sit, reading or working, and see you in your study."

"I won't have to say goodbye to you this way much longer," said Alexander, taking his leave.

She closed his mouth with her hand.

The next day Alexander set out to see Lizaveta Alexandrovna to make known what she had known for a long time, and to ask her advice and help. Pyotr Ivanych was not at home.

"Well good!" she said after hearing his confession. "You're no longer a boy. You can be the judge of your feelings and do as you wish with yourself. Only don't be in a hurry: get to know her well."

"Oh, dear Aunt, if you knew her! How many virtues!"

"For example?"

"She loves me so much..."

"That is, of course, an important virtue, but it's not the only thing you need in a marriage."

Then she told him several general truths about the married state, about what a wife and what a husband should be.

"But wait a bit. Autumn is coming now," she added. "Everyone will be going back to the city. There I'll call on your fiancée, we'll become acquainted, and I'll take up your cause in earnest. Don't let her go; I'm convinced you'll be a very happy husband."

She rejoiced.

Women adore marrying off men; sometimes they even see that for some reason the marriage will not and should not bond, yet they further it in every way.
They care only about arranging the wedding, then they leave the newlyweds to
their own devices. Heaven knows why they bother.

Alexander asked his aunt not to talk to Pyotr Ivanych until the matter was settled.

The summer had gone by in a flash; even the boring autumn dragged past.
Another winter set in. Aduyev's meetings with Yuliya were just as frequent.

She had apparently made a strict count of the days, hours, and minutes they
could spend together.

"Will you leave for work early tomorrow?" she sometimes asked.

"Around eleven."

"Then come to see me at ten, we'll have breakfast together. Couldn't you skip
it altogether! It's as if I were alone then, without you..."

"But how? my country... my duty..." Alexander would say.

"That's all very fine! But tell them you love and are loved. Do you imagine
your department head never loved? If he has a heart, he'll understand. Or bring
your work here; who prevents your working here?"

Another time she did not let him go to the theater and practically never let
him visit friends. When Lizaveta Alexandrovna came to call, for a long time
Yuliya couldn't come to her senses when she saw how young and pretty
Alexander's aunt was. She had imagined an aunt like most aunts, along in years,
and not pretty, and here, if you please, was a woman around twenty-six or twen-
ty-seven and a beauty! She made a scene in front of Alexander and began to let
him go less frequently to see his uncle.

But what was her jealousy and tyranny compared to Alexander's? He had convinced himself of her attachment to him, he saw that it was not in her nature to
betray him or grow cold, and—still he was jealous, and how jealous! It was not
the jealousy of an excessive love, where the tormenting pains in one's heart cause
weeping, groaning, and whining, and there is trembling for fear of losing one's
happiness—it was, rather, an indifferent, cold, mean jealousy. He tyrannized the
poor woman out of love more than others tyrannize from hate. It would seem to
him, for example, of an evening with guests that she didn't look at him long and
tenderly and often enough; he would look around like a beast—and woe if at that
time there was a young man near Yuliya, or even a man no longer young, but simply a man, or sometimes a woman—a thing. Insults, cutting remarks, black suspicions and reproaches hailed down. She had to justify herself then and do
penance through various sacrifices and unconditional obedience: not talk with
this one, not sit there, not go over there, endure sly smiles and the whispering of
sly observers, blush, turn pale, compromise herself.

If she received an invitation somewhere, before answering she, first of all, cast
a questioning glance at him, and he no sooner frowned than, pale and trembling,
that very moment she refused. Sometimes he would give permission—she would
get ready, dress and prepare to get in the carriage—when suddenly in a caprice of
the moment he would pronounce a threatening veto—and she would take off her
clothes. Afterwards he might begin to ask her pardon, suggest going, but when
was there time to dress again and harness the carriage? It would be left at that. He
was not only jealous of good looks, great intelligence and talent, but even of
monsters, and, finally, of anyone whose face he simply didn't like.

Once some guest arrived from that part of the country where her relatives lived. The guest was an older, plain man, who talked the whole time about the harvest and his case before the Senate, until Alexander, bored with listening, went to the next room. There was nothing to be jealous about. Finally the guest began to say goodbye.

"I've heard," he said, "that you're at home Wednesdays; wouldn't you let me join the company of your friends?"

Yuliya smiled and made ready to say "Please do!"—when suddenly from the next room there sounded a whisper louder than any cry: "I do not wish it!" Yuliya, shaken, hastily repeated these words aloud to the guest.

But Yuliya endured everything. She locked herself away from guests, never went out and sat in private with Alexander.

They continued to revel in bliss methodically. Having exhausted their whole store of known and ready enjoyments, she began to invent new ones, and to vary the pleasures in which this world was rich even without them. What a talent of inventiveness Yuliya displayed! But even her talent became exhausted. Repetition set in. There was nothing to wish for and experience.

There was not a single place out of town they hadn't visited, no play they hadn't seen together, no book they hadn't read and discussed. They had learned the feelings, ways of thinking, virtues and faults of one another, and nobody hindered them from carrying out their plans.

Sincere outpourings became rare. They sometimes sat for whole hours without saying a word. But Yuliya was happy and silent..

From time to time she would exchange a question with Alexander and get back a "yes" or "no"—and was content. If he didn't smile and didn't answer anything, she'd begin to watch every movement, every look and interpret them in her own way, and in that case you couldn't fend off her reproaches.

They stopped talking about the future because Alexander felt some kind of embarrassment about that, an awkwardness he could not explain to himself, and he tried to change the subject. He began to consider, reflect. The magic circle, in which his life was enclosed by love, burst out in places, and in the distance sometimes there appeared to him the faces of friends and a series of dissipated pleasures, or splendid balls with a crowd of beauties, or his eternally occupied and busy uncle, or his abandoned work...

One evening he was sitting at Yuliya's in this state of mind. It was snowing hard outdoors. The snow was beating against the windows and sticking in flakes to the panes. Inside one heard the monotonous ticking of the pendulum on the table clock and, infrequently, Yuliya's sighs.

For want of something to do Alexander cast his eyes round the room, then looked at the clock—ten. And he had still to sit some two hours more. He yawned; his glance rested on Yuliya.

Leaning with her back to the fireplace, she stood, inclining her pale face to her shoulder and following Alexander with her eyes, with an expression not of distrust and interrogation, but of languor and happiness. Apparently she was struggling with a secret emotion, with a sweet dream, and seemed weary.

Her nerves were so strongly involved that the very palpitation of languor subjected her to pathological weariness. Torment and bliss were indistinguishable in her.

Alexander answered her with a dry, restless look. He went up to the window and began to drum lightly with his fingers on the glass as he looked out at the street.

From the street came a mixed sound of voices and the carriages driving past.

In windows everywhere lights shone, shadows flew by. It seemed to him that there where there was more light a merry crowd had gathered. There, perhaps, a lively exchange of thoughts, of fiery, volatile feelings was taking place; there people were living loudly and joyously. And over there in that dimly lighted window probably some worthy worker sat industriously at his labor. And Alexander realized he had been dragging out an empty, stupid existence for almost two years now—and that's two years off the total of one's life—and all for love! Then and there he turned against love in resentment.

"What kind of love is this!" he thought. "Some kind of sleepy love without energy! This woman surrenders to feeling without a struggle, without exertion, without resistance, like a victim. A weak woman without character, she would have bestowed her love on the first man who came along; if it hadn't been me, she would have fallen in love even with Surkov, and she even started to love him, yes! However she defends herself—I saw it! Let someone more dashing and skillful than I come along, she'd yield to him! It's simply immoral! Is that love! Where is the sympathy of souls which sensitive people preach about? And weren't our souls drawn to each other—to be joined forever, it seemed; who would have thought otherwise! The Devil knows what this is, you can't make sense of it!" he whispered with vexation.

"What are you doing there? What are you thinking about?" asked Yuliya.

"So..." he said, yawning and sat on the sofa further away from her, seizing the corner of an embroidered pillow with one hand.

"Sit here, closer."

He didn't and didn't answer anything.

"What's the matter with you?" she went on, coming nearer to him. "You're insufferable today."

"I don't know..." he said wearily, "I feel something... as if I..."

He didn't know what to answer her or himself. He still hadn't properly explained to himself what was happening to him.

She sat down beside him, began to talk about the future and gradually brightened. She painted a happy picture of family life, joked at times and concluded very tenderly.

"You are my husband! Look," she said, pointing all around, "Soon all this will be yours. You will rule in this house as in my heart. I'm independent now, can do what I want, go wherever I want, but then nothing will move from its place without your order. I will be bound by your will, but what a beautiful chain! Forge it quickly, oh when?... All my life I've dreamed of such a man, of such a love... and here the dream is fulfilled... and happiness close... I hardly believe it... Do you know, it seems a dream to me. Isn't this the reward for my past sufferings?..."

It was painful for Alexander to hear these words.

"And if I fell out of love with you?" he asked suddenly, trying to give his voice a joking tone.

"I would box your ears!" she answered, taking him by the ears, then sighed and fell deep in thought because of this single joking remark. He was silent.

"Why, what's the matter with you?" she suddenly asked with animation. "You're silent, you hardly listen to me, look to the side..."

Then she moved toward him and putting her hand on his shoulder, began to speak quietly, almost in a whisper, on the same theme, but not so positively. She reminded him of the beginning of their intimacy, the beginning of love, its first signs and first joys. She almost sighed from the languor of her emotions; on her pale cheeks two spots turned pink. They gradually took fire, her eyes sparkled, then grew languid and closed halfway, she was breathing deeply, and her words were hardly audible as she played with Alexander's soft hair with one hand; then she looked into his eyes. He quietly freed his head from her hand, took a comb from his pocket and carefully combed the hair she had disarranged. She got up and looked at him fixedly.

"What is the matter with you, Alexander?" she asked, worried.

"Why are you bothering me! How do I know?" he thought, but was silent.

"Are you bored?" she suddenly said, and her voice betrayed both question and doubt.

" Boring!" he thought, "that's the right word! Yes! This is a torturing, murderous boredom! It's a month since this worm crawled into my heart and started gnawing at it... Oh God! What am I to do? And she's discussing love and marriage. How am I to bring her to reason?"

She sat down at the piano and played several of his favorite pieces. He didn't listen and still went on thinking his own thoughts.

Yuliya let her hands fall. She sighed, wrapped herself in her shawl and threw herself into the other corner of the sofa, from where she sadly observed Alexander.

He took his hat.

"Where are you going?" she asked in astonishment.

"Home."

"It isn't eleven o'clock yet."

"I must write to Mama; I haven't written her in a long while."

"Long? You wrote her day before yesterday."

He was silent, there was nothing to say. He had in fact written and somehow in passing had told her at the time, but forgotten. But love doesn't forget a single detail! In the eyes of love everything that concerns the beloved is an important fact. In the mind of a loving person a multiple fabric is woven out of observations, subtle considerations, recollections, surmises about everything that surrounds the beloved, that takes place in his world, or influences him. In love one word, a hint, suffices... why not even a hint!—a glance, a hardly noticeable movement of the lips is enough to constitute a surmise, and then become a consideration, and from there a decisive conclusion and then one either torments oneself or discovers bliss as a result of one's own thought. The logic of those in love, sometimes wrong, sometimes amazingly right, quickly throws up a structure of surmises and suspicions, but the force of love, even more quickly, razes it to the foundation; often a single smile, a tear, at most two or three words suffice—and you can say farewell to suspicions. Nothing can undermine or deceive this kind of monitoring. A person in love might suddenly take into his head something another person would not dream of even in sleep, yet he will not see what goes on under his nose; he might see with a penetration equal to clairvoyance, yet be shortsighted to the point of blindness.

Yuliya jumped up from the sofa like a kitten and seized him by the hand.

"What does this mean? Where are you going?" she asked.

"Really nothing, nothing. I'm just sleepy; I didn't sleep much last night, that's all."

"Didn't sleep much! Then why did you say earlier this morning that you slept nine hours and even that your head had started to ache from it?"

Another mistake.

"But my head does ache," he said, becoming a little embarrassed, "that's why I'm going."

"But after dinner you said the ache had gone."

"Heavens! What a memory you have! This is unbearable! Well, I simply want to go home."

"You mean you're not comfortable here? What do you have there at home?"

Looking straight into his eyes, she shook her head suspiciously. Somehow he calmed her and left.

"What if I don't go to Yuliya's today?" was the question Alexander asked himself upon awakening the next morning.

He walked up and down in his room a few times. "Right, I won't go!" he added, his mind made up. "Evsei! I'm getting dressed." And he set out to wander about the city.

"What fun, how pleasant to go walking alone!" he thought, "to go where you want, stop, read a sign, look in a store window, set off this way, that way... it's so wonderful! Freedom is a great gift! Yes! that's right—freedom in the broad, elevated sense means to go walking alone!"

He tapped with his stick along the sidewalk, merrily bowed to acquaintances. Walking along Morskaya Street, he saw a familiar face in the window of a house. An acquaintance beckoned to him to come in. He looked—oh! why that's Dumé! and went in, had dinner, stayed till evening, then went to the theater, and afterwards to supper. He tried not to think about home; he knew what awaited him there.

True, upon his return he found up to half a dozen notes on the table and a sleepy lackey in the hall. The servant had been told not to leave until he came. In the notes there were reproaches, questions and traces of tears. The next day he had to explain. He excused himself with work at the office. Somehow they made peace.

Three days later the same thing happened again on his and her side. Then again and again. Yuliya grew thin, didn't go anywhere or receive any visits but kept quiet because reproaches made Alexander angry.

A couple of weeks later Alexander arranged with friends to choose a day and go out on the town doing come what may, but the same morning he received a note from Yuliya with the request that he spend the day with her, and come early. She wrote that she was ill, sad, that her nerves were suffering and so on. He became angry, but went to warn her that he could not stay, that he had a lot of things to do.

"Yes, of course: dinner at Dumé's, theater, rides in the hills—very important business...," she said wearily.

"What does this mean?" he asked with vexation. "You're apparently having me watched? I won't stand for it." He got up and wanted to leave.

"Stop, listen!" she said, "let us talk."

"I have no time."

"One minute; sit down."

He sat down, unwillingly, on the edge of a chair.

Folding her arms, she scrutinized him, as if trying to read on his face in advance the answer to what she wanted to say.

He fidgeted in his place from impatience.

"Quickly! I have no time!" he said dryly.

She sighed. "You don't love me then?" she asked, slightly shaking her head.

"The same old song!" he said, smoothing his hat with his sleeve.

"How she has bored you!" she answered.

He got up and began walking around the room in rapid paces. A moment later sobbing was heard.

"This is the last straw!" he said almost with rage, stopping in front of her. "Haven't you tormented me enough!..."

"I've tormented you!" she exclaimed and started to sob more violently.

"This is insufferable!" said Alexander, getting ready to leave.

"All right, I won't, I won't!" she hastily began, wiping her tears. "You see, I'm not crying; but don't go, sit down."

She tried to smile, but even so the tears trickled down her cheeks. Alexander felt pity. He sat down and began to jiggle his foot. He started to pose question after question to himself and came to the conclusion that he had cooled to Yuliya, he did not love her. And why? God knows! She loved him more and more every day; and wasn't that the reason? Heavens! What a contradiction! All the conditions for happiness were there. Nothing prevented it, no other feeling had distracted him, but he had cooled. Oh, life! But how to calm Yuliya! Sacrifice himself? Drag out boring, long days with her; pretend—he couldn't. But not to pretend meant to face tears every minute, listen to reproaches, torment her and himself... If he began talking to her all of a sudden about his uncle's theory of betrayals and cooling off... now I ask you: she wouldn't understand anything; she'd cry and then what could be done?

Seeing that he was silent, Yuliya took his hand and looked him in the eyes. He slowly turned away and quietly freed his hand. He not only did not feel attracted to her, but felt a cold and unpleasant shudder run through his body from her touch. She doubled her caresses. He did not respond to them and became still colder, gloomier. She suddenly snatched her hand away from him and flared up. Feminine pride, offended self-love, shame awakened in her. She straightened up her head and posture and blushed in chagrin.

"Leave me!" she said abruptly.

He left promptly without any objection. But when the sound of his steps began to die down, she rushed after him.

"Alexander Fyodorych! Alexander Fyodorych!" she cried.

He turned.

"Where are you going?"

"Why you told me to leave!"

"And you're even glad to run away. Stay!"

"I have no time!"

She took him by the hand—and again tender, passionate speeches, prayers and tears poured out. He betrayed no sympathy either by glance, word, or movement—he stood as if made of wood, shifting from one foot to the other. His coldness drove her mad. He was showered with threats and reproaches. Who would have recognized in her the gentle woman with weak nerves? Her curls came loose, her eyes burned with a feverish gleam, her cheeks flamed, the features on her face seemed almost to dissolve. "How ugly she is!" thought Alexander, looking at her with a grimace.

"I'll have my revenge!" she said. "You think it's so easy to play with a woman's fate? You crept into my heart with flattery and hypocrisy, gained complete possession of me and then left me when I was no longer able to throw you out of my thoughts... No! I shall not let you go, I'll follow you everywhere and always. You won't get away from me no matter where you go. If you go to the country, I'll go after you; if you go abroad, I'll go there too, everywhere and forever. I won't part easily with my happiness. I don't care what kind of life I lead... I have nothing more to lose, but I'll poison your life. I'll get even, I'll have my revenge; I undoubtedly have a rival! It can't be that you've left me just like that... I'll find her—and you'll see what I'll do: you'll wish you'd never been born! With what pleasure I'd hear of your death... I could kill you myself!"

"How stupid! How absurd this is!" thought Alexander, shrugging his shoulders.

Seeing that Alexander was indifferent to threats too, she suddenly changed to a quiet, sad tone, then looked at him in silence.

"Have pity on me!" she said, "don't leave me. What shall I do now without you? I won't survive the separation. I shall die! Think about it: women love differently—more tenderly, more strongly than men. Love is everything for them, especially for me. Others flirt, love society, noise, and fuss. I've never grown accustomed to that: I'm different. I love quiet, solitude, books, music, but you more than everything in the world..."

Alexander showed impatience.

"Well, all right, you don't love me," she continued in a lively manner, "but keep your promise. Marry me, only be with me... You'll be free. Do what you want, even love whomever you want, if only I see you sometimes, even rarely... Oh, in God's name take pity, take pity!"

She began to cry and could not go on speaking. Agitation had exhausted her; she fell on the sofa, closed her eyes, her teeth were clenched, her mouth contorted convulsively. She had an attack of hysterics. An hour later she regained control, came to. Her maid was fussing about her. She looked around. "And where is...?" she asked.

"The gentleman has gone!"

"He's left!" she repeated despondently and sat for a long while in silence without moving.

The next day she wrote note after note to Alexander. He didn't come and didn't answer. The third, the fourth day, the same thing. Yuliya wrote to Pyotr Ivanych, inviting him to come see her about an important matter. She disliked his wife because she was young, pretty, and, as his aunt, related to Alexander.

Pyotr Ivanych found her seriously ill, almost dying. He spent some two hours with her, then set off to see Alexander.

"What a hypocrite, really!" he said.

"What's this about?" asked Alexander.

"Look at him, as if this weren't his doing. Says he doesn't know how to make a woman fall in love with him and then actually drives her crazy."

"I don't understand, Uncle..."

"What's so hard to understand about it? You understand! I was at Tafayeva's; she's told me the whole thing!"

"What!" muttered Alexander in great embarrassment. "Told everything!"

"Everything. How she loves you! You lucky man! So, here you were weeping that you didn't find passion. Here's passion for you; be comforted. She's going crazy, she's jealous, she weeps and rages... But why are you both involving me in your affairs? Now you've begun shunting your women off on me. That's the last straw; I've wasted the whole morning with her. I thought she wanted me on some business, maybe to mortgage her estate with the Estate Trust Council... she made it sound like that, but, see what she wanted me for—really, a fine business!"

"Why did you go to see her?"

"She asked me, complained about you. Indeed, aren't you ashamed of neglecting her so? Four days without showing up—is that a joke? Poor woman, she's dying. Get up and go quickly."

"What did you tell her?"

"The usual, that you also love her insanely, that you'd looked for a tender heart for a long time, that you were terribly fond of *sincere outpourings* and you too couldn't live without love. I said she was worked up about nothing—you would return; I advised her not to push you hard, to allow you to have fun sometimes... otherwise, I said, you'd bore each other... well, what's usually said in such cases. She became very cheerful, let out the secret that you both planned to marry, that my wife was intervening in this. And you didn't say a word to me—what kind of people are you! Well, then, so be it! This woman has something; you two will get along. I told her you'd carry out your promise without fail... I did my best for you just now, Alexander, out of gratitude for the service you did me... assured her you loved her *so passionately, so tenderly.*"

"What have you done, Uncle!" hastily began Alexander, changing color. "I... I don't love her any more!... I don't want to get married! I feel as cold as ice toward her!... I'd sooner drown myself... than..."

"Come, come, come!" said Pyotr Ivanych with pretended surprise. "Am I hearing you right? Wasn't it you who said—do you remember?—that you scorned human nature and especially women's, that there wasn't a heart in the world worthy of you? What else did you say? God help me remember..."

"For Heaven's sake, Uncle, not another word. Your reproach is enough, why give me a moral lesson too? Do you think I don't understand... Oh, people, people!"

Suddenly he began to chuckle and his uncle with him.

"There, that's better." said Pyotr Iyanych. "What's your opinion now of that... what's her name? Pashenka, the one with the wart?"

"Uncle, that's not generous!"

"No. I'm only talking so as to find out whether you still look down on her?"

"Let all that be for Heaven's sake, and instead, help me now to get out of this terrible plight. You're so wise, so reasonable..."

"So! Now you're giving me compliments, flattery ! No, get married, go ahead."

"Not for anything, Uncle! I implore you, help!"

"I've made a start, Alexander. Good that I guessed about your pranks long ago."

"What do you mean, long ago!"

"Why this: I've known about your affair from the very beginning."

"No doubt Aunt told you."

"Not at all! I told her. What's complicated about that? Everything was written on your face. Come don't be distressed; I've already helped you."

"How? When?"

"This morning. Don't get excited: Tafayeva won't bother you any more..."

"How did you manage? What did you tell her?"

"It'd take a long time to repeat, Alexander—it's boring."

"But you might have told her God knows what. She hates me, scorns me..."

"Isn't all that unimportant? I calmed her down—and that's enough. I said you couldn't love, that bothering about you wasn't worth it..."

"What did she answer?"

"She's even glad that you left her!"

"You say glad!" said Alexander thoughtfully.

"Yes, glad!"

"You didn't notice either regret or sadness in her? She doesn't care at all? Why, that's awful!"

He began to pace round the room excitedly.

"Glad, quite calm!" he insisted, "now I ask you! I'm going to see her at once."

"People are crazy!" remarked Pyotr Ivanych. "That's the heart for you: live by it—and everything will be in a fine fix. Wasn't it you who feared she'd send for you? Weren't you the one who asked for help? And now you've gotten excited because after separating from you she's not dying of grief."

"She's glad, content!" said Alexander, pacing back and forth, and not listening to his uncle. "Aha! so she didn't love me! Neither grief nor tears. No, I'll go see her."

Pyotr Ivanych shrugged his shoulders.

"Have it your way; I can't leave it like this, Uncle!" Alexander added, reaching for his hat.

"Well, go to her, then. But you won't pull free, and don't you come bothering me afterwards. I'm not going to intervene. I did it now only because I myself had gotten you into this. But enough, why are you still depressed?"

"It's shameful to live in this world!" said Alexander with a sigh.

"And shameful not to be working at anything," his uncle added. "Enough! Come see us today. After dinner we'll have a good laugh at your adventure, and then we'll go for a drive to the factory."

"How small I am, a nothing!" said Alexander pensively. "I have no heart! I'm pitiful, a beggar in spirit!"

"And all because of love!" Pyotr Ivanych interrupted. "What a stupid preoccupation—leave it to some Surkov or other. You're a capable fellow, you can busy yourself with something more important. You've done enough chasing after women."

"But look, you love your wife, don't you?..."

"Yes, of course. I've grown very accustomed to her, but that doesn't prevent me from doing my work. Well, goodbye, come to dinner."

Alexander sat, confused and morose. Evsei came stealing up to him with a boot, into which he had plunged his hand.

"Please, take a look, Sir," he said, imploring, "what a shoe polish! You polish and it comes out just like a mirror, and it costs only a quarter ruble."

Alexander came to, mechanically took a look at the boot, then at Evsei.

"Go away!" he said. "You're a fool!"

"You should send me back to the country..." Evsei said again.

"Go away, I tell you, go away!" shouted Alexander, almost weeping. "You've tormented me, you and your boots will drive me to the grave. .. you... barbarian!"

Evsei made a fast exit to the front hall.

IV

"Why doesn't Alexander come to our house? I haven't seen him for some three months," Pyotr Ivanych asked his wife one day as he returned home from somewhere or other.

"I've really lost hope of seeing him ever again," she answered.

"Why, what's the matter with him? In love again maybe?"

"I don't know."

"Is he well?"

"He is."

"Write to him, please; I must have a talk with him. At the office there are job changes again, but I don't think he knows. I don't understand his lack of interest."

"I've already written and invited him ten times. He says he's too busy, but actually he plays checkers with some peculiar people or goes fishing. It would be better to go there yourself, you could find out what's happened to him."

"No, I don't want to. Send a servant."

"Alexander won't come."

"Let's try."

They sent a servant, who quickly returned.

"So, what news; is he at home?" asked Pyotr Ivanych.

"He's at home, he sends you greetings."

"What's he doing?"

"He's lying on the sofa."

"What, at this hour?"

"The gentleman, you know, lies there all the time."

"Why, what do you mean, sleeping?"

"No, not at all, Sir. I thought so too at first, the master's napping, but no, his eyes are open, he's happy to stare at the ceiling."

Pyotr Ivanych shrugged his shoulders.

"Will he come here?" he asked.

"By no means, Sir. 'Give him my greetings,' he says. 'Tell Uncle to pardon me. I'm not well,' he says; and to you too, Ma'am, he sends greetings."

"What's the matter with him then? This is astonishing, really! Just going to pieces like this! Tell them not to unharness the carriage. There's no escape, I've got to go myself. But, really, this is the last time."

Pyotr Ivanych found Alexander on the sofa. When his uncle came in, he raised his head and sat up.

"You're not well?" asked Pyotr Ivanych.

"That's right...," answered Alexander, yawning.

"What are you doing?"

"Nothing."

"You can spend your time without doing anything?"

"I can."

"I heard today, Alexander, something about Ivanov's being promoted at the office."

"Yes, he's being promoted."

"Who gets his job?"

"Ichenko, they say."

"And you?"

"Me? Nothing."

"Why nothing? Why isn't it you?"

"They're not giving it to me. What's the use; true, I don't deserve it."

"I ask you, Alexander, you have to do something. If you went to see the director."

"No," said Alexander, shaking his head.

"Apparently you don't care?"

"I don't care."

"Look, this is the third time they've passed you by."

"I don't care. Let them."

"Look here, you'll have something to say when your former subordinate starts telling you what to do, or when you have to get up and bow when he comes in."

"All right, I'll get up and bow."

"And your self-esteem?"

"I haven't got any."

"Surely you have some interests in life?"

"None. I had some, but they disappeared."

"That's impossible. Some interests are replaced by others. But why have yours disappeared, when other people's haven't? It's too soon for that, it seems to me. You're not thirty yet..."

Alexander shrugged his shoulders.

Pyotr Ivanych by now no longer wanted to continue this conversation. He called all this caprice, but he knew that upon returning home there would be no avoiding his wife's questions, and therefore, unwillingly, he went on: "You might find some distraction, might go to social events," he said. "You could read."

"I don't want to, Uncle."

"People are beginning to talk about you, that you... that is... have had a breakdown because of love, are doing Heaven knows what, going around with peculiar people... For me that alone would be reason enough to go out."

"Let them say what they want!"

"Listen, Alexander, joking aside. That's all unimportant. You can bow or not bow, go to social events or not. But remember, like everyone, you have to have a career of some kind. Do you ever think of that?"

"Of course, I've already thought about it."

"What then?"

"I've drawn up a circle of activity for myself and I don't wish to step outside the circle. Within it I am master, that's my career."

"That's laziness."

"Perhaps."

"You don't have the right to lie on your side when as long as you have the strength for it you can do something. Is your work finished?"

"I'm doing something. No one will accuse me of idleness. In the morning I work at the office, but to labor beyond that—that's simply a luxury, an arbitrary obligation. Why should I bother?"

"Everybody bothers for some reason—one because he thinks it's his duty as long as his strength lasts, another for money, a third for honor... Why are you an exception?"

"Honor, money! Especially money! Why that? Look, I have enough to eat, something to wear, that's enough."

"And you're badly dressed now," remarked his uncle. "You're saying you need only that?"

"Only that."

"And the luxury of intellectual and spiritual pleasures, and art..." Pyotr Ivanych was about to begin imitating Alexander's tone: "You can move forward, you have a higher destiny, your duty calls you to noble labor... And your striving toward higher things—have you forgotten?"

"God be with them! God be with them!" said Alexander, disturbed. "And you, Uncle, have begun to talk wildly! That didn't use to be your custom. You aren't doing it for me, are you? You're wasting your breath! I did strive for higher things—remember? What was the result?"

"I remember how suddenly you wanted to be a minister of state right away, and then a writer. But when you saw that the way to a high calling is a long and difficult road, that talent is required of a writer, then you drew back. Many, like you, come here with higher views and don't see their chance when it's under their very nose. Just as you need paper to write—they take one look, and they've had it... I'm not talking about you; you've proved you can work and be something in time. Indeed it is boring to wait a long time. We want it all at once; if that doesn't happen, we feel depressed."

"But I don't want to strive higher. I want to stay as I am. Don't I have the right to choose my occupation for myself, whether or not it's beneath my abilities—what's the difference? If I do my work conscientiously—I do my duty. Let them reproach me with an incapacity for higher things: that wouldn't hurt me at all, even if it were true. You yourself said there's poetry in a modest corner, but now you're reproaching me for choosing the most modest one. Who'll forbid me to go down several steps and stand on the one I like? I don't want a higher destiny—do you hear, I don't want it!"

"I hear you! I'm not deaf yet, only this is all pitiful sophistry."

"It doesn't matter. So I've found my place and shall stay in it all my life. I've found simple, plain people; it doesn't matter that they're limited in intelligence. I play checkers with them and go fishing—and that's fine! Let me be punished for it, as you think; let me do without awards, money, honors, significance—everything that so flatters you. I renounce it forever..."

"You want to pretend calm and indifference to everything, but in your words resentment boils up. You're talking as if in tears, not words. There's a lot of rage in you; you don't know on whom to pour it out because only you yourself are to blame."

"So be it!" said Alexander.

"What do you want then? Shouldn't a person want something?"

"I want to be left alone to be in my dark corner, to be allowed not to bother about anything and stay quiet!"

"And is that really life?"

"Rather to my mind the life you lead isn't life, therefore I'm right."

"You want to remake life in your way; I imagine it would be a good one. According to you, I imagine, everybody would be walking in pairs of lovers and friends amid rose bushes..."

Alexander said nothing.

Pyotr Ivanych looked at him in silence. Alexander had again grown thin. His eyes were sunken. Premature wrinkles had appeared on his cheeks and forehead.

His uncle became alarmed. He did not much believe in spiritual sufferings, he feared the beginning of some physical ill was hidden beneath this apathy. "Suppose," he thought, "the fellow goes crazy, and you inform his mother; that will lead to a correspondence! If you don't watch out, she'll turn up here."

"Well, Alexander, I see you're disillusioned," he said. "What if I turn him back," he thought, "to his favorite ideas. Wait, I'll pretend..."

"Listen, Alexander," he said. "You've let yourself go terribly. Throw off this apathy. It's not good! And why? Perhaps you took too much to heart my sometimes careless criticism of love and friendship. Look, I said it in jest, in order to moderate the exaltation in you, which is somehow out of place in our positive century, especially here in St. Petersburg where everything is regulated, not only fashions, but also passions, business affairs and pleasures, everything is weighed out, checked out, evaluated... a limit set for everything. Why should one person openly depart from this general order? Do you really think I'm without feeling, that I don't recognize love? Love is a beautiful feeling; there's nothing more sacred than the union of two hearts, that friendship, for example... I'm inwardly convinced that feeling must be constant, eternal..."

Alexander burst out laughing.

"What's the matter?" asked Pyotr Ivanych.

"You're talking wildly, Uncle. Shall I get you a cigar; we'll light up, you'll go on talking and I'll listen."

"Why, what's the matter with you?"

"Why, nothing. You've decided to ensnare me! But at one time you called me a person of some intelligence! Do you want to toy with me like a little ball—that's insulting! One isn't a boy forever. The school I've been through has been good for something. How you've launched into oratory! As if I have no eyes? You're just trying to trick me, but I've seen through it."

"I've attempted what's beyond me," thought Pyotr Ivanych. "I'd better send him to my wife."

"Come to see us," he said, "my wife very much wants to see you."

"I can't, Uncle."

"Is that nice of you to forget her?"

"Maybe it's very bad, but pardon me for Heaven's sake and don't expect me now. Wait a little while longer; I'll come."

"Well, as you wish," said Pyotr Ivanych. He waved his hand and went home.

He told his wife that he was washing his hands of Alexander; let him do as he wanted, but he, Pyotr Ivanych, had tried all he could and was through with him now.

After escaping Yuliya, Alexander threw himself into a whirlpool of noisy merrymaking. He recited lines by a famous poet of ours:

> Let's go where joy draws breath,
> Where the noisy whirl of amusements roars,
> Where men don't live but throw life and youth away!
> In merry games at a joyful table,
> Drunk with the moment's false happiness,
> I inure myself to worthless dreams,
> Accept my fate with the help of wine,
> And calm the heart's cares,
> Make thoughts stop flying,
> Command my eyes ne'er to see
> The silent splendor of the skies, etc.

A circle of friends turned up and with them the unavoidable *goblet*. The friends contemplated their faces which were reflected in the foaming moisture and in their lacquered boots. "Away with grief," they exclaimed, exulting, "away with cares! Throw away, destroy, burn to ashes, drink up life and youth! Hurrah!" Glasses and bottles flew to the floor with a crash.

For a while the freedom, noisy gatherings, and his carefree life compelled Alexander to forget Yuliya and his sadness. But it was always one and the same thing—dinners in restaurants, the same faces with blurry eyes, every day the same stupid and drunken ravings of his companions, and besides, a constantly sick stomach; no, this wasn't for him. The delicate organism of Alexander's body and his soul, which was inclined to a sad, elegiac note, did not withstand these amusements.

He fled from *merry games at the joyous table* and found himself alone in his room in solitude with himself and his forgotten books. But a book would slide out of his hands, the pen did not obey his inspiration. Schiller, Goethe, Byron revealed the dark side of humanity to him—he didn't notice the bright side; he wasn't in the mood for it.

But how happy he had once been in that room! He hadn't been lonely; a lovely ghost had been nearby then to shelter him in the day at his absorbing work and keep watch at night at his bedside. Dreams had lived with him there, the future was clothed in a cloud, though not a heavy one portending foul weather, but rather a morning cloud hiding a bright dawn. Something was concealed behind the cloud, probably happiness... But now? Not only his room but the whole world had become empty for him, and within him dwelt cold and sadness...

Looking into life, and questioning his heart and his head, he saw with horror that neither here nor there had he a single dream left, not a single rosy hope: they were all behind him. The cloud had parted; naked reality spread out before him like the steppe. Heavens! What a boundless expanse! What a boring, cheerless view! The past had perished, the future is destroyed, there is no happiness. Everything is an illusion—but life goes on!

Even he himself didn't know what he wanted, only how much there was that he didn't want!

His head felt as if it were in a fog. He didn't sleep, yet seemed to be unconscious. Depressing thoughts dragged through his head in an unending chain. What could entice him, he wondered. Enchanting hopes, freedom from care—no! He knew everything that lay ahead. Honor, striving for awards? Why, what did he want with them? Was it worth struggling for some twenty or thirty years like a fish against the ice? And does that warm the heart? Does it comfort the soul when several people bow deeply before you, but perhaps think to themselves: "The devil take you!"

Love? No, indeed! He knew it by heart, and he'd already lost the capacity to love. Yet his all too ready memory, as if to mock him, reminded him of Nadenka, but not of the innocent, naive Nadenka—he never recalled her—but unfailingly Nadenka the traitor with the entire setting, the trees, path, flowers, and in the midst of it all, that little snake with the familiar smile, with her blush of languor and shame... and always for the other man, not for him! With a groan he grasped for his heart.

"Friendship," he thought, "is another stupidity! I know it all, there's nothing new, the past won't be repeated, but may it live!"

He didn't believe anybody or in anything, and did not lose himself in pleasure; he consumed it, as a man with no appetite consumes a delicacy, coldly, aware that boredom will immediately set in, knowing it's impossible to fill spiritual emptiness with anything. If you trust feeling, it will deceive you; it will only agitate the soul and add several wounds to the earlier ones. When he saw people bound together by love and beside themselves with exaltation, he would smile ironically and think, "Wait, you'll come to your senses. After the first joys jealousy will begin, scenes of reconciliation, tears. Living together, you'll bore each other to death, but if you separate, you'll both begin to weep. Come together again—and it's still worse. People are crazy! They quarrel constantly, sulk at each other, are jealous, then make it up for a minute, only to quarrel more violently. That's their love and devotion! And they insist on calling it all *happiness* even while they're foaming at the mouth or they have tears of despair in their eyes. You can keep your friendship... it's like a *bone you'd throw to your dogs!*"

He was afraid to desire, knowing that often, just as you are about to obtain what you want, fate will snatch happiness out of your hands and offer something quite different which you didn't want at all—some kind of trash. And if fate finally does grant your wish, it's only after first torturing, exhausting, debasing you in your own eyes and then throwing it at you, as one throws a tidbit to a dog. First you make him crawl up to the tasty morsel, look at it, hold it on his nose, roll over in the dust, stand on his hind paws and then—catch!

The periodic tides of happiness and unhappiness in life also frightened him. He did not foresee any joys, but always without fail grief; it can't be avoided—everyone is subject to the general law. To all is issued an equal portion of both happiness and unhappiness, it seemed to him. Happiness had ended for him, and what kind of happiness was it? Phantasmagoria, deception. Only grief was real, and it lay ahead. There would be illnesses and old age and various losses too, perhaps even poverty... As his aunt from the country would say, all these *blows of fate* lay waiting for him, and what comforts would there be? A lofty poetic destiny had deceived him. A heavy burden was being put upon him, and this was called duty! There were pitiful benefits—money, comfort, rank... You can have them! Oh, how sad to consider life, understand what it's like and not understand why it is!

Such was his misery and he could not see any way out of the depths of these doubts. His experiences only exhausted him in vain and added no health to his life, did not cleanse the air, gave no light. He didn't know what to do, turned from side to side on the sofa, began going through his friends in his mind—and grew still sadder. One was an excellent civil servant who enjoyed respect and was known as a good administrator. Another had surrounded himself with a family and preferred a quiet life to all the vain goods of this world, envying no one, desiring nothing. A third... yes, what? They all somehow had arranged their lives, settled down and were going their clear and predictable way. "Only I alone... yes, what sort am I?"

Here he began to probe within: could he be an administrator, some kind of squadron commander? Could he content himself with family life? And he realized that neither one, nor the other, nor the third would content him. Some little devil kept wriggling in him, whispering to him, that this was too petty for him, that he must fly higher... but where and how—he couldn't decide. He'd been mistaken about being an author. "What am I to do, what should I begin?" he asked himself and didn't know what to answer. So vexation gnawed at him. But, after all, to be an administrator or a squadron commander... Not really; the time had passed; you have to begin from the start.

Despair squeezed tears from his eyes—tears of vexation, envy, ill-will toward everyone, the most tormenting tears. He bitterly regretted that he had not listened to his mother and had fled the provinces.

"In her heart dear Mama sensed the distant grief," he thought. "There these unquiet impulses would have had an undisturbed sleep. There the stormy agitation of this complicated life would not have existed. In due course all the human feelings and passions would have touched me, self-love and pride and ambition—all would have touched my heart in small measure within the narrow limits of our district and all would have been fulfilled. I would have been first in the province! Yes, everything is relative! The godly spark of heavenly fire which burns more or less in all of us would have flashed unnoticed in me and quickly have gone out in the idle life there, or it would have begun burning in my attachment to my wife and children. My existence would not have been poisoned. I would have lived out my destiny proudly. My path in life would have been quiet and seemed to me both simple and comprehensible. My life would have been within my strength; I would have endured the struggle with it... And love? It would have bloomed luxuriously and filled my whole life. Sophie would have loved me in tranquillity. I would not have lost my belief in anything, I'd have plucked only roses without encountering thorns or even experiencing jealousy—for lack of competition! Why should I have been drawn so strongly and blindly into the distance, the fog, the unequal and unknown struggle with fate? And how wonderfully I understood both life and people then, as I might still have understood them even now, though now I understand nothing. I expected so much then of life and not having considered it carefully, would still be expecting something from it even now. I discovered so many treasures in my soul; and where did they go? I peddled them about the world, offered the sincerity of my heart, my first ardent passion—and what did I receive? Bitter disillusionment. I learned that all is deception, nothing is permanent, that it is impossible to rely either on yourself or others—and I began to fear both others and myself... In the midst of this analysis I could not recognize the little things of life and be content with them, like Uncle and many others... And now here I am!"

Now he wanted but one thing, to forget the past, to enjoy peace and the sleep of the soul. He grew ever colder toward life and regarded everything with sleepy eyes. In crowds of people, in the noise of gatherings he found boredom; he fled them, but boredom followed.

He was surprised at how people can enjoy themselves, be constantly busy with something or other, get excited every day over new interests. He found it strange others were not walking about sleepily, that they didn't weep or talk about pangs and mutual sufferings, when not chatting about the weather, and if they did talk, it was about pangs in the legs or another place, about rheumatism or hemorrhoids. Only the body caused them concern, and they didn't even mention the soul! "Empty, worthless people, animals!" he thought. And sometimes he would then fall into deep meditation. "There are so many of them, these worthless people," he told himself, worried, "while I am only one. Can it be... they are all... empty... wrong... while I?..."

Here it seemed to him that everyone except him alone was to blame, and he grew even more unhappy because of this.

He stopped seeing old friends, and the idea of drawing close to anyone new chilled him. After talking to his uncle he sank deeper into sleepy apathy. His soul was plunged in complete drowsiness. He surrendered to a kind of indifference, lived in idleness, stubbornly turned away from everything that recalled the educated world even a little.

"However you get through life, just get through it!" he would say. "Everyone is free to understand life as he will, and, then, after you die..."

He sought out conversations with people who were mean and bitterminded, with cruel hearts, and he spoke openly only when he heard fate being viciously ridiculed. Or he spent time with people beneath him in intellect and upbringing, most of all with the old man Kostyakov, to whom Zayezzhalov wanted to introduce Pyotr Ivanych.

Kostyakov lived in a part of St. Petersburg called Peski, and he would walk along the street there wearing a glossy leather cap and a robe belted with a bandana. He shared his room with a cook, with whom he played the card game "Trumps" in the evening. If there was a fire, he was the first at the scene and the last to go. When he passed a church in which there was a funeral service, he pushed his way through the crowd to look the dead man in the face and then accompanied him to the cemetery. In general, he was a passionate worshipper of ceremony of any kind, whether merry or sad. He also liked being present at unusual events of whatever kind: fights, fatal accidents, the cave-in of a ceiling, and so on, and read the newspaper accounts of such cases with special pleasure. In addition, he also read medical books, "so as to know what's inside a person," he said. In the winter Alexander played checkers with him and in the summer went fishing outside the city. The old man chatted about this and that. On their way to the fields, he talked about the grain and the sowing; when they walked along the bank, about the fish and the river boats, and going along the street he made remarks about the houses, their construction, materials and the income from them... He never talked about abstractions. He looked at life as something good if you had money, and if not, the other way round. Such a person was not dangerous to Alexander and could not awaken any spiritual agitation in him.

Alexander was trying to stifle the spiritual in himself as diligently as hermits try to mortify the flesh. He was silent at the office; if he met acquaintances, he got rid of them with two or three words, saying he had no time, and ran off. Yet he spent time with Kostyakov every day. Sometimes the old man would sit all day at Alexander's, other times invite him to his house to eat cabbage. He had already taught Alexander to make homemade liquor, solyanka soup and meat balls. Then they would set off together to a nearby village—to open country. Kostyakov had a lot of acquaintances everywhere. He talked with the peasants about how they were getting on, he joked with the women—he was, indeed, the jester Zayezzhalov had praised. Alexander allowed him full freedom of speech but remained silent himself for the most part.

He already felt that ideas of the world he'd left behind pursued him ever less often, churned less rapidly in his head, and as they found neither reinforcement nor opposition in the environment, they went unexpressed and died without multiplying. Within him his soul was as untended and empty as a neglected garden. Not much more was needed to make it a total wilderness. A few months more—and farewell! But here's what happened.

One day Alexander was fishing with Kostyakov. Dressed in a belted tunic and his leather cap, Kostyakov had set up on the bank a few rods of different sizes—rods for deep water, rods with cork floats, and rods with small and larger bells. He smoked a short pipe as he watched this battery of rods, Aduyev's among them, without daring to wink an eye, while Alexander stood leaning against a tree and looked in the other direction. For a long time they stood this way in silence.

"You have a bite, look, Alexander Fyodorych!" Kostyakov suddenly said in a whisper.

Aduyev looked at the water and again turned away. "No, it seemed so to you because of the ripple," he said.

"Look, look!" cried Kostyakov, "a bite, really, a bite! Oh, oh! Pull, pull! Hold on!"

Indeed, the float dove down in the water, the line quickly played out after it, and after the line even the rod began crawling out from the bush. Alexander reached for the rod, then for the line.

"Not so hard, lightly, not that way... what are you doing?" cried Kostyakov, skillfully intercepting the line. "Goodness! What a weight! Don't jerk—lead, lead, otherwise it'll break. Like this, to the right, to the left, this way, toward the shore. Move away! Keep on; now pull, pull, only not suddenly, that's right, that's right..."

On the surface of the water an enormous pike showed up. It quickly started to circle, flashing its silver scales and whipping with its tail to the right, then to the left, splashing them both with spray. Kostyakov turned pale.

"What a pike!" he cried, almost frightened, and stretched out over the water, fell, stumbled against his hooks and grabbed with both hands for the pike as it twisted above the water. "Now to the shore, to the shore, that way, keep on! It'll be ours there, however it twists. See how it slides, like a devil! Oh, what a fish!"

"Oh, my!" someone repeated from behind.

Alexander turned around. Two steps away from them stood an old man and, arm in arm with him, a pretty young girl, tall, bareheaded, and with an umbrella in her hands. Her brows drew slightly together in a frown. She bent forward a little and much involved, followed Kostyakov's movement with her eyes. She didn't even notice Alexander.

This unexpected apparition confused Aduyev. He let go the rod. The pike bounced back into the water, gracefully swished its tail and whirled into the deep water, pulling the line after it. All this happened in a single moment.

"Alexander Fyodorych! How could you?" cried Kostyakov like a madman and began getting hold of the line. He seized it and dragged out only the end, but without the hook and without the pike.

Quite pale, he turned to Alexander, showing him the end of the line and looked at him with rage for a whole minute in silence, then spit.

"If ever I go fishing with you, may I be accursed!" he declared and went back to his rods.

At this point the girl noticed Alexander was looking at her, blushed and retreated. The old man, apparently her father, bowed to Aduyev. Aduyev gloomily returned the bow, threw away his fishing rod and sat down on a bench under a tree about ten steps away.

"Even here there's no peace!" he thought. "Here's some Oedipus with his Antigone. Again a woman! There's no place to escape! Heavens, there are masses of them everywhere!"

"Alas! you fishermen!" said Kostyakov meanwhile, arranging his rods and angrily glancing at Alexander from time to time. "What's the use of your catching fish—you'd better catch mice, sitting at home there on your sofa! What's the point of fishing if the fish slips out of your hands? It was almost in your mouth, all but fried! It's a wonder it didn't walk off your plate!"

"Are you getting bites?" asked the old man.

"Yes, but you see," answered Kostyakov. "Though I've got six rods over here, just one cussed little perch came nibbling so as to mock me. But over there at the same time, what should turn up—you should have seen the big rod, that one with the cork: a pike, maybe ten pounds, and we let it get away! Well, they say the beast runs at the hunter! However that may be, if he'd broken loose from me, I would have gotten him in the water. But here the pike climbs in our teeth by himself, and we're asleep... and we still call ourselves fishermen! What kind of a fisherman is that! Are there fishermen like that? No, a real fisherman wouldn't blink an eye, even if a cannon were fired beside him. And this is a fisherman? What do you go fishing for?"

The girl had managed to see meanwhile that Alexander was a quite different sort from Kostyakov. Alexander was not dressed like Kostyakov; his height, years, manners, indeed everything about him was different. She quickly noticed signs of upbringing in him and read ideas on his face; even the shadow of sorrow did not escape her.

"But, look, he ran away!" she thought. "Strange, it seems I'm not the kind to run away from..."

The girl straightened up proudly, let her lashes fall and then raised them again and gave Alexander an unfavorable glance.

She indeed felt vexed. She drew her father's attention away and majestically walked past Aduyev.

The old man again exchanged bows with Alexander as they parted, but his daughter did not deign to give him even a glance.

"Let him realize that people aren't paying him any attention at all!" she thought, glancing on the side to see if Aduyev was looking.

Though Alexander indeed didn't look at her, still he involuntarily assumed a more picturesque pose.

"Look at him! He doesn't even cast a glance!" thought the girl. "What arrogance!"

The next day Kostyakov lured Alexander to go fishing again, and thus was cursed by his own oath.

For two days nothing disturbed their solitude. At first Alexander looked around, as if afraid, but not seeing anyone, regained his composure. The second day he pulled out an enormous perch. Kostyakov halfway made peace with him.

"Still, that's not a pike!" he said with a sigh. "We had happiness in our hands but didn't know how to make use of it; that doesn't happen twice! And again nothing for me! Nothing on six rods."

"Just ring your little bells!" said some peasant who stopped in passing to have a look at the success of their fishing. "Maybe the fish will come to hear the good news..."

Kostyakov gave him an angry look. "Shut up, you ignorant ninny!" he said, "peasant!"

The peasant went away.

"Blockhead!" Kostyakov cried after him. "Once a swine, always one. Laugh at your own kind, accursed devil! You're a dumb swine, I say, peasant!"

God forbid you should tease a hunter at a moment of bad luck!

The third day, as they fished in silence, training their unmoving glance on the water, a rustle was heard from behind. Alexander turned and started as if bitten by a mosquito, neither more nor less. The old man and young girl were there.

Aduyev, giving them a sideward look, hardly answered the old man's bow, but apparently expected this visit. Usually he went fishing in very careless dress. But this time he had put on a new topcoat and coquettishly tied a blue scarf round his neck, put his hair in order, even, it seemed, curled it a bit; he'd begun to resemble an idyllic fisherman. After waiting as long as good manners required, he walked away and sat down under a tree.

"*Cela passe toute permission!*" thought Antigone, flaring up in anger.

"Excuse us!" said Oedipus to Aduyev, "perhaps we're bothering you?..."

"No!" answered Aduyev. "I'm tired."

"Are they biting?" the old man asked Kostyakov.

"How can they bite when people talk an arm's length away," answered Kostyakov angrily. "Just now some kind of gnome came through with foolish chatter—why would they bite after that? So you apparently live nearby in the neighborhood?" he asked Oedipus.

"There's our summer cottage, the one with the balcony," he answered.

"Is it expensive, pray?"

"Five hundred rubles for the summer."

"It seems like a good cottage, well-managed, and there are a lot of outside sheds. Probably cost the owner some thirty thousand."

"Yes, about."

"So. And is this your daughter?"

"She is."

"Yes, Sir. A splendid young lady! Are you taking a walk?"

"Yes, we are. If you live in the country, you have to take walks."

"Quite so, quite so, how could you not; the weather's good, not like last week. What weather that was, oh my, my! God prevent more of the like. We'll be harvesting winter crops."

"God willing, it'll turn nice."

"God willing!"

"So, you're not catching anything just now!"

"I'm not, but he—see here, have a look."

He showed the perch.

"I can tell you," he continued, "it's unusual to have his luck! Unfortunately he doesn't have his mind on it; otherwise with his luck we'd never come home empty."

He sighed.

Antigone began to listen more attentively, but Kostyakov fell silent.

The appearance of the old man and his daughter began to be repeated more and more often. Even Aduyev deigned to notice them. Sometimes he too exchanged a word or two with the old man, but he still said nothing to the daughter. She at first felt irritated, then insulted and finally became sad. If Aduyev had spoken to her or even paid her ordinary attention, she would have forgotten him, but this way it was quite otherwise. A person's heart, it seems, lives on contradictions; without them, he wouldn't even have a heart.

Antigone was about to consider some terrible plan of revenge, but then gradually abandoned it.

Once when the old man and his daughter approached our friends, after a short wait Alexander put his rod on a bush and, as he usually did, sat down in his place and mechanically looked now at the father, now at the daughter.

They stood in profile to him. He saw nothing special in the father. A white shirt, homespun trousers and a flat hat with broad brims faced in green velvet. But the daughter, though! How gracefully she leaned on the father's arm! The wind now would blow her curls off her face as if intent on showing Alexander her pretty profile and white neck, then half catch up her little silk cape, showing her well-shaped waist, then play with her dress, uncovering her tiny foot. She looked pensively at the water.

For a long while Alexander could not take his eyes off her and felt a feverish shiver run through his body. He turned away from the temptation and began whipping the tops off flowers with a stick.

"Oh! how well I know what this is!" he thought. "Give it free rein and it will take off. Here you have love ready-made—how stupid! Uncle's right. But animal feeling alone will not tempt me. No, I will not lower myself to that."

"May I fish a little?" the girl asked Kostyakov shyly.

"You may, Miss, why not?" he answered, giving her Aduyev's rod.

"So there, you have a companion!" said the father to Kostyakov, and leaving his daughter, he set off to wander along the bank. "See it, Liza, catch some fish for supper," he added.

Silence lasted for several minutes.

"Why is your companion so gloomy?" Liza asked Kostyakov quietly.

"He's been passed by for promotion the third time, Miss."

"What?" she asked, frowning slightly.

"The third time, I say, they haven't given him the job."

She shook her head. "No, that can't be!" she thought. "That isn't it!"

"You don't believe me, Miss? I swear by my soul! And he let go the pike, remember, for that reason too."

"It's not that, not that," she thought, this time convinced: "I know why he let the pike go."

"Oh, oh," she suddenly cried out, "look, it's bobbing, it's bobbing!"

She pulled and caught nothing.

"The fish broke away!" said Kostyakov, looking at the rod, "you see, when it got the worm. It was probably a big perch. But you don't know how, Miss. You didn't let him take the hook properly."

"Oh, do you really have to know how to do this too?"

"As in everything," said Alexander automatically.

She blushed and quickly turned round, in turn dropping the rod in the water. But Alexander was already looking the other way.

"How do you get to the point of knowing how?" she said with a slight tremble in her voice.

"Practice more often," answered Alexander.

"So that's it!" she thought with a shock of pleasure, "that is, come here more often—I understand! Good, but I'll torment you, Mr. Barbarian, for all your arrogance..."

That's the translation of Alexander's answer which her coquetry gave her. But he said nothing more that day.

"She'll think, if you please, God knows what!" he said to himself, "she will begin to put on airs, play the coquette... that's stupid!"

From that day on the old man and his daughter came by every day. Sometimes Liza came without the old man and with her nurse. She brought work and books with her and sat under the tree; she was quite indifferent to Alexander's presence.

She thought in this way to touch his pride and, as she said, *torment* him. Out loud she chatted with her nurse about the house and housekeeping to show that she didn't even see Aduyev. And he sometimes really did not see her, once he had caught sight of her and dryly bowed—and he said not a word.

Noting that this ordinary maneuver was unsuccessful, she changed her plan of attack and would herself now and then start talking to him; sometimes she borrowed his rod. Gradually Alexander became more communicative with her, but he was very careful and did not allow any openness. Was it calculation on his part or still his *former wounds for which there was no cure* after all, as he said? Anyway, he was quite cold with her, even in conversation.

One day the old man had a samovar brought out on the bank. Liza poured tea. Alexander stubbornly refused, saying he didn't drink tea in the evening.

"All this tea drinking leads to greater intimacy... acquaintance... I don't want it!" he thought.

"What are you saying? Why yesterday you drank four glasses!" said Kostyakov.

"I don't drink outdoors," Alexander hastened to add.

"You're missing something!" said Kostyakov. "It's wonderful tea, aromatic, I'd say around fifteen rubles a pound. Please, some more, Miss; indeed with rum it would be good!"

They even brought rum.

The old man urged Alexander, who abruptly refused. When Liza heard the refusal, she pouted. She began trying to get out of him reasons for his unfriendliness. However slyly she guided the conversation to that subject, Alexander still more slyly turned it away.

This secrecy only stimulated her curiosity and perhaps even a different feeling in Liza. On her face, till then clear as the summer sky, there appeared a cloud of disturbance, thoughtfulness. She often looked sadly at Alexander, turned her eyes away with a sigh, lowered her gaze to the ground, and for her part thought, it seemed: "You're unhappy! perhaps disappointed in love... Oh, how I would know how to make you happy! How I would take care of you, how love you... I would defend you from fate itself. I would..." and so on.

Great numbers of women think this way and great numbers deceive those who believe this song of the sirens. Alexander seemed to notice nothing. He talked with her as he would talk with a friend, with his uncle—not a trace of that tenderness which unintentionally creeps into the friendship of a man and a woman and makes their relations different from friendship. For this reason they say that there isn't and cannot be friendship between a man and a woman, that what is called friendship between them is nothing but the beginning or the remains of love, or, indeed, love itself. Yet, looking at Aduyev's manner with Liza, one could believe that such friendship exists.

Once only he partly showed or wanted to show her his manner of thinking. He took from the bench the book she had brought and opened it. It was *Childe Harolde* in a French translation. Alexander shook his head, sighed, and silently put the book back in its place.

"You don't like Byron? You're against Byron?" she said. "Byron is such a great poet—and you don't like him!"

"I haven't said anything, and you've already attacked me," he answered.

"Why did you shake your head?"

"True. I'm sorry this book fell into your hands."

"Sorry for what, the book or me?"

Alexander was silent.

"Why shouldn't I read Byron?" she asked.

"For two reasons," said Alexander after a moment's silence. He laid his hand on hers, whether the better to persuade her, or because she had a soft, white little hand. He began to speak softly, measuredly, letting his eyes move now over her curls, now her neck, now her waist. In time with these movements his voice gradually rose.

"First," he said, "because you're reading Byron in French, and therefore, the beauty and power of the poet's language are lost for you! Look, what a pale, colorless pitiful language this is! It's the ashes of the great poet; it's as if his ideas had floated away in water. Second, because I would not advise you to read Byron, because... he perhaps will awaken in your soul vibrations that otherwise would not resound as long as you live..."

Here he pressed her hand strongly and expressively, as if by this he wanted to give weight to his words.

"Why should you read Byron?" he continued. "Perhaps your life will flow quietly like this stream. You see how small, slight it is. It reflects neither the whole sky nor the clouds. On its banks there are neither cliffs nor sharp slopes. It flows playfully. Ripples just barely mark its surface. It reflects only the green of the banks, a shred of sky, a tiny cloud... Probably your life would flow thus, but you're bringing on yourself vain agitations, storms. You want to look at life and people through a dark glass... Let it be, don't read it! Look at everything with a smile, don't look into the distance, live day by day, don't consider the dark sides of life and people, otherwise..."

"Otherwise what?"

"Nothing!" said Alexander, as if coming to.

"No, tell me: you've probably experienced something or other?"

"Where's my rod? Allow me, it's time for me to go now."

He seemed disturbed that he had spoken out so incautiously.

"No, one more word," Liza began. "Admit that a poet should make the reader feel with him. Byron is a great poet. Why don't you want me to feel with him? Do you think me so stupid, trivial that I shan't understand?..."

She was offended.

"Not quite that. Feel with what is peculiar to your feminine heart; seek what's in tune with it, otherwise terrible cacophony can result... in both head and heart." Here he shook his head as if hinting that he himself was the victim of such.

"One person will show you a flower," he said, "and make you enjoy its fragrance and beauty, while another will point out only the poisonous sap in the calyx... then both beauty and fragrance will be lost for you... He'll make you deplore the fact that the sap is there, and you'll forget that the fragrance is there also... There's a difference between these two people and between sympathy for them. Don't look for poison, don't get to the bottom of everything that happens to us and around us; don't seek unnecessary experience; that's not what leads to happiness."

He fell silent. She listened to him trustingly and thoughtfully.

"Talk to me, talk to me," she said with childlike submission. "I'm ready to listen to you for days on end, to obey you in everything..."

"Me?" said Alexander coldly. "I beg you! What right have I to tell you what to do?... Excuse me for letting myself make a suggestion. Read what you want... *Childe Harolde* is a very good book, Byron, a great poet!"

"No, don't pretend! Don't talk like that. Tell me what I should read."

With pedantic solemnity he tried to suggest several historical and travel books to her, but she said they had bored her at school. Then he recommended Walter Scott, Cooper, several French and English writers—men and women—and two or three of the Russians, trying the while, as if unintentionally, to show off his literary taste and fine feeling. After that there wasn't any conversation of the sort between them.

Alexander kept wanting to run away. "What are women to me!" he said. "I can't love, I've had it with them..."

"All right, all right!" Kostyakov objected to this. "So get married, then you'll see. I myself only wanted to play around with young girls and women, but when the time came for the ceremony, I could think of nothing else—someone pushed me so to get married!"

And Alexander did not run away either. All his former dreams began to stir in him. His heart began to beat faster. Liza's waist would flash before his eyes, or her small foot, or her curls, and his life grew somewhat brighter again. Kostyakov hadn't called him for some three days; instead, he dragged Kostyakov fishing himself. "Again! Again the same thing!" said Alexander, "but I shall be firm!"— and meanwhile he hurried to the stream.

Each time Liza would be impatiently awaiting the arrival of the friends. Each evening the cup of aromatic tea with rum would be made for Kostyakov—and perhaps Liza owed it to this lure that they did not fail to come even a single evening. If they were late, Liza and her father would be coming to meet them. When bad weather kept the friends at home, there'd be no end to reproaching them and the weather.

Alexander thought and thought and decided to stop his trips there for a time, Heaven knows why—he didn't know why himself, and he didn't go fishing for a whole week. Neither did Kostyakov. At last they set out.

A whole mile before the spot where they fished, they met Liza and her nurse. She cried out when she caught sight of them, then became suddenly embarrassed and blushed. Aduyev bowed coldly. Kostyakov launched into conversation.

"So here we are," he said. "You weren't expecting us? Hee, hee, hee! I see you weren't, even the samovar isn't here! What a long time, Miss, what a long time since you've seen us! Are they biting? I kept wanting to come, but I couldn't persuade Alexander Fyodorych here; he sat at home... or no, that is, he lay on his back the whole time."

She glanced reproachfully at Aduyev.

"What does that mean?" she asked.

"What?"

"You didn't come for a whole week?"

"Yes; I haven't been here for a week, it seems."

"Why then?"

"Well, I didn't want to..."

"Didn't want to!" she said with astonishment.

"Yes, why?"

She was silent, but seemed to be thinking. "How could you not want to come here? I wanted to send Papa to the city to see you," she said, "but I didn't know where you live."

"To the city to see me? What for?"

"A fine question!" she said, insulted. "What for? To find out whether something had happened to you, were you sick?..."

"Why do you care?..."

"Why do I care? Heavens!"

"Heavens what?"

"Why do you ask 'what'! Why, you see... I have your books..." She grew embarrassed. "Not to come for a week!" she added.

"Do you suppose I have to be here every day without fail?"

"Without fail!"

"Why?"

"Why, why!" She looked at him sadly and repeated, "why, why!"

He looked at her. What was this? Tears, dismay and joy and reproaches? She was pale, had grown somewhat thin, her eyes had reddened.

"So here we have it! Already!" thought Alexander. "I didn't expect it so soon!" Then he laughed loudly.

"'Why?' you say. Listen...," she continued. A kind of resolve gleamed in her eyes. She obviously had prepared herself to say something important, but at that moment her father came up to them.

"Till tomorrow," she said, "tomorrow I must have a talk with you. I can't today. My heart is too full... Tomorrow you'll come? Yes, do you hear? You won't forget us? Won't abandon us?..."

And she ran away without waiting for an answer.

Her father looked fixedly at her, then at Aduyev and shook his head;

Alexander looked after her in silence. He apparently pitied her and was vexed with himself that without noticing he had brought her to this state; blood did not rush to his heart, but to his head.

"She loves me," thought Alexander on the way home. "Heavens, how boring! How annoying! Now we mustn't even come here, yet the fish bite wonderfully at this spot... it's a shame!"

But at the same time inwardly, it seems, for some reason he was not dissatisfied with this, but grew cheerful and talked the whole time to Kostyakov.

His obliging imagination, as if on purpose, drew him a full-length portrait of Liza with luxurious shoulders, shapely waist, not to forget her little foot. A strange sensation began to throb in him, again a tremor ran through his body, but did not reach the soul—and died. He observed this sensation from the beginning to the very end.

"Animal!" he muttered to himself. "So that's the kind of thought that goes round in your mind... Ah! Nude shoulders, bust, tiny foot... Exploit trust and inexperience... deceive... Well, good, deceive and then what? The same boredom and besides, pangs of conscience, perhaps, and why? No, no! I won't let myself, won't lead her on... Oh, I'll stand firm! I feel in myself enough purity of soul, nobility of heart... I won't surrender and won't seduce her."

Liza waited for him all day with a tremor of pleasure, but then her heart fell; she felt downcast without knowing why; she grew sad and almost wished Alexander wouldn't come. When the appointed hour arrived and still no Alexander, her impatience turned into tormenting melancholy. With the last ray of the sun, every hope vanished; she began to cry bitterly.

The next day she revived again, was again cheerful in the morning, but toward evening she knew ever greater sorrow and was dying of both fear and hope. Again they didn't come.

The third and fourth day, the same thing. But hope always drew her to the river bank. Hardly would a boat show in the distance or two human figures be glimpsed along the bank, but she'd start to tremble and feel faint from the burden of joyous expectation. But when she'd see it wasn't they in the boat, or the figures weren't they, she'd drop her head to her chest dispiritedly and despair would descend more strongly upon her soul... A minute later sly hope would again whisper to her the comforting supposition of some delay—and her heart would again start beating in expectation. But Alexander held back, as if intentionally.

Finally when she was sitting one day, half ill and hopeless, at her place under the tree, she suddenly heard a rustle, turned and shuddered in joyous fright: Alexander stood before her, his arms folded in a cross.

She stretched out her hands to him with joyous tears and for a long time couldn't regain her composure. He took her by one hand and hungrily looked into her face, he too with emotion.

"You've grown thin!" he said quietly. "Are you suffering?"

She shuddered.

"How long it is since you've come!" she said.

"And you've waited for me?"

"I?" she answered excitedly. "Oh, if you knew!"

She finished her answer with a hard squeeze of his hand.

"But I've come to say goodbye to you!" he said and stopped, watching to see how she'd take it.

She looked at him with fright and disbelief.

"It's not true," she said.

"It's true!" he answered.

"Listen!" she said, shyly looking around in all directions. "Don't go away, for Heaven's sake, don't go away! I'll tell you a secret... Here Papa will see us from the little windows; let's go to our garden, to the summer house... it faces out toward the field, I'll show you the way."

They set out. Alexander did not take his eyes off her shoulders, shapely waist and felt a feverish tremor.

"Of what importance is it," he thought, walking behind her, "that I go? Look, so I'll only... take a look how it is there in their summer house... her father invited me; look, I could go straight there and openly... But I'm far from temptation, really far, and I'll show that. Here I've come on purpose to say I'm leaving.... though, indeed, I'm not going anywhere! No, Devil! you won't tempt me." But here, it seems, it was as if Krylov's little devil, who appeared from behind the stove to the hermit, had whispered to him, "But why did you come to say this, there was no need for that. You need only not have come and two weeks later you'd have been forgotten..."

Yet it seemed to Alexander he was acting nobly, coming for a heroic deed of self-sacrifice to fight temptation face to face. The first trophy of his victory over himself was a kiss he snatched from Liza; then he put his arm around her waist and told her he wasn't going anywhere, that he invented this so as to test her, find out whether she had any feeling for him. Finally, he completed his victory by promising to come to the summer house the next day at the same hour. Walking home, he went over what he had done and first cold, then heat came over him. His heart stood still in horror, and he did not believe himself. Finally, he resolved not to appear on the morrow—and arrived earlier than the appointed time.

This was in August. It was already getting dark. Alexander promised to come at nine o'clock, but arrived at eight, alone, without a fishing rod. Like a thief he made his way to the summer house, now fearfully looking around, now running top-speed. But someone got there ahead of him. This person hurriedly, panting, ran into the summer house and sat on the couch in the dark corner.

Some one was watching for Alexander, it seemed. He quietly opened the door, went on tiptoe in great excitement up to the couch and quietly took by the hand—Liza's father. Alexander shuddered, jumped back, wanted to run, but the old man seized him by the coat-tail and sat him down by force beside him on the couch.

"What does this mean, Sir, your coming here?" he asked.

"Why... for fish..." muttered Alexander, hardly moving his lips. His teeth were chattering. The old man was not at all terrible, but Alexander, like every thief caught in the act, trembled as if in a fever.

"For fish!" repeated the old man derisively. "Do you know what it means to fish in troubled waters? I've been watching you for a long time and now at last I know what you are. I've known my Liza from infancy. She's good and trusting. But you—you're a dangerous scoundrel..."

Alexander wanted to get up, but the old man held him there by the hand.

"Yes, Sir, don't get angry. You pretended to be unhappy, slyly avoided Liza, so she'd fall for you, made sure she had, yes, and wanted to make use of the situation... Do you call this a noble action? What are we to call you?"

"I swear on my honor, I did not foresee the consequences..." said Alexander in a voice of deep conviction. "I didn't want..."

The old man was silent for several minutes.

"Maybe that's true!" he said. "Perhaps not for love, but by chance, for want of something to do, you've turned a poor little girl's head, not knowing yourself what would come of it. If you succeeded—fine; if not—you're none the worse for it. In Petersburg there are lots of such headhunters. Do you know what they do to such men about town?"

Alexander sat with downcast gaze. He lacked the spirit to justify himself.

"In the beginning I thought better of you, but I was mistaken, very much mistaken! Why, what a quiet one you pretended to be! Thank Heaven, I realized in time. She doesn't need to see us together. You will go away and, of course, will never return. She will think you deceived her, and this will teach her a lesson. Only see to it that you never come here. Find another place to fish, and if you don't... I'll show you the door in a very unfriendly way... It's your good luck that Liza can still look me straight in the eye. I've watched her the whole day... Otherwise you wouldn't be leaving here this way... Goodbye for good!"

Alexander wanted to say something, but the old man opened the door and almost pushed him out.

In what state Alexander left—let the reader judge, if only he won't scruple to put himself in Alexander's place for a minute. Tears even gushed from our hero's eyes, tears of shame, of rage at himself, of despair...

"Why am I alive?" he said in a loud voice. "Repulsive, murderous life! But I, I... No, though I lacked the firmness to withstand temptation... I do have enough spirit to put an end to this useless, shameless existence."

With rapid steps he walked to the stream. It was black. Over its waves some kind of long, fantastic, distorted shadows played. The bank where Alexander stood was low.

"It's impossible to die here!" he said contemptuously and went out on a bridge a hundred paces from there. Alexander leaned his elbows on the railing in the middle of the bridge and began looking at the water. In his thoughts he said farewell to life, sent sighs in his mother's direction, blessed his aunt, even forgave Nadenka. He melted as tears of emotion flowed over his cheeks... He covered his face with his hands... We'll never know what he would have done when suddenly the bridge began to move under his feet. He looked around: Heavens! He was on the brink of the precipice; before him gaped the grave. Half the bridge had separated and was floating away... Ships were passing through; another minute—and goodbye forever. He gathered all his strength and made a desperate leap... to the far side. There he stopped, breathed deep and seized his heart.

"You did have a fright, Sir, didn't you?" the watchman asked him.

"Indeed, friend, I almost fell through the middle," Alexander answered in a trembling voice.

"Heaven forbid! Would you call that close?" said the watchman, yawning. "Year before last one young gentleman did fall that way."

Alexander set off for home, holding onto his heart with his hand. At times he looked back at the river and the separated bridge, stopped, then, trembling, turned away at once and quickened his pace.

Meanwhile Liza dressed coquettishly, and without either her father or her nurse sat out every evening under the tree till late at night.

The time of dark evenings began and she still waited, but neither hide nor hair of the friends was to be seen.

Autumn came. The yellow leaves falling from the trees covered the shore. The green faded, the river took on a leaden hue, the sky was always gray, a cold wind blew with a fine rain. The banks and the river grew empty. No merry songs or laughter or resonant voices were heard along the banks, and boats and canoes stopped scurrying back and forth. Not a single insect buzzed in the grass, not a bird chirped on the tree; only jackdaws and crows brought on a melancholy mood with their cries; and the fish ceased to bite.

But Liza still waited. She needed without fail to have a talk with Alexander: to disclose a secret to him. She still sat on the bench under the tree in her short warm jacket. She had grown thin; her eyes had become a bit hollow, her cheeks were tied in a handkerchief. Her father found her thus one day.

"Come, you've had enough of sitting here," he said, frowning and shivering from the cold. "Look, your hands have turned blue, you're freezing. Liza! Do you hear? Let's go."

"Where?"

"Home; we're moving to the city today."

"Why?" she asked, surprised.

"What do you mean why? It's autumn outdoors; only we alone are left in the country."

"Oh, goodness!" she said. "Even in winter it'll be nice here; let's stay."

"Why, what an idea! Enough, enough, let's go!"

"Wait!" she said in an imploring tone, "the beautiful days will still come back."

"Listen!" answered her father, caressing her cheek and pointing to the place where the friends used to fish, "they won't be back..."

"Won't be back!.." she repeated questioningly, sadly, then gave her father her hand, and quietly with bowed head she went home, looking back at times.

And Aduyev and Kostyakov had long been fishing somewhere in the opposite direction from this place.

V

Gradually Alexander succeeded in forgetting both Liza and the unpleasant scene with her father. He became calm, even cheerful, even laughed heartily at Kostyakov's shallow jokes. This man's view of life made him laugh. They drew up plans for going somewhere further and building a hut on the river bank where there were lots of fish and living there the rest of their days. Alexander's soul again began to sink in the sludge of limited ideas and material existence.

But fate did not sleep, and he didn't manage to drown altogether in such sludge.

In the autumn he received a note from his aunt with an urgent request to take her to a concert because his uncle was not feeling altogether well. Some artist or other, a European star, had arrived.

"What, to a concert!" said Alexander, much disturbed. "Go to a concert, into that crowd again, into the very glitter of tinsel, lies, pretense. .. No, I won't go."

"Go on; look, it costs as much as five rubles," remarked Kostyakov, who was with him.

"A ticket costs fifteen," said Alexander, "but I'd gladly give fifty not to go."

"Fifteen!" cried Kostyakov, clapping his hands. "What rascals! Curses! To come here to swindle us, do us out of our money! Damned cannibals. Don't go, Alexander Fyodorych. Spit on it! Some kind of thing would be all right; you'd take it home, put it on the table, eat it. But only to listen to this, yes and pay fifteen rubles for it! You could buy a colt for fifteen rubles!"

"Sometimes people pay even more," remarked Alexander, "for an evening's pleasure."

"An evening's pleasure! Why, you know what—let's go to the baths; we'll spend the evening splendidly. Whenever I get bored, I go there—and it's a great pleasure. You go around six and come out at twelve, and you get warm and rub your body, and sometimes you start a pleasant acquaintance. A cleric or a business man or an officer comes. They start talking about business perhaps or about the end of the world... You wouldn't want to leave! And for altogether sixty kopecks each. Your friends don't know where to spend the evening!"

But Alexander went with his aunt. With a sigh he got out last year's tailcoat, which he had not worn for so long, and pulled on white gloves.

"White gloves at five rubles, makes twenty?" added up Kostyakov, who was present while Aduyev dressed. Twenty rubles, then, you've thrown out the window on a single evening. Listen, that's astonishing!"

Alexander had lost the habit of dressing properly. He went to work in the morning in a comfortable old civil-service uniform; he spent the evening in an old frock coat or overcoat. He felt ill at ease in the tails. It was tight in one spot; in another there was something missing; his neck felt hot in the satin scarf.

His aunt greeted him cordially, grateful that he had decided for her sake to quit his seclusion, but no word passed about his way of life and occupation.

After finding a seat in the hall for Lizaveta Alexandrovna, Aduyev leaned against a column in the shadow of a broad-shouldered music lover and began to feel bored. He quietly yawned behind his hand but hadn't managed to close his mouth when deafening applause greeted the artist. Alexander didn't even look at him.

The introduction was played. After a few minutes the orchestra became quieter. The last sounds were joined by others, barely audible, playful at first, carefree, as if to awake memories of childhood games; noisy and merry voices were heard, which sounded like children. Next the sounds became more fluent and heroic; they seemed to express carefree youth, daring, excess of life and strength. Then they flowed more slowly, quieter, as if expressing a tender outpouring of love, a spiritual conversation, and, growing weaker, gradually died down to a passionate whisper and imperceptibly became silent...

No one dared move. The crowd of people froze in silence. Finally a single *Oh!* burst from everyone and was carried in a whisper around the hall. The crowd was about to move, but suddenly the sounds awoke again, streamed forth in a crescendo, then fragmented into a thousand cascades, and began to bounce, crowding and pushing each other. They thundered as if in jealous reproaches, they seethed with the rage of passion. The ear had not quite managed to catch them when suddenly they broke off, as if the instrument had no more strength or voice. Under the artist's bow there broke forth a dull, jerky groan; then weeping, imploring sounds were heard, and everything ended with a sick, prolonged sigh. One's heart broke: the sounds seemed to sing of betrayed love and hopeless anguish. They had sounded all the sufferings and all the grief of the human soul.

Alexander trembled. He raised his head and looked through tears over his neighbor's shoulder. A thin German, bending over his instrument, stood before the crowd and powerfully commanded it. He finished and dispassionately wiped his hands and forehead with a handkerchief. A roar resounded in the auditorium and there was thunderous applause. And suddenly this artist in his turn bowed before the crowd and began to make deep bows and give thanks.

"And he bows to the crowd," thought Alexander, looking shyly at this thousand-headed hydra, "he, who stands so far above it!..."

The artist raised his bow—and everyone immediately fell silent. Hesitating, the crowd again coalesced in a single motionless body. Other sounds flowed, majestically and triumphantly. The sounds made the listener straighten up, raise his head, look upward. They aroused pride in his heart, gave birth to dreams of glory. The orchestra softly began to play the second part in the piece, which seemed like the distant murmur of the crowd, the voice of the people...

Alexander turned pale and bent his head. These sounds, as if intentionally, distinctly told the story of his past, his whole bitter and disappointed life.

"Look, what a face on that man!" somebody said, pointing to Alexander. "I don't understand how anyone can show his feelings that way; I heard Paganini, and I didn't even move an eyebrow. "

Alexander cursed his aunt's invitation and the artist and most of all the fate that did not let him forget himself.

"And why? What was her purpose?" he thought. "What did she accomplish with me? What's the use of reminding me of my helplessness, the uselessness of a past which cannot be reversed?"

After taking his aunt home, he wanted to leave, but she held him back by the hand.

"Won't you come in?" she asked reproachfully.

"No."

"Why not?"

"It's already late; some other time."

"So you refuse me even this?"

"You more than anyone."

"Why?"

"It would take a long while to explain. Good night."

"Half an hour, Alexander, do you hear, no more. If you refuse, it means you never had even a hair's breadth of friendship for me."

She asked with such feeling and so persuasively that Alexander hadn't the heart to refuse and he let his head droop as he followed her. Pyotr Ivanych was in his study.

"Have I really earned only disdain from you, Alexander?" asked Lizaveta Alexandrovna, seating him near the fireplace.

"You're mistaken: it isn't neglect," he answered.

"Then what does it mean? What should we call it? How many times have I written to you, invited you to come here; you haven't come and finally stopped answering my notes."

"It isn't disdain..."

"What is it then?"

"Well," said Alexander and sighed. "Good night, dear Aunt."

"Wait! What have I done to you? What is the matter with you, Alexander? Why are you like this? Why are you indifferent to everything? Why don't you go anywhere? Why do you live in company not of your kind?"

"That's the way it is, dear Aunt. I like this way of life. I like living calmly. This is my kind of life..."

"Your kind? Do you find food for mind and heart in such a life, with such people?"

Alexander nodded his assent.

"You're pretending, Alexander; you've been very hurt by something and won't talk about it. Before, you used to know whom you could tell about your grief. You knew you'd always find comfort or at least sympathy. But now do you really have no one?"

"No one!"

"You believe no one?"

"No one."

"Do you really not remember sometimes your dear mama, her love for you... her caresses?.. Hasn't it really occurred to you that perhaps someone here too loves you, if not as she does, still at least like a sister, or better still, like a friend?"

"Goodbye, dear Aunt," he said.

"Goodbye, Alexander: I shan't keep you longer," his aunt answered. Tears came to her eyes.

Alexander was about to take his hat, but then he laid it down and looked at Lizaveta Alexandrovna.

"No, I can't run away from you; I haven't the strength!" he said. "What are you doing to me!"

"Be the old Alexander again, even for a minute. Tell me, entrust it all to me."

"Indeed, I can't be silent with you; I'll tell you everything that's in my heart," he said. "You ask why I've been hiding from people, why I'm indifferent to everything, why I haven't been seeing even you... Why? You know that I've been disgusted with life for a long time and I've chosen a way of living in which one can feel less. I don't want anything, I don't seek anything except calm, the sleep of the soul. I've come to know all the emptiness, the void of life, and deeply scorn it. *He who has lived and thought can never look on mankind without disdain.*[16] Activity, tasks, worries, recreation—I became sick and tired of it all, I don't want to achieve and strive for anything. I have no goal because when you try for something, you achieve it—only to realize it's an illusion. Joys are past for me; I've cooled toward them. In the educated world, among people, I feel the disadvantages of life more strongly, but at home, alone, far from the crowd I've become numb; no matter what may happen in this somnolence I don't notice either other people or myself. I do nothing and I don't see my deeds or those of others, and I'm at peace... I don't care. There can be no happiness, but unhappiness cannot get to me..."

"That's awful! Alexander, at your time of life," said his aunt, "such indifference to everything..."

"What are you surprised about, dear Aunt? Separate yourself for a minute from the narrow confines in which you are enclosed. Look at life, at the world. What is it?... What was great yesterday, means nothing today. What you wanted yesterday, you don't want today. Your friend of yesterday is your enemy today. Is it worth bothering about something, loving, becoming attached, quarreling, making up—in a word, living? Isn't it better to sleep in both mind and heart? I sleep; that's the reason I don't go anywhere, and especially not to see you. I was about to fall completely to sleep, but you're waking up my mind and heart and pushing them back into the abyss again. If you want to see me cheerful, healthy, perhaps even alive, even, if you will, in Uncle's sense happy—leave me where I am now. Let these emotions calm down, let my dreams fade, my mind go numb, let my heart turn to stone, my eyes lose the habit of tears, my lips of smiles—and then in a year, maybe two, I'll come to see you wholly ready for any test; then you'll not awaken me, however you try, but now..." He made a desperate gesture.

"Look, Alexander," quickly interrupted his aunt, "in one minute you've changed. You have tears in your eyes. You're still quite the same; don't pretend, don't hold back your feelings, give them free rein..."

"What for? I won't be the better for it! I'll only torture myself the more. This evening has destroyed me in my own eyes. I've seen clearly that I haven't the right to blame anyone for my melancholy. I myself have ruined my life. I dreamed of glory, Heaven knows why, and neglected my business, I've ruined my modest vocation and can't make up for the past—it's too late! I fled the crowd, disdained it—but this German with his deep, powerful soul and poetic nature does not flee from the crowd; he's proud of their applause. He understands that he's a barely noticeable link in the infinite chain of humanity. He too knows everything I know; sufferings are familiar to him. People listened as he told in sounds of his whole life, both its joys and sorrows and happiness, and also the soul's grief—he understands it. How small I suddenly became today, nothing in my own eyes with my sadness, sufferings! He awakened in me the bitter awareness that I am proud—and powerless... Alas, why did you invite me? Goodbye, let me go..."

"What am I to blame for, Alexander? You're not saying I could awaken bitterness in you—I?..."

"That's just the trouble! Your angelic, kind face, dear Aunt, gentle speeches, friendly hand squeeze—all that disturbs and touches me. I want to cry, to live again, suffer... but what for?"

"What do you mean, what for? Stay with us always; and if you think me even a little bit worthy of your friendship, you will then find comfort in another person. I'm not the only such... others will value you."

"Yes! You think that will comfort me? You think I shall trust that momentary compassion? You are, true, a woman in the noblest sense of the word. You were made for the joy, the happiness of a man, but can one count on that happiness? Can one guarantee that it is firm, that today or tomorrow fate won't turn this happy life upside down—that's the question! Can one believe anything and anybody, even oneself? Isn't it better to live without any hopes and feelings, not expect anything, not seek any joys and therefore not mourn any losses?"

"You can't escape fate anywhere, Alexander. Even where you are now, it will always pursue you..."

"Yes, true. Only there fate has nothing to play with; instead, I play with it. Look how a fish will get away from the fisherman when he's already stretched out his hand for it, how it will start raining just when you are setting out for town, or how the weather will be fine but you feel like... so it's really ridiculous..."

Lizaveta Alexandrovna had no more arguments. "You will get married... you'll love..." she said indecisively.

"I get married! Just one more thing! Do you really think I'd entrust my happiness to a woman, even if I fell in love with her, which is also impossible? Or do you really think I'd undertake to make a woman happy? No, I know we'd deceive one another and both deceive ourselves. Uncle Pyotr Ivanych and experience have taught me..."

"Pyotr Ivanych! Yes, he's much to blame!" said Lizaveta Alexandrovna with a sigh, "but you had the right not to listen to him... and you'd be happy in marriage..."

"Yes, in the country, of course; but now... No, dear Aunt, marriage is not for me. By now I can't pretend when I fall out of love and stop being happy. I can't help but see if my wife pretends either; we'd both be slyly pretending, as... for example, Uncle and you do..."

"We?" asked Lizaveta Alexandrovna with astonishment and fear.

"Yes, you! Tell me now: Are you happy, as you once dreamed you'd be?"

"Not as I dreamed... but happy in a different way than I dreamed, more reasonably, perhaps more so—isn't it all unimportant?..." answered Lizaveta Alexandrovna, embarrassed. "And you too..."

"More reasonably! Oh, dear Aunt, *you* should not talk thus; that's Uncle's word! I know this happiness according to his method; it's more reasonable. Good, but is it more so? You see, to him everything's happiness; there is no unhappiness. Let him have it his way! No! My life is over; I've grown weary, tired of living..."

Both fell silent. Alexander looked at his hat; his aunt considered what else could prevent his leaving.

"But your talent!" she said suddenly in a lively way.

"Alas! dear Aunt! You want to laugh at me! You've forgotten the Russian proverb: *Don't beat a man when he's down.* I don't have any talent, decidedly not. I have feeling, I had a lively imagination. I took dreams for creativity and created. Not long ago I found some of my old sins, read them—and I had to laugh myself. Uncle's right in having made me burn everything there was. Oh, if I could bring back the past! I wouldn't have used it so."

"Don't despair altogether!" she said. "Each of us has his heavy cross to bear..."

"Who's this must bear a cross?" asked Pyotr Ivanych, entering the room. "Greetings, Alexander! Your cross, is it?"

Pyotr Ivanych was bent over and hardly moved his legs when he walked.

"Only it isn't the cross you think," said Lizaveta Alexandrovna. "I'm speaking of the heavy cross Alexander bears..."

"What else is he bearing now?" asked Pyotr Ivanych, letting himself down into the armchair with greatest care. "Ouch! what pain! What a punishment!"

Lizaveta Alexandrovna helped him sit down, put a pillow under his back and moved a stool under his feet.

"What is the matter with you, Uncle?" asked Alexander.

"You see, I'm carrying a heavy cross! Oh, the small of my back. This is a real cross: this is the reward for long service. Oh, Heavens!"

"It's your own doing that you sit so much; you know this climate," said Lizaveta Alexandrovna. "The doctor told you to walk more, but you won't. In the morning he writes, and in the evening plays cards."

"What, should I start to walk the streets yawning with boredom and wasting time besides?"

"So, you're punished."

"You won't escape it here, if you choose to work in business. Who doesn't have lumbago? It's almost a kind of business man's distinguished service cross. Oh! you can't straighten up your back. Well, what are you busy with Alexander?"

"Everything as before."

"Ah! So that way your back won't start hurting. That's surprising, really!"

"Why are you surprised; aren't you yourself partly to blame that he's become what he is..." said Lizaveta Alexandrovna.

"I? Now I like that! I taught him to do nothing!"

"Quite right, Uncle, you have no cause for surprise," said Alexander. "You very much helped circumstances to make of me what I am now, but I don't blame you. I am myself to blame that I didn't know how—or, better, wasn't able to use your lessons as I should have because I wasn't prepared for them. Perhaps you're partly to blame because you at once understood my nature and nevertheless wanted to transform it. As an experienced person, you should have known that's impossible... You awakened in me a contest between two different views of life and could not reconcile them. What was the result? Everything in me turned to doubt, a kind of chaos, Uncle!"

"Ouch, my back!" groaned Pyotr Ivanych. "Chaos! So you see, out of chaos I tried to make something."

"Yes! But what did you make? You confronted me with life in its ugliest nakedness and at an age when I should have been seeing it only from the bright side."

"That is, I tried to show you life as it is so that you didn't get false ideas in your head. I remember what a brave fellow you were on your arrival from the country. You had to be forewarned that you couldn't be like that here. I forewarned you perhaps against many mistakes and stupidities! If it weren't for me, you might have made once again as many as you did!"

"Perhaps. Only you've left one thing out of consideration, Uncle—happiness. You've forgotten that a man is happy in his delusions, dreams and hopes; reality doesn't make one happy..."

"What crazy ideas you carry about! You brought that opinion straight from the Asian border. In Europe we long ago stopped believing that. Dreams, games, illusion—all that's good for women and children, but a man must know his business as it is. Do you think that's worse than deceiving yourself?"

"Yes, Uncle. Whatever you say, happiness is woven of illusions, hopes, trust in people, confidence in oneself, then of love and friendship... But you assured me that love is nonsense, an empty feeling, that it's easy and even better to go through life without it, that to love passionately—is not a great achievement, that we don't outshine the animals in that..."

"Just remember how you wanted to love, you composed bad verses, talked in a wild language, and so bored to death your... was it Grunya, whatever her name! Is that the way to gain a woman's love?"

"How then?" Lizaveta Alexandrovna dryly asked her husband.

"Ouch, how my back pains stab!" groaned Pyotr Ivanych.

"Then you insisted," Alexander continued, "there is no deep, harmonious love, but only habit..."

Lizaveta Alexandrovna, silent and in deep thought, looked at her husband.

"That is, I, do you see, I talked to you so as to, in order that you... oh, oh, my back!"

"And you told that," Alexander continued, "to a twenty-year-old boy for whom love was everything, whose activity, goal—everything turned on that feeling by which he could be saved or lost."

"You talk as if you were born two hundred years ago!" muttered Pyotr Ivanych. "You should have lived under Tsar Gorokh."[17]

"You explained to me," said Alexander, "your theory of love, deceptions, infidelities, coolnesses... what for? So that I knew everything before I began to love. So that when I loved, I indeed analyzed my love, as a schoolboy studies the anatomy of the body under his teacher's guidance and, instead of the beauty of forms, sees only muscles, nerves..."

"Yet, I remember, it didn't stop you from going crazy over that... what's her name—Dasha?"

"Yes, but you didn't let me be deceived. I would have found Nadenka's betrayal an unfortunate chance and waited till I didn't need love. But you immediately were on hand with your theory and showed me that was the universal rule. So at twenty-five I lost my faith in happiness and life, and grew old in my soul. You rejected friendship, called it habit, named yourself my best friend, and that probably as a joke, doubtless because you succeeded in proving there is no friendship."

Pyotr Ivanych listened and with one hand massaged his back. He made objections carelessly like a man who, it seemed, could with a single word annihilate all the accusations brought against him.

"And you had a good understanding of friendship," he said. "You wanted your friend to playact the same comedy as, they say, those two fools in antiquity... what were their names? One of them remained behind as a hostage while his friend went off to keep an appointment... Now, if everyone acted like that, the whole world would be an insane asylum!"

"I loved people," Alexander continued, "and believed in their worth, I considered them brothers, and would have reached out to them in warm embrace..."

"Yes, just what we needed! I do remember your embraces," interrupted Pyotr Ivanych, "you absolutely pursued me with them then."

"And you showed me what they're worth. Instead of guiding my heart in its attachments, you taught me not to feel, but to analyze and observe people and be wary of them. I observed them—and lost my love for them!"

"Who could tell you'd take it like that! You're so quick, you see, I thought this would only make you more lenient toward them. I know them but haven't come to hate them..."

"What, you love people?" asked Lizaveta Alexandrovna.

"I've grown accustomed... to them."

"Grown accustomed!" she repeated in a monotone.

"He, too, would have grown accustomed," said Pyotr Ivanych, "only he was already badly spoiled earlier in the country by his auntie and the yellow flowers; that's why he's been so slow growing up."

"I believed then in myself," Alexander began again. "You showed me I was worse than others—I took to hating even myself."

"If you looked at the matter more coolheadedly, you'd see that you're neither worse nor better—which is what I wanted of you. Then you'd not hate either others or yourself; you'd only bear people's stupidities with greater equanimity and you'd pay more attention to your own. I know my own value, I see that I have faults, but I do admit I love myself a lot."

"Ah! so you *love* in this instance and haven't *grown accustomed!*" coldly remarked Lizaveta Alexandrovna.

"Ouch, my back!" groaned Pyotr Ivanych.

"Finally, at one blow without forewarning or pity you destroyed my best dream: I thought I had a spark of poetic talent. You cruelly proved to me that I was not made to be a priest of literature. You painfully tore that splinter out of my heart and offered me work that I found repulsive. Without you I would have written..."

"And you'd be known to the public as an untalented writer," interrupted Pyotr Ivanych.

"What do I care about the public? I would have bothered about myself. I would have attributed my failures to meanness, ill-will and would gradually have grown used to the notion that one doesn't have to write and would have tried something else by myself. Why are you surprised that I became depressed after finding out everything?"

"Well, what is your response?" asked Lizaveta Alexandrovna.

"I don't want to speak to that," replied her husband. "How shall I respond to such nonsense? Am I to blame that when he came here, Alexander imagined everything was yellow flowers, love, and friendship; that all people do here is write verse or listen to it, though sometimes for variety's sake they try prose?... I proved to you that a man must work, in general everywhere and here especially, and work a lot, even to the point of pain in his back... that there are no yellow flowers. There's rank and money, and that's much better! That's what I wanted to prove to you! I did not doubt that you'd finally understand what life is, especially as it's understood nowadays. Indeed, you did understand, but even when you saw there aren't many yellow flowers or verses in life, and when you realized what life is—still it's a big mistake to think that with this realization you have the right to be downcast; others don't notice it and therefore live and sing for joy. Well, what are you complaining about? What do you want? Another man in your place would bless his fate. Neither need nor illness nor real grief has touched you. What do you lack? Love perhaps? Haven't you had enough? You've loved twice and been loved. You've been betrayed, you've called it quits. We decided you do have friends such as others seldom have, not false friends. True, they don't throw themselves into water for you or crawl up on a burning pyre, and they don't much care for embraces either, for those are extremely stupid, after all—just understand that at last! But, for all that, you'll always get advice, help, and even money from your friends. And isn't that what friends are? In time you'll get married. You have a career ahead of you. Just get busy, and with that you'll make your fortune. Do everything like others—and fate will not pass you by; you'll come into your own. It's ridiculous to imagine you're a special great man, when you were not created such! So what are you grieving about?"

"I'm not blaming you, Uncle; on the contrary, I can respect your intentions and truly thank you for them. It can't be helped that they weren't successful. And likewise don't blame me. We did not understand each other—that was our misfortune. What can please and suit you, or someone else, or a third person—doesn't please me..."

"Please me, another, or a third person! You're not speaking to the point, dear fellow! Am I really alone in thinking and acting as I was teaching you to think and act? Look around, look at most people—the *crowd*, as you call it. Not the people in the country; they won't get there for a long while, but consider the modern, educated, thinking and working mass. What do they want and what are they striving for? How do they think? You'll see it's just what I was teaching you. It's what I was demanding of you—I didn't invent all this."

"Who did then?" asked Liza Alexandrovna.

"Our time."

"So you must without fail follow all the ideas that are thought up in your time?" she asked. "Are they all sacred and true?"

"They're all sacred!" said Pyotr Ivanych.

"What! Is it true that one must reason more than feel? Not give free rein to the heart, restrain the impulses of feeling, not yield or believe in sincere outpourings?"

"Yes," said Pyotr Ivanych.

"Act at every moment according to a system rather than trust people, consider everything unreliable and live only for yourself?"

"Yes."

"And it's sacred truth that love is not the main thing in life, that one must love one's work more than a beloved person, on whose devotion one mustn't count either, and believe that love will necessarily end in coldness, betrayal, or habit; that friendship is habit? Is all this true?"

"It has always been true," answered Pyotr Ivanych. "Only formerly they didn't want to believe it, but now it has become a generally known truth."

"Is it also a sacred truth that everything must be examined, calculated, and considered, that one mustn't let oneself dream and delight in something known to be an illusion just so as to be happy this way?..."

"That's sacred because it's reasonable," said Pyotr Ivanych.

"Is it true too," continued Lizaveta Alexandrovna, "that one must act reasonably even toward those close to one's heart... for example, toward one's wife?..."

"My back has never before hurt this much... Ouch!" said Pyotr Ivanych, writhing in his chair.

"Your back indeed! A wonderful time we live in! I have to admit."

"Very wonderful, my dear. Nothing gets done by caprice. Everywhere reason, cause, experience, gradual progress, and, therefore, success. Everything moves toward perfection and the common good."

"Perhaps, Uncle, there's truth in your words," said Alexander, "but it doesn't comfort me. I know everything according to your theory, look at things with your eyes. I'm a pupil of your school, but meanwhile I find life boring, difficult, unendurable... Why is that?"

"Why, for not being accustomed to the new order. You're not alone in that; there are others who haven't caught up. They're all *martyrs*. It's really too bad about them, but what can you do. You can't keep back a whole people for a handful of them. For everything you accuse me of," said Pyotr Ivanych after a moment's consideration, "I have a single and main justification. Do you remember when you arrived here, after a five-minute conversation with you, I advised you to go back? You didn't obey. Why do you now attack me? I told you in advance that you'd not get accustomed to the real order of things, but you counted on my guidance, asked for my advice... talked in high-flown language about modern achievements of the mind, about the strivings of mankind... about the practical tendencies of this century—so here you have it! It was impossible for me to be your nursemaid from morning till night, or make the sign of the cross over you. I talked business to you because you asked me to, and what came of that doesn't concern me. You're not a child and not stupid. You can judge yourself... Instead of doing your business, you now groan over some girl's betrayal, now suffer from a spiritual void, now from superfluity of emotions—what sort of life is that? Why, it's torture! Look at today's youth: what fine fellows! How everything hums with intellectual activity and energy, how easily and skillfully they manage with all that nonsense called *palpitations, sufferings...* and the Devil knows what else in your old language!"

"How easily you judge!" said Lizaveta Alexandrovna, "and aren't you sorry for Alexander?"

"No. Now if his back hurt, I'd feel sorry. That's no invention, no dream, no poetry, but real grief... Ouch!"

"At least instruct me, Uncle, what I'm to do now. With your mind, how would you solve this problem?"

"What to do? Why, go to the country."

"To the country!" repeated Lizaveta Alexandrovna. "Are you in your right mind, Pyotr Ivanych? What will he do there?"

"To the country!" repeated Alexander, and they both looked at Pyotr Ivanych.

"Yes, to the country. You'll see your mother there and comfort her. You say you're looking for a calm life. Here, right now, everything agitates you, but where is it calmer than on the lake with your auntie... Really, go. And who knows? perhaps you'll even... Ouch!" He seized his back.

Two weeks later Alexander resigned from the civil service and came to say goodbye to his aunt and uncle. Alexander and his aunt were sad and silent. Lizaveta Alexandrovna had tears in her eyes. Pyotr Ivanych alone spoke.

"Neither career, nor fortune!" he said, shaking his head. "Was it worth coming here; you've shamed the Aduyev family!"

"That's enough, Pyotr Ivanych," said Lizaveta Alexandrovna, "you've overdone it with your career talk."

"How, indeed, my dear, can one do nothing for eight years!"

"Farewell, Uncle," said Alexander. "I thank you for everything..."

"You're welcome. Farewell, Alexander! Won't you need money for the road?"

"No, thank you. I have some."

"What is this, he never takes any! To refuse again is the last straw! Well, go with God, with God."

"And aren't you sorry to part with him?" said Lizaveta Alexandrovna.

"Mm!" roared Pyotr Ivanych. "I've grown accustomed to him. Remember, Alexander, that you have an uncle and a friend—do you hear? And if you need a government or other job and the contemptible metal, dare to ask me; you'll always find both the one and the other and the third."

"And if you wish sympathy," said Lizaveta Alexandrovna, "comfort in grief, warm reliable friendship!"

"And sincere outpourings," added Pyotr Ivanych.

"... so, remember," continued Lizaveta Alexandrovna, "that you have an aunt and a friend."

"Now that, my dear, won't preoccupy him in the country. He'll have everything: flowers and love and outpourings and even an aunt."

Alexander was deeply moved; he couldn't say a word. Saying goodbye to his uncle, he was about to embrace him, though not so energetically as eight years before. Lizaveta Alexandrovna was bathed in tears.

"Oof! it's as if a mountain had been lifted from my shoulders!" said Pyotr Ivanych, when Alexander was gone, "as if even my back had gotten better!"

"What did he do to you?" said his wife through her tears.

"What? Simply a torment, worse than the factory people. If they begin fooling around, then you give them a beating, but with Alexander what are you going to do?"

Alexander's aunt spent the whole day weeping, and when Pyotr Ivanych asked about dinner, he was told none had been prepared. The mistress had locked herself up in her study and had not received the cook.

"Still trouble with Alexander!" said Pyotr Ivanych. "What a martyrdom with him!"

He muttered and muttered, then went to the English Club for dinner.

The stage coach slowly dragged itself out of town in the early morning, taking Alexander and Evsei with it.

Alexander had stuck his head out of the carriage window and was trying by all means to put himself in a melancholy mood; finally, he poured out his feelings in internal monologue.

They drove past barbers, dentists, dressmakers, gentlemen's mansions. "Farewell," he said, nodding his head and holding on to his thinning hair, "farewell, oh city of false hair, false teeth, cotton imitations of natural things, round hats, city of polite snubs, artificial feelings, lifeless boredom! Farewell, grandiose morgue of the soul's deep, strong, tender, and warm emotions. Here I faced up to contemporary life for eight years, but with my back to nature, which turned away from me. I expended my life forces and grew old at twenty-nine, but there was a time...

> "Farewell, farewell, oh city,
> Where once I loved, where now I weep,
> And where my heart is buried deep![18]

"I stretch out my arms to embrace you, wide fields, beneficent fields and meadows of my homeland; take me to your bosom; I shall revive and my soul shall arise!"

Here he read the poem by Pushkin which begins, "A vandal artist...," wiped his moist eyes, and hid in the depth of the carriage.[19]

VI

The morning was a beautiful one. A light ripple barely flecked the surface of the lake, familiar to the reader, in the village of Grachi. One's eyes involuntarily squinted from the blinding gleam of the sun's rays, which ignited diamond and emerald sparks in the water. The weeping birches bathed their branches in the lake, and here and there the banks were overgrown with sedge in which large yellow flowers were hidden, resting on broad floating leaves. Sometimes light clouds moved across the sun, as if suddenly it had turned away from Grachi. Then the lake, the grove and the village all grew dark for a moment; only the distance glowed brightly. The cloud would pass, and again the lake would shine and the meadows would be truly flooded with gold.

Since five in the morning Anna Pavlovna had been sitting on the balcony. What brought her out, the sunrise, the fresh air or the singing of the lark? No, she has kept her eyes fixed on the road that goes through the grove. Agrafena came to ask for the keys, and Anna Pavlovna gave them up without taking her eyes off the road, and didn't even ask what for. The cook appeared; without looking at him either, she gave him a lot of orders. She had ordered dinner for ten people on the following day.

Again Anna Pavlovna was alone. Suddenly her eyes sparkled, all the strength of her body and soul was concentrated on seeing. Something black had come into view on the road. Something was moving, but calmly, slowly. Oh dear! This load was going downhill. Anna Pavlovna frowned.

"Here comes someone in a heavy wagon!" she muttered. "No, let them go around, everyone cuts through here."

Irritated, she again sat down in her chair and again with quivering expectation trained her gaze on the orchard, not noticing anything around her. But around her there was something to notice; the background began to change significantly. The noon air, heated by the rays of the sun, became oppressive and heavy. Now even the sun hid. It became quite dark. The wood and the distant villages and the grass—all were clothed in a neutral, somehow foreboding color.

Anna Pavlovna came to and looked up. Goodness! From the west a black shapeless patch tinged with copper at the edges was drifting toward her like a live monster and moving quickly toward the village and the grove, spreading what looked like enormous wings to the sides. Everything in nature grew distressed.

The cows hung their heads; the horses switched their tails, blew through their nostrils and snorted, shaking their manes. The dust under their hooves did not rise, but, heavy like sand, was strewn under the wheels. The cloud approached threateningly. Soon a distant, loud, hollow sound was rolling slowly nearer.

Everything turned quiet, as if awaiting something unknown. Where had those birds gone which had so playfully soared upward and sung when the sun was shining? Where were the insects which buzzed so variously in the grass? Everything hid and was silent; even the inanimate objects, it seemed, shared the sinister foreboding. The trees stopped swaying and banging each other with their branches. They straightened up and only rarely bowed with their tops among themselves, as if mutually forewarning of a nearby danger in a whisper. The cloud had already encircled the horizon and formed a kind of leaden impenetrable vault. In the village everyone was trying to get home in time. A minute of solemn, general silence set in. Then a fresh little breeze swept through from the wood, like an advance messenger; it blew coolness into the face of the voyager, made a rustle in the leaves, banged shut the gates of a village house in passing, and then, after whirling up a circle of dust on the street, died down in the bushes. Right after it a violent windstorm advanced, slowly pushing a pillar of dust along the road; it soon broke into the village, ripped off several rotten boards from the fence, carried away a thatched roof, twisted up the skirt of a peasant girl carrying water, and chased roosters and hens down the street, fanning out their tails.

It passed. Again quiet. Everything is running about and hiding. Only a stupid ram has no sense of what's coming; indifferent, he chews his cud, standing in the middle of the street, and looks in one direction without understanding the general alarm. A little feather and a straw are circling along the road, trying to follow close after the wind.

Two or three big drops of rain fell—and suddenly lightning flashed. An old man got up from his resting place and hurriedly led his grandchildren inside; his old woman, crossing herself, hastily closed the window.

A thunderclap resounded, and swallowing human noises, triumphantly, majestically rolled away in the air. A frightened horse tore itself loose from the horse hitch and ran about, rope attached, in the field while a peasant vainly pursued him. And the rain sprinkled, even lashed, ever faster and faster, and drummed on roofs and windows harder and harder. A small white hand fearfully shoved out on the balcony an object of her tender care—flowers.

At the first bolt of thunder Anna Pavlovna crossed herself and left the balcony.

"No, obviously one can't hope for anything today. He's probably stopped somewhere because of the storm, perhaps for the night."

Suddenly the noise of wheels was heard, only not from the grove, but from the other side. Someone drove into the courtyard. Aduyeva's heart stopped beating.

"Why from there?" she thought. "Surely he didn't want to arrive secretly? Really now, there's no road there."

She did not know what to think, but soon everything became clear. The next minute Anton Ivanych entered. His hair had turned silver and he himself had grown fat; his cheeks were puffed from doing nothing and overeating. He was wearing the same frock coat and wide pants.

"I was waiting and waiting for you, Anton Ivanych," began Anna Pavlovna. "I thought you wouldn't come. I was about to despair."

"How could you think that! To whom else, dear lady. True! I'm not to be lured to visit everyone... only not to visit you... I was delayed, not by my fault. You see,

I'm making my rounds with a single horse now."

"How's that?" asked Anna Pavlovna absentmindedly, moving toward the window.

"This is how, dear lady; since the christening at Pavel Savich's the piebald has been lame. Their coachman had the crazy idea of laying an old barn door over the ditch. Poor people, you see! Didn't have a new board. But there was a nail or hook on the door, whatever—Devil knows! The horse, treading on this, shied so to the side she almost broke my neck... such rascals! So, since that time she's been lame... You see such misers there! You won't believe, dear lady, how it is in their house; in some almshouses they keep the paupers better. Yet in Moscow in stores on Kuznetsky Most, people go through about ten thousand in a year!"

Anna Pavlovna listened to him absentmindedly and slightly shook her head when he finished. "But look, I got a letter from Sashenka, Anton Ivanych!" she interrupted. "He writes he'll be here around the twentieth. So I've been beside myself for joy!"

"I heard, dear lady. Proshka was saying so, but at first I wasn't clear what he was talking about. I thought he'd already arrived; I actually broke out in sweat for joy."

"May God give you health, Anton Ivanych, for loving us."

"How could I not love you! Why, look, I carried Alexander Fyodorych in my arms; he's the same as one of my family."

"Thank you, Anton Ivanych; God will reward you! But I have practically not slept for another night and haven't let my people sleep; how awful if he came and we were all dozing—a fine state of affairs! Yesterday and the day before I walked to the grove, and would have gone today, except that my wretched age is getting the better of me. Insomnia plagued me at night. Sit down, Anton Ivanych. Look, you're soaked through; don't you want to have a drink and lunch? Dinner will be late perhaps; we'll wait for our dear guest."

"Well, perhaps I'll have a snack. As for the other, I must admit, I've had lunch!"

"Where did you manage to do that?"

"I stopped at the crossroads at Marya Karpovna's. I had to go past there, you see. More for the horse than for me, I gave her a rest. It's no joke in today's heat to clock off eight miles. There in passing I had a bite to eat. Good that I didn't obey and stay, however much they urged me; if I had, the storm would have kept me there all day."

"So, how is Marya Karpovna?"

"She's well, thank God! She sends you greetings."

"I humbly thank you. And her daughter, Sofiya Mikhailovna, and her husband, how are they?"

"Fine, dear lady; they're expecting their sixth child. In two weeks it's due. They asked me to stop by around that time. But there's such poverty at their house that I wouldn't even take a look. It would seem they had enough children, but no. Amazing!"

"What you do say!"

"Really, now! Inside, all the door and window frames have warped. The floor gives way under your feet. The roof leaks. And they haven't the wherewithal to fix it. They serve soup, a bun and mutton—and that's really all. But how eagerly they invite you!"

"Amazing, and she was out to catch my Sashenka, that crow!"

"What was she thinking of, dear lady, trying to catch such a falcon! I can't wait to see him. Such a handsome fellow, I'm sure! I've been suspecting something, Anna Pavlovna: hasn't he won the heart of some princess or countess there and hasn't he come to ask your blessing and invite you to the wedding?"

"Do you think so, Anton Ivanych!" said Anna Pavlovna, dissolved in joy.

"Really!"

"Oh, you dear man, may God give you health!... Yes, here I was about to forget it. I've wanted to tell you and there I forgot; I've been thinking and thinking what is this, and it's been on the tip of my tongue. And you see, no use, it would have been lost. Will you have a bite of lunch first, or shall I tell you now?"

"It doesn't matter, dear lady; indeed, tell me during lunch; I won't miss a single bite, not a single word, so now then."

"That is," Anna Pavlovna began when they had brought lunch, and Anton Ivanych had sat down at table, "so I dreamed..."

"But look, aren't you too going to eat?" asked Anton Ivanych.

"Oh my! How could I think of eating now! I couldn't swallow a bite, I didn't finish even a cup of tea just now. So I dreamed that I was sitting like this, and there in front of me stood Agrafena with a tray. I dreamed I said to her, 'How is it,' I said, 'that tray you have is empty,' but she didn't answer and kept looking at the door. 'Oh, goodness!' I thought to myself in my dream, 'why is she staring over there?' So I too began looking that way. I looked and suddenly Sashenka came in, so sad, came up to me and said, yes, just as if I weren't dreaming, he said, 'Farewell, dear Mama, I'm going far away, look there,' and pointed to the lake, and 'I won't come back any more,' he said. 'Where are you going, my dear?' I asked, but my heart so ached. I dreamed he didn't answer, but only looked at me so strangely and pitifully. 'So where have you come from, darling?' I thought I asked again. And he sighed deeply and again pointed to the lake. 'From the depths,' he said almost inaudibly, 'from the water folk.' I was then so wholly shaken—and I woke up. My pillow was all wet with tears. And now that I'm awake, I can't get hold of myself. I sat on my bed and just wept. I was flooded in tears and wept. As soon as I got up, I immediately set the little lamp to glimmering in front of the Virgin of Kazan. Perhaps her merciful intercession will keep him from all sorts of misfortunes and calamities. Such doubts came over me, really! I can't understand; what might this have meant? Hasn't something happened to him? What a storm..."

"It's all right, dear lady, to weep in a dream; it's a good sign!" said Anton Ivanych, cracking an egg against his plate. "He'll be here tomorrow without fail."

"But I was just thinking, shouldn't we go after lunch as far as the grove to meet him. Somehow we'd get through to there. You see how awfully muddy it's suddenly gotten there."

"No, he won't be here today; I have a sign!"

At this minute the wind brought the distant sound of troika bells, which then suddenly ceased. Anna Pavlovna held her breath.

"Oh!" she said, relieving her heart with a sigh, "and I was just thinking..."

Suddenly again.

"Heavens, goodness! Isn't that troika bells?" she said and rushed to the balcony.

"No," answered Anton Ivanych, "it's a colt with bells round its neck grazing quite near here. I saw it on my way. I even shooed it, or it would have gotten into the rye. Why don't you have it hobbled?"

Suddenly the bells began to sound as if right under the balcony and flooded in louder and louder.

"Oh, dear Sir! It's really so; he's coming, coming here! It's really he!" cried Anna Pavlovna. "Oh, oh! Run, Anton Ivanych! Where are the servants? Where's Agrafena? No one's here! As if he were coming to a strange house, goodness!"

She quite lost control. And the bells rang as if in the room with them.

Anton Ivanych jumped up from his chair.

"It's he! Yes!" cried Anton Ivanych. "There's Evsei too on the driver's seat! Where's your icon, bread and salt? It's a sign... What kind of confusion is this here! No one would have thought! And you, Anna Pavlovna, what are you doing, just standing there, not going to meet him? Run fast!"

"I can't!" she managed to say with difficulty, "my legs are paralyzed."

With these words she sank into a chair. Anton Ivanych snatched up a slice of bread from the table, put it on a plate, stood a saltshaker beside it and was about to rush to the door.

"Nothing is prepared!" he grumbled.

But into the same door to meet him three lackeys and two maids burst in. "He's coming! He's coming! He's arrived!" they cried, pale and frightened as if robbers had come.

Following behind them, Alexander too appeared.

"Sashenka! You, my dear!..." exclaimed Anna Pavlovna and suddenly stopped and looked at Alexander in amazement.

"But where is Sashenka?" she asked.

"Why, it's me, Mama dear!" he answered, kissing her hand.

"You?" She took a good look at him. "You, is it really you, my dear?" she said and warmly embraced him. Then suddenly she looked at him again.

"Why, what's the matter with you? Are you not well?" she asked, worried, not releasing him from her embraces.

"I'm fine, Mama dear."

"Fine! But what has happened to you, my darling. Did I send you away like this?"

She pressed him to her heart and began to cry bitterly. She kissed him on the head, the cheeks, the eyes.

"Where is your hair? It was like silk!" she added through her tears. "Your eyes shone like two stars, your cheeks were blood-red and milk-white, you were altogether like a ripe apple! Evidently wicked people got hold of you, envied your good looks and my happiness. Didn't your uncle look out for you? And I even thought I handed you from my hands to his as to a sensible person! He didn't know how to keep my treasure! You, my darling..."

The old woman wept and rained caresses on Alexander.

"Obviously to dream of tears leads to no good!" thought Anton Ivanych. "What is this you're doing, dear lady, wailing over him as if he were dead," he whispered, "it's no good, a bad sign." Aloud he said, "Greetings, Alexander Fyodorych! God has brought about your return and our meeting again in this world."

In silence Alexander gave him his hand. Anton Ivanych went to see whether they had taken everything out of the cart; then he began to call together the servants to greet the master. But they already were all crowded into the entry and vestibule. He lined them all up and instructed them how to greet the master, who was to kiss the master's hand, who his shoulder, who only the hem of his clothing and what to say the while. They chased one boy away altogether, telling him, "First go and wash your face and wipe your nose."

Evsei, wearing a strap as a belt and covered with dust, greeted the servants, who surrounded him. He gave them presents from St. Petersburg, to one a silver ring, to another a birch tobacco box. On seeing Agrafena, he stopped as if turned to stone and looked at her silently with stupid delight. She looked at him from the side, scowling, but immediately betrayed herself; she laughed for joy, then was about to begin crying, then suddenly turned away and frowned. "Why don't you speak?" she said. "Such an idiot, doesn't even greet me!"

But he couldn't say anything. With the same stupid smile he went up to her. She hardly let him embrace her.

"See what the Devil's brought home," she said angrily, looking at him on the sly from time to time, but in her eyes and smile she expressed greatest joy. "So those Petersburg folk have turned your heads, your master's and yours. What a little mustache you've grown!"

He took from his pocket a little paper box and gave it to her. In it were bronze earrings. Then he got a package out of a bag in which a big scarf was wrapped.

She seized both the one and the other and without looking at them, thrust them into a cupboard.

"Show us your presents, Agrafena Ivanovna," said several of the servants.

"What is there to look at? Haven't you ever seen anything? Go away from here! Why have you crowded in here?" she cried at them.

"Here's one more!" said Evsei, giving her another package

"Show us, show us!" insisted several.

Agrafena tore the paper and several packs of used, but still almost new cards were strewn from it.

"Look what he found to bring me!" said Agrafena. "Do you think I have nothing to do but play cards? Really! Did you think I was going to play with you!"

She hid the cards too. An hour later Evsei was again sitting in his old place between the table and the stove.

"Heavens! What peace!" he said, now drawing up, now stretching out his legs. "Is this all they do here? But with us in Petersburg it's simply a slave's life! Isn't there something to eat, Agrafena Ivanovna? We haven't eaten anything since the last post stop."

"You haven't lost your old habit? Really! How you fall upon it; clearly they didn't really feed you there."

Alexander went through all the rooms and then the garden, stopping at every bush, every bench. His mother accompanied him. Her gaze was fixed on his pale face, she kept sighing but was afraid to cry. Anton Ivanych had frightened her. She questioned her son about his life, but could not learn the reasons why he'd become thin and pale, and where his hair had disappeared to. She invited him to eat and drink, but refusing everything, he said he was weary from travelling and wanted to sleep.

Anna Pavlovna looked to see whether the bed was well made, scolded the maid that it was hard, had her make it again in her presence and didn't go away until Alexander had lain down. She went out on tiptoe, threatened the servants so they wouldn't dare speak out loud, or breathe, and would walk without shoes. Then she sent for Evsei. Agrafena came with him too. Evsei bowed to the mistress and kissed her hand.

"Whatever has happened to Sashenka?" she asked in a threatening manner. "Why has he changed so, huh?"

Evsei was silent.

"Why are you silent?" said Agrafena. "Do you hear, the mistress is asking you?"

"Why has he gotten so thin?" said Anna Pavlovna. "Where has his pretty hair gone?"

"I can't say, Madam!" said Evsei, "that's a question for the master!"

"You can't say! Then which way were you looking?"

Evsei didn't know what to say and didn't answer.

"You found someone trustworthy, Ma'am," said Agrafena, looking lovingly at Evsei. "Be good now! What did you do there? Tell the mistress! Or she'll give it to you!"

"Are you saying, Ma'am, I didn't do my best!" said Evsei fearfully, looking now at the mistress, now at Agrafena. "I served in good faith and truth; just ask Arkhipych..."

"What Arkhipych?"

"The doorman there."

"Really, how he hedges!" remarked Agrafena. "Why do you listen to him, Ma'am! You should shut him up in the shed, then he'd begin to talk!"

"I'm ready not just to do my masters' bidding," Evsei went on. "I'd even die on the spot. I'll swear on the icon..."

"You're all good with words," said Anna Pavlovna, "but when it comes to doing deeds, then you're not there! Clearly you looked after your master well—you allowed my darling to lose his health. You looked after him! I'll teach you..."

She threatened him.

"You mean I didn't, Ma'am? In eight years only one shirt got lost, and thanks to me, the worn ones are mended."

"Where did it go to?" angrily asked Anna Pavlovna.

"It got lost at the laundress's. I reported it at the time to Alexander Fyodorych, so as to take off the cost from her pay, but he said nothing."

"You see, scoundrel," remarked Anna Pavlovna, "she was tempted to steal good linen!"

"How could I not take care!" continued Evsei. "May God give that everyone do his duty as I did. The master'd still be asleep and I would already have run to the bakery and back..."

"What rolls did he eat?"

"White ones, good ones."

"I know, white, but were they the rich milk rolls?"

"Look, what a blockhead!" said Agrafena, "he doesn't even know how to say words sensibly, though he's lived in the capital!"

"By no means, Ma'am," answered Evsei, "hard rolls."

"Hard rolls! Oh, you villain! murderer, robber!" said Anna Pavlovna, reddening with anger. "So you didn't think to buy him milk rolls? And you were taking care!"

"But the master, Ma'am, didn't order..."

"Didn't order! To my darling it's all the same; whatever you put before him, he'll eat. And you didn't think about that? Did you really forget that he always ate milk rolls here? To buy him hard rolls! Really, did you stash the money some other place? I'll show you! Well, what else? Speak..."

"Then, when he finished breakfast," Evsei continued, intimidated, "he'd go to work and I'd get his boots. I'd keep polishing them the whole morning, always again and again, sometimes all of three times. When he'd take them off in the evening—I'd clean them again. How, Ma'am, can you say I didn't take care of him? Why, I didn't see such boots on any of the gentlemen. Pyotr Ivanych's were worse polished, though he has three lackeys."

"Why is he this way then?" said Anna Pavlovna, softened.

"It must be from writing, Ma'am."

"Did he write a lot?"

"A lot, every day."

"What did he write then? Some kind of documents probably, weren't they?"

"Must have been, Ma'am, documents."

"And why didn't you restrain him?"

"I did, Ma'am. 'Don't sit there, Alexander Fyodorych,' I'd say. 'Why don't you go for a walk? The weather's good, lots of gentlemen take walks. What's this writing? You'll hurt your lungs; your Mama will be angry...'"

"And what'd he say?"

"'Go away,' he'd say, 'you're a fool!'"

"And he's right, a fool!" said Agrafena.

At this Evsei looked at her, then went on again looking at the mistress.

"But didn't his uncle restrain him then?" asked Anna Pavlovna.

"Not he, Ma'am! He'd come, and if he found him idle, then he'd fall upon him. 'What,' he'd say, 'you're not doing anything? Here,' he'd say, 'you're not in the country. You have to work,' he'd say, 'not lie on your side! You're always dreaming!' he'd say. And then he'd give him a good scolding besides..."

"How did he scold?"

"'Provincial...' he'd say... and go on and on... he'd scold so that sometimes I wouldn't listen."

"A plague on him!" said Anna Pavlovna, spitting. "Give him some rascals of his own to rail at! My boy needed holding back... Heavens, goodness, merciful Lord!" she exclaimed, "whom can you count on nowadays if even your own relatives are worse than a wild beast? Even a dog shields its pups, and there an uncle works his blood nephew to death. And you, big fool that you are, couldn't tell his uncle not to bark that way at the master, but leave him alone. Let him yell at his own wife, the wench! You see he found someone to abuse! 'Work, work!' Let him die at his work himself! He's truly a dog, God forgive me! He found a slave to work!"

After this there was silence.

"Has Sashenka been this thin for long?" she then asked.

"About three years now," answered Evsei. "Alexander Fyodorych began to feel quite down and didn't eat much... Suddenly he began to lose weight and more weight; he melted away like a candle."

"Why did he feel so down?"

"God knows, Ma'am. Pyotr Ivanych deigned to say something to him about that. I would have listened, but it was beyond me; I made no sense of it."

"But what did he say?"

Evsei thought for a minute, trying, evidently, to remember and moving his lips.

"He called him something, but I've forgotten what..."

Anna Pavlovna and Agrafena looked at him and awaited the answer with impatience

"Well?.." said Anna Pavlovna.

Evsei was silent.

"So, simpleton, say something," added Agrafena, "the mistress is waiting."

"Dis... I think, disill... disillu... sioned..." Evsei got out at last.

Anna Pavlovna looked with amazement at Agrafena, Agrafena at Evsei, Evsei at both, and all three were silent.

"What's that?" asked Anna Pavlovna.

"Disill... disillusioned, that's it, I remembered!" answered Evsei in a decisive voice.

"What kind of calamity is that now? Heavens! Is it a sickness perhaps?" asked Anna Pavlovna with sadness.

"Oh, dear, it doesn't mean depraved maybe, Ma'am?" Agrafena hastily blurted out.

Anna Pavlovna turned pale and spat.

"How can you say such a thing!" she said. "Did he go to church?"

Evsei became slightly embarrassed.

"You can't say, Ma'am, that he went a lot...," he answered indecisively. "You can almost even say that he didn't go... The gentle folk there, all respect to them, don't go to church much..."

"Well, that's the reason!" said Anna Pavlovna with a sigh and crossed herself. "Clearly my prayers alone were not enough for God. My dream did not lie: my darling has been in the very depths!"

Now Anton Ivanych came in.

"Dinner will get cold, Anna Pavlovna," he said. "Isn't it time to wake Alexander Fyodorych?"

"No, no, Heaven forbid!" she answered. "He said not to. 'Eat without me,' he said. 'I have no appetite. It's better for me to sleep,' he said. 'Sleep will strengthen me. Perhaps I'll want something by evening.' So, here's what you do, Anton Ivanych: don't be angry with me, an old woman; I'll light the lamp before the icon and pray while Sashenka is napping. I don't feel like eating, but you have dinner by yourself."

"Good, dear lady, good. I'll do as you ask; count on me."

"But please do me a favor," she continued. "You are our friend and love us so much. Call in Evsei and question him properly why Sashenka has become thoughtful and thin, and why he's lost his hair? You're a man. It'll be easier for you... Did they offend him there? After all, there are such villains in the world... Find out everything."

"Good, dear lady, good; I'll get it all out of him, find out everything. Send Evsei to me while I'm eating—I'll do everything you ask!"

"Good day, Evsei," he said, sitting down at table and thrusting his napkin behind his tie, "how are you?"

"Good day, Sir. How did we live there? Not well. But you prospered here."

Anton Ivanych spat. "Don't criticize your betters, fellow. It's easy to go too far," he added and began to eat his soup. "Well, how did you get on there?" he asked.

"So-so, not terribly well."

"Good food, I bet? What did you eat?"

"What, Sir? At the store you buy some cold meat in aspic and some cold meat pie—and that's dinner!"

"Why at the store? And your own oven?"

"They didn't cook at home. Bachelors there don't cook."

"You don't say!" said Anton Ivanych, putting down his spoon.

"That's right, Sir. And they brought the master's dinner from a restaurant."

"What a gypsy way of life! Oh, how could he help getting thin! Here, have a drink on me!"

"I thank you most humbly, Sir! I shall drink to your health!"

A silence followed. Anton Ivanych ate.

"What do cucumbers cost there?" he asked, putting a cucumber on his plate.

"Ten for forty kopecks."

"Really?"

"I swear it, Sir, and that's not all, Sir. Shameful to say, but sometimes they send in pickles from Moscow."

"You don't say, Heavens! Well, how can anyone help getting thin!"

"Where would you find there a cucumber like that!" Evsei went on, pointing to a cucumber, "you wouldn't even dream of such! They're tiny things, rubbish there. Here you wouldn't even look at them, but gentlemen eat them there. It's a rare house, Sir, that bakes bread. Putting up cabbage in vinegar, or beef in brine, bottling mushrooms—they do none of that there."

Anton Ivanych shook his head, but said nothing because he had stuffed his mouth full. "How do they live then?" he asked, chewing.

"There's everything at the store. And what's not in that store is somewhere in a deli, and what isn't there is in a pastry shop, and if you don't find it there, go to the English store—and the French have everything!"

Silence.

"So, how much for young pigs?" asked Anton Ivanych, serving himself almost half one.

"I don't know, Sir. We didn't buy them. Some high price, two rubles maybe."

"Oh my, my, my! How could you help getting thin! What high prices!"

"Good families don't eat them much, it's more the government clerks who do."

Again silence.

"So then you did live badly there?" asked Anton Ivanych.

"May you never have it so bad! The beer there is even thinner than the kvas here. From having kvas in your belly all day it's like something boiling! The only good thing there is the boot polish, it's so good you can't admire it enough, and a wonderful smell, good enough to eat!"

"You don't say!"

"I swear to God!"

Silence.

"So, that's the way it is?" asked Anton Ivanych, chewing thoroughly.

"Yes, it is, Sir."

"You ate badly?"

"Badly. Alexander Fyodorych ate that way and very little. He quite lost the habit of eating. For dinner there they don't eat even a pound of bread."

"How could you help getting thin!" said Anton Ivanych. "All because it's expensive, is it?"

"It's expensive too, Sir, but also there is no custom of eating your fill every day. Gentlemen eat, so to speak, on the sly once a day, and then, if they manage it, around five o'clock, sometimes at six they snatch a bite and let it go at that. For them that's the last thing they think of. First they finish all their business, and then, indeed, they eat."

"What a way to live!" said Anton Ivanych. "How could you help getting thin! It's a wonder you didn't die there. And the whole time was like that?"

"No, Sir. On holidays the masters, when they sometimes gather, Heaven forbid, how they eat! They'll drive to some German restaurant, and, do you hear, eat up a hundred rubles worth. And what they drink—God keep us!—worse than we ever do! Sometimes at Pyotr Ivanych's there'd be guests. They'd sit down at table around six and get up from it at four in the morning."

Anton Ivanych opened his eyes wide.

"What you do say!" he said, "and they eat all that time?"

"They eat all that time."

"It'd be worth seeing; it's not our way! What do they eat?"

"What, indeed, Sir. Nothing to look at! You can't tell what you're eating. The Germans put God knows what in their food; you wouldn't want to take it in your mouth. Even the pepper isn't the same there. They pour into the gravy something out of foreign vials... Once Pyotr Ivanych's cook treated me to gentlemen's food and I was nauseated for three days. I look, there's an olive in the food; I thought, like an olive here too, I bite into it—look, but it's a tiny little fish. I began to feel sick, spat it out, took another—there, too, the same thing, yes, and in all of them... oh dear! Devil take the cursed fellows!"

"Are you saying they put this in intentionally?"

"Heaven knows! I asked and the boys just laugh; they say, 'Listen, that's the way it comes.' But what kind of food is it? They begin, as is proper, by serving a hot dish with pirogi, only they're are as small as a thimble. You put around six in your mouth at once, try to chew them; you look—they're gone, melted away... After the hot dish they suddenly serve something sweet, then beef, and then something frozen and then some kind of grass and then the roast... and I couldn't eat it."

"So the stove wasn't heated for cooking at your house? Well, how could you not get thin!" said Anton Ivanych, getting up from table.

"I thank you, my God," he began aloud with a deep sigh, "that you have fed me with these heavenly gifts—what's the matter with me, that's a slip of the tongue: earthly gifts—and don't deprive me of your heavenly kingdom."

"Clear the table; the masters won't have dinner. For this evening prepare another little pig... or isn't there a turkey? Alexander Fyodorych likes turkey; I expect he's hungry. And now bring me a bit of fresh hay to the little attic room; I'll rest for an hour or so, then wake me for tea. If Alexander Fyodorych so much as stirs, make sure you wake me."

When he got up from his nap, he went to see Anna Pavlovna.

"Well, what did you learn, Anton Ivanych?" she asked.

"Nothing, dear lady. I humbly thank you for the hospitality... and I slept so sweetly. The hay was so fresh, fragrant..."

"Your health, Anton Ivanych. So, what does Evsei say? You asked him?"

"How could I not ask! I learned everything: it's nothing! Everything will correct itself! The whole thing, it seems, comes from the bad food there."

"The food?"

"Yes, judge for yourself: the cucumbers forty kopecks for ten, a baby pig two rubles, and all the food from the pastry shop, and you don't eat your fill. How could you help getting thin? Don't worry, dear lady, we'll get him back on his feet, we'll cure him. Have more birch liqueur made; I'll give you the recipe, I got it from Prokof Astafich; so give him a wine glass or two morning and evening, and it's good before dinner; possibly with holy water... do you have some?"

"I have some, indeed; you brought it."

"Yes, I do remember I did. Choose food with more fat. I ordered a young pig or turkey roasted for supper."

"Thank you, Anton Ivanych."

"You're welcome, dear lady. Shouldn't you order pullets in white sauce too?..."

"I will..."

"Why must you do it yourself? What am I there for? I'll take care of it... let me."

"Do take care of it, you help me like one of the family."

He went out and she thought about it.

Her woman's instinct and mother's heart told her food was not the main reason for Alexander's pensiveness. She began with wily, slant allusions to find out the cause, but Alexander did not understand her allusions and did not answer. So two or three weeks passed. A great many young pigs, chickens and turkeys went their way in Anton Ivanych's direction, but Alexander was still pensive and thin, and his hair did not grow.

Then Anna Pavlovna decided to have a direct talk with him.

"Listen, my dear Sashenka," she said one day, "you've been here a month now and I haven't seen you smile even once. You walk around like a dark cloud, you look at the ground. Or is nothing dear to you here in the place where you were born? Apparently a foreign place was dearer. Are you homesick for there perhaps? My heart breaks when I look at you. What has happened to you? Tell me: What do you need? I will spare nothing to get it. If someone has offended you, I'll take care of him."

"Don't worry, dear Mama," said Alexander. "It's just the way it is, nothing's wrong! I've grown up, become more reasonable, and for that reason, more thoughtful...

"But why thin? And where's your hair?"

"I can't say why... You can't tell all that's happened in eight years... Perhaps my health has suffered a little..."

"What pains you?"

"I have pains both here and there." He pointed to head and heart. Anna Pavlovna felt his forehead with her hand.

"You don't have any fever," she said. "What ever was this? Does your head throb?"

"No... really..."

"Sashenka! Let's send for Ivan Andreich."

"Who's Ivan Andreich?"

"A new doctor; it's two years since he came. He's really a marvelous doctor! He prescribes almost no medicines. He makes some kind of tiny little pills himself—and they help. Here our Foma suffered from stomach trouble; three days and nights he howled to high heaven. The doctor gave him three tiny pills and like magic the pain was gone! See the doctor, darling!"

"No, Mama dear, he won't help me. This will go away by itself."

"But why are you so tired of life? What is this misfortune?"

"It's just that way..."

"What do you want?"

"I don't know myself. I'm just bored."

"How very strange, Heavens!" said Anna Pavlovna. "You like the food, you say; you have all the comforts and you have a good rank... What else perhaps? But you're bored! Sashenka," she said quietly after a moment's silence, "isn't it time for you... to get married?"

"What do you mean! No, I'm not getting married."

"But I have a girl in mind—pretty as a doll, a pink, tender little thing, so thin you can almost see through her. Such a slender shapely little waist. She went to a boarding school in the city, owns seventy-five serfs and has twenty-five thousand cash and a splendid trousseau, made in Moscow, and she's of good family... What about it? Sashenka? I've already talked with her mother at coffee, and joking, threw out a word. She seemed to prick up her ears for joy..."

"I'm not getting married," repeated Alexander.

"What, never?"

"Never."

"Heaven have mercy! What will come of that? We're all human; but you alone are like God knows what! It would be such a joy for me! If only God would send me grandchildren to fuss over. Really, marry her; you'll fall in love with her..."

"I won't fall in love, Mama dear; I've already fallen out of love."

"How could you fall out of love without marrying? Whom did you love there?"

"A girl."

"Why didn't you marry her?"

"She betrayed me."

"How could she betray you? You weren't yet married to her!"

Alexander was silent.

"Fine girls you have there: they love before marriage! She betrayed you! What a loathsome creature! Happiness itself was within her grasp, and she didn't know how to appreciate it, the good-for-nothing! If I'd seen her, I'd have spit in her face. What did your uncle think? Who was it she found better, that I'd like to see... But what of it, is she the only one in the world? You'll fall in love again."

"I did love another time."

"Whom?"

"A widow."

"Well, and why didn't you marry her?"

"I betrayed her."

Anna Pavlovna looked at Alexander and didn't know what to say.

"You betrayed!" she repeated. "Obviously some kind of loose woman!" she then added. "It's a real pitfall there, God forgive me. They love before marriage without a church ceremony, they betray... What does go on in this world as soon as you look closely! Clearly the Last Judgment is coming... Well, tell me, don't you want anything! Perhaps the food is not to your taste? I'll send for a cook from the city..."

"No, thank you; everything's fine."

"Perhaps you're bored all by yourself; I'll send for neighbors."

"No, no. Don't get excited, Mama dear! It's quiet for me here, it's fine. It will all pass... I haven't got my bearings yet."

This was all Anna Pavlovna could achieve.

"No," she thought. "Without God clearly you don't get anywhere." She suggested that Alexander drive with her to communion in the nearest village, but he overslept twice, and she could not bring herself to wake him. Finally she invited him to go to evening mass. "Fine," said Alexander, and they went. His mother quickly entered the church and took her place at the very front. Alexander remained standing at the door.

The sun had started to set and was throwing slanting rays, which now played on the golden frames of the icons, now lit the dark and severe countenances of the saints and with its splendor completely obscured the weak and tentative flickering of the candles. The church was almost empty. The peasants were at work in the fields. Only in the corner at the exit were a few old women crowded together, their heads tied with white handkerchiefs. Others, mourning and resting cheek in hand, sat on the stone step of the side altar and from time to time emitted loud and heavy sighs, Heaven knows whether about their own sins or about domestic affairs. Others had fallen to the ground and lay prostrate for a long time praying.

The fresh little breeze which came through the iron screen on the window would partly raise the cloth on the altar, or play with the priest's gray hair, turn a page in the book and extinguish the candle. The footsteps of the priest and deacon reverberated loudly over the stone floor in the empty church; their voices resounded wearily in the vaults. On high in the cupola the daws cried resonantly and the sparrows chirped, flying across from one window to another, and the noise of their wings and ringing of the bells sometimes drowned out the service...

"As long as a man's life forces are in turmoil," thought Alexander, "as long as his wishes and passions are in play and he's alive emotionally, he flees the soothing, meaningful and solemn perceptions to which religion leads. He comes looking for comfort in it with waning, spent forces, wrecked hopes, with the burden of years..."

Little by little at the sight of familiar objects recollections awakened in Alexander's soul. He ran through his childhood and youth up to the trip to Petersburg, remembered how, as a child, he repeated prayers after his mother, how she assured him a guardian angel stands on watch for a human soul and eternally fights with the Evil One, how, pointing to the stars, she told him they were the eyes of God's angels who look at the world and count the good and evil deeds of people, how the dwellers in Heaven weep when there are more evil deeds than good deeds, and how they rejoice when the good deeds exceed the evil ones. Showing him the blue of the distant horizon, she said that was Zion... Alexander sighed, as he came to from these recollections.

"Oh, if I could still believe in this!" he thought. "My youthful beliefs are gone and what have I learned that's new and true?... Nothing; I've found doubts, explanations, theories... and I'm still further from the truth than before... What good is this dissent, this philosophizing?.. Heavens! When the heat of belief does not warm the heart, is it really possible to be happy! Am I the happier?"

The service ended. Alexander came home still more bored than when he went. Anna Pavlovna did not know what to do. Once he woke up earlier than usual and heard a rustling behind the head of his bed. He looked around: some old woman was standing over him and whispering. She immediately disappeared as soon as she saw he had noticed her. Under his pillow Alexander found some kind of grass; around his neck hung an amulet.

"What does this mean?" Alexander asked his mother. "What manner of old woman was in my room?"

Anna Pavlovna was embarrassed.

"That's Nikitishna," she said.

"What Nikitishna?"

"Why, you see, my dear... you won't be angry?"

"Well, what is it? Tell me."

"She... they say, helps many people... She only whispers on water and breathes on a sleeping person—and everything goes away."

"For the third year at the widow Sidorikha's," said Agrafena, "a fiery snake kept flying down the chimney at night..."

Here Anna Pavlovna spat.

"Nikitishna," continued Agrafena, "conjured the snake; it stopped flying..."

"Well, what about Sidorikha," asked Alexander.

"She gave birth; the child was such a skinny one and black! It died the third day."

"Where did you get her from?" he asked

"Anton Ivanych brought her," answered Anna Pavlovna.

"You like listening to that fool!"

"Fool! Oh, Sashenka, how can you? You should be ashamed. Anton Ivanych, a fool!

"How have you managed to say such a thing? Anton Ivanych is our benefactor, our friend! "

"Here, dear Mama, take the amulet and give it back to our friend and bene-factor. Let him hang it round his own neck."

From that time on he began to lock his door at night.

Two or three months passed. Gradually the solitude, quiet, the domestic life and all the material benefits accompanying it helped Alexander return to health. And the laziness, freedom from care and absence of any moral shocks brought back to his soul the peace Alexander had sought in vain in Petersburg. There, imprisoned in stone walls, fleeing from the world of ideas and the arts, he had wanted to fall asleep like a toad, but agitations of envy and impotent desires constantly awakened him. Every phenomenon in the world of science and art, every new famous person made him ask, *"Why isn't this me? Why am I not in his place?"* There at every turn he encountered people he would compare himself unfavorably to... There he would often fall, there he saw his weaknesses as in a mirror, there he had been at the mercy of his inexorable uncle who attacked his way of thinking, his laziness, and unfounded desire for fame, there in that elegant world and multitude of talents he had cut no figure. Finally, people there try to harness life to known conditions, explain its dark and mysterious places, giving no rein to feelings, passions and dreams, and thus depriving life of its poetic allure. They want to give it some kind of boring, monotonous, heavy form...

But here what ease! He was better, more intelligent than everyone! Here he was universally worshipped for several miles around. Besides, here with every step his soul was open to peaceful, soothing impressions in the face of nature. The murmur of the streams, the whisper of the leaves, the cool and sometimes the very silence of nature—everything gave birth to thought, awakened feeling. In the garden, in the field, at home recollections of childhood and youth came to him. Anna Pavlovna, sitting next him sometimes, seemed to guess his thoughts. She helped him renew his memory of little things dear to his heart from his life, or told him those things he didn't remember at all.

"These willows here," she said, pointing to the garden, "were planted by your father. I was carrying you. I used to sit here on the balcony and look at him. He'd work for a while, work, and look up at me, and the sweat would pour from him in floods. 'Ah! you're there?' he'd say, 'somehow I feel so gay working!' And he'd go at it again. And there's the puddle where you used to play with the children. You were such an angry child, always something not to your taste—and you'd cry out at the top of your lungs. Once Agashka—that's the one married now to Kuzma—his is the third *izba* from the circle road—she somehow pushed you and banged your nose so it bled and your father beat and beat her; I implored him all I could."

Alexander supplemented these recollections with others of his own... "See, here on this bench under the tree," he thought, "I sat with Sofiya and was happy then. And see there between two lilac bushes I got my first kiss from her..." And he saw it all again... He smiled at these recollections and sat through whole hours on the balcony, greeting or saying goodbye to the sun, listening to the birds singing, the lapping of the lake and the hum of unseen insects.

"Goodness! How lovely it is here!" he said under the influence of these gentle impressions, "far away from restlessness, from that trivial life, that anthill, where man:

...in throngs, hemmed in by fences,
Tastes not the morning cool, nor senses
The vernal perfume of the downs...[20]

"How you tire of living there, and how you rest your soul here in this simple, uncomplicated straightforward life! The heart is renewed here, the breast breathes freer and the mind is not tormented by trying thoughts and insoluble choices in its disputes with the heart; both are in harmony, nothing needs to be resolved. Without worry or the burden of thought, with a somnolent heart and mind and a slight excitement you let your glance slide from the grove to the pasture, from the pasture to the hill and then you look deep into the infinite blue of the sky."

Sometimes he went over to the window which opened on the courtyard and the street into the village. There he saw another picture, reminiscent of Teniers, of a full and busy family life. Barbos, the dog, would be stretched out full length in the heat near the stable, his muzzle on his paws. A dozen hens greet the morning wildly running and clucking; the roosters would be fighting. Along the street the herd is being driven to the field. Sometimes one cow, fallen behind the herd, moos sadly as she stands in the middle of the street, looking around in all directions. Men and women with rakes and scythes on their shoulders are on their way to work. At times the wind will snatch two or three words of their talk and carry it to the window. Over there a peasant cart crosses over the little bridge with a rumble, behind it a load of hay slides along lazily. Blond, wirehaired children wander about the meadows, holding up their long shirts. In view of this picture Alexander began to understand the poetry of a *gray sky*, a *broken fence*, a *garden gate*, a *muddy pond* and the Russian *stomping dance*. He changed his tight elegant tailcoat for a loose robe of domestic handwork. And in every feature of this peaceful life, in every impression—morning, night, meal and rest times—the ever-watchful eye of maternal love was on him.

Her joy knew no bounds at seeing how Alexander filled out, the red came back to his cheeks, his eyes took on life with a peaceful gleam. "Only his hair doesn't grow," she said, "and it was like silk."

Alexander often took walks in the neighborhood. Once he met a crowd of peasant women and girls on their way to the woods to look for mushrooms, joined them and spent the whole day. When he got home, he praised the girl Masha for her agility and skill, and Masha was taken into the house to *look after the master*. He drove sometimes to watch the field work and learned from experience things about which he had often written and translated for the magazine. "How often we fibbed about this," he thought, shaking his head, and began to go into the subject deeper and more persistently.

Once in bad weather he tried working, sat down to write and was pleased with the beginning of an essay. He needed some book or other for reference; he wrote to St. Petersburg and they sent the book. He started working seriously. He sent for more books. In vain Anna Pavlovna tried to persuade him not to write so as not to *overstrain his lungs;* he wouldn't hear of it. She sent Anton Ivanych. Alexander wouldn't listen to him either and went on writing. When he had not only not lost weight from writing, but after three or four months had gained some, Anna Pavlovna calmed down.

A year and a half passed this way. All would have been well, but at the end of this time Alexander again became thoughtful. He had no wishes, or whatever ones he had were easily fulfilled; they did not go beyond the limits of family life. Nothing bothered him, no cares, no doubts, but he was bored! Gradually the narrow domestic circle got on his nerves. His mother's efforts to please began to annoy him, and Anton Ivanych disgusted him, he was even tired of his work and nature did not enchant him.

He sat silently at the window, looked indifferently at his father's willows now, and listened with annoyance to the lapping of the lake. He began to think about the reason for this new melancholy and discovered he was homesick—for St. Petersburg! With perspective on what had passed he began to regret it. The blood was still warm in his veins, his heart beat, soul and body demanded activity... He needed something to do again, Heavens! He almost burst into tears at this discovery. He had thought his boredom would go away, that he would adapt to the country, become accustomed. No, the longer he lived there, the worse his heart ached; he again longed for the abyss he already knew.

He had made his peace with the past. It became dear to him. Hate, his dismal look, gloom, unfriendliness to people had been mitigated by solitude and thought. The past came back to him in a brighter light, and even the traitress Nadenka appeared almost in rays of light. "What am I doing here?" he asked with vexation. "Why am I wilting? Why must my talents be extinguished? Why am I not to shine with my work? I've become more reasonable now. How is Uncle better than I? Can I really not make my way? So I haven't succeeded till now, I didn't take hold—well that's that, I've come to my senses now and it's time I did! But how my departure will grieve my dear mama! Still, after all, I must go; I can't perish here! Take this one or that one there—they all left home... And my career and my fortune?... Only I have stayed behind... and for what? Why?" He walked up and down, discontent, and didn't know how to tell his mother of his intention to leave.

But his mother soon freed him of that difficulty: she died.

Here is what he finally wrote to his aunt and uncle in St. Petersburg.

To his aunt:

> Before my departure from Petersburg, you, dear Aunt, sent me off with tears in your eyes, with precious words which are graven in my memory. You said if ever I should need warm friendship or sincere sympathy, then in your heart there would always be a space for me. That moment has come, when I've understood the full value of those words. Those rights over your heart, which you so magnanimously gave me, are for me the guarantee of peace, quiet, comfort, calm and perhaps the happiness of my whole life. About three months ago my dear mama died: I shan't add another word. You know by her letters what she was for me and will understand what I have lost in her... I am now running away from here for always. But where, solitary pilgrim, should I turn if not to those places where you are?... Say one word: Shall I find in you what I left a year and a half ago? Have you not put me out of your memory? Will you agree to the boring obligation of healing my new and deep wound with your friendship, which has already often saved me. I set all my hope on you and another powerful ally—activity.
>
> "You are surprised—aren't you? You find it strange to hear this from me, to read these lines in a calm tone, unlike my usual. Don't be surprised and don't fear my return. No scatterbrain, no dreamer, no disappointed man, or country boy will come to you, but just a person like so many in

Petersburg, such as I long since should have been. Especially prepare Uncle on this score. When I look at my past life, I feel embarrassed and ashamed both for others and myself. But it couldn't be otherwise. Look when I've at last found myself—at thirty! The hard school I went through in Petersburg and my thinking in the country have thrown bright light on my fate. At considerable distance from Uncle's lessons and my own experience I've understood them more clearly here, and I see where they long ago should have led me; I see how pitifully and unreasonably I turned away from the direct goal. I'm calm now. I don't torture or torment myself, yet don't boast of this. Perhaps this calm derives at present from egoism. I feel, by the way, that soon my view of life will clear to a point where I'll discover another source of calm—a purer one. Now I still can't help regretting that I've already reached that borderline where—alas!—youth ends and it beomes time to consider, verify, and analyze every excitement—the time of consciousness.

Though perhaps my opinion about people and life has changed but little, still a lot of hopes have vanished, a lot of wishes gone; in a word; illusions are lost. Consequently I need not fear being wrong or deceiving myself in many things and many people,

And that's very comforting from one point of view! Now I see the future more clearly. The hardest part lies behind me. Emotions aren't frightening because few are left. I've been through the most important and I bless them. I'm ashamed to remember how, imagining myself a martyr, I cursed my lot, life. Cursed! What pitiful childishness and ingratitude. How late I realized that sufferings cleanse the soul, that they alone make a person bearable to both himself and others, elevate him... I admit now that not to experience sufferings means not to experience the fullness of life; in suffering there are many important factors, and here, perhaps, we won't live to see how they are resolved. I see in such disturbances the hand of Providence, which, it seems, assigns man a neverending task—to strive forward, to achieve a goal designated from on high while struggling every minute with deceptive hopes and tormenting barriers. Yes, I see how inevitable in life are this struggle and these deceptive hopes and tormenting barriers, how without them life would mean not living but standing still, sleep... If struggle ends, look—life ends too. A person was busy, loved, enjoyed, suffered, experienced crises, did his work and therefore lived!

Do you see how I reason. I've emerged from darkness; I see how everything I've been through till now was some kind of difficult preparation for my real life's road, a complex knowledge for living. Something tells me that the rest of the way will be easier, quieter, more understandable... The dark parts have been illumined, the complicated knots have untied themselves. Life begins to seem good, not evil. Soon I shall say again how good life is, but say it not as a youth enraptured by a momentary enjoyment, but with full consciousness of its true joys and its sorrows. For that reason even death is not terrible; it presents itself not as a scarecrow but a marvelous experience. And now an unfamiliar calm has come to prevail. Childish vexations, flareups of wounded self-love, infantile irritability and a comic anger at the world and people which resembled the anger of a pug dog at an elephant—it's as if they never were.

I've made friends again with people with whom I long ago fell out of friendship—with people who, as I note in passing, are the same here as in

Petersburg, only harder, more blunt and ridiculous. But I don't get angry at them here, and there I certainly shan't either. That's a sample of my meekness for you. The strange fellow Anton Ivanych comes to stay with us as if to share my grief; tomorrow he'll go to my neighbor for a wedding, and then to someone else—to fulfill the obligation of a midwife. But neither grief nor joy prevents his eating four times a day at everyone's house. I see it's all the same to him whether a person dies, is born or gets married, and I'm not repelled or vexed to see him... I suffer him and don't chase him away... A good sign—don't you think, dear Aunt? What will you say to yourself after reading this word of praise?"

To his uncle:

Dearest best Uncle and along with this, Your Excellency!
    With what joy I learned that your career too is successfully complete—you achieved success in wealth long ago! You are Acting Privy Councillor and Director of Chancery! I dare to remind Your Excellency of the promise you gave me upon my departure: 'If you need work, or need an occupation or money, turn to me!' you said. And here I am needing work and an occupation; of course, I'll need money. A poor man from the provinces dares to ask for work and a position. What fate awaits my request? Not the one which formerly awaited the letter from Zayezzhalov when he asked help with his affair?... As for *creativity*, which you had the cruelty to mention in one of your letters, then... Isn't it a sin for you to stir up long forgotten stupidities when I myself blush for them?... Oh, Uncle, oh, Your Excellency! Who hasn't been young and somewhat stupid? Who hasn't had some strange, so-called *cherished* dream which was never meant to be realized? Take my neighbor on the right: He imagined himself a hero, a giant—a hunter before the Lord... He wanted to astonish the world by his heroic deeds... and it ended with his resigning from the service with the rank of ensign, not having been in a war. He peacefully sets out potatoes and sows turnips. Another neighbor on the left dreamed of remaking the whole world and Russia according to his ideas, but after copying documents for some time in a government office, he left for here and till now hasn't been able to rebuild his old fence. I thought creative talent had been given me from on high and wanted to disclose new undiscovered secrets to the world, not suspecting that these were no secrets and I was no prophet. We're all ridiculous. But tell me who, without blushing for himself, would dare to expose with abusive denunciation these youthful, noble, fiery, though not altogether realistic dreams? Who hasn't in his time nourished a fruitless wish, hasn't made himself the hero of a glorious deed, a solemn epic, a thundering tale? Whose imagination hasn't been carried away to fabulous, heroic times? Who hasn't wept in sympathy with the noble and beautiful? If such a person should be found, let him throw the first stone at me—I envy him. I blush for my youthful dreams, but respect them. They're a guarantee of purity of heart, the sign of a noble soul predisposed to the good.
    You, I know, will not be persuaded by these arguments. You need a positive, practical argument. Here it is: Tell me how talents would be recognized and refined if young people repressed in themselves these early inclinations, if they did not give free rein and space to their dreams, but

slavishly followed the indicated direction without trying out their strengths? After all, isn't it a law of nature that youth must be unruly, fiery, sometimes crazy and stupid, and that everyone's dreams are mitigated with time, as mine are now. Was your own youth really free of these sins? Recall, dig deep in your memory. I see you from here with your calm, never agitated gaze shaking your head and saying: no, nothing! Allow me to expose you, for example, at least in love... Do you deny it? Don't, for the evidence is in my hands... Remember that I could research the matter at the place of action. The scene of your love suit is before my eyes—it's the lake. Yellow flowers still grow on it. One, which I've pressed, I have the honor to present to Your Excellency enclosed as a sweet reminder. But there is a more terrible weapon against your persecutions of love in general and mine in particular—it's a document... You frown? And what a document!!! You've grown pale? I stole the precious antique from my old auntie, from her no less ancient breast and shall bring it with me as an eternal piece of evidence against you and a defense for myself. Tremble, Uncle! That's not all; I know in detail the whole history of your love. My auntie tells me every day at breakfast and supper and before bedtime, and I enter all these precious materials in a special memoir. I shall not fail to hand it to you personally, along with my essays on agriculture, which I've been working on here for a year now. For my part, I consider it my duty to assure my auntie of the immutability of your *emotions* toward her, as she says. When I am favored to receive from Your Excellency an answer assenting to my request, I shall have the honor of making my appearance, bringing dried raspberries and honey and presenting several letters which the neighbors promise to provide me with concerning their needs, with the exception of Zayezzhalov, who has died before the settlement of his lawsuit.

EPILOGUE

Here is what happened to the principal characters of this novel four years after Alexander's second arrival in Petersburg.

One morning Pyotr Ivanych was walking back and forth in his study. He was no longer the once hearty, robust, well-built Pyotr Ivanych with ever the same calm gaze, head held proudly high, and erect posture. Whether from years or circumstances he seemed to have drooped. His movements were not so hale and hearty, his gaze not so firm and self-assured. Many gray hairs gleamed in his sideburns and on his temples. It was obvious that he had celebrated the fifty-year jubilee of his life. He walked slightly bent. It was especially strange to see on the face of this imperturbable calm man—such as we have known him till now—not so much a worried as a melancholy expression, which, nevertheless, still had something characteristic of Pyotr Ivanych.

He seemed to be in a quandary. He would take two steps and suddenly stop in the middle of the room, or with rapid paces he'd measure off two or three times the distance from one corner to the other; apparently an unaccustomed thought had struck him.

In the armchair next to the table sat a short, stout man with an honorary medal round his neck, wearing a frock coat buttoned clear to the top, and one leg crossed over the other. He lacked only the cane with a big gold knob, that classic cane by which the reader at once used to recognize a doctor in novels and stories. Perhaps a doctor needs this stick, with which, for want of something to do, he goes walking and for whole hours sits with his patients, comforts them and often combines in his person two or three roles—physician, practical philosopher, friend of the house, and so on. But this is all well and good where people live spread out with room to spare, are seldom ill and where a doctor is more a luxury than a necessity. But Pyotr Ivanych's doctor was a Petersburg doctor. He didn't know what it meant to walk on foot, although, indeed, he prescribed exercise for his patients. He was a member of some council or other, secretary of some association or other, and professor and physician for several government institutions and. for the poor; he was unfailingly present at consultations; he also had an enormous practice. He did not even take off his left glove and wouldn't have taken off the right if it hadn't been necessary to feel a pulse; he never unbuttoned his frock coat and almost never sat down. From impatience the doctor had already often recrossed his legs several times. It had long been time for him to go, but Pyotr Ivanych had still said nothing. At last:

"What is to be done, Doctor?" asked Pyotr Ivanych, suddenly stopping in front of him.

"Go to Kissingen," answered the doctor. "It's the only way. The attacks have begun to recur too often in your case..."

"Oh dear! You're always talking about me!" interrupted Pyotr Ivanych. "I'm talking about my wife. I'm past fifty, but she's in the full flower of life. She must live, and if her health is beginning to fail at this time..."

"Here you're already foreseeing her end!" remarked the doctor. "I told you only my fears for the future, and for now there's still nothing... I only wanted to say that her health... or her poor health, and so she's... seemingly not quite normal..."

"Isn't it all the same? You made your remark in passing, yes and forgot it. But ever since, I've been watching her constantly and every day I discover new, disquieting changes in her—and it's been three months now that I've known no peace. Why didn't I notice earlier—I don't understand! My position and my business rob me of time and my health... and look, now, indeed, that of my wife too."

He again started pacing around the room. "Did you question her today?" he asked after a moment's silence.

"Yes, but she doesn't notice anything in herself. At first I assumed a physiological cause; she had no children... but, it seems, no! Perhaps the cause is purely psychological..."

"Still easier!" Pyotr Ivanych remarked.

"But perhaps, indeed, there's nothing. There are decidedly no suspicious symptoms! It's this way... You've sat too long here in this swamp climate. Go to the south. Breathe fresh air. Gather new impressions and see what happens. Spend the summer in Kissingen; take the cure of the waters. Then the autumn in Italy, the winter in Paris. I assure you that the accumulation of mucus, of irritation... will completely disappear!"

Pyotr Ivanych almost didn't listen to him.

"Psychological cause!" he said half aloud and shaking his head.

"That is, do you see why I say psychological," said the doctor. "A person who didn't know you could suspect some kind of worries here... or not worries... but suppressed desires... sometimes there is a need, a lack... I wanted to bring you to the notion..."

"Need, desires!" interrupted Pyotr Ivanych. "Her every wish is anticipated; I know her taste, habits. And need... Hm! You see our house, know how we live."

"A fine house, a wonderful house," said the doctor. "A marvelous cook and what cigars! And what of that friend of yours who lives in London... Has he stopped sending you sherry? I haven't seen it this year at your house..."

"How cunning fate is, Doctor! Have I really not been careful with her?" Pyotr Ivanych began with a fervor not characteristic of him. "I've weighed, it seems, every step... No, something went wrong... and when at the height of success, of such a career... Alas!" He waved his hand and went on walking.

"Why are you getting so excited?" said the doctor. "There's decidedly nothing dangerous. I repeat to you what I said the first time, that is, that her organism is unaffected; there are no destructive symptoms. Anemia, some decline in strength... That's all!"

"A trifle!" said Pyotr Ivanych.

"Her failing health is negative and not positive," the doctor continued. "Do you think she's the only one? Look at all the non-natives here; what are they like? Leave, leave here. But if you can't go, distract her, don't let her sit. Please her, take her out. More movement for body and spirit; the one and the other are part of her unnatural falling asleep. Of course, in time it can attack the lungs or..."

"Goodbye, Doctor! I shall go to her," said Pyotr Ivanych, and went with rapid steps to his wife's study. He stopped at the door, quietly moved aside the door hanging and fixed on his wife his worried gaze.

She... What did the doctor notice in her that was special? Anyone seeing her for the first time would find in her a woman like many in Petersburg. True, she was pale, her gaze dull, her blouse spread freely and evenly over her flat shoulders and smooth chest, her movements slow, almost limp... But you can't say red cheeks, bright eyes and fiery movements distinctively characterize our beauties, can you? Nor charm of body shape... Neither Phidias nor Praxiteles would find a Venus here for their chisel.

No, you mustn't look for plastic beauty in our northern belles. They're not statues; the poses of antiquity in which the beauty of Greek women has been immortalized doesn't come naturally to them. Indeed, there's nothing on which to build those poses. We don't have those impeccably correct contures of the body... Sensuality doesn't pour from northern eyes in liquid rays; that naive-lustful smile such as burns on a southern woman's mouth does not melt on their half-open lips. Our women receive as their portion a different, higher beauty. The chisel cannot capture the gleam of thought in the features of their faces, the struggle of the will with passion, the play of emotional movements, inexpressible in language, along with innumerable fine nuances of cunning, seeming naiveté, anger and kindness, hidden joys and sufferings, all those transient lightning flashes breaking forth from the core of the soul...

However that might be, a person seeing Lizaveta Alexandrovna for the first time would not have noticed anything wrong with her. Only one who had known her before, who remembered the freshness of her face, the brightness of her shining glances in which it used to be hard to distinguish the color of her eyes— they drowned so deeply in the luxurious, trembling waves of light—only one who remembered her magnificent shoulders and shapely bust, such a one would look at her now with painful surprise; his heart would contract with pity, if he was close to her, as Pyotr Ivanych's heart now doubtless contracted, though he feared to admit it to himself.

He quietly entered her study and sat down beside her. "What are you doing?" he asked.

"Why I'm going through our expense book," she answered. "Imagine, Pyotr Ivanych, last month around fifteen hundred rubles went for food alone. That's unheard of!"

He took the book from her without saying a word and put it on the table.

"Listen," he began, "the doctor says that my illness may get worse here; he advises taking the waters abroad. What do you say?"

"What should I say? In this, I think, the doctor's opinion is more important than mine. We must go if he so advises."

"But you? Would you want to take this trip?"

"If you want to."

"But perhaps you'd rather stay here a while?"

"Good, I'll stay."

"Which of the two?" asked Pyotr Ivanych with some impatience.

"Dispose for yourself and of me as you will," she answered with limp indifference. "If you say so, I'll go; if not, I'll stay here..."

"It's impossible to stay here," remarked Pyotr Ivanych. "The doctor says your health too has somewhat suffered... from the climate."

"Where did he get that idea?" said Lizaveta Alexandrovna, "I'm healthy; I don't feel anything wrong."

"A long journey," said Pyotr Ivanych, "also can be tiring for you. Don't you want to stay a while with your aunt in Moscow while I'm abroad?"

"Good, I'll go to Moscow if you please."

"Or shouldn't we both go to the Crimea for the summer?"

"Good, to the Crimea then."

Pyotr Ivanych couldn't stand it. He got up from the sofa and began, as in his own study, to walk about the room. "Is it all the same to you wherever you are?" he asked.

"All the same," she answered.

"Why?"

Without answering anything to this, she picked up again the expense book from the table. "It's up to you, Pyotr Ivanych," she started to say. "We must cut expenses. Fifteen hundred rubles for food alone..."

He took the notebook from her and threw it under the table. "Why are you so preoccupied with this?" he asked. "Or do you begrudge the money?"

"How can I not be preoccupied? After all, I'm your wife! You yourself taught me... and now you reproach me for my concern... *I'm doing my work!*"

"Listen, Liza!" said Pyotr Ivanych after a brief silence, "you're trying to transform your nature, overrule your will... That's no good. I never forced you. Don't tell me these trifling things" (he pointed to the notebook) "could preoccupy you? I've given you complete freedom..."

"Heavens! What do I need freedom for?" said Lizaveta Alexandrovna. "What shall I do with it? Till now you have so well, so reasonably disposed for both me and yourself that I've lost the habit of having my way. Continue to do so in the future, and I don't need freedom."

Both fell silent.

"For a long time," Pyotr Ivanych began again, "I haven't heard any kind of request from you, any wish or capricious fancy."

"I don't need anything," she remarked.

"You have no kind of special... hidden wishes?" he asked with concern, fixedly looking at her.

She hesitated whether to speak or not.

Pyotr Ivanych noticed this. "Say, for Heaven's sake, say what it is!" he went on. "Your wishes shall be mine, I'll carry them out like the law."

"Well, good," she answered. "If you can do that for me... then... cancel our Fridays... these dinners exhaust me..."

Pyotr Ivanych considered. "You live all closed up even so," he said after a moment's silence. "But when our friends stop coming to see us Fridays, you'll be altogether a hermit. Though, please; if you want this—it shall be done. What will you do?"

"Give me your bills, books, business deals... I'll work on them..." she said and reached under the table to pick up the expense book.

This seemed to Pyotr Ivanych a badly concealed pretense. "Liza!" he said reproachfully.

The little book remained under the table.

"And I've been thinking whether we shouldn't renew some acquaintances we had completely abandoned? To do that I wanted to give a ball so as to create some distraction for you, so you might go out yourself..."

"Oh, no, no!" began Lizaveta Alexandrovna, frightened. "For Heaven's sake, that isn't necessary! How could we have... a ball!"

"Why does this frighten you so? At your age a ball hasn't lost its interest. You can still dance..."

"No, Pyotr Ivanych, I beg you, don't plan things!" she said quickly. "To worry about what to wear, get dressed up, receive the crowd, drive out in a carriage—Heaven protect me!"

"It seems you want to spend your whole life in a blouse."

"Yes, if you'd permit, I'd never take it off. Why get all dressed up? It's a waste of money, and superfluous bother without any use."

"Do you know what?" suddenly said Pyotr Ivanych. "They say Rubini has been engaged to sing here this winter. I asked them to reserve a box for us. What do you think?"

She didn't answer.

"Liza!"

"It's no use..." she said shyly. "I think that too will be tiring for me... I get tired..."

Pyotr Ivanych bowed his head, walked to the fireplace, and leaning his elbow on it, looked at her... how should we say this?—with sorrow, no, not with sorrow, but with anxiety, with worry and with fear.

"Why this, Liza"—he was going to say, "indifference," but didn't even finish; he could not utter the word.

He looked at her for a long time in silence. In her lifelessly dull eyes, in her face, which lacked the play of lively thought and feelings, in her listless pose and slow movements, he perceived the cause of that indifference he was afraid to ask about. He had guessed the answer earlier when the doctor had merely called his attention to his fears. He had then realized and begun to guess that in methodically cutting off his wife from all inclinations which could harm their conjugal interests, he had not at the same time given her in himself any compensations for those joys not sanctioned by law which she would have encountered out of wedlock—he saw that her domestic world was nothing but a fortress inaccessible to temptation, where, instead, at every step barriers and patrols prevented every lawful manifestation of feeling...

The methodicalness and dryness of his relationship to her had unfolded without his consent and will to the point of cold and subtle tyranny and over what?

Over the heart of a woman! For this tyranny he paid her with wealth, luxury, all the external conditions, as he saw it, for her happiness—a terrible mistake, the more so because his mistake stemmed not from ignorance, not from his crude understanding of the heart—he knew it well—but from lack of concern, from egoism! He forgot that she had no civil service job, did not play cards, owned no factory, that an excellent table and the best wine have little value in a woman's eyes, yet, nevertheless, he compelled her to lead this life.

Pyotr Ivanych was kind, and if not out of love of his wife, then from his sense of justice he would have given Heaven knows what to correct this wrong, but how? He spent many nights without sleep from the time the doctor told him his fears about Lizaveta Alexandrovna's health, nights of trying to find a way to reconcile her heart with her real situation and to restore her diminishing strength. And now, standing at the fireplace, he was thinking of this very thing. It occurred to him that perhaps the embryo of a dangerous disease was already hidden in her, that she was already dead from her colorless, empty life.

Cold sweat broke out on his forehead. He was lost in cures, feeling that to discover them took more heart than head. And where was he to get that? Something told him that if he could fall at her feet, enclose her in embraces and with a voice of passion tell her that he lived only for her, that she was the goal of all his labors, activity, career, striving, that his methodical conduct with her had been inspired only by a burning, persistent, jealous wish to secure her heart for himself... He understood that such words would have the effect of reanimating a corpse, that she would suddenly flourish with health and happiness, and it wouldn't be necessary to go to a spa.

But to say something and prove it are two different things. To prove it, one must indeed have passion. And deep in his soul Pyotr Ivanych found not a trace of passion. He felt only that his wife was essential to him—true, but the same as the other essentials of life, essential out of habit. Perhaps he wouldn't be averse to pretending, playing the part of a lover, however ridiculous it might be at fifty to start suddenly speaking the language of passion. But can you deceive a woman with passion when there is none? Would he have enough heroism and ability to carry this role far enough to satisfy the demands of the heart? And wouldn't offended pride kill her completely when she noticed that what several years ago would have been a magic potion for her, was now offered her as medicine? No, in his precise manner he weighed and judged this late step and couldn't decide to take it. He intended to achieve perhaps the same thing, but in a different way since this was now necessary and possible. For three months now a thought had been stirring in his mind which earlier would have seemed to him nonsensical, but now—another matter! He had kept it in case of emergency. Now the emergency had come, and he decided to carry out his plan.

"If this doesn't help," he thought, "then there's no salvation! Let come what may!"

With firm steps Pyotr Ivanych went up to his wife and took her by the hand. "You know, Liza," he said, "what an important part I play at the office. I consider myself the most active official in the ministry. This year I shall be nominated for the rank of Privy Councillor, and, of course, I'll get it. Don't think my career will stop there. I can go still further... and would have gone..."

She looked at him with astonishment, waiting to see what this would lead to. "I have never doubted your abilities," she said. "I'm completely convinced you won't stop halfway but will go to the end of the road..."

"No, I shan't; in a day or so I shall hand in my resignation."

"Resignation?" she asked with surprise, straightening up.

"Yes."

"Why?"

"Hear me out. You know that I bought out my partner, and the factory belongs to me alone. It brings me forty thousand in pure profit without any attention. It runs like a self-winding machine."

"I know. So what about it?" asked Lizaveta Alexandrovna.

"I shall sell it."

"What do you mean, Pyotr Ivanych! What is the matter with you?" said Lizaveta Alexandrovna, looking at him, frightened. "What is all this for? I am confused, I can't understand..."

"You really can't understand?"

"No!" said Lizaveta Alexandrovna, perplexed.

"You can't understand that, seeing how bored you are, how your health suffers... from the climate, I would place less value on my career and the factory and that I would take you away from here, devote the rest of my life to you?... Liza! Did you really think me incapable of sacrifice?" he added reproachfully.

"So this is for me!" said Lizaveta Alexandrovna, hardly in control of herself. "No, Pyotr Ivanych!" she began in strong agitation, "for Heaven's sake, no sacrifice for me! I shan't accept it, do you hear? I decidedly won't take it! That you should stop working, achieving distinction, growing rich—and for me! God forbid! I'm not worth this sacrifice! Forgive me: I was insignificant for you, meaningless, weak in understanding and appreciating your high goals, noble labors... Such a woman as I was not the one you needed..."

"Magnanimity too!" said Pyotr Ivanych, shrugging his shoulders. "My intentions are immutable, Liza!"

"Heavens, Heavens, what have I done! I was thrown like a stone on your path; I'm holding you back. What a strange fate is mine!" she added almost with despair. "If a person doesn't want to, he doesn't have to live... Will God not pity me and take me? To hold you back..."

"You think wrongly that this sacrifice is hard for me. Enough of leading this wooden life! I want to rest, have peace, but where shall I find peace except alone with you?... We'll go to Italy."

"Pyotr Ivanych!" she said, almost weeping, "you are kind, noble... I know you are capable of magnanimous pretense... but perhaps your sacrifice is useless, perhaps it's already... late, and you're throwing away your concerns..."

"Spare me, Liza, don't think ahead that far," objected Pyotr Ivanych. "Otherwise you'll see that I'm not made of iron... I tell you again that I want to live not by reason alone. Not everything in me is frozen yet."

She looked at him fixedly with distrust. "And that is... sincere?" she asked after a moment's silence. "You truly want peace, are going away not just for me?"

"No, for myself too."

"But if for me, I'm not worth anything, not anything..."

"No, don't say that! I'm not well, I'm tired... want to rest..."

She gave him her hand. He kissed it with warmth.

"So we'll go to Italy?" he asked.

"Good, we'll go," she answered in a monotone.

Pyotr Ivanych felt as if a mountain had been taken from his shoulders. "We'll be doing something," he thought.

They sat for a long time, not knowing what to say to each other. We'll never know who would have broken the silence first if they had remained by themselves. But now in the next room hurried steps were heard. Alexander appeared.

How he had changed! He had filled out, grown bald, and how ruddy he'd become!

With what dignity he carried his little protruding belly and the order of merit round his neck! His eyes shone with joy. With special feeling he kissed his aunt's hand and pressed his uncle's.

"Where do you come from?" asked Pyotr Ivanych.

"Guess," answered Alexander portentously.

"You're moving at full gallop today," said Pyotr Ivanych, looking at him questioningly.

"I'll bet you can't guess why!" said Alexander.

"Ten or twelve years ago once, I remember, you came running in to see me like this," remarked Pyotr Ivanych. "You even broke something in my room too... Then I guessed at once that you were in love, but now... you aren't again? No, it can't be; you're too sensible to..."

He glanced at his wife and suddenly fell silent.

"You haven't guessed?" asked Alexander.

His uncle looked at him and went on thinking. "It's not... are you getting married?" he said hesitantly.

"You guessed it!" solemnly exclaimed Alexander. "Congratulate me."

"Indeed? To whom?" asked both uncle and aunt.

"To Alexander Stepanych's daughter."

"Really? Why she's a wealthy bride," said Pyotr Ivanych. "And her father... no objection?"

"I've just come from them. Why shouldn't her father agree? On the contrary, he listened to my proposal with tears in his eyes. He embraced me and said that now he could die in peace, that he knew to whom to entrust the happiness of his daughter... 'Just follow in the footsteps,' he said, 'of your uncle!'"

"Did he say that? You see, even now—not without your uncle!"

"And what did the daughter say?" asked Lizaveta Alexandrovna.

"Why... she... like, you know, all young girls," answered Alexander, "didn't say anything, only blushed. And when I took her by the hand, then her fingers played in my hand as if on the piano... as if they were trembling."

"She didn't say anything!" remarked Lizaveta Alexandrovna. "Did you really not take the trouble to find out anything from her before you made the proposal? Don't you care? Why are you getting married?"

"What do you mean why? Am I always to be on the loose like this! I'm tired of living alone. The time has come, dear Aunt, to settle down, put down roots, set up one's own household, fulfill one's duty... The bride is pretty, rich... Uncle here will give you reasons to get married; he goes into detail..."

Pyotr Ivanych said nothing, but without his wife's noticing sent Alexander a sign not to refer to him; Alexander did not see his hand wave, however.

"But if she doesn't like you?" said Lizaveta Alexandrovna. "Perhaps she can't love you—what do you say to that?"

"Uncle, what should I say? You speak better than I... Why, look, I'll quote your very words," he went on, not noticing that his uncle was squirming in his seat and signalling with coughs to stop this talk. "If you marry for love," said Alexander, "love will pass and you'll live by habit. If you marry not for love, you'll come to the same result; you'll get accustomed to your wife. Love is one thing, and marriage is another. These two things don't always go together, and it's better when they don't... Isn't that so, Uncle? At least you taught me so..."

He glanced at Pyotr Ivanych and suddenly stopped, seeing that his uncle was giving him a ferocious look. With mouth wide open in amazement he looked at his aunt, then again at his uncle and fell silent. Lizaveta Alexandrovna thoughtfully shook her head.

"Well, so you're getting married?" said Pyotr Ivanych. "Well, it's time now, my blessing! But then you wanted to marry at twenty-three."

"Youth, Uncle, youth!"

"Perhaps so, youth."

Alexander considered and then smiled.

"What is it?" asked Pyotr Ivanych.

"It's that an absurd thing has occurred to me..."

"What?"

"When I loved," answered Alexander pensively, "then marriage wasn't granted..."

"And now you're getting married, but love isn't granted," added his uncle, and both started to laugh.

"We can deduce from that, Uncle, that you are right in assuming habit to be the main thing..."

Pyotr Ivanych again made a ferocious face at him. Alexander fell silent, not knowing what to think.

"You're marrying at thirty-five," said Pyotr Ivanych. "That's the right way. But do you remember how you raged then in convulsions, you cried out that unequal marriages distressed you, that the bride is lured like a victim, decked out in flowers and diamonds, and pushed into the arms of an elderly man, mostly unattractive and bald. Show me your head."

"Youth, youth, Uncle. I did not understand the essential thing," said Alexander, smoothing his hair with his hand.

"'The essential thing,' you say," Pyotr Ivanych continued. "But do you remember how much you were in love with that—what was her name?..."

"Come, come, Uncle, enough," said Alexander, blushing.

"Where is the 'colossal passion, the tears'?..."

"Uncle!"

"What? Enough of yielding to 'sincere outpourings,' enough of plucking yellow flowers! 'You're tired of living alone'?"

"Oh, if that's it, Uncle, I shall prove that I'm not the only one who's loved, raged, been jealous, wept... allow me, allow me: I have in my possession a written document..."

He took from his pocket a folder, and after digging quite a while in the papers, dragged out some kind of ancient, almost ruined, yellowed little sheet of paper.

"Here, dear Aunt," he said, "is the proof that Uncle was not always such a reasonable, ironic, pragmatic person. He, too, knew sincere outpourings and transmitted them on paper that was not official with the government seal, and he wrote with special inks besides. For four years I've dragged this scrap around with me and always waited for an occasion to expose Uncle. I was about to forget about it, but you yourself reminded me."

"What nonsense is this? I don't understand anything," said Pyotr Ivanych, looking at the scrap.

"Why here, take a look."

Alexander carried the little paper up to his uncle's eyes. Suddenly Pyotr Ivanych's face darkened.

"Give it to me! Give it to me, Alexander!" he cried hastily and wanted to snatch the scrap. But Alexander swiftly withdrew his hand. Lizaveta Alexandrovna looked at them with curiosity.

"No, Uncle, I won't give it to you," said Alexander, "until you confess here in Aunt's presence that you once loved like me, like everyone... Or otherwise this document will be given into her hands as an eternal reproach to you."

"Barbarian!" cried Pyotr Ivanych, "what are you doing to me?"

"You don't want to confess?"

"Well, well, I did love. Give it to me."

"No, pardon me, say you raged and were jealous?"

"Well, I was jealous, I raged..." said Pyotr Ivanych, frowning.

"Wept?"

"No, I didn't weep."

"That's not true! I heard it from my aunt; admit it."

"My tongue won't get it out, Alexander. Here, shall I cry now?"

"Dear Aunt, here's a document."

"Show it to me; what is it?" she asked, stretching out her hand.

"I've wept, wept! Give it to me!" Pyotr Ivanych howled in despair.

"On the lake?"

"On the lake."

"And plucked yellow flowers?"

"I did. So a pox on you altogether! Give it to me!"

"No, I haven't finished. Give me your word of honor that you'll consign my stupidities to eternal oblivion and stop beating me with them."

"My word of honor."

Alexander handed over the scrap of paper. Pyotr Ivanych seized it, lighted a match and burned it then and there.

"Tell me at least what is this?" asked Lizaveta Alexandrovna.

"No, my dear, I won't tell you that even at the Last Judgment," answered Pyotr Ivanych. "You mean I really wrote that? It can't be."

"You did, Uncle!" interrupted Alexander. "I'll tell you if you want, what he wrote; I know it by heart: 'My adored angel...'"

"Alexander! I will never speak to you again!" screamed Pyotr Ivanych in anger.

"They're blushing as if for a crime—and for what!" said Lizaveta Alexandrovna, "a tender first love." She shrugged her shoulders and turned away from them.

"There's so much... stupidity in such love," said Pyotr Ivanych, soft and wheedling. "But with you and me we didn't even mention sincere outpourings, or flowers, or moonlight walks... yet you do love me..."

"Yes, I very much... have grown accustomed to you," answered Lizaveta Alexandrovna vacantly.

Pyotr Ivanych began smoothing his sideburns pensively.

"What, Uncle," asked Alexander in a whisper, "isn't that as it should be?"

Pyotr Ivanych signalled to him as if to say, "Be quiet."

"Pyotr Ivanych can be forgiven for thinking and acting like that," said Lizaveta Alexandrovna. "He's been that way for a long time and none of us has known him otherwise. But from you, Alexander, I didn't expect this change..." She sighed.

"What did you sigh for, dear Aunt?" he asked.

"For the old Alexander," she answered.

"You didn't really want me, dear Aunt, to stay the same as I was ten years ago?" Alexander objected. "Uncle is right to say that this stupid dreaminess..."

Pyotr Ivanych's face began to turn furious, and Alexander fell silent.

"No, not like that," answered Lizaveta Alexandrovna, "not like ten, but like four years ago. Do you remember the letter you wrote me from the country? How good you were there!"

"I think I was still dreaming then," said Alexander.

"No, you didn't dream. You understood then and had your own view of life; you were admirable then, noble, reasonable... Why didn't you stay that way? Why was this only in words, on paper, but not in deed? This admirable quality shone forth like the sun from behind clouds—for a minute..."

"You're trying to say, dear Aunt, that now I... am not reasonable and... not noble..."

"Heaven forbid, no! But now you're reasonable and noble... in another way, not my way..."

"What is to be done, dear Aunt?" said Alexander with a resounding sigh. "It's the time we live in. I keep up with the time; you have to stay in step. Look, I refer you to Uncle, I quote his words..."

"Alexander!" ferociously said Pyotr Ivanych. "Let's go for a minute to my study; I must have a word with you."

They went into the study.

"What is this passion that's come over you today to refer to me?" asked Pyotr Ivanych. "Don't you see what condition my wife is in?"

"What is it?" asked Alexander, alarmed.

"Don't you notice anything? It's that I am quitting government service, my business—everything and going with her to Italy."

"What are you saying, Uncle!" exclaimed Alexander in amazement. "Why this year you're due to get Privy Councillor..."

"But you see, Madam Privy Councillor is not well..."

He walked back and forth three times in the room. "No," he said, "my career is finished! My business is at an end; fate will not let us go on... Done is done!" He waved his hand. "Let us talk rather of you," he said. "You, it seems, are following in my footsteps..."

"I'd like to, Uncle!" added Alexander.

"Yes!" continued Pyotr Ivanych. "At a little over thirty Collegiate Councillor, a good civil-service salary, making a lot of money on the side, and just at the right moment marrying a rich girl... Yes, the Aduyevs do well! You very much take after me; you lack only the pains in the small of your back..."

"I do, though, sometimes feel a stab..." said Alexander, touching his spine.

"All that's very fine—except, of course, the pain in your back," continued Pyotr Ivanych. "I admit, I didn't think anything sensible could come of you when you arrived here. You were always full of metaphysical questions, had your head in the clouds... But all that passed—and thank Heaven! I would tell you to keep on following in my footsteps in everything, only..."

"Only what, Uncle?"

"Only. .. I'd like to give you several bits of advice... about your future wife..."

"What's this? This is interesting."

"Perhaps better not!" continued Pyotr Ivanych after a moment's silence. "I'm afraid of somehow making things worse. Do as you know best; perhaps you'll find out yourself... Let's talk about your marriage instead. They say your bride has a dowry of two hundred thousand—is that so?"

"Yes, her father's giving her two hundred, and a hundred were left her by her mother."

"So that's three hundred!" cried Pyotr Ivanych almost frightened.

"And her father said today too that he would put all five hundred of his serfs completely at our disposal now on condition we pay him eight thousand annually. We will all live together."

Pyotr Ivanych jumped up from his chair with his characteristic liveliness. "Stop, stop!" he said. "You've overwhelmed me. Did I hear aright? Repeat, how many?"

"Five hundred serfs and three hundred thousand capital..." Alexander repeated.

"You're not joking?"

"What do you mean joking, Uncle?"

"And the estate is not mortgaged?" asked Pyotr Ivanych quietly, not moving from his place.

"No."

His uncle, crossing his arms on his chest, looked at his nephew with respect for several minutes. "Career and fortune, both at once," he said almost to himself, admiring him. "And what a fortune! And so suddenly! Everything! Everything!... Alexander!" he added proudly, solemnly, "You are of my blood, you are an Aduyev! So be it, embrace me!"

And they embraced.

"That's the first time, Uncle!" said Alexander.

"And the last!" answered Pyotr Ivanych. "This is not an ordinary event. So, you won't, I guess, be needing any of the contemptible metal? Do call on me at least just once!"

"Oh! I do need some, Uncle. There are a great many expenses. If you can give me ten or fifteen thousand..."

"I had to twist your arm—it's the first time!" proclaimed Pyotr Ivanych.

"And the last, Uncle. This is not an ordinary event," said Alexander.

NOTES

1. The hero of Alexander Pushkin's verse epic, *The Bronze Horseman*.

2. Quoted from Pushkin's poem, "I remember the wonderful moment..." written in 1825 for his neighbor in the country, Anna Petrovna Kern.

3. Frédéric Soulié (1800-47), French Romantic, author of Gothic novels, predecessor of Eugène Sue and Alexandre Dumas père.

4. Alexander Pushkin, *Eugene Onegin*, trans. Walter Arndt (Ardis, 1992), VI, 17: 6-10.

5. Alexander Pushkin, "The Commander."

6. Alexander Pushkin, *Eugene Onegin*, I, 49:13, trans. Walter Arndt.

7. Alexander Pushkin, *Collected Narrative and Lyrical Poetry*, trans. Walter Arndt (Ardis, 1984), p. 40.

8. LaFontaine's seventeenth-century classic French fables were reworked by Ivan Krylov (1769-1844) in satiric nineteenth-century Russian versions which became proverbial in Russia.

9. A reference to Alexander Griboedov's satiric verse play *Woe from Wit*, Act III, scene 9. Upon his arrival at Famusov's ball, the card-sharp and man-about-town Zagoretsky presents the daughter of the house, Sophie, with tickets for the next day's sold-out theater show and boasts about the obstacles he had overcome in order to obtain them.

10. "Hardly were we leaving the gates of the Peloponnesian peninsula," *Phaedra*, 1677.

11. Gustave Drouineau, *The Green Manuscript* (1831); Eugène Sue, *The Seven Mortal Sins* (1847-49); Jules Janin, *The Dead Ass* (1829).

12. Heinrich Jung-Stilling, Pietist, 1740-1817, part of whose work, *Heinrich Stillings Jugend* (Heinrich Stilling's Youth), Goethe edited, Strasburg, 1777.

13. Christian Felix Weisse, 1726-1804, Anacreontic poet, author of musical works for the Leipzig stage, publisher of *Kinderfreund* (The Children's Friend), a didactic weekly for youth, 24 vols., 1775-82.

14. "Now I've got it!"

15. The first line, "Beatus ille qui procul negotiis..." from Horace's *Epode* II, *Iambics*, 41-31 B.C.

16. Alexander Pushkin, *Eugene Onegin*, I: 46, trans. Walter Arndt.

17. An allusion to the Russian version of *pays de Cocaigne* or *Schlaraffenland*, where roast partridge flew about with a fork in them, ready to eat, and the streams flowed with cranberry juice; see *Afanasiev's Tales*, No. 130.

18. Pushkin, *Eugene Onegin*, I, Stanza 50, trans. Walter Arndt.

19. From Pushkin's "Renewal" (Vozrozhdenie), first published in 1828. The last four lines read: "My aberrations disappear thus/ From my tormented consciousness/ And the visions return/ Of my early pure youth."

20. Alexander Pushkin, *The Gypsies*, in Alexander Pushkin, *Collected Narrative and Lyrical Poetry* (Ardis, 1984), trans. Walter Arndt.

Alexander Goncharov

An Ordinary Story

Stage Adaptation in Three Acts
by Viktor Rozov

Translated by
Marjorie L. Hoover

Dramatis personae

Alexander Aduyev
Anna Pavlovna, his mother
Pyotr Ivanovich Aduyev, Alexander's uncle
Elizaveta Alexandrovna, Pyotr's wife

Marya Karpovna
Sofiya (Sonya), her daughter } Anna Pavlovna's neighbors

Anton Ivanovich
Pospelov, Alexander's friend
Marya Mikhailovna Lyubetskaya
Nadenka, her daughter
Count Novinsky
Yuliya Pavlovna Tafayeva
Surkov

Agrafena
Evsei
Vasily } servants
Marfa

Civil servants
Tafayeva's guests
Aduyev's servants
Alexander's auntie

Places of action

The Aduyev country estate, in and around St. Petersburg, Pyotr Ivanovich's house, Alexander's attic room, Lyubetskaya's summer cottage, Tafayeva's house

ACT I

Scene 1

The Aduyev living room. Confusion amid preparations for a departure. Servants constantly rush in and out. Agrafena and Evsei are packing a trunk.

EVSEI. Goodbye, goodbye... It's our last day, Agrafena Ivanovna.

AGRAFENA. And thank God! Let the Devil take you away, we'll have more room... Just get out of my way, there's nowhere to move!

EVSEI. Someone else will take my place.

AGRAFENA. You devil!

EVSEI. God willing... it's not Proshka...

AGRAFENA. Just let go of me, damn you! And what if I do take up with Proshka!

EVSEI. God will reward you for your goodness...

AGRAFENA (*cries out*). He's actually glad... Be glad then! (Rushes out of the room.)

EVSEI (*after her*).

(*Enter Anna Pavlovna, carrying a pile of sheets, which she puts in the trunk, and Alexander, who carefully puts manuscripts in a case.*)

ANNA PAVLOVNA. Sashenka!

ALEXANDER. What is it, Mama?

ANNA PAVLOVNA. Where are you going, my dear, and why?

ALEXANDER. What do you mean? To Petersburg. Why... so as to... I feel within me...

ANNA PAVLOVNA. Listen, Sasha, it isn't too late. Change your mind, stay!

ALEXANDER. Stay! How can I! I've made up my mind!

ANNA PAVLOVNA. Are you really unhappy here? And what about Marya Karpovna's daughter, dear Sonya... Why you're blushing! God keep her, how she loves you, my dear!

ALEXANDER. Look, Mama, really... She just...

ANNA PAVLOVNA. Yes! Yes, as if I didn't see... Don't go! What will you find in Petersburg! Heaven knows what you'll see and suffer. Cold and hunger and need—you'll endure all sorts of things... But here, come look... (*Goes to the window and beckons to him, but he is busy looking through manuscripts.*) See with what beauty God has dressed our fields! We'll harvest up to four thousand bushels in rye alone. And over there we have wheat and barley... But you're not listening. (*She goes back to the trunks, goes on packing.*) Look, Sashenka, notice where I'm putting things... At the very bottom of the trunk I'm packing a dozen sheets, twenty-two pairs of socks... Do you know what I've thought of doing? I'm putting your wallet with money and the letter to your uncle in one of your socks... Uncle Pyotr Ivanovich will certainly be glad. After all,. it's been seventeen years since we've exchanged a word, that's the truth... Leave your papers alone, you'll tire yourself out and break your back!

ALEXANDER (*stops sorting his papers and listens to his mother*).

ANNA PAVLOVNA. I still have a lot to tell you. (*Wiping her tears.*) Where was I,

I wanted to say... What was it? Above all, take care of your health. If you get sick, God forbid!... say a serious illness, write me. I'll gather all my strength and come... Don't walk the streets at night. Stay away from people who look brutish. Save your money, save it for a rainy day, spend wisely. Money, the wretched stuff, is the cause of all kinds of good and evil. Don't throw it away, don't take a fancy to unnecessary luxuries, but don't deny yourself things you can afford either. Don't succumb to drink, it's man's prime enemy. And one more thing (*lowers her voice*)—watch out for women. I know them! There are shameless women who'll throw themselves around the neck of a man like you as soon as they see him...

ALEXANDER. Enough, Mama...

ANNA PAVLOVNA. Just a minute, one more word. Don't cast your eye on married women, that's a great sin. But if you do fall in love, and a nice girl is willing, why then... (*She lowers her voice still further.*) You can let Sonya go... Indeed, what was Marya Karpovna dreaming of!

ALEXANDER. Sofiya? No, Mama, I shall never forget her.

ANNA PAVLOVNA. Come now, my dear, don't get excited... After all, I was just... And will you remember your mother?

ALEXANDER. Look what foolish things you're saying! Forget you! May God punish me...

ANNA PAVLOVNA. Stop, Sasha, stop! What fate are you provoking for yourself?

(*As Anna Pavlovna speaks, the ring of approaching carriage bells is heard They quiet down, apparently, when the carriage reaches the porch. Marya Karpovna and her daughter Sonya come in the door.*)

ANNA PAVLOVNA. Marya Karpovna, darling! (*They embrace and weep.*) Sonya, hello, my dear! (*She exchanges greetings with Sonya.*)

SONYA. Hello...

(*Anna Pavlovna and Marya Karpovna leave the room. Alexander and Sonya are alone. They throw themselves into each other's arms.*)

SONYA. Sasha, dear Sasha!

ALEXANDER. Sweet Sonya!

SONYA. Sasha!

ALEXANDER. Sweet Sonya! (*They kiss and weep.*)

SONYA. You'll forget me there...

ALEXANDER. Oh, how little you know me!

SONYA. You will, you will! You'll be famous...

ALEXANDER. I'll come back, believe me, and no other girl will ever...

SONYA. Here, take these quickly... This is a lock of my hair, and here's a little ring. (*She gives Alexander the keepsakes, which he kisses passionately. And again.*) Sasha!

ALEXANDER. Sweet Sonya!

SONYA. Sasha!

ALEXANDER. Sweet Sonya!

(*They embrace and kiss. A carriage bell is heard. Anton Ivanovich appears in the door. Anna Pavlovna and Marya Karpovna enter from the next room; with them Alexander's aunt.*)

ANTON IVANOVICH (*to Anna Pavlovna*). Good day, Madame!
ANNA PAVLOVNA. Thank you for coming. Such sorrow... (*Greetings all around.*)
Please come sit down at the table and have something to eat for the road.

(*They all take places around the table. Anna Pavlovna weeps.*)

ANTON IVANOVICH. It disgusts me to see you like this, Anna Pavlovna, and
there's no one to punish you for it. If there were, he'd beat and beat you...
ANNA PAVLOVNA. My only son, and he's leaving... I shall die and there'll be no
one to bury me.
ANTON IVANOVICH. And what are we here for! Am I a stranger to you then?
Would you keep such a young eagle shut up? Set him free; he'll spread his
wings... You'll see what wonders he'll accomplish! He'll go straight to the top...
ANNA PAVLOVNA. If only you're right... Have something to eat, ladies and
gentlemen. (*She fills the glasses.*)
MARYA KARPOVNA. You'll see, Anna Pavlovna, how he'll rise in the world!
Petersburg will gape to see so bright a young man!
ANTON IVANOVICH (*rising*). To your health, Alexander Fyodorovich! Have a
good trip! And come back soon. And get married! What, Sofiya Vasilievna, are
you blushing?
SONYA. I wasn't... I just...
ANTON IVANOVICH. Oh, youth, youth... Well, in the name of the Father, the
Son and the Holy Spirit...

(*The sound of bells from a fast-approaching carriage. The door bursts open. It is
Alexander's friend, Pospelov.*)

ALEXANDER (*jumping up from the table*). Pospelov!
POSPELOV. Aduyev! (*They embrace.*)
ALEXANDER. Where have you come from? How?
POSPELOV. From home. I galloped round the clock-just to say goodbye to you.
ALEXANDER. A friend, a true friend! Till death do us part, right? (*They embrace.*)
POSPELOV. To the grave! I too dream of going to Petersburg. It's our duty,
Alexander! Our duty! Society needs the best minds, honest hearts, pure souls...

As long as we burn for freedom,
As long as hearts beat for honor...

(*Pospelov and Alexander go on talking quietly together; they take each other by the hand,
as if swearing an oath*):

My friend, we'll dedicate to our country
The noble impulses of our soul!

ANNA PAVLOVNA (*in tears*). Dear Sasha!
POSPELOV. You shouldn't shed tears, dear Anna Pavlovna, but be proud of
your son! He feels confined here, it's suffocating. We have no place here for
big projects which... (*He embraces Alexander.*) On your way! On your way! And
write! Write!

(*Exclamations. Farewells. People pick up chests, bundles, and trunks and go out.*)

ANNA PAVLOVNA (*with a cry*). Goodbye, goodbye, my dear! Shall I see you again?... (*She embraces Alexander.*)

(*Anton Ivanovich and Marya Karpovna tear her away from Alexander and take her on the porch.*)

AUNTIE (*detaining Alexander. Furtively*). Sasha, can you keep important secrets?
ALEXANDER. Yes, Auntie.
AUNTIE (*pulling a letter in a blue envelope from her bosom*). Give this to your uncle, Pyotr Ivanovich. And tell him that I always keep the yellow flower and his letter with me—here. (*She points to her breas.t.*)
ALEXANDER. What flower?
AUNTIE. You don't have to know that. He'll understand... (*Embarrassed.*) Embrace him for me. (*She kisses Alexander and makes the sign of the cross over him.*)
POSPELOV (*at the door*). Alexander, what are you waiting for!
ANNA PAVLOVNA (*on the threshold*). My darling! Farewell! (*She almost falls into the arms of Auntie and Pospelov. Alexander disappears. The bells of the departing carriage are heard.*) He's gone!

Scene 2

The study of Alexander's uncle, Pyotr Ivanovich Aduyev in Petersburg. Morning. Pyotr Ivanovich in his dressing gown. He takes from a tray a letter in a blue envelope, opens it and reads.

PYOTR IVANOVICH. "Dearest brother, Pyotr Ivanovich, gracious sir!" What sort of sister is this! (*Calls.*) Vasily! (*A servant enters.*) Where's this letter from?
VASILY. A young gentleman came, said his name was Alexander Fyodorovich Aduyev and you're his uncle. He promised to call about this time.
PYOTR IVANOVICH. So that's it! Tell this gentleman when he comes that as soon as I got up I left town for the factory and I'll be back in three months, maybe ten. You may go... (*Reads.*) "I shall remember to the grave how we walked around our lake together and you—at risk of life and health—waded up to your knees in the water and got a big yellow flower for me... And do you still have that ribbon you pulled out of my bureau despite my cries and pleading?" Did I pull out a ribbon?! "I have sentenced myself to an unmarried life..." Oh, the poor old maid... It's clear why she still has the yellow flower on her mind. (*He tears up the letter, throws it in the wastebasket and opens the second letter.*) "My dearest brother-in-law, Pyotr Ivanovich! With God's blessing my precious Sasha has left on a long journey. I am sending him straight to you and I told him not to stay anywhere else but with you..." Stupid old woman... "I remembered, dear brother-in-law, how seventeen years ago we sent you off and how we lamented then and wept..." (*Stops to think. Calls.*) Vasily!

(*Vasily enters.*)

When my nephew comes, don't turn him away. Better also reserve the room upstairs that used to be rented. (*Goes on reading.*) "Protect him from wine and cards. At night you'll doubtless sleep in the same room. Dear Sasha is accustomed to lying on his back! For that reason he groans piteously and tosses; wake him gently and make the sign of the cross—it will stop at once. And in summer cover his mouth with a handkerchief. He lets his mouth gape wide in his sleep, so the wretched flies crawl in toward morning. In case of need, don't leave him without money..."

VASILY (*enters*). Your nephew Alexander Fyodorovich has come...

(*Alexander practically runs in. Vasily exits. Alexander tries to embrace his uncle, but he blocks the attack with a powerful handshake.*)

ALEXANDER. Dear Uncle!

PYOTR IVANOVICH (*keeping his nephew at a distance*). How do you do...

ALEXANDER. Aunt Marya Pavlovna asked me to embrace you...

PYOTR IVANOVICH. Your aunt should have become wiser with age, but I see she's still as foolish as years ago! Sit down here opposite me, I'll go ahead with changing my clothes without ceremony; I've business...

ALEXANDER. Excuse me, Uncle...

PYOTR IVANOVICH. For what?

ALEXANDER. I didn't come directly to you, but stayed on the way at the coach inn...

PYOTR IVANOVICH. And you did just right. How could you have come to me without knowing whether or not you could stay. I've found you an apartment here in the building.

ALEXANDER. Uncle, I thank you for this kindness! (*He tries to embrace Pyotr Ivanovich.*)

PYOTR IVANOVICH. Sit down, sit down, there's nothing to thank me for. You're my relative; I'm doing my duty, that's all... I'm going out, I've got my civil service work and my factory.

ALEXANDER. I didn't know you had a factory, Uncle.

PYOTR IVANOVICH. Glass and porcelain... By the way, it's not mine alone, we're three partners.

ALEXANDER. Is business good?

PYOTR IVANOVICH. Yes, decent. One partner, true, isn't very reliable. He squanders everything, but I'm able to keep a tight rein on him... Well, goodbye. Have a look at the town now, have dinner somewhere, and you may come to see me in the evening. We'll have a talk. But I've forgotten—what's your name?

ALEXANDER. Alexander.

PYOTR IVANOVICH. Oh, Vasily! (*Vasily enters.*) Show him the room and help him move in. (*He stops, looks at Alexander.*) Yes... it will be hard for you here.

ALEXANDER. Why?

PYOTR IVANOVICH. There are stars in your eyes. (*Exits.*)

VASILY. This way, sir.

(*Alexander remains standing, puzzled.*)

Scene 3

The room into which Alexander has by now moved. He is writing a letter at the desk. Evsei is polishing boots in the entryway.

EVSEI. What a life they have here! At Pyotr Ivanovich's they light the stove once a month. People dine at someone else's house... Good Lord, they're strange people, indeed! But still they're called Petersburgers. Where we come from, every dog laps from his own dish.

(*The bell rings. Pyotr Ivanovich enters and walks through to Alexander's room. Alexander hastily covers something with his hand.*)

PYOTR IVANOVICH. Hide it, hide your secrets, I'll look the other way. Well, is it hidden? I came to see if you've gotten settled. Good day.
ALEXANDER. Good day, Uncle...
PYOTR IVANOVICH. Are you content?
ALEXANDER. Very.
PYOTR IVANOVICH (*laughs, looks around the room*). I started out worse. (*Sits down in the armchair.*) Tell me now, why did you come here?
ALEXANDER. I came to live here...
PYOTR IVANOVICH. If you mean by that to eat, drink, and sleep, then it wasn't worth the trouble... For you won't succeed either in eating or sleeping here as you would in the country.
ALEXANDER. I meant something else, Uncle.
PYOTR IVANOVICH. To rent a first-floor apartment on Nevsky Prospect, have your own carriage, announce a weekly day "at home" to receive guests?
ALEXANDER. As you put it, Uncle, it looks as if I myself don't know why I came.
PYOTR IVANOVICH. That's just about it.
ALEXANDER. I'll tell you. I was drawn by an irresistible striving, a thirst for noble activity. There surged in me the desire to clarify and realize... these hopes...
PYOTR IVANOVICH. Do you perhaps write poetry?
ALEXANDER. And prose, Uncle... May I show you?
PYOTR IVANOVICH. No, no, some time later. I was just asking.
ALEXANDER. But why?
PYOTR IVANOVICH. Just the way you talk...
ALEXANDER. Is it bad then?
PYOTR IVANOVICH. No, maybe it's good, but wild... It seems you want to say, insofar as I can understand, that you came here to seek your fortune, rise in the world.
ALEXANDER. If you choose to understand it that way...
PYOTR IVANOVICH. A good idea, but you came in vain...
ALEXANDER. Why? I hope you're not saying that from your own experience.
PYOTR IVANOVICH. A reply to the point... You're right. I've done well and my business is not doing badly. But as far as I can see, you and I are very different people.
ALEXANDER. I don't dare compare myself with you at all.
PYOTR IVANOVICH. That's not the point. You may be ten times better and

brighter than I. But I see you've been protected. How are you to endure what I have endured?

ALEXANDER. Perhaps I can accomplish something if you don't deprive me of your advice and experience.

PYOTR IVANOVICH. I'm afraid to advise you. But I won't refuse to give you my opinion, if you wish. You can listen or not, as you desire.

ALEXANDER. I shall try to adapt to a contemporary view, Uncle. Just today, looking at these enormous buildings and ships, I thought about the achievements of contemporary humanity; I understood the excitement of this rationally busy crowd...

PYOTR IVANOVICH. "The rationally busy crowd!" Indeed, you had better stayed home! Do you perhaps know that the likes of you, promising young men, have come to the capital not by the tens or the hundreds but by the thousands. They all have a thirst for noble activity, success, and fortune... And where are they now?

ALEXANDER. I hope I have enough courage and strength...

PYOTR IVANOVICH (interrupting). Well, it's good you've come, you can't turn back... Let's see, perhaps we'll succeed in making something of you... What's this you've dropped? What is it?

ALEXANDER (picking up a little packet he had dropped from the desk). It's nothing...

PYOTR IVANOVICH. Hair, it seems. Truly, nothing... So I've seen one thing; now show me what you've hidden in your hand. (Alexander opens his fist and shows a ring in his hand.) What's this? Where is it from?

ALEXANDER. These, Uncle, are material tokens of spiritual relationships.

PYOTR IVANOVICH. What? Let me see these tokens.

ALEXANDER. From Sofiya, Uncle. She gave them to me in parting to remember her by.

PYOTR IVANOVICH. And you brought these things nine hundred miles! You'd have done better to brink a sack of dried raspberries! (He takes the lock of hair and the ring, weighs them on his palm, wraps them in a bit of paper and throws them out the window.)

ALEXANDER (cries out). Uncle!

PYOTR IVANOVICH. What?

ALEXANDER. What's a name for what you've done?

PYOTR IVANOVICH. Ejection of non-material tokens out the window and into the canal—all kinds of junk and trifles.

ALEXANDER. You call these "trifles"!

PYOTR IVANOVICH. And what did you think they were? Half of your heart? I come to see him on business and what's he busy with here? Sitting and thinking about junk.

ALEXANDER. Does that interfere with business, Uncle?

PYOTR IVANOVICH. Very much. Time is passing and you have Sofiya and her tokens on your mind. You must forget Sofiya and her tokens now.

ALEXANDER (firmly). I shall never forget her, Uncle!

PYOTR IVANOVICH. Of course. Why, if I hadn't thrown away your keepsakes, you'd have remembered her for, say, one extra month.

ALEXANDER. Have you never loved anyone?

PYOTR IVANOVICH. I couldn't stand tokens.

ALEXANDER. But, in my opinion, the sacred emotion of love...

PYOTR IVANOVICH. I know this sacred love... At your age you need only see a lock of hair, a tiny shoe, a garter, or touch a hand—and sacred, uplifting love begins to run through your whole body. Give it reign, and soon... Your love, unfortunately, lies in the future; there's no way to escape it. But accomplishment will escape you if you don't begin to work at it... I've almost found a job for you.

ALEXANDER. You've found one! Uncle, I'm most grateful to you. (*He kisses his uncle on the cheek.*)

PYOTR IVANOVICH (*wiping his cheek with a handkerchief*). You seized your opportunity... Why wasn't I on my guard? Well, listen now. Tell me what you know, what do you think yourself fitted for?

ALEXANDER. I know theology, civil, criminal, natural and common law, diplomacy, political economy, philosophy, aesthetics, archeology...

PYOTR IVANOVICH. Hold on, hold on... But do you know how to write decently in Russian?

ALEXANDER. What a question! (*Goes out to the entryway and looks for certain papers in a small trunk.*)

PYOTR IVANOVICH (*lights a cigar with a sheet of paper; takes the letter Alexander was writing, glances through it, and reads aloud*): "My uncle is a good man, it seems, very intelligent, but altogether prosaic; he's always busy with business and calculations. All impulses of love and friendship are quite foreign to him, as is all striving for beauty. Sometimes I see something like Pushkin's demon in him. He doesn't believe in love and the like, says there is no happiness, and no one ever promised it. There is only life, which is divided equally between good and evil, that is, contentment, success, health, and quiet, on the one hand, and discontent, failure, anxiety, illness, and so forth, on the other. He doesn't have any strong impressions and doesn't love beauty, it seems. I don't think he has read even Pushkin..."

ALEXANDER (*returning with manuscripts, horrified*). What are you reading, Uncle?

PYOTR IVANOVICH. A letter to some Pospelov was lying here—probably your friend... Excuse me, I wanted to take a look at how you write.

ALEXANDER. And you read it all?

PYOTR IVANOVICH. Yes, almost. Why?

ALEXANDER. Oh, my goodness! (*Covers his face with his hands.*)

PYOTR IVANOVICH. Why what's wrong, what's the matter with you?

ALEXANDER. And you say that calmly—aren't you angry, don't you hate me?

PYOTR IVANOVICH. No. Why should I fly into a rage?

ALEXANDER. Aren't you angry? Prove it, Uncle.

PYOTR IVANOVICH. What do you want me to do?

ALEXANDER. Embrace me.

PYOTR IVANOVICH. Forgive me, I can't.

ALEXANDER. Why?

PYOTR IVANOVICH. Because there's no rhyme or reason for such behavior. Now if you were a woman, it would be another matter; in that case it's done without reason, prompted by another impulse.

ALEXANDER. And you don't think me a monster?

PYOTR IVANOVICH. Do you think whoever writes nonsense is a monster?

ALEXANDER. But to read such bitter truths about yourself...

PYOTR IVANOVICH. You imagine you wrote the truth?

ALEXANDER. I was mistaken, of course. I'll correct it.

PYOTR IVANOVICH. Do you want me to dictate the truth to you?

ALEXANDER. Of course.

PYOTR IVANOVICH. Sit down and write. (*Alexander sits down at the desk, takes pen and paper.*) "Dear friend," have you got that? "My uncle isn't stupid or mean; he wants the best for me..."

ALEXANDER (*jumping up*). Uncle, I know enough to appreciate...

PYOTR IVANOVICH (*dictating*). "...though he doesn't throw himself around my neck. He says he doesn't love me, and with good reason—you can't begin to love someone in two weeks. And I don't love him yet, though I assure him I do..."

ALEXANDER. That's not so, Uncle!

PYOTR IVANOVICH. Don't lie, don't lie! "But we're beginning to get accustomed to each other." Have you got that?

ALEXANDER. I have.   ·

PYOTR IVANOVICH. Well, what else do you have here? "Matter-of-fact spirit... demon." Write: "My uncle's neither a demon, nor an angel, but a human being like everybody. He thinks and feels in an earthly fashion, assuming that if we live on earth, then we mustn't fly away to heaven where we're not wanted for the time being, but instead we should busy ourselves with those human affairs to which we're called. He assures me I'll forget you and you me. This seems crazy to me and probably to you too, but he advises me to get used to the idea so we both won't fool ourselves. Uncle likes to be doing things and advises me to do the same, and I so advise you. He's not always thinking about his government work and his factory, and he knows Pushkin and more by heart."

ALEXANDER. You do, Uncle?

PYOTR IVANOVICH. Write... "He reads in two languages everything good that comes out in all fields of human knowledge. He loves art and often goes to the theater. But he doesn't run about, waste his time, cry 'oh' and 'ah', because he finds that childish. He thinks you have to control yourself and not foist your impressions on someone else because no one else needs them. Also, he doesn't talk wildly and advises me not to, and I advise you not to. Write me less often and don't expend your time for nothing." Your friend so-and-so. And the month and day.

ALEXANDER. How can I send a letter like that: "Write less often"?

PYOTR IVANOVICH. I'm only telling you my opinion. You asked me to yourself; I shan't make you send it—I'm not your nanny. (*Alexander looks for another letter.*) Are you looking for something?

ALEXANDER. I'm looking for the other letter—to Sofiya.

PYOTR IVANOVICH. Where is it? Really, I didn't throw it out the window.

ALEXANDER. Uncle! Look, you lit your cigar with it!

PYOTR IVANOVICH. I did? Now how could I do that... and not notice... Just imagine, I burned up such a treasure. Well, then... You are able to write Russian. Tomorrow we'll go to the government offices... And what's this pile of papers you've dragged out? (*He points to the papers Alexander has brought in from the hall.*)

ALEXANDER. These are my scholarly papers. I would like to show them to the department head. Especially one project I worked on...

PYOTR IVANOVICH. Ah... one of those projects which was completed a thousand years ago or else is impossible and not necessary to complete.

ALEXANDER. How will my department head find out about my capabilities?

PYOTR IVANOVICH. He'll know in a flash. He's a master at finding out. And what job do you want to take on?

ALEXANDER. I don't know, Uncle, what I should...

PYOTR IVANOVICH. There are jobs for ministers of state, their deputies, directors, vice-directors, department heads, head clerks, their assistants, civil servants with special portfolio, to name but a few...

ALEXANDER. Well, for the beginning, the job of head clerk sounds good...

PYOTR IVANOVICH. Of course, of course... Then three months later you're promoted to director and in a year minister. Is that your idea?

ALEXANDER. The department head has probably told you where there's a vacancy...

PYOTR IVANOVICH. Yes, we'd better rely on him, or he'll doubtless be offended, and he's a stickler for the rules. He's a stern taskmaster... What else do you have there?

ALEXANDER. You asked me to show you my poetry.

PYOTR IVANOVICH. I did? Somehow I don't remember.

ALEXANDER. I think my job is one thing, but my soul thirsts for...

PYOTR IVANOVICH. You mean, beside your government job you want to work at something else. Well, how about translation? That's very laudable. Of what? Literature?

ALEXANDER. Yes, Uncle.

PYOTR IVANOVICH. Are you sure you have talent?

ALEXANDER. I hope...

PYOTR IVANOVICH. Without it, you know, you'll be a menial in art, and what's the use of that? Talent—that's something else again. You can go far with that. And, besides, it's money in the bank. It's worth a hundred serfs.

ALEXANDER. You measure talent in terms of money?

PYOTR IVANOVICH. How else would you suggest? The more they read you, the more money they pay you... Show me what you have there.

> ...Hiding in the ether
> Stars tremble in unsteady gleaming,
> And, as if in mutual accord,
> Keep strict silence...

(*Reads the rest to himself. Yawns.*) Not bad, not good.

ALEXANDER. Here's a translation from Schiller.

PYOTR IVANOVICH. Enough... So you know some languages too?

ALEXANDER. I know French, German, and a little English.

PYOTR IVANOVICH. Congratulations! You should have said so long ago. This isn't a time for modesty. I'll find you some literary work right away.

ALEXANDER. That will be wonderful! I have a desire to express so much...

PYOTR IVANOVICH. Listen, make me a gift of your projects and works.

ALEXANDER. A gift? Gladly, Uncle. I'll make a table of contents of all my articles in chronological order.

PYOTR IVANOVICH. No, that won't be necessary. Thank you for the gift... Evsei! (*Evsei enters.*) Take these papers to my servant Vasily.

ALEXANDER. Why Vasily? I can take them to your study myself.

PYOTR IVANOVICH. He asked me for the wherewithal to paper some wall or other.

ALEXANDER. Wallpaper?

PYOTR IVANOVICH. You've made a present of them now. And what do you care what use I make of your present?

ALEXANDER (*pressing his papers to his breast in despair*). But these are my works, my dreams, my...

PYOTR IVANOVICH (*forcefully pulling the papers away from him*). Listen to me, Alexander. Later you won't blush and you'll thank me. There, take them away, Evsei... (*Evsei exits.*) Well, now it's nice and clean in your room, no trifles. It's up to you whether you fill it with trash or something useful. Let's go to the factory—we'll walk around, distract ourselves and take a look at how they work there. Begin a new life, Alexander, begin anew! Petersburg is a beautiful but hard city. Don't expect concessions from it. (*Alexander stands and covers his face with his hands.*) Well, are you coming with me?

ALEXANDER (*quietly, softly*). I'm coming, Uncle...

Scene 4

On the stage there are only single desks. Goverment clerks sit behind the desks. Enter the head of the department and with him Alexander. The clerks' pens begin to scratch more diligently.

DEPARTMENT HEAD. Ivan Ivanovich! (*One clerk jumps up from his desk, runs over to the department head, stands at attention.*) Pass me your snuff box! (*Ivan Ivanovich offers his snuff box. The department head takes a pinch and sniffs it. He points to Alexander.*) Try him out!

IVAN IVANOVICH (*to Alexander*). If you please... (*Leads Alexander to a desk.*) Do you have a good hand?

ALEXANDER. Hand?

IVAN IVANOVICH. Yes, handwriting. Here, try copying this document. (*Alexander writes. Ivan Ivanovich takes the document, looks at it and goes to the department head.*) He writes badly, Sir...

DEPARTMENT HEAD (*inspecting the document*). Yes, it's bad. He can't do originals. Well, let him copy leaves of absence for the time being, and then when he's gotten a bit more accustomed, give him documents. Perhaps he'll do. (*Exits.*)

IVAN IVANOVICH (*takes Alexander to an empty desk, shows him a chair*). Please... (*Moves a pile of documents over to him.*) Copy these... (*Alexander sits down at the desk and writes. Ivan Ivanovich walks around him, watches how he writes.*) You must put in a hyphen here.

ALEXANDER. And is the way I wrote it really worse?

IVAN IVANOVICH. Maybe it's even better, but you can't do that here.

ALEXANDER. Why?

IVAN IVANOVICH. You can't.

ALEXANDER. Do you pretend doing it your way changes anything?

IVAN IVANOVICH. A lot.

ALEXANDER. What?

IVAN IVANOVICH. The rules. So, please, no innovations.

ALEXANDER (*writes, speaks quietly*). You have to be patient, patient.

Scene 5

A garden at the Lyubetsky's country cottage. A summer-house, a bench, bushes. Nadenka with a cup of milk in her hands.

ALEXANDER (*rushing in*). Nadezhda Alexandrovna!

NADENKA. Alexander Fyodorovich!

ALEXANDER. You were waiting for me! Heavens, how happy I am!

NADENKA. I was waiting for you? I wouldn't dream of it! You know I'm always in the garden.

ALEXANDER. Are you angry?

NADENKA. What for? What an idea!

ALEXANDER. Give me your hand then... What's this, you're drinking milk?

NADENKA. I'm having dinner.

ALEXANDER. You're having dinner at six o'clock and dining on milk!

NADENKA. Of course you find milk a strange thing for dinner after your luxurious meal at your uncle's. But here in the country we live modestly.

ALEXANDER. I didn't have dinner at Uncle's. I told him yesterday I wasn't coming.

NADENKA. Where have you been till now?

ALEXANDER. I sat through the day at the office, until four o'clock.

NADENKA. But it's six now. Don't lie; admit you were tempted by dinner and the pleasant company.

ALEXANDER. Word of honor, I didn't go to Uncle's... If I had, then how could I have gotten here by now?

NADENKA. Do you think this is early? (*Alexander tries to come close to Nadenka.*) Don't come near me. I can't bear to look at you!

ALEXANDER. Enough of playing games, Nadezhda Alexandrovna!

NADENKA. I'm not playing games at all... Tell me where you've been till now!

ALEXANDER. I ate a quick meal in a restaurant...

NADENKA. Quick you say! Poor thing! You must be hungry. Do you want some milk?

ALEXANDER. Oh, give me, give me your cup... (*Stretches out his hand, but Nadenka finishes drinking the milk and turns the cup upside down.*)

NADENKA. Look, Alexander Fyodorovich, shall I hit that bug with a drop, that one crawling along the path? Oh dear, I hit her. Poor thing, she'll die! (*She picks up the bug, puts it on the palm of her hand and breathes on it.*)

ALEXANDER. How taken you are with the bug!

NADENKA. Poor thing! Look, she'll die... What have I done! (*The bug starts to crawl on her hand and Nadenka throws it on the ground with a sharp jerk, then crushes it with her foot.*) Nasty bug! So where were you?

ALEXANDER. I told you...

NADENKA. Oh yes, at your uncle's... (*She sets off towards the house.*)

ALEXANDER. Where are you going?

NADENKA. Where? What do you mean where? That's good! To see Mama.

ALEXANDER. Why? Perhaps we'll bother her. (*They stand in silence looking at each other. Enter Nadenka's mother, Marya Mikhailovna.*)

MARYA MIKHAILOVNA. Alexander Fyodorovich!

ALEXANDER. How do you do, Marya Mikhailovna. (*Kisses her hand.*)

MARYA MIKHAILOVNA. Why didn't you come to dinner? We waited for you till five o'clock.

ALEXANDER. I was held up at the office. I beg you never to wait for me later than four o'clock.

MARYA MIKHAILOVNA. That's just what I said. But Nadenka here kept saying, "Let's wait."

NADENKA. I! Mama, what do you mean! It was I who kept saying, "It's time for dinner, Mama." But you said, "No, we must wait a bit, Alexander Fyodorovich hasn't been to see us for a long time. Probably he'll come to dinner today."

MARYA MIKHAILOVNA. Hear, hear! Oh, she really has no conscience! Putting her words in my mouth. I said, "Wherever can Alexander Fyodorovich be now? It's already four-thirty." "No," says she, "we must wait, Mama..."

ALEXANDER. Nadezhda Alexandrovna! Am I really so fortunate that you were thinking of me?

NADENKA. Don't come near me! Mama's joking, and you're ready to believe her!

MARYA MIKHAILOVNA. Don't believe her, Alexander Fyodorovich! Why are you pretending? Probably Alexander Fyodorovich is happy to hear you were thinking of him. I'll order you something to eat. (*Exits.*)

NADENKA. You don't deserve it! To keep us waiting so long!

ALEXANDER. Nadenka! (*They embrace and kiss.*) Like a dream!

NADENKA. What are you doing! You forget yourself! I shall tell Mama!

ALEXANDER. Nadezhda Alexandrovna! Don't destroy my bliss with reproach.

NADENKA. Do you love me very much?

ALEXANDER. Very much. (*They kiss again.*)

NADENKA. Can there be sorrow in the world?

ALEXANDER. Unfortunately there is.

NADENKA. What sorrow?

ALEXANDER. There is poverty.

NADENKA. Poverty? Can the poor possibly not feel what we felt just now! So then they're not poor. (*Laughs.*)

ALEXANDER. Angel! Angel! (*Squeezes her hand.*)

NADENKA. Ouch, you're squeezing so hard it hurts! (*Alexander covers her hand with kisses.*) Do you know, people say that what happens once can never happen again! Therefore this moment will never be repeated!

ALEXANDER. Oh no! That's not so! We'll be close all our lives...

NADENKA (*interrupting*). Oh stop, stop... I get frightened when you talk like that...

ALEXANDER. What is there to be afraid of? Can't we believe in ourselves?

NADENKA. I don't know.

ALEXANDER. Why? We must believe! Nothing will get the better of us, just as now in this garden no sound disturbs the solemn silence.

VOICE OF MARYA MIKHAILOVNA (*Off-stage*). Alexander Fyodorovich! The clotted milk's been on the table for a long time.

NADENKA. At the moment of our inexpressible bliss suddenly the clotted milk is served. (*Laughs, runs off.*)

ALEXANDER (*alone*). And Uncle tries to tell me that happiness is an illusion, that you mustn't believe in anything unconditionally, that life is without conscience! Why did he want to deceive me so cruelly! No, this is life! This is the way I imagined it. This is the way it ought to be, the way it is and will be. This is the way I myself will make it! Otherwise it isn't life! (*Runs out in pursuit of Nadenka.*)

Scene 6

Pyotr Ivanovich's study. He's working at his desk.

ALEXANDER (*rushes in, excited and cheerful.*) Hello, Uncle!

PYOTR IVANOVICH. Hello, Alexander! How is it I haven't seen you for a long time? Why, what's the matter with you? You have such a festive look. Have you been promoted or given a medal? (*Alexander shakes his head.*) Or you've come into money?

ALEXANDER. No.

PYOTR IVANOVICH. Why do you look like the commander of a regiment?

ALEXANDER. Don't you notice anything in my expression?

PYOTR IVANOVICH. A kind of silly look... Wait... Are you in love? There, I guessed it, didn't I? That's it. Why didn't I guess it right off! So that's why you've gotten so lazy...

ALEXANDER. I'm not lazy. I'm young.

PYOTR IVANOVICH. Therefore stupid.

ALEXANDER. In love with Nadenka Lyubetskaya.

PYOTR IVANOVICH. I didn't ask who... Whoever, they're all the same kind of silly fool... What Lyubetskaya? The one with the wart?

ALEXANDER. What wart?

PYOTR IVANOVICH. Right by her nose. Haven't you noticed it yet?

ALEXANDER. You're confusing things. It's the mother, you mean, who has a wart near her nose.

PYOTR IVANOVICH. Well, no matter.

ALEXANDER. No matter! Nadenka! You really didn't notice her? To see her once and not notice!

PYOTR IVANOVICH. What's so special about her? What's there to notice? She doesn't have a wart, you say?...

ALEXANDER. Haven't you talked enough about that wart! How can you say she's like those wooden, affected debutantes? You won't hear any vulgar commonplaces in her conversation... Will some corset indeed forever inhibit the sigh of love and the cry of a tormented heart? Will there never be room for feeling?

PYOTR IVANOVICH. Everything will be revealed later to her husband. There are foolish girls who prematurely reveal what they should hide or repress, and then later make up for it with tears and tears... There's no counting them!

ALEXANDER. Is this a matter for calculation too, Uncle?

PYOTR IVANOVICH. As everything, my dear fellow.

ALEXANDER. In your opinion you have to control even feeling like steam: now let out a little, now suddenly stop, open the valve, shut it off...

PYOTR IVANOVICH. Yes, nature gave man that valve for a purpose—it's his reason. And you don't always use it—that's too bad!

ALEXANDER. Really, Uncle, it's sad to listen to you! Things aren't like that! Life is beautiful! (*With a sweeping gesture he embraces Pyotr Ivanovich.*)

PYOTR IVANOVICH. Alexander! Close the steam valve! You've let all the steam escape! Look what you've done! In one second two stupidities—mussed up my hair and spattered my letter with ink... Look at yourself in the mirror for God's sake. Well, can there be a stupider face? And you're not stupid!

ALEXANDER *(laughs)*. I'm happy!

PYOTR IVANOVICH. So what should I do now with my letter?

ALEXANDER. I'll scrape off the spots and it won't be noticeable. (*Throws himself at the desk, and bumps it so that a small statue falls and breaks.*)

PYOTR IVANOVICH. Third stupidity, Alexander, and it's worth fifty rubles.

ALEXANDER. I'll pay for it, I'll pay!

PYOTR IVANOVICH. "I'll pay," you say! That would be the fourth stupidity... I see you want to tell about your happiness. Well, it can't be helped. (*Sits down in the armchair.*) Tell your story, but be quick about it.

ALEXANDER. No, Uncle, these things can't be told.

PYOTR IVANOVICH. Still, I see you want to tell. But on the other hand... stop, I'll tell it myself.

ALEXANDER. That'll be amusing!

PYOTR IVANOVICH. Very amusing! Listen. Yesterday you and your beauty had some time alone.

ALEXANDER *(impressed)*. Did you have me followed?

PYOTR IVANOVICH. What's this, you think I keep spies in my pay to watch you?

ALEXANDER. How do you know then?

PYOTR IVANOVICH. Sit down, sit down, for God's sake, and don't come near my desk—you'll break something... Everything's written on your face. I'll read from there... So you declared your love. You both were very silly in the usual way. It began from some little thing when you were left alone, from some embroidery...

ALEXANDER. You didn't guess right! We were in the garden...

PYOTR IVANOVICH. A flower then, maybe a yellow one. You asked whether she liked the flower. She answered yes. "Why?" you said. "I don't know," she said, and you both were silent because you wanted to say something quite different. Then you looked at each other, smiled, and blushed.

ALEXANDER. Oh, Uncle, Uncle, how can you!

PYOTR IVANOVICH. Then you began to talk about how only now had you realized the value of life when you saw her... what's her name? Marya, is it?

ALEXANDER. Nadenka...

PYOTR IVANOVICH. And how you were waving your arms, I imagine! You probably broke a cherry tree or a whole apple tree.

ALEXANDER. Uncle! You were spying on us!

PYOTR IVANOVICH. Yes, I was sitting behind a bush there.

ALEXANDER. How do you know everything?

PYOTR IVANOVICH. Since Adam and Eve it's been the same old story for everyone, with slight variations. Know the character of the actors and you'll know the variants. It's all happened again and again... And it's stupid!

ALEXANDER. How many times have I vowed to keep what goes on in my heart a secret from you!

PYOTR IVANOVICH. Why didn't you keep your vow? Here you've come and bothered me...

ALEXANDER. No, let me be forever stupid in your eyes, but I cannot live with your notions of life and people. If they're true, I don't want to live. I don't want to live under such conditions, do you hear? I don't want it!

PYOTR IVANOVICH. I hear you, but what am I to do? After all, I can't deprive you of life... I have the feeling you'll still break a lot more of my things. But it really doesn't matter: love is love, no one's keeping you from it. It's not our custom that at your age one should be so preoccupied with love; still, it shouldn't happen to such a degree that you abandon work...

ALEXANDER. But my work—it's like some kind of bureaucratic machine which grinds away without pause or rest, as if there were no people but only wheels and springs... And my literary work consists of translating "How to Derive Molasses from Potatoes" and "Abstracts from German Economists."

PYOTR IVANOVICH. Enough said, you're not working on abstracts... Oh my, what I think of love at age twenty!

ALEXANDER. What kind of love do you want, Uncle? Love at forty?

PYOTR IVANOVICH. I don't know how love is at forty, but at forty-two...

ALEXANDER. Like yours?

PYOTR IVANOVICH. If you will, like mine.

ALEXANDER. That is, no love.

PYOTR IVANOVICH. How do you know?

ALEXANDER. As if you could love!

PYOTR IVANOVICH. Why not? Don't you think I'm human? Only I love with reason.

ALEXANDER. Reasonable love! That's a fine love that keeps its head!

PYOTR IVANOVICH (*interrupting sharply*). Wild animal love loses its head, but a reasonable love must keep it; otherwise, it isn't love...

ALEXANDER. What is it then?

PYOTR IVANOVICH. Something vile, as you say.

ALEXANDER. You... love? (*Laughs.*) Whom then, Uncle?

PYOTR IVANOVICH. You'd like to know?

ALEXANDER. I would.

PYOTR IVANOVICH. My fiancée.

ALEXANDER. Not... a fiancée! (*Walks up to his uncle.*)

PYOTR IVANOVICH. Not too close, not too close, Alexander; close the valve!

ALEXANDER. That means you're getting married?

PYOTR IVANOVICH. So I am.

ALEXANDER. And not a word to me! You didn't share it with me...

PYOTR IVANOVICH. I avoid sharing in general and have long been against it, especially in marriage.

ALEXANDER. You're so calm... and so hellishly cold in discussing love.

PYOTR IVANOVICH. Hellish coldness—that's something new! People say it's hot in hell.

ALEXANDER. Do you know what, Uncle? Perhaps... No, I can't keep a secret from you... I might be getting married too!

PYOTR IVANOVICH. Close the valve, Alexander!

ALEXANDER. Go on joking, go on joking, Uncle!

PYOTR IVANOVICH. Ought you to be marrying?

ALEXANDER. What do you mean?

PYOTR IVANOVICH. At your age!

ALEXANDER. I'm twenty-three.

PYOTR IVANOVICH. A fine time! At that age only peasants marry when they need a woman to work in the house.

ALEXANDER. But if I'm in love with a girl...

PYOTR IVANOVICH. By no means do I advise you to marry a woman you're in love with.

ALEXANDER. This is something new—I've never heard that...

PYOTR IVANOVICH. There are a lot of things you've never heard of!

ALEXANDER. I've always thought there shouldn't be marriage without love.

PYOTR IVANOVICH. Marriage is one thing and love another. You have to look, choose...

ALEXANDER. Choose?

PYOTR IVANOVICH. Yes, choose. That's the reason I don't advise you to marry when you fall in love. You see, love passes—that's the horrid truth.

ALEXANDER. That's the rudest lie and slander.

PYOTR IVANOVICH. Love will pass, I repeat, and then the woman who seemed the ideal of perfection to you will seem very imperfect perhaps, and then there's nothing you can do. Love prevents you from seeing that she lacks certain qualities necessary in a wife.

ALEXANDER. So you're getting married by calculation?

PYOTR IVANOVICH. With calculation, but not calculating... But you shouldn't get married at all now. Tell me, why are you getting married?

ALEXANDER. What do you mean why? Nadenka—is my wife! (*Covers his face with his hands from happiness.*)

PYOTR IVANOVICH. There, you see, you don't know yourself.

ALEXANDER. My heart stops beating at the very thought... But she says we must wait a year, that we are young and must test ourselves...

PYOTR IVANOVICH. She's the one who suggested it? How old is she?

ALEXANDER. Eighteen.

PYOTR IVANOVICH. And you're twenty-three. Well, my boy, she's twenty-three times more intelligent than you. A year from now! By then she'll deceive you!

ALEXANDER. Uncle, with whom have you been living your whole life?

PYOTR IVANOVICH. I've lived with people, loved women.

ALEXANDER. She deceive me! A woman who is sincerity and purity incarnate...

PYOTR IVANOVICH. But a woman all the same, so probably she'll deceive.

ALEXANDER. And now will you say that I'll cheat on her too?

PYOTR IVANOVICH. It's not out of the question.

ALEXANDER. Who do you think I am?

PYOTR IVANOVICH. A human being.

ALEXANDER. They're not all alike.

PYOTR IVANOVICH. I know! I know! A decent person doesn't doubt the sincerity of an oath when he gives it to a woman, but then he betrays her, or grows cold toward her, and doesn't know why himself. This does not happen by intent, and there's nothing vile about it. Nature hasn't allowed us to love forever.

ALEXANDER. I'm happy now and I thank God. And I don't want to know what lies ahead.

PYOTR IVANOVICH. The first half of your phrase is so reasonable that a man in love shouldn't say it. But the second half, pardon me, won't get you anywhere. "I don't want to know what lies ahead."

ALEXANDER. So what do you advise, Uncle? When a moment of bliss arrives, must one take a magnifying glass and examine it?

PYOTR IVANOVICH. No, the opposite; reduce it so as not to make a fool of yourself for joy...

ALEXANDER. And if a moment of sorrow comes, should that also be examined in your miniaturizing glass?

PYOTR IVANOVICH. No, magnify it. A sorrow is easier to overcome when you imagine the unpleasantness twice as large as it is... But what's the use of explaining to you when you're delirious... Oh dear, it's almost one o'clock. Not another word, Alexander. Run along... I shan't listen. Dine with me tomorrow, there'll be something interesting.

ALEXANDER. Tomorrow, Uncle, I...

PYOTR IVANOVICH. What?

ALEXANDER. I've been invited to the country.

PYOTR IVANOVICH. Probably to the Lyubetskys?

ALEXANDER. Yes.

PYOTR IVANOVICH. Well, as you wish! Remember about your work, Alexander. I'll tell the editor what you're busy with...

ALEXANDER. I'll finish the abstracts of the German economists without fail!

PYOTR IVANOVICH. You'd best begin them first...

ALEXANDER (*laughing and throwing open his arms, goes up to his uncle to embrace him*). Uncle!

PYOTR IVANOVICH (*escaping behind the desk*). Run along, run along, you unfortunate fellow! You're not going to make it in life, you just won't! (*Alexander leaves.*) But one could envy him. No, that's stupid! (*Sits down and writes. A moment later he comes to his senses and tears up what he was writing. Starts writing again.*) Phooey! He's confused me.

Scene 7

The Lyubeysky garden, the same as in scene 5. Nadenka and Alexander are standing near a bench.

NADENKA. No, no, you can't speak to Mama today; that nasty Count is sitting with her!

ALEXANDER. Count? What Count?

NADENKA. You don't know what Count! Count Novinsky, you know, our neighbor. His country home is here; how many times you yourself have praised his garden!

ALEXANDER. Count Novinsky at your house! What has he come for?

NADENKA. I really don't know yet myself.

ALEXANDER. Is he... an old man?

NADENKA. An old man! What are you talking about? He's young and handsome!

ALEXANDER. You've already managed to notice he's handsome!

NADENKA. That's nice! Does it take long to notice that? I've already talked with him. He's very charming. He asked what I do, talked about music, asked me to sing something, but I know almost nothing. This winter without fail I'll ask Mama to get me a singing teacher.

ALEXANDER. I thought, Nadezhda Alexandrovna, that this winter you would have an occupation beside singing...

NADENKA. What?

ALEXANDER. What, indeed!

NADENKA. Oh... yes...

(*Enter Marya Mikhailovna and the Count.*)

MARYA MIKHAILOVNA. May I introduce you, Count? This is Alexander
  Fyodorovich Aduyev.
COUNT NOVINSKY (*bowing to Alexander*). Are you related to Pyotr Ivanovich
  Aduyev?
ALEXANDER (*coldly*). My uncle.
COUNT NOVINSKY. I often see him socially.
ALEXANDER. You might. What's strange about that?
COUNT NOVINSKY. Your uncle is an intelligent and pleasant man!
ALEXANDER (*remains silent*).
NADENKA (*in a low voice to Alexander*). Aren't you ashamed! The Count is so
  friendly to you, while you...
ALEXANDER (*in the same quiet voice*). I don't need his friendly gestures; don't
  repeat that word...
MARYA MIKHAILOVNA. Dinner is served, ladies and gentlemen!

(*They all seat themselves around a garden table. They eat.*)

ALEXANDER (*quietly to Nadenka*). He's at a house for the first time, yet shame-
  lessly eats enough for three!
NADENKA. So what! He's hungry!
ALEXANDER (*abruptly gets up from the table*). Unfortunately, I cannot stay any
  longer; I have work. Goodbye, Marya Mikhailovna! (*Turns to Nadenka*). Till
  tomorrow.
NADENKA. We won't be at home tomorrow.
ALEXANDER. Well, the day after tomorrow.
NADENKA. Good...

(*Alexander bows to all; exits.*)

COUNT NOVINSKY. What a pleasant young man... awfully young... and pleasant.

(*They all go on eating.*)

Scene 8

*The same garden. Nadenka and the Count in riding dress. Marya Mikhailovna is agi-
tated. Alexander is visible hiding behind a bush.*

MARYA MIKHAILOVNA. Sit tighter, Nadenka! Look after her, Count, for
  Heaven's sake!
NADENKA (*gaily*). Don't worry, Mama, we're just going once around the grove.
  I already know how to ride... Count! Shall we ride around once more?
ALEXANDER (*quietly*). Again!
COUNT NOVINSKY. Very well.

(*Nadenka and the Count confer about something in whispers. They go toward the horses.*)

ALEXANDER (*jumps out from behind the bushes and cries out*). Nadezhda Alexandrovna!

(*Everyone stands still as if transfixed. Pause.*)

MARYA MIKHAILOVNA (*coming to her senses*). Oh, it's you, Alexander Fyodorovich!

COUNT NOVINSKY (*bows to Alexander, who doesn't respond*).

NADENKA. You're right, Count. Alexander is like a child. (*She looks angrily at Alexander and goes to the horses. The Count walks behind her.*)

MARYA MIKHAILOVNA (*follows*). Slow down, slow down, for Heaven's sake, slow down! (*Walks up to the bench, sits down.*) Well, let the young people have their fun, but you and I will chat for a while, Alexander Fyodorovich... Why haven't we seen hide nor hair of you for two weeks? Have you stopped loving us?

ALEXANDER. I fear, Marya Mikhailovna, that you no longer love me.

MARYA MIKHAILOVNA. It's a sin for you to fear that, Alexander Fyodorovich! I love you as if you were family. Now I don't know about Nadenka. Why, she's still a child. What sense has she? Every day I repeat to her, "What does it mean that we don't see Alexander Fyodorovich, why doesn't he come? I keep expecting him." Nadenka even sometimes says, "What is it, Mama, whom are you waiting for? I'm hungry and the Count too, I think.'"

ALEXANDER. So the Count... visits often?

MARYA MIKHAILOVNA. Yes, almost every day. "But what about Alexander Fyodorovich," I say, "is he coming?" "He's not coming," she'll say, "it's no use waiting."

ALEXANDER. She...spoke like that?

MARYA MIKHAILOVNA. Yes! And now this horseback riding! Really, we weren't brought up at all this way. And now, it's terrible to say, ladies have even started to smoke...

ALEXANDER. Did this begin a long time ago?

MARYA MIKHAILOVNA. Why, I don't know. They say it became the fashion about five years ago. It's all from the French, you know...

ALEXANDER. Not that; I mean, has Nadezhda Alexandrovna been riding for long?

MARYA MIKHAILOVNA. About a week and a half. The Count is so kind! Look at all those flowers! All from his garden... And they ride every day now... You're not ill are you, Alexander Fyodorovich?

ALEXANDER. Something hurts in my chest...

MARYA MIKHAILOVNA. What is it, does it ache, gnaw, or stab?

ALEXANDER. All three!

MARYA MIKHAILOVNA. You must not neglect it... Do you know what? Take liniment and rub your chest hard at night until it's red. And instead of tea, drink herb tea, I'll give you the recipe.

(*The sound of approaching horses is heard. Nadenka and Count Novinsky enter. Nadenka is breathing hard.*)

MARYA MIKHAILOVNA (*running to Nadenka*). Just look how you've tired yourself out, you can hardly breathe. This riding will do you no good!

COUNT NOVINSKY (*to Alexander*). Do you want to ride with us, Alexander

Fyodorovich? I have an excellent horse for you.

ALEXANDER. No, thank you.

COUNT NOVINSKY. Do you know how? How much fun it is!

ALEXANDER. I can't spend my time with trifles. I have work.

COUNT NOVINSKY. Important business?

ALEXANDER. Yes... I'm doing abstracts of German economists.

COUNT NOVINSKY. That's interesting. I thought you had a factory or mill or a shipyard.

NADENKA. Shall we go riding again tomorrow, Count?

COUNT NOVINSKY. With pleasure.

MARYA MIKHAILOVNA. That's enough, Nadenka, you're bothering the Count.

COUNT NOVINSKY. I enjoy these outings, Marya Mikhailovna.

MARYA MIKHAILOVNA. Wouldn't you like tea with jam, Count?. I made the jam myself.

COUNT NOVINSKY. With pleasure.

(*Marya Mikhailovna and the Count exit. Alexander and Nadenka remain alone.*)

ALEXANDER. Nadezhda Alexandrovna!

NADENKA (*coldly*). Will you come to see us tomorrow?

ALEXANDER. I don't know, why?

NADENKA. I'm only asking, will you?

ALEXANDER. You'd like me to?

NADENKA. Will you come to see us tomorrow?

ALEXANDER. No.

NADENKA. And the day after?

ALEXANDER. No, I'm not coming for a whole week, maybe two... not for a long time!

MARYA MIKHAILOVNA (*returns for a moment to fetch the scarf she left on the bench*). Don't forget to rub your chest with liniment, Alexander Fyodorovich! (*Exits.*)

ALEXANDER. Nadezhda Alexandrovna!

NADENKA (*looking into the distance*). Tell me please, what's that smoke over there? A fire or one of those factory furnaces?

ALEXANDER (*shaking his head*). And you are like the others, like all of them!

NADENKA. What do you mean? I don't understand you.

ALEXANDER. Nadezhda Alexandrovna, I haven't the strength to bear this torture any longer.

NADENKA. What torture? Really, I don't know...

ALEXANDER. Don't pretend; tell me, is this you? Are you the same person you were?

NADENKA (*decisively*). I'm still the same!

ALEXANDER. You haven't changed toward me?

NADENKA. No. I'm just as friendly to you, I think; I receive you just as cheerfully...

ALEXANDER (*struck by the lie*). Is this you? Heavens! A month and a half ago right here...

NADENKA. What smoke is that on the other shore, I would like to know.

ALEXANDER. Please don't! Please don't!

NADENKA. Why, what have I done to you? You stopped coming to see us—as you wish... To keep you against your will...

ALEXANDER. As if you didn't know why I stopped coming! And the Count?

NADENKA. What Count?

ALEXANDER. What Count! Will you also say that you don't care about him?

NADENKA. You're mad!

ALEXANDER. Yes, you're right! My reason is failing with each passing day... How can you treat someone this way who loves you more than anything in the world, who forgot everything for you, and you...

NADENKA. What have I done?

ALEXANDER (*enraged by her cold calm*). What do you mean? You have forgotten! I remind you that here on this very spot you swore a hundred times to belong to me. "God hears our vows," you said. You ought to blush before Heaven and these trees, before every blade of grass... You've committed perjury!

NADENKA (*recoiling from Alexander in horror*). Ooh! How angry you are! Why are you angry? I did not refuse you. You had not yet spoken to Mama... How do you know?

ALEXANDER. Speak to her after what you've done?

NADENKA. What have I done? I don't know...

ALEXANDER. What? I'll tell you. What do these meetings with the Count mean, these horseback rides?

NADENKA. I can't run away from him! And the horseback riding means... that I love to ride... It's so pleasant: you gallop... Oh, that horse Lucy is such a darling! Did you see her? She already knows me...

ALEXANDER. But the change in your treatment of me? Why is the Count at your house every day from morning till evening?

NADENKA. Oh, heavens! How do I know? How ridiculous you are! It's Mama's wish.

ALEXANDER. That's not so! Your mama wants what you want. For whom are these flowers? All for Mama?

NADENKA. Yes, Mama loves flowers...

ALEXANDER (*paying no attention to what she says*). But what do you talk to him about in a low voice? See, you're turning pale. You feel your own guilt. To destroy a person's happiness, forget, ruin everything... Hypocrisy, lies, betrayal! How could you stoop to that? A rich count, a society lion, condescended to cast a kindly glance on you—and you melted, fell on your knees before this tinsel sun. Where's your sense of shame!!! Don't let me find the Count here! Do you hear? Give him up, cease all relations with him, let him forget the way to your house!!! I will not have it!!! (*In a rage Alexander seizes Nadenka by the hand.*)

NADENKA (*in a shrill voice*). Mama! Mama! Come here!

(*Marya Mikhailovna enters, running. After her Count Novinsky.*)

MARYA MIKHAILOVNA. What has happened to you? What is the matter? Why did you cry out?

NADENKA. Alexander Fyodorovich... isn't well!

MARYA MIKHAILOVNA. What a fright you gave me, you crazy girl! What's the matter if he's sick? I know his chest hurts. What's so terrible about it? It's not consumption! Let him rub it with liniment—it will all go away...

(*Count Novinsky takes his leave, bowing. Marya Mikhailovna also exits.*)

ALEXANDER. Farewell, Nadezhda Alexandrovna...

NADENKA. Farewell.
ALEXANDER. When will you let me come to see you?
NADENKA. When it suits you.

(*They stand in silence.*)

ALEXANDER. Nadezhda Alexandrovna...
NADENKA. I can't listen to you, you were...
ALEXANDER. I was to blame. I shall speak differently now, I give you my word. You won't hear a single reproach. An explanation is unavoidable... You did, after all, give me permission to ask your mama for your hand. After what has happened, I must repeat the question. Answer just one question for me briefly and sincerely, and our explanation will be over at once... Don't you love me any more?
NADENKA. What an idea! You know how Mama and I have always valued your friendship... have always been glad to see you...
ALEXANDER. Listen, leave Mama out of this. Be the old Nadenka for a minute... and answer directly...
NADENKA (*remains silent*).
ALEXANDER. Answer, Nadezhda Alexandrovna. A single word will free me from torment and you from this unpleasant explanation.
NADENKA. What are you asking me about? I'm quite lost... my head is truly in a fog...
ALEXANDER. I'm asking, has someone taken my place in your heart? One word, yes or no, decides everything. Does it take long to say?
NADENKA (*remains silent*).
ALEXANDER. Yes or no?
NADENKA (*remains silent*).
ALEXANDER. Yes or no?
NADENKA (*very quietly*). Yes... (*Pause.*)
MARYA MIKHAILOVNA (*entering*). Alexander Fyodorovich! In which ear do you hear a ringing?
NADENKA. Mama is asking you a question...
ALEXANDER. Ah?
MARYA MIKHAILOVNA. In which do you hear a ringing? Come, quickly!
ALEXANDER (*gloomily*). In both!
MARYA MIKHAILOVNA. What ears you have! In the left! But I was guessing whether the Count would come tomorrow!
NADENKA. Leave us, Mama! And don't listen. (*Marya Mikhailovna exits.*) Forgive me! I don't understand it myself... It all happened unexpectedly, against my will... I don't know how... I could not deceive you...
ALEXANDER. I shall keep my word, Nadezhda Alexandrovna! I shall not speak a word of reproach. I thank you for your sincerity... You have helped a lot... today... It was hard for me to hear that "yes," but it was harder for you to say it... Farewell, you won't see me any more—a reward for your sincerity... But the Count, the Count! What will it lead to? The Count will not marry you. What are his intentions?
NADENKA. I don't know...
ALEXANDER. Heavens! How blind you are!
NADENKA. He can't have bad intentions...
ALEXANDER. Be careful, Nadezhda Alexandrovna!

NADENKA. Farewell, Alexander Fyodorovich! (*Exits.*)
ALEXANDER (*remains alone; suddenly begins to sob.*)

Curtain

ACT II

Scene 9

Pyotr Ivanovich's study. Late evening. Pyotr Ivanovich, seated at his desk in his dressing gown, is writing. Elizaveta Alexandrovna, entering, goes over to her husband, puts her arms around his neck, kisses him.

ELIZAVETA ALEXANDROVNA. Aren't you tired?
PYOTR IVANOVICH (*kissing her hand*). No, Liza.
ELIZAVETA ALEXANDROVNA. I didn't think that I'd have such an intelligent husband.
PYOTR IVANOVICH. Are you being ironical?
ELIZAVETA ALEXANDROVNA. What do you mean! You're wonderful!
PYOTR IVANOVICH. You don't need money?
ELIZAVETA ALEXANDROVNA. No, I'm happy with you even without it.
PYOTR IVANOVICH. Without it, Liza, nobody can ever be happy.
ELIZAVETA ALEXANDROVNA. Why has Alexander stopped coming to see us?
PYOTR IVANOVICH. Apparently he doesn't feel the need. When he does, he'll come.
ELIZAVETA ALEXANDROVNA. I've taken a liking to him.
PYOTR IVANOVICH. You have a lot in common. Only you're more intelligent.
ELIZAVETA ALEXANDROVNA. Alas, I'm stupid too.
PYOTR IVANOVICH. Don't slander yourself. I wouldn't have married a stupid woman. Just as you wouldn't have married a stupid man.
ELIZAVETA ALEXANDROVNA. I love *you*, Pyotr Ivanovich.
PYOTR IVANOVICH. My mind, you mean.
ELIZAVETA ALEXANDROVNA. I don't know... Goodnight.
PYOTR IVANOVICH. Goodnight...

(*Elizaveta Alexandrovna exits. Pyotr Ivanovich finishes writing his document, puts out one candle, and taking up the other, heads for the bedroom. Alexander enters. He has grown thinner and more mature, and speaks in a drier and more certain tone.*)

PYOTR IVANOVICH. Nephew! Of late it's been no use expecting you in the daytime, but now all of a sudden, bang!—in the middle of the night! How are you? (*They exchange greetings.*) Are you well?
ALEXANDER. Yes, I move, eat, and drink, therefore I'm well.
PYOTR IVANOVICH. You haven't gambled away everything or lost money?

ALEXANDER. You just can't imagine any grief not connected with money!

PYOTR IVANOVICH. What kind of grief is it, if it's not worth a red cent?

ALEXANDER. When you hear what has happened, you'll be horrified...

PYOTR IVANOVICH. Tell me, I haven't been horrified for a long time. (*Looks at his nephew.*) By the way, though, it isn't hard to guess. No doubt someone's deceived you.

ALEXANDER (*jumps up, wants to say something, but sits down again*). Could anyone have foretold it!

PYOTR IVANOVICH. You had not to foretell it, but foresee it!

ALEXANDER. And you can reason about it so calmly...

PYOTR IVANOVICH. Why, what's it to me?

ALEXANDER. Yes, I forgot. You wouldn't care even if the whole town burned to the ground or fell apart.

PYOTR IVANOVICH. Please! And my factory?

ALEXANDER. I won't get any comfort from you, nor do I ask it. I'm asking your help as a relative.

PYOTR IVANOVICH. Gladly. Are you sure you don't need money?

ALEXANDER. If my unhappiness were only lack of money, I'd bless my fate!

PYOTR IVANOVICH (*serious*). Don't say that... Are you staying here long, Alexander?

ALEXANDER. Yes, I need all your attention. Why?

PYOTR IVANOVICH. I was about to go to bed without supper, but now...

ALEXANDER. You're able to eat supper?

PYOTR IVANOVICH. Yes, and very much so. But you really won't join me?

ALEXANDER. No, and you won't choke down a bite either when you learn that this is a matter of life and death.

PYOTR IVANOVICH. Of life and death? Yes, then that is indeed very important... but, by the way—let's try perhaps to swallow something. (*Rings the bell. Vasily enters.*) Ask what there is for supper. (*Vasily exits.*) On an empty stomach, you know, it's awkward...

ALEXANDER. Do you know Count Novinsky?

PYOTR IVANOVICH. We're acquaintances... Why?

ALEXANDER. I congratulate you on such a friend. He's a scoundrel!

PYOTR IVANOVICH. I've known him for five years and always considered him a decent fellow.

ALEXANDER. Since when have you been defending people, Uncle?

PYOTR IVANOVICH. And since when have you begun to berate them and stopped calling them angels?

(*Vasily brings in supper, puts it on the table and exits.*)

ALEXANDER. Until I learned differently, but now... I'm completely to blame that I didn't listen to you when you advised me to beware of everyone...

PYOTR IVANOVICH (*starting to eat*). I'd advise it again: it doesn't hurt to beware... If the person proves to be a scoundrel, you won't be deceived, but if he's a decent fellow, you'll be pleased to have made a mistake.

ALEXANDER (*contemptuously*). Show me where there are any decent people!

PYOTR IVANOVICH. Why, take you and me, for example. The Count, since we've already mentioned him, is a decent person too. Isn't that enough... Not everyone's bad.

ALEXANDER. Everyone, everyone!

PYOTR IVANOVICH. And you?

ALEXANDER. I? At least I shall take through life a heart free of meanness.

PYOTR IVANOVICH. Well, good, let's see. But what has the Count done to you?

ALEXANDER. What has he done? He's robbed me of everything.

PYOTR IVANOVICH. Be more precise. Under the word "everything" one can mean Heaven knows what, say, money. But the Count wouldn't do that...

ALEXANDER. Everything! Life!

PYOTR IVANOVICH. Look, you're alive!

ALEXANDER. Unfortunately, yes!

PYOTR IVANOVICH. Ah! He's taken your girl, hasn't he, this... what's her name? Yes, he's good at that; it's hard for you to compete with him. A charmer! A charmer!

ALEXANDER. He'll pay dearly for his mastery... I won't yield without a fight!

PYOTR IVANOVICH. How provincial!

ALEXANDER. I'll destroy this wretched womanizer!

PYOTR IVANOVICH. Don't act like a barbarian!

ALEXANDER. I'll wipe him off the face of the earth!

PYOTR IVANOVICH (*continuing to eat*). By the way, did he say whether he'd received a china dinner service from abroad?

ALEXANDER (*threateningly*). We're not talking about china, Uncle! Did you hear what I said?

PYOTR IVANOVICH (*grunts affirmatively*). Mm-m!

ALEXANDER. Listen attentively at least once in your life. I came on business. Will you agree to be my second?

PYOTR IVANOVICH. The cutlets are quite cold!

ALEXANDER. Are you laughing at me, Uncle?

PYOTR IVANOVICH. Judge for yourself; how can one listen seriously to such nonsense, asking someone to be his second in a duel!

ALEXANDER. What do you mean?

PYOTR IVANOVICH. It's obvious—I won't do it.

ALEXANDER. Good. I'll find someone else.

PYOTR IVANOVICH. Listen, Alexander. The Count is not going to fight with you, I know him.

ALEXANDER (*flying into a rage*). Refuse to fight! I didn't suppose he was so base!

PYOTR IVANOVICH. He isn't base, only intelligent.

ALEXANDER. So that makes me stupid in your view?

PYOTR IVANOVICH. N... no, in love. Tell me, now, whom are you especially angry at—the Count or her... what's her name... Anyuta is it?

ALEXANDER. I hate him, disdain her.

PYOTR IVANOVICH. Let's begin with the Count. Let's assume he accepts your challenge. Let's even assume that you find some fool of a second—what will be the result? The Count will kill you like a fly.

ALEXANDER. It's not certain who will kill whom.

PYOTR IVANOVICH. Probably he'll kill you.

ALEXANDER. Divine judgment will decide the matter.

PYOTR IVANOVICH. Well, as you like—but God will decide in his favor. It's said that the Count puts bullet after bullet on the mark at fifteen paces, and you don't even know how to shoot. Suppose even that divine judgment permits such an injustice and you somehow accidentally even kill him. What's the sense in that? Do you think you'd get your beauty's love back that way? She'd begin to hate you, while you'd be conscripted into the army...

ALEXANDER. What am I to do in my situation?

PYOTR IVANOVICH. Nothing! Leave it as it is—it's already ruined.

ALEXANDER. Leave it as is! Milk flows in your veins, not blood!

PYOTR IVANOVICH. Stop talking nonsense, Alexander! Don't you think there are lots of girls in the world like your... Marya or Sofiya, what's her name?

ALEXANDER. Her name is Nadezhda.

PYOTR IVANOVICH. Nadezhda? And who was Sofiya then?

ALEXANDER (*grudgingly*). Sofiya... That was in the country

PYOTR IVANOVICH. Do you see? There Sofiya, here Nadezhda, somewhere else Marya. The heart is a deep well; you probe for a long while to reach bottom. The heart keeps on loving till old age...

ALEXANDER. The heart loves once!

PYOTR IVANOVICH. The heart keeps on loving until it loses its strength. If one love fails, the heart is only quiescent, it is silent until the next love. If the next love is thwarted, the capacity to love remains unfulfilled until the third or fourth time. Some people love happily the first time, they're the ones who shout that it's possible to love only once. As long as a person is healthy...

ALEXANDER. You keep talking about physical, material love, Uncle...

PYOTR IVANOVICH. What sort of thing is material love? There is no such love, just as there isn't any uniquely ideal love. Both soul and body play equal parts in love; if not, love is incomplete. We are not spirits and not beasts... Where did I leave off? Oh, yes! You'll be drafted into the army... Besides, after this scandal your girl won't let you come near her... And why do you want to wipe the Count off the face of the earth? Do you think he was obliged to inquire whether your girl was taken by someone else? He fell in love too; was he at fault in that? At fault for enjoying himself? And you, did you contend for her?

ALEXANDER. That's what I want to do now.

PYOTR IVANOVICH. With an oak club in your hands? You should have fought a duel of a different kind with the Count.

ALEXANDER. Cunning is contemptible!

PYOTR IVANOVICH. Is resorting to blows better? Awáken love by whatever means, but maintain it by intelligence. Cunning is but one part of intelligence; there's nothing contemptible in that.

ALEXANDER. I prefer to suffer rather than resort to cunning!

PYOTR IVANOVICH. Well, then, suffer, if you enjoy it... Oh, the provinces! Oh, Asia! No, to be happy with a woman requires a lot. You must know how to make a woman of a girl according to a well-thought-out plan, a method, if you will... You must cunningly take possession of her heart, mind, and will; you must subordinate her taste and habits to yours, so that she sees things through you, is of the same mind as you... A complete schooling is necessary...

(*The door opens. On the threshold Elizaveta Alexandrovna appears.*)

ELIZAVETA ALEXANDROVNA (*calmly*). And the wife must not show that she understands this great schooling of her husband's and must institute a little of her own, but not gossip about it over a bottle of wine... (*She changes the candles on the table and exits.*)

PYOTR IVANOVICH. I boasted too soon. Let that be a lesson!

ALEXANDER. Are you afraid?

PYOTR IVANOVICH. Why should I be afraid? I made a mistake, so I must find a way to redeem it... What were we talking about? Oh yes, it seems you wanted to kill her... what's her name?

ALEXANDER. I despise her too deeply.

PYOTR IVANOVICH. But tell me, why do you despise her?

ALEXANDER. To pay me back with ingratitude...

PYOTR IVANOVICH. What had she to be grateful for? Do you mean you loved her to be nice to her? You wanted to do her a favor perhaps? You shouldn't have shown her the depth of your feelings. A woman cools when a man completely declares himself. Was it her fault she began to love the Count? Why does a certain man die, a certain woman go crazy? How can we answer such questions? Love must end some time; it can't last a century.

ALEXANDER (begins to sob). How she changed! How she began to dress up for the Count! If only I had the comfort that I lost her because of circumstances; if she had been forced... or if she had even died... then it would be easier to endure... But this way, no, no... another man! I don't want to live, I don't want to live, I don't want to live...

PYOTR IVANOVICH (walking around his study, lost in thought, calls out). Liza! (Elizaveta Alexandrovna enters. They stand at a distance from Alexander speaking in whispers.) What am I to do with Alexander? I've quite worn myself out with him. He's begun to bawl... (Whispers something in her ear.)

ELIZAVETA ALEXANDROVNA. Poor fellow... Let me try, I'll go to him.

PYOTR IVANOVICH. You won't get anywhere, it's his nature. He quite takes after his aunt. I've been reasoning with him for some time.

ELIZAVETA ALEXANDROVNA. You only reasoned?

PYOTR IVANOVICH. And convinced him. He agreed with me.

ELIZAVETA ALEXANDROVNA. I don't doubt it. You're very reasonable and... cunning!

PYOTR IVANOVICH. Thank Heaven, if that's so. Well, it seems I've done all that can be done.

ELIZAVETA ALEXANDROVNA. It seems you have, but he's still crying.

PYOTR IVANOVICH. I'm not to blame, I've done everything to comfort him.

ELIZAVETA ALEXANDROVNA. What have you done?

PYOTR IVANOVICH. Talked a whole hour... my throat's even gone dry...

ELIZAVETA ALEXANDROVNA. And he's still crying? Amazing! Let me try. And you meanwhile think over your new method...

PYOTR IVANOVICH. What, what do you mean?

(Elizaveta Alexandrovna does not answer, but goes over to Alexander. Pyotr Ivanovich exits. Elizaveta Alexandrovna strokes Alexander on the head. Alexander raises his head, and seeing his aunt, takes hold of her hand and presses it to his cheek.)

ALEXANDER. Dear Aunt, I don't want to live, I don't want to live.

ELIZAVETA ALEXANDROVNA (giving Alexander time to regain his calm). She's a bad woman, Alexander. The Count is an immoral, sly person. Fate has guided you correctly, separating you from everything filthy and false...

ALEXANDER. But I love her and can't live without her!

ELIZAVETA ALEXANDROVNA. Alexander, you can be a very great and famous person. You have talent. Your poetry, the story you've been writing is so touching... Put your sufferings down on paper, let others weep through your tears and feel the joy and beauty of your suffering... Don't surrender to grief, Alexander, however great... You're a strong person, stand taller than others...

(*She goes on stroking his head. Alexander has become quiet. The tears are gone from his eyes; he shows only quiet sorrow. He gets up, bows farewell to his aunt and starts toward the door.*) (*Elizaveta Alexandrovna calls after him.*) Write, Alexander, write. I believe in your star...

Scene 10

Nevsky Prospect. This scene can be set in front of the curtain and the sound design might be a recording of the sound of passing vehicles, hoofbeats, the roar of the crowd, the ringing of distant bells. The shadows of people walking to and fro are reflected.

ALEXANDER (*in a Byronic mood stands leaning against the wings on one side as Pospelov enters from the other. Alexander rushes to his friend and embraces him*). Pospelov!

POSPELOV (*wearing the ribbon of a government award around his neck, rather coldly*). Hello, Aduyev.

ALEXANDER. Have you been here long?

POSPELOV. Long enough. And, as you can see, I've gotten ahead. And you?

ALEXANDER. I—no... Oh, how glad I am to see you! A kindred soul!

POSPELOV (*laughing*). Enough! You're still the same old dreamer... But why are you so gloomy?

ALEXANDER. Listen to what people have done to me!

POSPELOV (*worried*). Have you been robbed?

ALEXANDER. No, worse!

POSPELOV. Do you need help? Can I be of help to you in your government job?

ALEXANDER. People have robbed me of my soul. Let me tell you how I was treated...

POSPELOV. Excuse me, Aduyev, I've been invited to a formal dinner; persons who can be helpful to me will be there...

ALEXANDER. Dinner? Important persons? But you're my first friend, and I am yours...Remember how we swore an oath!

POSPELOV. The empty enthusiasm of youth... When you get on in years, you begin to understand...

ALEXANDER. Understand what? What? How vile life is!

POSPELOV. On the contrary—how pleasant... No, undoubtedly you've had some trouble at work... Come to see me... (*He gets out his card and gives it to Alexander, who doesn't take it.*) We'll talk. Word of honor, I'm ready to help you.

ALEXANDER. Yes, but listen! I'm talking about love...

POSPELOV. About love? Love is a wonderful thing! I'll tell you later a lot of funny things on that score... Right now I can't. Come to see me, we'll talk. (*Stuffs the card into Alexander's hand.*) I look forward to it. (*Exits.*)

ALEXANDER (*flabbergasted*). He didn't want to hear me out... dinner invitation... important people... Friendship! Sacred friendship! What is there in this world? (*Tears Pospelov's card into little pieces.*) Everything is a lie, a lie, a lie! And perhaps I'm supposed to become like everyone? Perhaps I'm really stupid? Everyone is this way! I don't want to be, can't be, shan't be!

(*The stage darkens.*)

Scene 11

Pyotr Ivanovich's study. He is sitting at his desk.

ELIZAVETA ALEXANDROVNA (*entering*). I've come to ask a favor of you. (*Pyotr Ivanovich gets out his wallet.*) No, don't worry, put your money away.
PYOTR IVANOVICH. Not to take money when it's offered! It's unbelievable!
ELIZAVETA ALEXANDROVNA. Alexander came to see me the day before yesterday.
PYOTR IVANOVICH. Has he been betrayed in love again perhaps?
ELIZAVETA ALEXANDROVNA. This time in friendship.
PYOTR IVANOVICH. Oh, I heard about his meeting with Pospelov...
ELIZAVETA ALEXANDROVNA. Let's talk with him... more gently.
PYOTR IVANOVICH. You're not demanding that I cry, are you?
ELIZAVETA ALEXANDROVNA. It wouldn't hurt.
PYOTR IVANOVICH. What's the good of that for him?
ELIZAVETA ALEXANDROVNA. A lot... and not only for him...
PYOTR IVANOVICH. What? (*Elizaveta Alexandrovna does not answer.*) I've been fussing over him for six years.
ELIZAVETA ALEXANDROVNA. Of course, how are we to find time for trivial matters?... We women spin people's fates. If a single feeling man turns up among them, capable of loving...
PYOTR IVANOVICH. Don't be angry. I did all I could. It was you who encouraged him to write a story.
ELIZAVETA ALEXANDROVNA. Why say it was I? He himself feels inclined to literary creativity.
PYOTR IVANOVICH. Enough, Liza! Inclination's neither here nor there—who isn't so inclined at his age? But to write a story, inclination alone is not enough...
ELIZAVETA ALEXANDROVNA. You're cruel to Alexander, Pyotr Ivanovich!
PYOTR IVANOVICH. Why cruel? I took his story, sent it to an editor I know over my signature, and pretending I wanted to achieve fame in my old age, asked him to print it, please. See, now I've received an answer from him.
ELIZAVETA ALEXANDROVNA. What does he say?
PYOTR IVANOVICH. I haven't opened it. I've invited Alexander. I need him for a job. Let him read it, he'll be glad to. Well, what do you want me to do with him?
ELIZAVETA ALEXANDROVNA. Give him an easy lesson...
PYOTR IVANOVICH. Scold him? Fine, I'm good at that.
ELIZAVETA ALEXANDROVNA. Don't scold him!
PYOTR IVANOVICH. Does he have money?
ELIZAVETA ALEXANDROVNA. You have only money on your mind! He'd be ready to give all his money for one kind word from his friend.
PYOTR IVANOVICH. We'll see what good will come of it...
ALEXANDER (*entering, bows*). You asked me to come, Uncle?
PYOTR IVANOVICH. I did. (*Alexander sits down in silence.*) You're complaining about your friend? But tell me, what did you want from him? A sacrifice of some sort? Was he supposed to climb up the wall?

ALEXANDER. People are incapable of rising to a conception of friendship as it ought to be...

PYOTR IVANOVICH. If they are incapable of it, then there ought not to be such friendship. (*Pause.*) So, what are you doing now?

ALEXANDER. Why, nothing...

PYOTR IVANOVICH. Too little... Well, do you read at least?

ALEXANDER. Yes.

PYOTR IVANOVICH. What?

ALEXANDER. Krylov's fables.

PYOTR IVANOVICH. A good book. But surely not just that?

ALEXANDER. Only that now. Heavens, what portraits of people, how true to life!

PYOTR IVANOVICH. Why do you dislike people so?

ALEXANDER. Why? For their baseness, their smallness of spirit.

PYOTR IVANOVICH. You're disheartened, that's all! You need to keep busy with something, then you won't inveigh against people for nothing! In what way are your friends bad? There are always decent people.

ALEXANDER.Yes! Whomever you take, you've got hold of some animal out of Krylov's fables.

PYOTR IVANOVICH. The Khozarovs, for example?

ALEXANDER. A whole family of animals!

PYOTR IVANOVICH. And the Lunins?

ALEXANDER. He is the very image of the ass. And she looks at you like the kind fox.

PYOTR IVANOVICH. What would you say about the Sonins?

ALEXANDER. Well, there's nothing good to say.

PYOTR IVANOVICH. And you don't like Volochkov?

ALEXANDER. A contemptible and, in addition, mean animal... (*Alexander even spits.*)

PYOTR IVANOVICH. So, now finish this gallery of portraits with ours. What kind of beasts are my wife and I? (*Alexander says nothing, only smiles ironically.*) Well, and what kind of beast are you yourself?

ALEXANDER. I haven't done harm to people!

PYOTR IVANOVICH. So you're right in everything? You came out of the water quite dry? Wait, I'll take you out into fresh water...

ELIZAVETA ALEXANDROVNA. Pyotr Ivanovich! Stop...

PYOTR IVANOVICH. No, let him listen to the truth. Tell me, please, Alexander, when you slandered your friends just now as donkeys, and foxes, and other animals, was there no slight ripple in your heart of something like a pang of conscience?

ALEXANDER. For what, Uncle?

PYOTR IVANOVICH. For the reason that you were cordially welcomed for several years running at the houses of these beasts. Let's assume that they acted slyly and planned intrigues against those from whom they could get something, but they had nothing to gain from you. It's not kind of you, Alexander! Let's go on. You say you have no friends, but I've always thought you have three.

ALEXANDER. Three? Once I had one, but he...

PYOTR IVANOVICH. Three... Let's begin by seniority. That one... Pospelov, it seems... After you hadn't seen each other for several years, a different friend would have turned away from you when you met, but he invited you to his house, offered you his services and help, and, I'm convinced, would even have given you money, and in our time money is the touchstone to test more than feeling... No, please introduce me to him; I see him as a decent fellow, but according to you, he's a villain... So, what do you think, who's your second friend?

ALEXANDER. Who? Why, no one.

PYOTR IVANOVICH. Huh? Liza, he doesn't even blush! And I, how do I rate with you, may I ask?

ALEXANDER. You're... a relative.

PYOTR IVANOVICH. That's a fine title! I thought I was more. That's not kind, Alexander. That's a character trait which is called vile even in grade-school copy books, and such as you don't find even in Krylov.

ALEXANDER. But you've always pushed me away...

PYOTR IVANOVICH. Yes, when you wanted to embrace me!

ALEXANDER. You laughed at me, at feeling...

PYOTR IVANOVICH. And why, to what end?

ALEXANDER (*gets up and holding out his arms, goes to his uncle*). Uncle!

PYOTR IVANOVICH. Sit down, I haven't finished! Your third and best friend I hope you'll name yourself...

ELIZAVETA ALEXANDROVNA (*interrupting*). Pyotr Ivanovich, don't try to be clever for Heaven's sake, let him be...

PYOTR IVANOVICH. Don't interfere!

ALEXANDER (*quite embarrassed*). I can appreciate my aunt's friendship...

PYOTR IVANOVICH. No, you can't. If you could, you wouldn't be looking at the ceiling to find a friend, but would point to her. If you truly felt her friendship, out of respect for her merits you wouldn't think ill of people. She alone should redeem in your eyes the faults of others. Who dried your tears and whimpered with you?

ALEXANDER. Oh, dear Aunt! You don't think, that I don't esteem... I swear!

ELIZAVETA ALEXANDROVNA. I believe you, I believe you, Alexander! Don't listen to Pyotr Ivanovich. He's making mountains out of molehills, glad of a chance to show off his intelligence. For Heaven's sake, stop, Pyotr Ivanovich.

PYOTR IVANOVICH. Right away, I'll finish right away. Just one last word! You said you do no wrong to others. Tell me now, do you love your mother?

ALEXANDER. What a question! I'd give my life for her...

PYOTR IVANOVICH. So tell me, when did you last write to her?

ALEXANDER. About... three weeks ago.

PYOTR IVANOVICH. No. Four months... Well, then, what kind of beast are you?

ALEXANDER. That long! (*Frightened.*) What's happened?

PYOTR IVANOVICH. The old woman is sick with grief.

ALEXANDER. Really! Oh, Heavens! Heavens!

ELIZAVETA ALEXANDROVNA. Not so! It's not so! She's not sick, but much grieved.

PYOTR IVANOVICH. You spoil him, Liza.

ELIZAVETA ALEXANDROVNA. And you are immoderately severe. There were certain difficulties which distracted Alexander for a time...

PYOTR IVANOVICH. To forget his mother for some girl—fine difficulties!

ELIZAVETA ALEXANDROVNA. Enough, for Heaven's sake!

ALEXANDER. Don't interrupt Uncle, dear Aunt. Let him thunder his reproaches. I've deserved worse, I'm a monster! (*Seizes his head in his hands.*)

PYOTR IVANOVICH. In the words of your favorite author, "Rather than trying to evaluate others, Better turn your fox eye on yourself." (*To his wife softly.*) I think I've done just as you asked. (*Gets up.*) But now I have good news for you, Alexander.

ALEXANDER. What is it Uncle?

PYOTR IVANOVICH (*taking out a sealed envelope*). An answer from the editor.

ALEXANDER. Give it to me, give it to me quickly! (*Opens the envelope.*)

PYOTR IVANOVICH. Read it aloud. We'll rejoice together.

ALEXANDER (*reading*). "What kind of mystification is this, my dearest Pyotr Ivanovich? You've signed this story. But who'd believe you! No, the fragile products of your china factory are much more solid than this piece of work..." (*Alexander's voice falls.*)

PYOTR IVANOVICH. I can't hear you, Alexander! Speak louder!

ALEXANDER (*continuing to read*). "Out of sympathy with the author of the story you probably want to know my opinion. Here it is: The author must be a young man. He's not stupid, but somehow pathologically angry at the whole world. In what an enraged, furious mood he writes! Probably he's disappointed! Oh, God, when will his kind die out! (*Alexander takes a deep breath.*) Pride, day-dreaming, the development of all sorts of emotional leanings and the stultification of the mind with the inevitable consequence—indolence—these are the causes of this evil. Learning, labor, a practical job—these are the remedies for it. This is what can bring our idle, sick youth to their senses."

ELIZAVETA ALEXANDROVNA. Don't go on, Alexander. Let be...

PYOTR IVANOVICH. Why? (*Taking the letter from Alexander, he finishes reading it.*) "Tell your *protégé* that, first of all, a writer only writes sensibly when he's not under the influence of personal enthusiasms and preferences. He should view life and people in general with a calm, bright eye; otherwise he'll express only his own ego which interests no one. The second and main condition is talent, and there isn't even a trace of it here."

ELIZAVETA ALEXANDROVNA. That's not so! The story is good, and he has talent, though he writes differently from others...

PYOTR IVANOVICH. The editor knows better than we, Liza, whether he has talent or not... Well, Alexander, how do you feel?

ALEXANDER. Calmer than one might have expected. I feel like a person who's been deceived in everything.

PYOTR IVANOVICH. No, like a person who has deceived himself and wanted to deceive others too... (*Holds out to Alexander the thick pile of his manuscript sheets.*) What shall we do with your manuscript, Alexander?

ALEXANDER. Don't you need to paper any screens?

PYOTR IVANOVICH. No, not now. (*Alexander begins to tear up the manuscript.*) Bravo! That's right!

ALEXANDER (*tearing with fanaticism*). Good, good! I'm free!

PYOTR IVANOVICH. What are you going to do now?

ALEXANDER. What? Now, for the time being, nothing.

PYOTR IVANOVICH. You can do nothing only in the country, but here... Why did you come here? Liza, excuse me, we two must talk man to man... Actually that's why I asked you to come here. (*Elizaveta Alexandrovna exits.*) Do you know my partner Surkov? (*Alexander nods.*) He's a good fellow, but very shallow. His greatest weakness is women. He's no sooner fallen for one then he goes and throws money around: surprises, presents; he begins to change his coach and horses... This is when he launches into big spending; his percentages are not enough, so he begins asking me for money. If I refuse, he starts talking about taking the capital.

ALEXANDER. What's all this leading to, Uncle?

PYOTR IVANOVICH. You'll soon see. Recently a young widow, Yuliya Pavlovna Tafayeva, returned here from abroad... Well, have you guessed?

ALEXANDER. Surkov fell in love with the widow?

PYOTR IVANOVICH. He's quite mad about her! And what else?

ALEXANDER. What else... I don't know...

PYOTR IVANOVICH. You're a fine one! Well, listen, Surkov has twice let it be known that he'll need money soon. If you don't help... Now have you guessed?

ALEXANDER. Surkov's asking for money, you don't have any. You want me to...

PYOTR IVANOVICH. No, that isn't it.

ALEXANDER. Then... Now I've got it...

PYOTR IVANOVICH. What have you got?

ALEXANDER. Strike me dead, Uncle, I don't understand anything!

PYOTR IVANOVICH. Get Tafayeva to fall in love with you.

ALEXANDER (*puzzled*). That's absurd!

PYOTR IVANOVICH. What's absurd about it?

ALEXANDER. I won't do it for anything!

PYOTR IVANOVICH. I beg you, Alexander, for the sake of the business...

ALEXANDER. I just don't want to see women. And what you propose...

PYOTR IVANOVICH. So don't even look at her... Just superficially... that'll be even better...

ALEXANDER. First of all, Uncle, it's a vile thing to do...

PYOTR IVANOVICH. It's only a trick that doesn't hurt anyone... At first Surkov will go mad with jealousy, but then cool off quickly—I know him. And our capital will be intact...

ALEXANDER. I can't.

PYOTR IVANOVICH. Too bad. I was even very much counting on you. And, it seems, until now I haven't overburdened you with requests.

ALEXANDER. But I don't like this one; it's even repugnant to me.

PYOTR IVANOVICH. Just suffer through it. One must, after all, do a few things one doesn't like. Help me out, Alexander, I beg you! It's terribly important to me. If you do this—do you remember the two vases you admired at the factory? They're yours.

ALEXANDER. Excuse me, Uncle, do you really imagine I'd take a present...

PYOTR IVANOVICH. Yes, why should you start troubling yourself for nothing, waste your time? When I do something for you, offer me a present—I'll take it. Help me out, Alexander, I beg you.

ALEXANDER (*undecided*). I can try...

PYOTR IVANOVICH. Well, good. Just have a try! I guarantee you'll succeed. On Thursday I'll introduce you to Tafayeva. This whole business will take a month, two at most. I know Surkov... Goodbye!

Scene 12

Tafayeva's drawing room. Several guests conversing in both Russian and French. Pyotr Ivanovich and Alexander enter and bow to the guests.

PYOTR IVANOVICH (*taking Alexander to Tafayeva*). Allow me, Yuliya Pavlovna, to introduce my nephew Alexander. (*Alexander kisses Tafayeva's hand. Everyone's eyes are on him.*) Isn't my friend Surkov here? Has he forgotten you?
TAFAYEVA. Oh, no! I'm very grateful to him; he comes to call on me.
PYOTR IVANOVICH. Where is he?
TAFAYEVA. Imagine, he gave his word to get me and my cousin without fail a box for tomorrow at the theater when, they say, none is to be had... He went for them just now.
PYOTR IVANOVICH. And he'll get them, I'll guarantee he will; he's a genius at that... Yes, here he is.

(*Surkov enters. He has in his hand a cane with a gold top in the shape of a lion's head. Surkov kisses Tafayeva's hand, bows to the guests. His gaze rests on Alexander.*)

SURKOV (*to Alexander*). You're here too, young man! (*Alexander bows.*)
PYOTR IVANOVICH (*under his breath to Alexander*). He has a presentiment! (*Surkov goes up to the ladies, kisses their hands.*) Ah! And he's got a cane. What does that mean? (*Aloud to Surkov.*) What's that?
SURKOV (*in passing*). I was getting out of the carriage recently... I stumbled and am a little lame.
PYOTR IVANOVICH (*again quietly to Alexander*). Nonsense! Did you notice the head of the cane—the gold lion's head? He bragged that he'd paid six hundred rubles for it, and now he's showing it off. That's an example for you of the means by which he works. Do battle with him and drive him out of the field... Remember the vases are yours and be inspired.
SURKOV (*to Tafayeva, waving the tickets*). Do you have a ticket for tomorrow?
TAFAYEVA. No.
SURKOV. Allow me to present you this. (*Gives the ticket to Tafayeva.*)
TAFAYEVA. Pyotr Ivanovich, won't you sit in my box?
PYOTR IVANOVICH. I'm very grateful, but tomorrow I'm engaged to be at the theater with my wife. But, here, let me present a young man to you in exchange...
TAFAYEVA. I wanted to ask him too. There are but three of us, my cousin and I, yes and...
PYOTR IVANOVICH. He'll take my place and, if necessary, he'll replace this dashing fellow. (*He points to Surkov.*)
SURKOV. I thank you, only it would have been better to propose a replacement earlier, before there was a ticket. Then I would have seen how I would be replaced.
TAFAYEVA. Oh dear, I'm very grateful for your kindness, but I didn't invite you to sit in the box because you have an orchestra seat. Surely you prefer to face the stage directly... especially at the ballet.

SURKOV. No, no, you're being sly, you don't think that. Exchange a place beside you—not for anything!

TAFAYEVA. But it's already promised...

SURKOV. How? To whom?

TAFAYEVA. Monsieur René. (*She points to a bearded foreigner.*)

MONSIEUR RENÉ. Oui, Madame m'a fait cet honneur.

SURKOV. I'm deeply obliged to you! (*Turning to Pyotr Ivanovich, points to Alexander.*) I owe this to you.

PYOTR IVANOVICH. No need to be grateful. But won't you sit in my box? My wife and I are only two. You haven't seen her for a long time, you could pay her court...

SURKOV (*in a hurry*). I'm leaving! Goodbye!

TAFAYEVA. So soon! Will you come to see us tomorrow in our box if only for a minute?

SURKOV. How sly of you! One minute, when you know that for a place beside you I'd give up a place in paradise.

TAFAYEVA. If theatrical paradise, I believe you! Let us go into the dining room, ladies and gentlemen.

(*Surkov is about to give his arm to Tafayeva, but Pyotr Ivanovich gives Alexander a slight push. Alexander stretches out his arm to Tafayeva, who takes it with pleasure as they go into the dining room. Pyotr Ivanovich takes Surkov's arm and the other guests follow.*)

Scene 13

At Tafayeva's house. Alexander and Tafayeva stand in close embrace; they kiss.

TAFAYEVA. Will you leave for work early tomorrow?

ALEXANDER. Around eleven.

TAFAYEVA. Then come here at ten, we'll have breakfast... Or couldn't you just not go at all?

ALEXANDER. But how? My country... My duty...

TAFAYEVA. Just tell them you love and are loved. (*They embrace.*) Surely your department head must have loved too. Your aunt made a bad impression on me. I assumed she was an elderly woman, not pretty... I forbid you to spend time with her, do you hear?

ALEXANDER. I promise, Yuliya! (*They embrace.*)

TAFAYEVA. We won't have to say goodbye this way much longer... What furniture do you want in your study?

ALEXANDER. I'd like walnut with dark-blue velvet upholstery.

TAFAYEVA. That's very nice... I'll put an armchair near your desk and sit and watch when you work. That will be wonderful, won't it?

ALEXANDER. Yes...

TAFAYEVA. You answered mechanically.... What were you thinking about?

ALEXANDER. About you...

TAFAYEVA (*embracing Alexander*). I can't be an hour without you.

ALEXANDER (*affectionately*). Yuliya, my dear, you mustn't love so absolutely... That's passion...

TAFAYEVA. Why not!
ALEXANDER. Passion can't be reasonable...
TAFAYEVA. You don't mean you love reasonably?
ALEXANDER. I? No, of course not! (*Passionately kisses her.*)
TAFAYEVA. Stay here!
ALEXANDER. I can't... I have business to attend to... Goodbye, my beloved...
TAFAYEVA. Till tomorrow! (*They kiss.*)

Scene 14

Alexander's room. Evsei in the entryway is, as usual, polishing boots to a high gloss and muttering to himself. Two big porcelain vases are new among the room's furniture. Enter Pyotr Ivanovich and Elizaveta Alexandrovna.

PYOTR IVANOVICH. I especially thank you. You did me a favor beyond my expectations! And you were so modest. "I can't," he says. "I don't know how!" Doesn't know how indeed! I've wanted to see you for a long time, but it was impossible to catch you. Well, I'm very grateful! Did you receive the vases undamaged?
ALEXANDER. I shall send them back.
PYOTR IVANOVICH. What's this? They're yours by all rights. You wrapped up this little deal... And my silly Surkov almost went crazy. Two weeks ago he ran in to my office quite beside himself. I knew at once... "Oh, it's you," I said. "What's the good news?" "Nothing good," he says. "I've come with bad news about your nephew." "Why, what's this?" I ask. "You frighten me, tell me right away!" At this he begins to shout. "You yourself complained," he says, "that he didn't work much, but you're the one who's taught him idleness. You introduced him to Yuliya, and now he sits at her house from morning to night." You see how he lies about you out of rage. Do you really sit there from morning till night, is it true?
ALEXANDER (*murmurs*). Yes... I sometimes... visit...
PYOTR IVANOVICH. "Sometimes"—that's different. I say to Surkov, "That's no big misfortune." And he to me. "What do you mean, 'no misfortune.' A young man must work... Why does he take her a bouquet of flowers every day? What does that cost in winter?"
ALEXANDER. Sometimes... that's true... I did bring...
PYOTR IVANOVICH. You see, again "sometimes." Not every day. Give me the bill. I'll pay. "They're always," he says, "taking walks, just the two of them, where there are few people."
ALEXANDER. I have several times... that's correct... gone walking with her...
PYOTR IVANOVICH. Even so, not every day. I knew he was lying. "This Alexander now! What a nephew!" In sum, Surkov exaggerated to the point of insisting you were up to your ears in love with Tafayeva.
ELIZAVETA ALEXANDROVNA. Pyotr Ivanovich!
PYOTR IVANOVICH. What?
ELIZAVETA ALEXANDROVNA. I forgot to tell you. A servant came just now with a letter from the Lukyanovs.
PYOTR IVANOVICH. I know, I know... where was I?

ELIZAVETA ALEXANDROVNA. Isn't it time we had dinner, Pyotr Ivanovich?
PYOTR IVANOVICH. We're going right now... Since you mentioned dinner, by
the way, Surkov says that you dine there almost every day, Alexander, espe-
cially Wednesdays and Fridays. The devil knows what lies he told, I got fed up.
Look, it's Friday today, and here you are. Come dine with us.
ALEXANDER (alarmed). Uncle, I can't. I have letters to write... translations...
PYOTR IVANOVICH. Well, do your work by all means, we won't prevent you...
You did your job, Alexander, and expertly. Don't bother with it further. You
needn't call on her any more. I can imagine how boring it is there! When you
need money, ask me! Let's go, Liza! (Noticing that Alexander is looking at Eli-
zaveta Alexandrovna.) I'll wait for you in the carriage, Liza! But don't take too
long, I'm hungry... (Exits.)
ALEXANDER (rushing toward Elizaveta Alexandrovna). Dear Aunt!
ELIZAVETA ALEXANDROVNA. Are you in love again, Alexander, as before?
ALEXANDER. No, much more happily! I don't choke from joy now, like an ani-
mal; I'm conscious of my happiness, I meditate on it, and for that reason it's
perhaps quieter, but fuller. What a difference between that other woman and
Yuliya! If you knew, dear Aunt, how many virtues she has!
ELIZAVETA ALEXANDROVNA. For example?
ALEXANDER. She loves me so!
ELIZAVETA ALEXANDROVNA. That is, of course, a great virtue...
ALEXANDER. The matter is.... I want... to marry her.
ELIZAVETA ALEXANDROVNA (hiding her surprise). You will be a very happy
husband, Alexander. Only don't hurry... don't be hasty.
ALEXANDER. I shall obey you, dear Aunt. Uncle likely is already angry. Forgive
me, dear Aunt; for him the process of digestion is more important than love.
ELIZAVETA ALEXANDROVNA. Do you think so?
ALEXANDER. Unquestionably... (He kisses Elizaveta Alexandrovna's hand. Exit
Elizaveta Alexandrovna. Alone, Alexander rushes into the hall. Feverishly he puts on
his outer garments, examines himself in the mirror, and rushes out headlong.)

Scene 15

Again the room at Tafayeva's; she sits in an armchair embroidering. Alexander, at the
other end of the stage, sits doing nothing; he looks at his watch, yawns, looks at Yuliya.

TAFAYEVA. What are you doing there? What are you thinking about?
ALEXANDER. Nothing... (Speaking his thoughts in an aside inaudible to Tafayeva.)
What kind of love is this! Some kind of sleepy love without energy. This woman
surrendered to feeling without resistance, without a struggle, like a victim. She
bestowed her love on the first man who came along.
TAFAYEVA. Sit here... closer...
ALEXANDER (without answering Tafayeva, continues his aside). If I hadn't been
there, she would have indeed fallen in love with Surkov... It's simply immoral!
TAFAYEVA. What's the matter with you?
ALEXANDER (gets up, goes to Tafayeva; aside). Is this love? The devil knows what
it is, you can't make sense of it!
TAFAYEVA. What's the matter with you?
ALEXANDER (sitting down in the armchair near Tafayeva). I don't know... I feel...

as if I...

TAFAYEVA. You will be my husband! Soon all this will be yours!

ALEXANDER (*aside*). What fun, how pleasant to go walking alone! To go where you want, stop, read a sign, look in a store window, set off this way, that way... it's so wonderful! Freedom is a great blessing! Yes! In the broad, highest sense, freedom precisely means to go out walking alone!

TAFAYEVA (*continuing*). You will rule in this house as in my heart.

ALEXANDER. And if I fell out of love with you?

TAFAYEVA. I'd box your ears! What's the matter with you? You're silent, you hardly listen to me, look to the side... What's the matter with you, Alexander?

ALEXANDER (*aside*). How she's latched on to me! I don't know why!

TAFAYEVA. Are you bored?

ALEXANDER (*aside, delighted*). Boring! That's the right word! That's it... That's it, boring... What am I to do? And she's discussing love and marriage...

TAFAYEVA. Are you bored, Alexander?

ALEXANDER. How can you ask! Not a bit! (*Gets up.*)

TAFAYEVA. Where are you going?

ALEXANDER. Home.

TAFAYEVA. It isn't eleven o'clock yet.

ALEXANDER. I must write to Mama, I haven't written her for a long while.

TAFAYEVA. What do you mean "long"? You wrote her day before yesterday.

ALEXANDER. Well, I'm just sleepy. I didn't sleep much last night, that's all.

TAFAYEVA. "Didn't sleep much!" Then why did you say earlier this morning that you slept nine hours? You even said that your head had started to ache from it!

ALEXANDER. But my head does ache... That's why I'm going.

TAFAYEVA. But after dinner you said the headache had gone.

ALEXANDER. Heavens! What a memory you have! This is unbearable! Well, I simply want to go home!

TAFAYEVA. You mean you're not comfortable here? What do you have at home?

ALEXANDER. Work.

TAFAYEVA. Yes, of course: dinner at Dumé's, rides in the hills—very important business!

ALEXANDER. What does this mean? You're apparently having me watched? I won't stand for it! (*Goes to the door.*)

TAFAYEVA. Stop, listen! Let's have a talk.

ALEXANDER. I haven't time.

TAFAYEVA. One minute. Sit down.

ALEXANDER (*unwillingly sits down on the edge of his chair*). Quickly, I have no time!

TAFAYEVA. You don't love me then?

ALEXANDER. The same old song!

TAFAYEVA. How she has bored you! (*Begins to weep.*)

ALEXANDER (*enraged*). This is the last straw! Haven't you tormented me enough!

TAFAYEVA. I've tormented you!

ALEXANDER. This is insufferable! (*Goes to the door.*)

TAFAYEVA. All right, I won't, I won't. (*Wipes away her tears.*) You see, I'm not crying. But don't go away, sit down. (*Alexander sits down on the edge of the chair; Tafayeva goes to him, kneels and strokes him. Alexander sits still, not responding to her caresses. Tafayeva jumps up, speaks in staccato jerks.*) Leave me! (*Alexander heads for the door. Tafayeva rushes after him.*) Alexander Fyodorovich! Alexander Fyodorovich! (*Alexander turns.*) Where are you going?

ALEXANDER. Why, you told me to leave.

TAFAYEVA. And you're even glad to run away. Stay!

ALEXANDER. I have no time. (*Looks at Tafayeva, aside*). How ugly she is!

TAFAYEVA. I'll have my revenge! You think it's so easy to play with a woman's fate? No, I shall not let you go, I'll follow you everywhere. You won't get away from me no matter where you go. If you go to the country, I'll follow you. Go abroad—I'll go there too, everywhere and forever. I shall pursue you everywhere. I don't care what kind of life I lead... I have nothing more to lose. But I'll poison your life—I'll get even, I'll have my revenge. I must have a rival. You can't just have left me like that... I'll find her—and you'll see what I'll do. You'll wish you'd never been born! With what pleasure I'd hear of your death... I could kill you myself!

ALEXANDER (*aside*). How stupid! How absurd this is!

TAFAYEVA (*continuing*). Have pity on me! Don't leave me! What shall I do now without you! I shall not survive our separation. I shall die! Think about it: women love differently—more tenderly, more strongly than men. Love is everything for them, especially for me. Others flirt, love society, noise and fuss. I'm different. I love quiet, solitude, books, music, but you—more than anything in the world! Well, all right, you don't love me, but keep your promise. Marry me, only be with me... You'll be free. Do what you want, even love whomever you want, if only I see you sometimes, even rarely... (*Falls on the sofa and begins to weep hysterically.*)

ALEXANDER (*aside*). She's dying from suffering and I don't care. I don't even feel pity for her. She's become unpleasant, even repulsive to me. What is this? (*Stands for a while, turns and leaves.*)

(*A maid enters, sees the sobbing Tafayeva, runs to her.*)

TAFAYEVA. But where is...

MAID. He's gone...

TAFAYEVA. Gone! Oh! (*Shriek.*)

(*Lights out.*)

ACT III

Scene 16

Alexander's room. Alexander is lying on the sofa, unshaven, eyes inflamed and vacant.

EVSEI (*entering, shows Alexander the shoes he is polishing*). Just look, Sir; this boot wax is remarkable—gloss like a mirror, and it costs only a quarter. And what a smell—you could eat it!
ALEXANDER. Go away! You fool!
EVSEI. We should send some to the country...
ALEXANDER. Go away, I tell you, go away! You torment me, you and your boots will be the death of me... you... savage! Savage! Savage! (*Pushes Evsei out of the room. Throws himself down on the bed again. Seizes his head in his hands.*)

(*Enter Pyotr Ivanovich and Elizaveta Alexandrovna.*)

ELIZAVETA ALEXANDROVNA (*quietly*). Why don't you ever come to see us Alexander Fyodorovich? For over half a year...
ALEXANDER. I've had no reason to.
PYOTR IVANOVICH (*cautiously*). Rumor has it you've been drinking a lot...
ALEXANDER. I gave it up.
PYOTR IVANOVICH. You were seeing some young woman in a garden house. The girl's father gave you a scolding... (*Alexander remains silent.*) And now, they say, you go off fishing and play checkers with old men. Is this true?
ALEXANDER. It is.
PYOTR IVANOVICH. Is this you?
ALEXANDER. Yes.
PYOTR IVANOVICH. And can you live without doing anything?
ALEXANDER. I can.

(*Pause.*)

PYOTR IVANOVICH. I heard that Ivanov is leaving his job, Alexander.
ALEXANDER. Yes, he is.
PYOTR IVANOVICH. Why aren't you getting his job?
ALEXANDER. They haven't done me the honor.
PYOTR IVANOVICH. You have to try for it.
ALEXANDER. No.
PYOTR IVANOVICH. Apparently you don't care?
ALEXANDER. No, I don't.
PYOTR IVANOVICH. This is the third time they've passed you by.
ALEXANDER. I don't care. Let them!
PYOTR IVANOVICH. And your self-esteem?
ALEXANDER. I haven't got any.

PYOTR IVANOVICH. Surely you have some interests in life?

ALEXANDER (*jumping up from the bed*). Let me be, Uncle! I tried to express my opinions, tried to do better... No one wanted any of it... Everywhere the machine went on turning. The convenient and eternal machine!

PYOTR IVANOVICH. But you must have some kind of career.

ALEXANDER. I've had it. I've marked out the circle of my activity—I'm the master here; this is my "career".

PYOTR IVANOVICH. That's laziness.

ALEXANDER. Perhaps.

PYOTR IVANOVICH. You can move forward. You have a higher destiny. Duty calls you to noble labor...

ALEXANDER. What's this? (*Laughs.*) You've begun talking wildly. That didn't use to be your custom. You aren't doing it for me, are you? You're wasting your breath!

PYOTR IVANOVICH. You want to pretend calm and indifference toward everything, but resentment boils up in your words... Shouldn't a person want something?

ALEXANDER. I want to be left alone in my dark corner.

PYOTR IVANOVICH. And is that really life?

ALEXANDER. Rather to my mind the life you lead isn't life. Therefore, I'm right. (*Lies down on the bed again.*)

PYOTR IVANOVICH. Well, Alexander, you're disillusioned, I see...

ELIZAVETA ALEXANDROVNA (*to her husband*). This is awful, he seems out of his mind...

ALEXANDER (*yells*). Pyotr Ivanovich and experience have taught me!

ELIZAVETA ALEXANDROVNA. Yes, he's much to blame! But you had the right not to listen to him.

ALEXANDER. I was young, he's experienced!

ELIZAVETA ALEXANDROVNA (*to her husband*). Do you hear?

PYOTR IVANOVICH (*seizing the small of his back*). Ouch, how my back hurts... It's a kind of sign of success among business people—back pains... Ouch!

ELIZAVETA ALEXANDROVNA. You should get married, Alexander... And you have literary talent!

ALEXANDER. Why do you beat a man when he's down, dear Aunt!

ELIZAVETA ALEXANDROVNA. It's you, you're to blame, Pyotr Ivanovich...

PYOTR IVANOVICH. I? Now I like that! I taught him to do nothing!

ELIZAVETA ALEXANDROVNA. There's nothing for you to be surprised about. You confused his notions of life. Everything in him turned to doubt, to chaos...

PYOTR IVANOVICH. Indeed, I tried to make something out of chaos...

ELIZAVETA ALEXANDROVNA. He believed in love, friendship, in the sacredness of duty... Now he believes in nothing...

PYOTR IVANOVICH. He should live in the land of Cockaigne...

ELIZAVETA ALEXANDROVNA. He believed in himself. But you tried to prove that he's worse than almost anyone else, and he began to hate himself.

PYOTR IVANOVICH. Impossible... Take me; I know my own value, I see that I have faults, but, I admit I love myself a lot.

ELIZAVETA ALEXANDROVNA. You love yourself—now that's unquestionably an objective to aim for—yourself!

PYOTR IVANOVICH. Oh, my back!

ELIZAVETA ALEXANDROVNA. With one blow, without pity, you destroyed his dream, his belief in his talent...

PYOTR IVANOVICH. He had none, Liza.

ELIZAVETA ALEXANDROVNA. But he did! Only it needed support and not ridicule and abuse... Why are you surprised that he lost heart? What pleases and suits you doesn't suit someone else, or a third person; it isn't right for others.

PYOTR IVANOVICH. Suit me, another, or a third person! Nonsense! That's enough, Liza! You've even become pale! You're not well!

ELIZAVETA ALEXANDROVNA. Don't worry about me, Pyotr Ivanovich. I'm all right...

PYOTR IVANOVICH. Am I really alone in thinking and acting this way? Look around you. What I demanded of him wasn't all invented by me.

ELIZAVETA ALEXANDROVNA. Who did then?

PYOTR IVANOVICH. Our time.

ELIZAVETA ALEXANDROVNA. Must one without fail follow all the ideas that are thought up in your time? Are they all sacred and true?

PYOTR IVANOVICH. They're all sacred!

ELIZAVETA ALEXANDROVNA. What! Is it true that one must reason more than feel?

PYOTR IVANOVICH. Yes.

ELIZAVETA ALEXANRDOVNA. And it's sacred truth that you must love your work more than a beloved person?

PYOTR IVANOVICH. That has always been true.

ELIZAVETA ALEXANDROVNA. Is it also true that you must act reasonably even toward those close to your heart... for example, toward your wife?

PYOTR IVANOVICH. Wait a minute... My back hurts abominably... Ouch!

ELIZAVETA ALEXANDROVNA. Your back, indeed! A wonderful time we live in! You can't say otherwise!

PYOTR IVANOVICH. Very wonderful, my dear. Everywhere there is reason, experience, gradual progress, and, therefore, success. Everything moves toward perfection and the common good. Look at the youth of today—what fine fellows! How everything hums with intellectual activity and energy! How easily and skillfully they manage with all that nonsense called "palpitations" and "sufferings"—and the Devil knows what else—in your language!

ELIZAVETA ALEXANDROVNA. You mean you're not sorry for Alexander?

PYOTR IVANOVICH. No. Now if his back hurt, then I'd be sorry for him.

ALEXANDER. Your back! Won't you ever understand, Uncle, that what you think is the cruel truth is in actual fact a lie! And I can't destroy it because it's an ironclad lie.

PYOTR IVANOVICH. That's true, Alexander, and that's the reason you can't break it.

ALEXANDER (*yells*). No, no! (*Again falls on the bed. Quiet. Speaks calmly*). Uncle, can you say what I ought to do?

PYOTR IVANOVICH. Yes, I can. (*Alexander sits up on the bed. He looks at his uncle in expectation.*) Go back to the country.

ELIZAVETA ALEXANDROVNA. Are you in your right mind, Pyotr Ivanovich?

ALEXANDER (*feverishly*). Yes, yes, yes! (*Laughs.*) Splendid! To the country! To the country! To the country! (*Walks back and forth and until Pyotr Ivanovich and Elizaveta Alexandrovna exit keeps repeating*) To the country! I haven't conquered! That's where I belong!

PYOTR IVANOVICH. Come, say goodbye before you leave. I've grown accustomed to you. Remember, you have an uncle and a friend. If you need... in a word, if you change your mind...

ELIZAVETA ALEXANDROVNA. And if you need sympathy and unfailing friendship...

ALEXANDER (*not listening to them, shouts*). Evsei! Evsei!

EVSEI (*entering*). What is your wish?

ALEXANDER. We're going to the country! Back home!

EVSEI. Glory to you, great Lord! At last you've come to your senses!

ALEXANDER. Get our things together!

EVSEI (*leaving*). At last, Lord! I'll light a candle...

ELIZAVETA ALEXANDROVNA. Alexander, perhaps you should think it over...

ALEXANDER. Leave me, I beg you, leave!

PYOTR IVANOVICH. (*leaving and leading Elizaveta Alexandrovna away*). No, he's not of the Aduyev clan, not ours... He's weak... a lesser character... (*Both exit.*)

ALEXANDER (*goes to the window, looks at the city and shakes his fist at it*). Ooh! Farewell, you stone coffin of the best human feelings, the soul's powerful emotions! Farewell, you unfeeling, greedy, lying city! You made me an old man at twenty-nine, killed everything human in me! You cursed, hateful place! May you drown in your swamps! May you be swallowed up again in water! May you... (*Weeping.*) I'm nothing! I'm nothing!

Scene 17

The dining room on the Aduyev country estate. Anna Pavlovna and Anton Ivanovich await Alexander's return.

ANTON IVANOVICH. Why are you so aimlessly pacing like this from room to room, Anna Pavlovna?

ANNA PAVLOVNA. Not so loud! (*Listens.*) No, that's not a carriage bell... (*She paces again, moving objects from one place to another.*)

ANTON IVANOVICH. I stopped by at Marya Karpovna's on the way—a disaster! (*Laughs.*) Sofiya Mikhailovna is expecting her sixth child soon. And they're so poor! I didn't even want to look... Why, she had set her cap for your Alexander Fyodorovich, the old crow... Please sit down, sit down! I expect he'll appear with medals, resplendent in his great success...

ANNA PAVLOVNA. Not so loud! (*Freezes. The sound of a bell is heard.*) Heavens, oh Lord! It's he! He's come! (*Sits down, too excited to move.*)

ANTON IVANOVICH (*running to the window*). It's he, all right! And there's Evsei on the box! Where's your icon? And the bread and salt? (*Snatches up bread and salt, puts them on a plate.*) And you, Anna Pavlovna, you go run to meet them yourself!

ANNA PAVLOVNA (*with difficulty*). I can't. My legs have given way... (*Alexander enters. Balding, thin, he walks calmly and evenly, without passion. Behind him, Evsei and Anna Pavlovna's servants with the baggage. Anna Pavlovna gets up with difficulty and goes toward Alexander.*) Sashenka! My dear!... (*Stops suddenly, looks at Alexander, as if at a stranger.*) But where is Sashenka?

ALEXANDER. Why it's me, Mama dear!

ANNA PAVLOVNA. Is it really you, my dear? No, this isn't you... What's the matter? Aren't you well?

ALEXANDER. I'm fine, Mama.

ANNA PAVLOVNA (*gradually coming to, manages to say*). Fine! But what has happened to you, my darling? Did I send you away like this? Where is your hair? It was like silk! Your eyes shone like two stars, your cheeks were blood-red and milk-white. You were just like a ripe apple! (*She grasps her heart.*)

ANTON IVANOVICH (*in her ear*). What's this, dear lady, you're wailing over him as if he were dead! Welcome, Alexander Fyodorovich! (*They greet each other.*)

ANNA PAVLOVNA (*coming to*). Come with me, your room is ready.

(*Anton Ivanovich takes leave, bowing; exits. Anna Pavlovna and Alexander go upstairs.*)

AGRAFENA (*to Evsei*). Why don't you speak? Such an idiot, doesn't even greet me! (*Evsei goes to Agrafena and embraces her.*) See what the Devil's brought home! So those Petersburg folk have turned your heads, your master's and yours. What a little mustache you've grown!

(*Evsei gives little presents to Agrafena.*)

ANNA PAVLOVNA (*returning, to Evsei*). Whatever has happened to Sashenka, huh?

EVSEI (*remains silent*).

AGRAFENA. Why are you silent? Do you hear, the mistress is asking you!

EVSEI. I can't tell you, Madam! That's a question for the master! It must be from writing, Ma'am.

ANNA PAVLOVNA. Did he write a lot?

EVSEI. A lot, every day.

ANNA PAVLOVNA. And why didn't you restrain him?

EVSEI. I did, Ma'am. "Don't sit there, Alexander Fyodorovich," I'd say; "you'll hurt your lungs; your mama," I'd say, "will be angry."

ANNA PAVLOVNA. And what did he say?

EVSEI. "Go away," he'd say, "you're a fool!"

AGRAFENA. And he's right, a fool!

ANNA PAVLOVNA. But didn't his uncle restrain him then?

EVSEI. Not he, Ma'am! He'd come, and if he found him idle, then he'd fall upon him. "What," he'd say, "you're not doing anything? Here," he'd say, "you're not in the country. You have to work!"

ANNA PAVLOVNA. A plague on him! Let him have some rascals of his own to rail at! Or let him yell at his wife, the wench! You see, he found someone to abuse with his "work! work!" A dog, he's truly a dog, God forgive me!... Has Sashenka been this thin for long?

EVSEI. It's been three years now since Alexander Fyodorovich began to feel quite down and didn't eat much.

ANNA PAVLOVNA. Why was he so low?

EVSEI. God knows, Ma'am. Pyotr Ivanovich deigned to say something to him about that. I would have listened, but it was beyond me, I made no sense of it.

ANNA PAVLOVNA. But what did he say?

EVSEI. He called him something, but I've forgotten what.

ANNA PAVLOVNA. Well?

AGRAFENA. So, simpleton, say something, the mistress is waiting.

EVSEI (*with difficulty*). Dis... I think, disill... disillu... sioned...

ANNA PAVLOVNA. What's that?

EVSEI. Disill... disillusioned, that's it! I remembered!

ANNA PAVLOVNA. What kind of calamity is that now? Heavens! Is it a sickness perhaps?

AGRAFENA. Oh dear, it doesn't mean depraved, maybe, Ma'am?

(*Alexander enters.*)

ANNA PAVLOVNA (*to the servants*). Go away!... Sit down, Sashenka, and eat! (*Both sit down at the table.*) My dear, if you'd only smile just once... Like a dark cloud, you only look at the ground. Has someone offended you? I shall find out!

ALEXANDER (*simply*). Don't worry, Mama... I've grown up, become more reasonable, and for that reason, more thoughtful.

ANNA PAVLOVNA. But why thin? And where's your hair?

ALEXANDER. I can't say why... You can't tell all that's happened in eight years... Perhaps my health has suffered a little...

ANNA PAVLOVNA. What pains you?

ALEXANDER (*pointing to his head and heart*). I have pains both here and there.

ANNA PAVLOVNA (*feels Alexander's forehead*). You don't have any fever... Does your head throb?

ALEXANDER. No... Yes...

ANNA PAVLOVNA. Shall I send for the doctor?

ALEXANDER. No, Mama, he won't help me. It will go away by itself.

ANNA PAVLOVNA. But why are you so tired of life? What is this misfortune?

ALEXANDER. It's just that way...

ANNA PAVLOVNA. What do you want?

ALEXANDER. I don't know myself. I'm just bored.

ANNA PAVLOVNA. Heavens, how very strange! Sashenka! (*In a low voice.*) Isn't it time you got married?

ALEXANDER. What an idea! No, I'm not getting married.

ANNA PAVLOVNA. But I have a girl in mind—pretty as a doll; a pink, tender little thing, so thin you can almost see through her.

ALEXANDER. I'm not getting married.

ANNA PAVLOVNA. What, never?

ALEXANDER. Never.

ANNA PAVLOVNA. Heaven have mercy! We're all human... you'll fall in love with her...

ALEXANDER. I've already fallen out of love, Mama.

ANNA PAVLOVNA. How could you fall out of love? Without marrying? Whom did you love there?

ALEXANDER. A girl.

ANNA PAVLOVNA. Why didn't you marry her?

ALEXANDER. She betrayed me.

ANNA PAVLOVNA. How could she betray you? You weren't married to her yet? Fine girls you have there—they love before marriage! She betrayed you! What a loathsome creature! Happiness itself was within her grasp and she didn't know how to appreciate it, the good-for-nothing! If I'd seen her, I'd have spit in her face... But what of it, is she the only girl in the world? You'll fall in love again.

ALEXANDER. I did love another time.

ANNA PAVLOVNA. Whom?

ALEXANDER. A widow.
ANNA PAVLOVNA. Well, and why didn't you marry her?
ALEXANDER. I betrayed her.
ANNA PAVLOVNA. You betrayed!... Obviously some kind of loose woman! A real pitfall there, God forgive me. What does go on in this world as soon as you look closely! (*In a sudden gesture she presses her hand to her heart again.*)
ALEXANDER. Don't get excited, Mama! It's quiet for me here, it's fine... Now I'm with you for good...

(*Anna Pavlovna straightens herself up at the table. Tears run down her face. Alexander sits motionless.*)

Scene 18

A spotlight pulls Alexander out of the darkness of his attic room, as he sits at his desk, feverishly writing.

ALEXANDER. "Dear Aunt, As you took leave of me, you promised me your friendship and sympathy if ever I needed them. The moment has come when I appreciate the full value of your words. Indeed, I reached it long ago! How much time has passed! An eternity! Mama died three months ago. I am now running away from here for good!" (*He stops writing and thinks aloud.*) What am I doing here? What am I languishing here for? Why am I wasting my talents? How is Uncle better than I? How are others better than I? They all set forth into the world... while I... I shall come back to you not as an oddball, a romantic dreamer, or a disillusioned man, but just a person like so many in Petersburg, such as I should have been long ago... You'll see what I'm capable of! (*He takes another sheet of paper and again writes feverishly.*) "Dear, kindest Uncle, and along with that, Your Excellency! I dare to remind you of the promise you gave me upon my departure. You said if I should need work, or need an occupation or money, to turn to you. And here I am needing work and an occupation, and maybe I'll need money too." (*Stops writing and thinks aloud.*) Leave here, leave! My best years are passing; I've accomplished nothing... "Uncle, I've understood how right you were in what you said. I've understood you, your soul, or, better still, your mind, because the soul—in actuality is nothing!"

Scene 19

Room in Pyotr Ivanovich's apartment. A certain disorder. Pyotr Ivanovich has grown older and lost his former self-assurance. A physician is with him.

PYOTR IVANOVICH. What am I to do, Doctor? Her health grows worse every day...
DOCTOR. It does indeed grow worse! I only wanted to say that she... is in a not

quite normal situation...

PYOTR IVANOVICH. Isn't it all the same? I don't understand why I didn't notice earlier! My government position and my business rob me of time and my health... and look, now, indeed, that of my wife too! Did you question her today?

DOCTOR. Yes, but she doesn't notice anything wrong... Perhaps there's a psychological cause....

PYOTR IVANOVICH. "Psychological cause"?

DOCTOR. That is, do you see why I say "psychological." A person who didn't know you could suspect some kind of worries in this case.... or suppressed desires... or sometime's it's a case of need...

PYOTR IVANOVICH (*interrupting*). "Need," "desires"! Her every wish is anticipated. I know her taste, her habits... How cunning fate is, Doctor! Haven't I been careful with her? I've weighed, it seems, every step... No, somewhere something went wrong. And when? At the height of success, of such a career... Alas!

DOCTOR. Why are you getting so excited? Anemia, a certain decline in strength... Go south this summer, to Italy in the fall, and next winter to Paris...

PYOTR IVANOVICH (*hearing steps*). Sh-sh... (*Elizaveta Alexandrovna enters.*) Goodbye, Doctor! (*Doctor, bowing, takes leave of Elizaveta Alexandrovna and Pyotr Ivanovich.*) What are you doing?

ELIZAVETA ALEXANDROVNA (*carrying the account books*). Why, I'm going through our expense book. Imagine, Pyotr Ivanovich, last month around fifteen hundred rubles went for food alone. That's unheard of!

PYOTR IVANOVICH. Listen, the doctor says that my illness may get worse here. He advises taking the waters abroad. What do you say?

ELIZAVETA ALEXANDROVNA. What should I say? We must go if he so advises.

PYOTR IVANOVICH. But you? Would you want to take this trip?

ELIZAVETA ALEXANDROVNA. If you want to...

PYOTR IVANOVICH. But perhaps you'd rather stay here?

ELIZAVETA ALEXANDROVNA. Good, I'll stay.

PYOTR IVANOVICH. Which of the two do you mean?

ELIZAVETA ALEXANDROVNA. If you say so, I'll go; if not, I'll stay here...

PYOTR IVANOVICH. The doctor says that your health too has somewhat suffered... from the climate.

ELIZAVETA ALEXANDROVNA. Where did he get that idea? I'm healthy; I don't feel anything wrong.

PYOTR IVANOVICH. Or should we both go to the Crimea for the summer?

ELIZAVETA ALEXANDROVNA. The Crimea would be fine too.

PYOTR IVANOVICH. Is it all the same to you wherever you are?

ELIZAVETA ALEXANDROVNA. All the same.

PYOTR IVANOVICH. Why?

ELIZAVETA ALEXANDROVNA. It's up to you, Pyotr Ivanovich; we must cut expenses... Fifteen hundred rubles for food alone...

PYOTR IVANOVICH (*snatches the account book out of her hands and throws it under the table*). Why are you so preoccupied with this? Or do you begrudge the money?

ELIZAVETA ALEXANDROVNA. How can I not be preoccupied? After all, I'm your wife. You yourself taught me... and now you reproach me for my concern. I'm doing my work!

PYOTR IVANOVICH (*after a pause*). Listen, Liza... I leave you complete freedom...

ELIZAVETA ALEXANDROVNA. What shall I do with it? I don't need freedom...

PYOTR IVANOVICH. For a long time I haven't heard any request from you, any wish, any capricious fancy.

ELIZAVETA ALEXANDROVNA. I don't need anything.

PYOTR IVANOVICH. You have no special... hidden wishes?

ELIZAVETA ALEXANDROVNA. Give me your bills, books, business deals... I'll work on them... (*Reaches for the account book under the table.*)

PYOTR IVANOVICH. Liza!... (*The book remains under the table.*) But I was thinking, shouldn't you renew some of your acquaintances?

ELIZAVETA ALEXANDROVNA. For Heaven's sake, please, no!

PYOTR IVANOVICH. Why not, Liza, it's... (*Elizaveta Alexandrovna doesn't answer.*) You know, I'm considered the most active official in the ministry. This year I shall be nominated a Privy Councillor, and, of course, I'll get it. Don't think my career will stop there. I can go still further...

ELIZAVETA ALEXANDROVNA. I'm completely convinced you won't stop halfway, but will go to the end of the road...

PYOTR IVANOVICH. No, I shan't go on. In a day or so I shall hand in my resignation.

ELIZAVETA ALEXANDROVNA. Resignation? Why?

PYOTR IVANOVICH. Hear me out. You know that I bought out my partner, and the factory belongs to me alone.

ELIZAVETA ALEXANDROVNA. I know. So what about it?

PYOTR IVANOVICH. I shall sell it.

ELIZAVETA ALEXANDROVNA. What do you mean, Pyotr Ivanovich! What's the matter with you? What's all this for? I'm confused, I can't understand...

PYOTR IVANOVICH. You *really* can't understand?

ELIZAVETA ALEXANDROVNA. No!

PYOTR IVANOVICH. You can't understand that seeing how bored you are, how your health suffers... from the climate, I would place less value on my career and the factory and would take you away from here, devote the rest of my life to you?... (*He kneels beside Elizavata Alexandrovna's chair.*) Liza! Did you really think me incapable of sacrifice?

ELIZAVETA ALEXANDROVNA. So this is for me! No, Pyotr Ivanovich, for Heaven's sake, no sacrifice for me! I shan't accept it, do you hear? I absolutely won't!

PYOTR IVANOVICH. My intentions are immutable, Liza!

ELIZAVETA ALEXANDROVNA (*with a cry of sorrow*). If a person doesn't want to, he doesn't have to live... Will God not pity me and take me?

PYOTR IVANOVICH. We'll go to Italy.

ELIZAVETA ALEXANDROVNA. But perhaps the sacrifice is useless, perhaps it's... too late...

PYOTR IVANOVICH. Spare me, Liza, don't think ahead that far. Otherwise you'll see that I'm not made of iron... I tell you again that I want to live not by reason alone! Not everything in me is frozen yet.

ELIZAVETA ALEXANDROVNA. And that is... sincere? You truly are going away not just for me?

PYOTR IVANOVICH. No, no! I'm not well, I'm tired of everything... Liza! It even seems to me that Alexander was right about some things long ago! (*He kisses her hand with warmth.*)

(*Steps are heard. Pyotr Ivanovich gets up from his knees. Alexander enters. He has put on weight, become bald and ruddy. He has a little belly and an award ribbon around his neck. His eyes sparkle with joy. He kisses his aunt's hand and squeezes his uncle's.*)

PYOTR IVANOVICH. Where have you come from?

ALEXANDER. I'll bet you can't guess!

PYOTR IVANOVICH. A while ago I'd have said you're in love...

ALEXANDER. You haven't guessed.

PYOTR IVANOVICH. It's not... are you getting married?

ALEXANDER. Yes! Congratulate me.

In unison: PYOTR IVANOVICH. Really?

            ELIZAVETA ALEXANDROVNA. Who is she?

ALEXANDER. To Alexander Stepanych's daughter. What do you say? I've just come from them. Her father embraced me and said that now he could die in peace. "Just follow in the footsteps of your uncle," he said.

ELIZAVETA ALEXANDROVNA. And what did the daughter say?

ALEXANDER. Why... she... like, you know, all young girls, didn't say anything, only blushed.

ELIZAVETA ALEXANDROVNA. She didn't say anything! Did you really not take the trouble to find out anything from her before you made the proposal! Don't you care? Why are you getting married?

ALEXANDER. What do you mean why? Am I always to be on the loose like this? I'm tired of living alone. The time has come, dear Aunt, to settle down, put down roots, set up one's own household, fulfill one's duty... The bride is pretty, rich... Uncle here will give you reasons to get married...

ELIZAVETA ALEXANDROVNA. But if she doesn't like you? Perhaps she can't love you?

ALEXANDER (*not listening*). Love is one thing and marriage another. These two things don't always go together, and it's better when they don't... Isn't that so, Uncle? At least you taught me so...

PYOTR IVANOVICH. You see, Alexander, Elizaveta Alexandrovna and I...

ALEXANDER. And remember how I wanted to marry that... What was her name?.... (*Chuckles.*) I've forgotten!

ELIZAVETA ALEXANDROVNA. Nadenka!

ALEXANDER (*goes on laughing*). Yes, yes! That's it! Youth! Uncle, if you'd like, I'll show you I'm not the only one who once love, raged, was jealous, wept...

PYOTR IVANOVICH. What's this?

ALEXANDER. A written document exists... (*Takes out a folder and pulls out of it a yellowed little sheet of paper.*) Here, dear Aunt, is proof that Uncle was not always such a reasonable and pragmatic person... My dying auntie took this dried-out scrap of paper from her dried-out breast to give to me as she lay dying. For a long time I've been waiting for an occasion to expose Uncle, but would keep forgetting.

PYOTR IVANOVICH. Give it here, Alexander!

ALEXANDER. Why here, take a look. (*He holds the paper before his uncle's eyes.*)

PYOTR IVANOVICH (*trying to seize it*). Give it to me...

ALEXANDER. Aha! You're blushing! No, Uncle, not until you confess here in Aunt's presence that you once loved like me and were, pardon me, "stupid" like everyone.... (*Unfolds the yellowed sheet.*) Listen, Aunt, and laugh with me at Pyotr Ivanovich. (*Reads.*) "My adored angel..."

PYOTR IVANOVICH (*shouts*). Stop!

ALEXANDER (*puzzled*). What's the matter! If you insist... (*Tears up the letter.*) I wanted to make Aunt laugh and to say that I'm not the only one...

PYOTR IVANOVICH (*going up close to Alexander, in a low voice*). Can't you see what condition my wife is in?

ALEXANDER. What condition?

PYOTR IVANOVICH. Nothing you can see on the surface now. But enough that I'm quitting government service, my business, and going with her to Italy...

ALEXANDER. What do you mean! Why, this year you're due to get Privy Councillor...

PYOTR IVANOVICH. Yes... But Madam Privy Councillor is not well...

ALEXANDER. But for that you're really turning down such a career...

PYOTR IVANOVICH (*aloud, unconcerned*). Is your bride's dowry large?

ALEXANDER. Three hundred thousand! (*Expectantly and triumphantly looks at his uncle and aunt.*) And I'm to be master of five hundred serfs. Three hundred dowry and five hundred serfs! Well? A government career and a fortune! Yet you, Uncle, said I'm not an Aduyev! And all this I owe to you... Why did you sigh, dear Aunt?

ELIZAVETA ALEXANDROVNA. For the Alexander you once were.

ALEXANDER (*laughing*). It can't be helped, dear Aunt. It's the times we live in! I'm keeping pace with the times, you can't lag behind! And the times, one must admit, are good! By the way, Uncle, are you getting ready to sell your factory? I could... Don't you think? And perhaps I could borrow from you for a short while around ten thousand... Ouch, my back! (*Joyously puts his hand to his back.*) What do you know? (*Chuckles.*) My back hurts. Oh, my back!

Curtain